Love Beyond Borders

Love Beyond Borders

Qubool hai, she had said

SURJITSINGH SIKH

BLUEJAY

Bluejay Books Pvt. Ltd.
A-8/76, Ist F loor
Sector 16, Rohini
Delhi 110 085
info@bluejaybooksindia.com

First published in 2014 by
Bluejay Books Pvt. Ltd.

Typeset by Eshu Graphic

Printed and bound in India

I dedicate this book to my dear daughter Manmeet. Her faith in my ability spurred me to start writing.

ACKNOWLEDGEMENTS

I thank my young grand children Sanjana and Deep, who initiated me in the use of computer, thus providing me the tools for the writing.

I am also thankful to Dr. Panna Jain and Dr. Anil Jain for their help.

I wish to acknowledge the technical assistance provided by Sajid Patel and Jasvinder Chhabda.

It was May 1993. Waqaar Ahmed was in the seventh heaven. After passing his M.B.B.S. with the top rank, he had secured admission to the Master's course in surgery at the prestigious King Edward Medical University of Lahore. He was on his way to fulfill his mother's dream. It was her ambition that her son, the only child, should be a surgeon. She herself was a doctor, a highly qualified specialist in obstetrics and gynecology. She held a Master's degree in the subject from the Lahore University, as well as an MRCOG of London. Waqaar at present was working as a junior house surgeon in Dr. Akhlaq's unit at the University Hospital. Dr. Aklhlaq was one of the highly rated surgeons of Pakistan, and the most sought after teacher of surgery at the University.

Waqaar was tall and handsome, almost six feet in height, and of wiry built. He had a light brown complexion and chiseled Punjabi features. He was a health freak. He rarely missed his daily sessions of workout at the gym. His assiduousness in physical exercise was matched by his mother's fastidiousness regarding his diet. The food at home was prepared under her instructions and supervision, and excluded all unhealthy items.

That day, he had just finished his work at the out-patient department, and had gone to the ward to complete the paper work of the new admissions. As he approached the first bed, he heard the ward telephone ring. A nurse called out to him.

"Dr. Waqaar, casualty department for you." She handed him the receiver.

"Hello," he said.

"Waqaar, this is Aslam." There was a note of urgency in the casualty officer's voice.

"Your father has just been brought in. He has had a serious accident. I have put in a venous line and sent his blood sample to the blood bank for urgent typing and matching. I am taking him straight to the Surgery I.C.U. Come over there at once."

Dr. Aslam disconnected the phone. Waqaar replaced the receiver. His face reflected a combination of annoyance and anxiety. His father got involved in frequent brawls and accidents when under the influence of alcohol. These incidents were getting on his nerves. He controlled himself, and instructed the senior nurse,

"Sister, my father has been admitted to the I.C.U. I am going there now. Tell Dr. Qureshi to manage today's admissions."

He almost ran to the I.C.U. Dr. Roderick, the Assistant surgeon on duty there, was examining his unconscious father. Dr. Mantoo, a Registrar in Anesthesiology was inserting an arterial line. The senior nurse was standing by, ready to hook up the monitors on to the patient. Dr. Roderick finished his assessment, and turned to Waqaar.

"I am sorry Waqaar, your father has a fractured skull, and at least half a dozen fractures of limbs, beside a few broken ribs. Both his tibias have compound fractures. His blood pressure is precariously low. In this condition, we cannot move him to the radiology department for X-rays, and scanning. That shall have to wait until his general condition improves. I must warn you that it looks like a losing battle."

He turned to Dr. Mantoo, "Transfuse four units of blood at full speed."

Dr. Nilofer, Waqaar's mother, had received the news of her husband's accident, and had arrived at the hospital. She did not enter the I.C.U, but watched the ongoing activities from outside through a glass panel. Dr. Aslam, who had earlier informed her of the accident, joined her there, and apprised her of her husband's condition. Aslam was an intimate friend of Waqaar, and knew his mother well. He made a sign to Waqaar to come out of the I.C.U. and escorted the mother-son duo to the visitors' room attached to the I.C.U.

"Waqaar, you stay here with Nilofer Auntie. We are there to look after Mahmood Uncle."

After Aslam left, Waqaar and his mother sat in silence for a long minute.

"How is he?" She made a succinct inquiry.

"Bad," his reply was equally terse.

Waqaar knew that there was no love lost between his parents, only a silent tolerance of each other. At this point, a nurse attached to the I.C.U. came in carrying a tray with the tea things, and placed it on a low table before them. She addressed Waqaar with the practiced professional perkiness.

"Thank God, our blood bank has a large quantity of AB type blood in stock. You know doctor, in spite of your father's blood type being rare, we have already received four units, and more are being cross-matched. Besides, we have a couple of donors standing by. Dr. Roderick says…"

The chatty nurse went on with her ramblings. She failed to notice that Waqaar had gone deathly pale. He jumped up from his chair, intending to rush to the I.C.U., but his mother gripped his arm and motioned him to resume his seat.

"But Ammi…" he started in agitation. His mother cut him short with a suggestive pressure on his arm, and a glance towards the nurse. Reluctantly, he resumed his seat. As soon as the nurse left the room, he again leapt up from his seat, and said in an urgent voice,

"They have got his blood type wrong. I must stop the transfusion."

"Sit down Vicky, my son, and do calm down," Waqaar's mother called him Vicky only on rare occasions, when she wanted to express intense tenderness towards him.

He remained standing, still gripped by agitation.

"For God's sake Ammi, you know your and my blood types. How can Abba's be type AB?"

"Mahmood is not your father."

His mother uttered the words with such measured casualness that for a few seconds they did not register on Waqaar's mind. Then he went utterly still, staring at his mother in disbelief, his face drained of blood. His mother's eyes, full of compassion, rested steadily on his face. Waqaar slumped down into a chair, and his body shuddered as if gripped by an ague. He slowly lifted his face, and his mother saw the questioning look in his eyes.

"My child, I have worried, ever since I encouraged you to take up medical studies, that a day would come when I would have to face this question..." She hesitated for a moment, and then said in a calm steady voice

"Mahmood is my lawful husband, but he is not your biological father."

Waqaar turned his face away. He gripped the armrests of the chair tightly, and stared with vacant eyes at nothingness. His jaw worked as he tried to speak, but no sound came from his lips. His mother pulled her chair next to his, and silently put her arm around his shoulders. Aslam walked in at this moment and saw mother and son *comforting* each other. He held Waqaar's hand and said with a feigned cheerfulness,

"Have heart friend, your father is a fighter, *Insha Allah* we shall win the battle."

Waqaar's "father" died that night. The entry in the hospital records showed that Mahmood Khan had died of severe head injury. The police recorded it as an accidental death from driving under the influence of alcohol.

*****

Waqaar went through the burial ceremonies of his "father" in a daze. He responded to the commiserations and condolences offered by relatives and friends like an automaton. A colossal emotional storm was raging within him. Conflicting thoughts gripped his mind, and his heart was wrenched by self-disgust. Until this day, whenever difficulties or doubts confronted him, he would run to his mother for advice and solace. Her pious demeanor and wise counsel never failed to put his mind at rest. She had been as much a friend to him as a mother. Now he was loath to be in her presence. He had taken a week's leave of absence from his hospital duties, and was staying at home in order to help in performing the last rites of his "father". However, he spent most of his time lying down in his bedroom under the pretext of being tired.

Nilofer was painfully aware of what her son was going through. She yearned to go to him, take him in her arms, and soothe his troubled mind. However, in her wisdom, she decided to leave him alone for the time being. She wanted him to weigh for himself the *misdeed* committed by his mother and indict her before she presented her defense.

Waqaar, in his wildest imaginations, had never thought that one day he would have to sit in judgment on his mother's conduct. For him, his mother had been a pious, compassionate woman, with an unblemished moral fiber. She had dedicated her life to caring for the poor sick. He had worshiped the ground she walked on. Now out of the blue, she had confessed to having a son out of the wedlock. A word kept reverberating in his mind - *Illegitimate. Illegitimate. I am illegitimate*! He started pacing the floor of his room, back and forth, back and forth. He abruptly halted in front of a framed photograph of his mother on his desk. He gazed at the angelic face. "Is this face only a put up mask of chastity? Underneath, is this woman capable of committing the heinous sin of adultery, and cheat on her husband?" His thought process halted abruptly. "Adulteress… I call my own mother an adulteress... I?" He was overwhelmed by a sense of self-remorse. He felt ashamed of his thoughts, which he considered, were no less than a filial blasphemy. He cursed himself for letting such profane thoughts about his mother enter his mind. However, his mother's words kept ringing in his ears,

"Mahmood is my lawful husband, but he is not your biological father."

Then his thoughts took another course. Was Mahmood her husband at all? Yes, he had seen a *nikah naama,* the marriage certificate in the family records, a legal document pronouncing a certain Nilofer, daughter of a certain Wazeer Ahmed, given in marriage to a certain Mahmood Khan, son of a certain Akbar Ali, against a sum of certain amount as *Mehr.* Nevertheless, ever since he could remember, he had never seen a trace of companionship between them. Why, he had hardly seen them exchange a few words. Whenever his "father" was at home, and this was not very frequent, as he spent most of his time on the farms, his mother had always kept out of his way. She had let the servants comply with his commands, and demands. The servants ran scared in his presence, as he was prone to lose temper for no obvious reasons. Waqaar had never seen his mother perturbed by her husband's tantrums. Once in a while, when he got so enraged that the house reverberated with his rants, Waqaar's mother dropped whatever she was doing and went to her husband,

"Mahmood, do calm down. You know losing temper is not good for you."

At such times, Waqaar noticed a peculiar expression on his mother's face. He could not decide whether it was pity or disdain. However, her words never failed to bring about the desired result. Mahmood calmed down immediately, always. Barring this situation, Waqaar had never seen his mother intervening in any of her husband's doings.

Waqaar could not recall a single occasion when his "father" might have shown any affection towards him, even when he was a child. He had only barked his orders at him, commanding him to do this, that, or the other. He hardly socialized with the family, and had very few friends. They were all illiterate or semiliterate men.

Ever since Waqaar had reached an age when he could understand the meaning of marriage, he had often wondered about the strange union of his parents. "How did my mother come to marry my father?" He had often thought. "She was a specialist doctor, and he a semi literate farmer. Moreover, he was incapable of any intellectual interaction. Surely, looking at their aloofness from each other, it could not have been a love marriage. Neither was it a child marriage. The marriage certificate was dated 1965. My mother was already a qualified doctor at the time. There must have been some compelling reason for her to have agreed to this atrocious arrangement."

Waqaar's thoughts again went to the Nikkah Naama. The inequitable contract had kept his poor mother chained to a man who had remained a stranger to her all these years. She had no way of breaking free of this chain. Her creed did not give a woman the right to demand a *talaque,* and get divorced from a disastrous marriage. A surge of pity for his mother welled up within him and wrenched his heart. All the self-pity left him. He cursed himself for having called her, even in his mind, an adulteress. What mortification she must have suffered when she had to tell her grown-up son that he was an illicit offspring of hers? He closed his eyes for a minute in an endeavour to calm himself, and then went looking for his mother.

He found her in her study, stretched out in a reclining chair, reading Allama Iqbal's *Shikwa.* There was a cup of tea on a side table. It had gone cold. He walked up to her with slow steps, and stood before her with bowed head.

"Have a seat son," her voice was as calm as ever.

After Waqaar had taken his seat, she went on in the same serene voice,

"I have no regrets whatsoever, and my *Allah* shall judge me on the day of the *Qayamat*. I have no intention of giving you an explanation."

"For God's sake Ammi," Waqaar choked on his words, "Who am I to ask you for an explanation?"

He could not go on. Tears rolled down his cheeks. A stony silence fell between them, both lost in their own thoughts. Waqaar resumed haltingly,

"You know Ammi, I feel sort of liberated, now that I know I am not an offspring of Mahmood Khan."

He made no further elaboration; neither did his mother make any comment. Long minutes of silence followed. Then he asked in a low but firm voice,

"Tell me Ammi, who *is* my father."

Nilofer did not answer him just then. She interlocked the fingers of her hands, and closed her eyes for a long time, as if weighing her answer. Then she spoke in a commanding tone.

"Vicky my son, I cannot, and shall not tell you his name. However, this much I shall tell you, he was an angel… my soul mate…my idol... I shall worship him until the doomsday. I do not know his whereabouts, as we have mutually decided not to seek each other out."

There was another long interval of silence before she spoke. There was a tender note in her voice.

"You must believe me Vicky, you are not a by-product of your parent's lust. Your birth was a very carefully planned event."

There was silence again.

She turned her chair to face him. There was a note of finality in her words.

"We shall never discuss this topic again."

Waqaar promised his mother that he would not mention the matter again, but he made one promise to himself too,

"*I shall find my father.*"

His mother, that day, had broken one promise she had made to herself. A promise never to let loose the memories she had locked up in her breast twenty-four years back. Today's dialogue with her son Vicky had shattered the lock, and the memories of her flight from a disastrous marriage, and meeting with another Vicky, came gushing out like surging storm water which had breached the dam.

It was January 16, 1966. Nilofer was sitting in the office of Dr. William Wise, the Professor of Obstetrics and Gynecology of the Welsh National School of Medicine, and the University Hospital of Wales, in Cardiff. The Commonwealth University, which had its offices in London, had awarded her a two-year scholarship, and had nominated Professor Wise her guide.

She had arrived at the Heathrow Airport the previous night. A courier from the office of the British Council had picked her up, and had deposited her at the Grosvenor Kensington Hotel, where the council had booked a room for her. As it was past midnight, she had gone straight to bed.

Next morning after breakfast, she had proceeded to visit the office of the British Council in the Spring Gardens. This was the first time she had ever left the shores of Pakistan. London was a strange place for her. The courier had, the previous night, given her brusque directions to the Council's office, and had handed her a small map of the underground railways.

"Please be at the Council office at nine in the morning," he had said, and had promptly disappeared.

She had asked, at the hotel reception, directions to Grosvenor underground station, and then had taken the tube to Spring Gardens. She had located the office without difficulty. The receptionist had escorted her to the office of Mrs. Pyke, the secretary. Mrs. Pyke had asked her what transport she had used to reach the office.

"I took the tube."

"Have you been to London before?"

"No, this is my first visit to Britain."

"I suggest that you should not use the tube for a while, as tube trains are a bit tricky for the newcomers."

Mrs. Pyke had opened a drawer of her desk, and had handed her a railway ticket and currency notes for fifty pounds.

"Here is your ticket to Cardiff. Your train leaves Paddington station at 11.41. The money is for your immediate needs. Once you are in Cardiff, you need to open an external account with a bank. Let us know your account number and the name of the bank. Your allowances will be deposited in your account every month."

Mrs. Pyke had rattled on,

"At the Cardiff Station, one of our officers will meet you. Her name is Miss Valerie. She has your description. She will be waiting for you at the exit barrier. She will drive you to the hotel, where a room has been booked for you. Please shift from the hotel as soon as your hospital allots you a room. If you have any question, please do ask now. If not, I shall say goodbye."

Nilofer had reached Cardiff at 1.36 in the afternoon. At the exit barrier, a young girl had raised her hand and waved to her.

"Miss Valerie?"

"Dr. Khan?"

They had spoken almost simultaneously. Miss Valerie's handshake and greeting had been much warmer than that of the courier at the Heathrow, or Mrs. Pyke's at the Council office. Later she was to learn that the Welsh and the Scots were generally warmer and more hospitable people than the English. Putting her luggage in the van, Miss Valerie had said,

"We have booked you in a nice little cosy hotel called the Lake View."

It was indeed a small and cosy place. Miss Valerie had surprised her by accompanying her to her room and making a quick inspection of it.

"The room is a bit small, but looks comfortable. Is there anything else I can do for you, Dr. Khan?" she had asked.

"Yes, Miss Valerie. May I request you to give me a lift in your car to the University Hospital?"

"Yes indeed, shall we go?"

As they drove down to the Hospital, Valerie said,

"Dr. Khan, you need to know that the University Hospital is popularly known as the Heath Hospital, because of its location in the Heath Park."

Nilofer had located the Department of Obstetrics and Gynecology on the second floor. Professor Wise's secretary Mrs. Davies, a rather bulky woman, had asked her to take a seat while she announced her arrival to the Professor. Within a few minutes, the Professor had emerged from his office,

"Hallo, Dr. Khan," he said, "welcome to Cardiff."

They had shaken hands, and the professor had escorted her into his office.

"Will you have a cup of coffee, Dr. Khan?"

"Yes sir," she replied, "Coffee would be welcome."

Professor Wise picked up his intercom, and spoke to his secretary.

"Mrs. D, will you get us some coffee please?

"Sir, what is the arrangement for my lodging?" Nilofer inquired.

"Oh yes, let us see," said the professor as he removed a file from the drawer of his desk. He consulted the papers and said,

"A room has been set aside for you at the Radnor House."

Mrs. Davies entered with two mugs of coffee on a tray and placed it on the desk.

"When can I start work?" Dr. Nilofer asked the professor.

"Well, Dr. Khan I suggest you take it easy for a couple of days, and get settled first. Meanwhile I shall set up a meeting with Dr. Joans for next Tuesday. Dr. Joans is our senior consultant Gynecologist. You contact me on Monday and I shall let you know the time for the meeting. The three of us shall then chart out your program and..."

The bleep of his intercom interrupted him. He put the receiver to his ear, listened for a moment and then said,

"That's lovely, Mrs. D, send him in right away."

The door opened, and a tall, lean man in a white coat entered. His features and complexion were that of an Asian. He had an open friendly handsome face.

"Good evening Professor," said the newcomer.

His accent amused Nilofer. It sounded like *goo evening.* There was an unsuccessful attempt at British pronunciation.

"Come in Vicky, come in," said the Professor, "meet Dr. Khan from Pakistan. She is here in Britain on a commonwealth scholarship. Dr. Khan, this is Dr. *Weekram,* our registrar in surgery."

The name Weekram gave no indication to Nilofer regarding the newcomer's nationality.

"Hi doctor," he greeted her, but did not offer to shake hands, and Nilofer, in her turn, just nodded her head in response. The newcomer then turned to the professor.

"Professor, I had dropped in to have a word with you about Mrs. Glen, but as you are busy at the moment, I could come back later."

"Do have a seat Vicky, and tell me about Mrs. Glen."

The two of them talked for a while about a patient on whom, Nilofer guessed, the surgery and gynecology teams had operated jointly. When Vicky got up to leave, the professor said,

"Oh Vicky, I have a favor to ask of you. A room has been allotted to Dr. Khan at the Radnor House. Could you please see that she gets settled there comfortably?"

"Sure, Professor, I'll do that right away. There should be no problem. I too am at the Radnor House."

*****

Nilofer and Vicky took leave of the Professor. As they walked towards the elevators, both remained silent for some time. Vicky was thinking how to strike conversation with his companion. These Muslim women are a bit unpredictable in their behavior. He had known an Indian Muslim woman doctor who would rebuff a compatriot male who offered to shake hands, saying it was against her culture, while she had no qualms shaking the hand of a white man. Nilofer too was reflecting on Vicky's demeanor in the Professor's office. Why had this man not offered to shake hands with her? Was he one of those religious zealots who considered physical contact with a stranger of opposite sex a taboo? Vicky made the first move at conversation. He spoke in Urdu.

"It sounds a bit strange, a lady being addressed as Khan."

"True, but it is no fault of the westerners," Nilofer replied in English. "The western people traditionally write their given name first, followed by the father's or husband's name, and end with the surname. We Muslims do not use surnames and hence these westerners mistakenly consider the suffix to the father's or husband's name as the surname, which is usually Khan, Ali, Ahmed, and so on."

Vicky was intrigued at her reluctance to converse in her national language. Nilofer was thinking it would be better to keep the conversation at a formal level. Speaking in Urdu will breed informality. She spoke in English again,

"May I know your formal name? I can't call you Vicky."

"It is Vikram, Vikram Kocher. I am from India. Everyone here calls me Vicky. They find it easy to pronounce." Now he too had switched to English.

"Well, I have no problem in pronouncing Vikram or Kocher."

"And I have no problem in speaking Urdu," Vicky could not resist having a dig at her.

She took it sportingly and just laughed off the jibe. Vikram noticed the peculiar way she laughed. Her laughter started soundlessly from her eyes, which opened wide, with a twinkle in them, and then it spread down her face to her lips. The corners of her mouth twitched once or twice and the lips opened in a broad smile; then came forth a short pleasing tinkle of laughter. The fleeting latent period that her smile took to reach from the eyes to the lips jabbed Vicky's memory briefly. Any way, her laughter broke the ice. Vicky had a way of putting people at ease. Nilofer was surprised at her own laughter. She had not laughed in the last three months, and had thought she would never smile again.

"I am not a westerner," he said, "and I know better than to call you Dr. Khan."

"Well, you can call me Dr. Nilofer."

They came to the Radnor House and took two flights of stairs to his room on the second floor.

"Can I offer you a cup of coffee?" Vicky continued to speak in English. To his surprise, his guest now chose to switch to Urdu.

"Is there a canteen nearby? I am famished. I haven't had lunch."

"I am sorry the dining hall is not open at this time. I can fix up a quick omelette and some bread if you like."

"That would be an act of kindness to a hungry soul." She seemed to discard her stiff attitude.

Vikram looked at his watch and said,

"Pardon me, but you will have to bear your hunger pangs for a few more minutes. I must first see to your room. The housekeeper is due to go off duty any time now."

He picked up the phone on his desk and dialed a three-digit number.

"Hi, Jenny dear," he spoke into the phone. "This is Vicky. I have here with me a Dr. Nilofer Khan from Pakistan. I am told she is to have a room here at the Radnor."

He listened for a few seconds and then said,

"That will be nice of you, thanks Jenny." He put the phone down and said to Nilofer.

"Your room number is 107 on the first floor. The housekeeper is leaving the key in the lock. You can occupy it whenever you want. And now you will have to excuse me, I have a hungry mouth to feed." He left the room.

Left alone, Nilofer proceeded to inspect Vikram's room. It was a large comfortable room with central heating. There was a high bedstead covered with a clean fresh looking bed sheet. A sky blue carpet covered the floor. A large wardrobe covered one whole wall. A large desk stood against the wall opposite to the wardrobe. Above the desk, fixed to the wall were the controls for the B.B.C. Radio.

A cute looking music system lay on a high glass shelf to the left of the desk. "So, our Vicky dear is fond of music," Nilofer thought. "A show off too, trying to impress me by addressing women workers as dears."

Vicky came back carrying a tray, which he placed on the desk. There was a plate of omelette, slices of bread and cake, and two cups of steaming coffee. As she proceeded to do justice to the frugal meal, Vicky sipped his coffee, and watched his guest in silence. She must be around twenty-five, he guessed. She was a bit above the average height for an Asian girl, may be five feet eight. She had a delicate face. There was a tiny, almost imperceptible mole just under the tip of her nose, which enhanced its exquisiteness. She had full, slightly pouting lips. The most stunning feature of her face was her eyes. They were large, and had a piercing look. Vikram could not help equating them with *cups of nectar*. However, a perpetual expression of dejection, and a sickly complexion overshadowed her pretty features. There is something tragic about this girl, Vikram guessed.

She looked up at him and asked hesitatingly,

"Does your phone have international link?" Seeing a questioning look in his eyes, she said,

"I would like to call my home in Lahore."

"Oh, for that we shall have to go through the hospital switch board." He consulted his watch and said,

"It must be around half past ten of night in Lahore. Would you like to call now?"

"Yes please, if it is possible."

He asked her to write down the Lahore number on a piece of paper, picked up the phone, and again dialed a three-digit number. It was answered instantly.

"Is this Miss Gauld? ... Oh, Hanna dear…"

Nilofer thought, "Here he goes again *dearing* the girls." Meanwhile Vikram was saying into the phone,

"…This is Vicky; I need to call Lahore in Pakistan. Shall I give you the number?"

He spoke the number slowly, and then silently held the receiver to his ear for about half a minute, and then said,

"Okay, we shall wait."

He replaced the receiver, and said to Nilofer,

"She has not been able to get through to Lahore. She will try again after five minutes.

As they waited, Vikram kept on an inconsequential dialogue, remarking on the treacherous, wet, and cold Welsh weather.

The phone rang and Vikram picked it up. He listened for a couple of seconds, and then passed on the receiver to Nilofer.

"Your party is on the line."

Nilofer spoke into the phone in the Punjabi language,

"Hello… It is me," she said, and then went on without a pause, "I have reached Cardiff…No…Yes…Okay."

She put the phone down. Vikram was surprised at the sheer brevity of the conversation. Usually a person calling home after reaching a foreign land had a cascade of questions to answer, effusive inquiries about the journey, about his well being, arrangements for lodging and boarding, and hordes of other things. Here was a woman from a conservative community who had traveled to a foreign land calling back home to announce her arrival in just one short phrase! The person on the other side of the line was her husband. That much Vikram had deducted from her words of address, or rather lack of them. This was not the way a young couple separated by thousands of miles would converse. There certainly was a discordant note. Nilofer interrupted his thoughts.

"I must see my room, and then get my luggage from the hotel."

They went down to room number107 on the first floor. The key was in the lock as the housekeeper had promised. The room was a replica of Vikram's room. Vikram showed her the facilities available to the lodgers. For every unit of four rooms, there was a separate block of showers and toilets, a common kitchenette with a refrigerator, an electric stove, a coffee percolator, crockery, and pots and pans. There was a small utility room with a washing machine, an electric iron, and ironing board.

"You don't really have to use these gadgets. A laundry bag is provided in each room. Put your linen for laundering in it. The bag will be taken away every Wednesday. Your linen will be washed and ironed, and returned to your room on Friday. The house cleaner will dust and hoover the room, and change the bed linen regularly. Any day you do not want your room to be disturbed, hang the 'do not disturb' sign on the doorknob. The breakfast lunch and supper are available at the dininghall, which I shall show you tomorrow morning."

"Why tomorrow? Am I to go hungry tonight?" Nilofer asked jokingly.

They had now switched over to Punjabi, interspersed with Urdu.

"How can I dare be that presumptuous? You are my guest this evening. I do not want you to start on an insipid, tasteless British supper. You shall be eating that for the rest of your stay here and may even learn to relish it. But tonight you shall have a spicy Bengali meal."

Nilofer made ready to protest, but he did not give her the opportunity, and went on,

"You must be tired. I suggest you have an hour's rest. I shall pick you up at seven. We shall collect your things from the hotel, and then have our dinner at a nice little place."

Before Nilofer could say anything, he left. As he walked up the stairs to his room, Vikram recalled the inflection of some of the Punjabi phrases Nilofer had used. That dialect was spoken in the northeast of Pakistan, around the district of Gujarat. Vikram considered asking Nilofer about it, but then thought better of it.

Nilofer lay down on the bed. She covered herself with a light blanket and fell asleep instantly. The insistent ringing of her phone woke her up. She opened her eyes. She was disoriented. For a few moments, she could not fathom where she was. Then slowly the room came into focus. She looked at her watch. She had slept for a full hour. She picked up the receiver.

"Sorry if I woke you up. It is time to go to your hotel," Vikram reminded her.

"Give me ten minutes and I shall be ready."

Vikram drove her to the Lake View Hotel. She asked him to wait at the reception, while she went up to her room and changed out of her crumpled dress into a fresh one. They retrieved her baggage, put it in his car's boot, and drove to a small eating-place run by a Bengali from East Pakistan. They took their seats, and a waiter placed two copies of the menu before them. She consulted the menu and then closed it.

"Will you please select for me."

Vikram summoned the waiter and ordered Bung tomato soup, Masala Chicken, and tandoori roti, to be followed by curried fresh water *Machh* and rice.

They ate in silence. Nilofer had always shunned talking while eating, and felt thankful to her host for making no attempt at conversation during the meal. She declined coffee after the meal and Vikram called for the bill.

They drove back to the Radnor House. Vikram carried her valise to her room. Before leaving, he said,

"My phone number is 211, same as the room number. Do call me if you need any help. I shall give you a tinkle at seven in the morning, and we shall go to the dining hall for breakfast."

Nilofer thanked him profusely for helping her and for the dinner, and said good night.

Next morning Vikram rang precisely at seven.

"Are you ready for the breakfast?"

"Yes." She said, "Ready and hungry."

She was surprised at feeling so hungry after the heavy dinner last night.

Perhaps the weather, she thought. She refused to admit to herself that the lifting of her mood in the amiable company last evening had restored her appetite. Her appetite had been blunted the last three months and she had been eating only sparsely.

They went to the dining hall, which was close to their quarters. The breakfast that morning consisted of orange juice, fried eggs, baked beans, and a steaklet. Nilofer eyed the little steak, and said,

"I hope it's not a pork preparation."

Vikram took some time to answer her.

"I don't think it is…But Dr. Nilofer, I would rather not analyze too closely the ingredients that go into the preparations of food here. If you do, you may end up starving. In this country, segregation of beef from pork is irrelevant. For all you know, the eggs on your plate may have been fried in lard, the pig fat."

A deep frown appeared on Nilofer's face. She folded her hands, and said,

"O my Allah the merciful, do pardon us, the sinners."

After breakfast, Vikram left for the hospital, and Nilofer returned to her room. She had plenty of free time at hand. Her work schedule was to be decided on Tuesday. Today was Friday. She had four days before she could start work. What should she do till then? She had no reading material to occupy her. Could she go out and buy some books? She did not know the town. She could not just go out and ask a stranger where one can buy books. She must ask Dr. Vikram. "Oh God!" she thought, "Am I not becoming too dependent on Vikram for everything?"

Suddenly she remembered that she had not offered a single *namaaz* since she had left home two days back. Missing namaaz was justified in travel, but not otherwise. She felt remorseful, "How did I forget it last evening and this morning?"

She looked at her watch, which she had now set to the British time. There were still three hours before the noon prayer – *Salat Al Zuhr*. The room was a bit too cold for her. She manipulated the knob of the radiator to raise the temperature. She reclined on the bed, and stared at the freshly painted ceiling. She dwelt on the recent events that had taken place back home. This agitated her, and a blanket of gloom wrapped her thoughts. She jumped out of bed, and started pacing the floor. When fifteen minutes of marching up and down did not help in soothing her mind, she changed into *kameez* and *salwar*, picked up her *dupatta*, and left the room. She walked down to the common room. The television set was on, and a doctor couple in white coats occupied the sofa against the sidewall. The man was a burly giant, and the woman's built was equally robust. The couple looked up as she entered, and then ignored her totally. Nor were they interested in the program, being aired on the T.V. They sat there snuggled together, cuddling and kissing, unconcerned of the company. Nilofer watched T.V. for a few minutes, and then turned her back to it in disgust. Such indecent programs! These would never be allowed in Pakistan, nor would such behavior by the spectators be tolerated.

She picked up the copy of *The Guardian* from the side table. The front page had a two-column item on the hostilities building up again between India and Pakistan, and the inept governance of her country under the military rule of General Ayub Khan. This news item only added to her gloom. She put the newspaper back, and returned to her room. She performed *woozoo,* the washing prior to prayer, and then took out from her bag the *musalah,* the praying carpet. She peered out of the window to see which direction was the west. It was a difficult task on a cloudy day. She spread the *musalah* and stood facing the direction she guessed was west. She said her *namaaz* very sedately and slowly. After finishing the prayer, she felt considerably calm. She rolled up the carpet and placed it in a corner of her wardrobe.

Exactly at one, there was a knock at the door.

"Time for lunch," Vikram said.

Without saying a word, she draped her dupatta over her shoulders, and followed him. Vikram sensed her somber mood, and made no attempt at conversation. When they emerged from the house, Nilofer looked up towards the sky and turned her face from side to side.

"Are you trying to locate the directions?

Nilofer was taken aback by the accuracy of his guess.

"Yes," she said, "I could not decide which way the west lay. I had to say namaaz, facing what I guessed was west."

Vikram chuckled,

"As such, Dr. Nilofer, God manifests in all directions, but if you want to face the *Kaaba* for your prayers, you must turn to South-East as it lies in that direction from the British Isles."

"*Haye Allah*!" She was utterly flustered, "That did not occur to me. How ignorant of me. *Parwardigar*, forgive me."

Vikram smiled again,

"Well, *Doctor Sahiba,* for your next *salat,* do face the Nurses' hostel. It lies in the South-East direction from the Radnor House."

Nilofer was surprised at a non-Muslim using the Arabic term salat, instead of namaaz, but she refrained from commenting. This time Vikram took her to a different dining hall. This one was attached to the Hospital. It was more crowded than the one in which they had their breakfast.

"When the staff members take a short lunch break from their work, they usually come here," Vikram informed her.

The main dish on the menu that day was fish.

"Friday is a no meat day in most European countries. All dining halls here serve fish on Fridays," Vikram continued her education.

There was choice of fried cod or smoked salmon. Nilofer selected the cod and picked up two cheese sandwiches to go with it. Vikram had smoked salmon with potato chips. They took a table, which had just been vacated by two young girls in nurse's uniform, and finished their meals in silence. Nilofer was thankful for Vikram's quietness. She had not yet overcome the disgust she had contracted in the common room. She cursed herself for imposing her foul mood on Vikram. She continued to avoid any conversation while Vikram escorted her to her quarters, before he left for the hospital.

That evening, at supper, she tried to make up for her earlier reticence, by striking a friendly conversation. She talked a bit about herself.

"I am doing a postgraduate course in obstetrics and gynecology at the King Edward University of Lahore. My scholarship here will be for two years. The time I spend here will be considered towards my Master's degree back home."

"Why don't you register for membership exam of the Royal College of Obstetrics and Gynecology?" Vikram asked.

"I don't know whether that will be permitted," she said.

Vikram advised her to wait for a month or so, and then take up the matter of membership with Professor Wise.

"He is a very considerate man. Meanwhile we should gather information on your eligibility for registration."

"Well, I thank you for being so considerate yourself," she said.

For the next three days, the two of them had all their meals together. Vikram took her around the campus and showed her various facilities provided to the inmates. Nilofer saw the two low buildings, housing the resident doctors; the multi-storied buildings of the undergraduate students, and the nurses' hostels, the indoor swimming pool and the canteen where the students could buy drinks at subsidized rates.

"Does this not amount to encouraging youngsters to drink?" she asked.

"Well, this is their culture," he said, "consuming alcoholic beverage is not considered improper here. Drinks are considered a delicacy."

On Tuesday morning, Nilofer went to Professor Wise's office where she met Dr. Cynthia Joans, the senior consultant Gynecologist. She was a middle-aged woman with a slight, almost reedy built. With her height of about five feet ten, she appeared to tower over Nilofer as she shook hands with her. Because of her tall thin built, her head and face looked disproportionately large. She had a slightly upturned nose and thin lips, which gave her an authoritarian appearance. When she spoke, she had a habit of pulling her mouth slightly to the right, which gave her a mocking look. She was the opposite of Professor Wise. While the professor was a polite, soft-spoken man, this woman talked brusquely which sounded almost rude. She hardly took a sip from the coffee that had been placed before her, and proceeded to outline the program for Nilofer.

"Professor, the first thing that Dr. Khan needs to do is to get registered with the General Medical Council. Once she receives her registration certificate, she has to have a medical insurance policy issued. Until then she should not handle patients. Even after she is registered and insured, she shall not be given independent responsibility of patients, as she is not an employee of the hospital. She shall work under the supervision of the consultant and the senior registrar."

Dr. Joans continued briskly as if she was in a hurry to be gone,

"Dr. Khan, you will not do any emergency work. Even if someone suggests it, you will refuse. Tell him or her that you are a visiting scholar and not on the hospital staff. Of course, you will participate in the out-patient, in-patient, as well as in the operative work. Nevertheless, all this will be under supervision. I suggest that you spend the initial six months in my unit, and the next six months in the unit of Dr. Collin Theodore. During the second year of your tenure, Professor Wise and I have agreed that you should be given the liberty to decide your own program."

She rose from her chair,

"Now if you will excuse me, I shall get to my work."

She turned to Nilofer,

"Tomorrow is our operating day. Be in the O.T. number nine, at eight sharp." She breezed out of the room.

Nilofer turned to the Professor as if to ask for leave.

"Finish your coffee Dr. Khan," he said.

While listening to the barrage of Dr. Joans, she had forgotten her coffee.

"Oh," she said and took a sip. It had gone cold. She finished it in two gulps and put the cup down. The Professor gave her a reassuring smile.

"Do not get ruffled by Joan's demeanor. Her bite is not as bad as her bark. You will soon find out that she has a heart of gold, and is a very talented doctor. I have only one thing to add to the program outlined by Joans. In the second year of your scholarship, you will be entitled to travel around the country visiting various hospitals relevant to your subject. The British Council shall bear your traveling expenses. We shall discuss the details of your traveling program at the appropriate time. Now I must say good bye and wish you a happy time with us."

That evening, at the dining table Nilofer told Vikram what had transpired at the meeting.

"You can learn a lot by being around Dr. Joans," Vikram said, "You must make full use of this opportunity. I would suggest that at the end of six months, behave as if you have forgotten to move to the unit of Dr. Collin Theodore, and continue to work with Dr. Joans. She too would act as if she has forgotten about your shifting to Theodore's unit."

Vikram saw the questioning look in Nilofer's eyes, and explained.

"Theodore has worked in the Indian army in the days of British Empire. He has not shed his superior attitude of the Raj era. He still looks down on the colored races as inferior people. Though the race relation regulations of this country do not permit any racial discrimination, Theodore has his own ways of putting down the colored staff working with him, without obviously infringing the regulations. The hospital authorities are aware of his veiled racial attitude, and will not take any notice if you, as a visitor, do not wish to be a part of his unit."

"I'll remember that, but at the moment I need some stationery. Can you suggest a store?

"I can do better than that. Tomorrow I should be done at the hospital by five in the evening. You trot down to my room as soon as you finish your day. We'll have our coffee and then I shall drive you down to the city centre and show you where you can buy your requirements."

Next day they went down to the city centre. Vikram gave her a guided tour.

"Marks and Spencer is the place for buying garments. You get good stuff, and at a reasonable rates. At British Homes you can get your home appliances, that is, if you plan to set up your domesticity in Britain," Vikram jested.

They entered Boots.

"This is the place that you shall be using most of the times. They deal in books, stationery, electronics, musical systems, optical appliances, toiletry, cutlery, crockery, pharmaceuticals, and hordes of things of daily requirement."

They approached a young girl behind the counter. Vikram addressed her.

"Excuse me miss, this is Dr. Khan. Will you please issue a doctor's concession card to her?"

"Yes sir," said the girl, and took out a blank card from the drawer of the counter.

"May I see your I.D. please?"

Nilofer removed her passport from the purse and offered it to the girl. The girl looked at the first page of the passport and said,

"This here, it does not say 'doctor'. Do you have any other I.D. which shows your work place?"

"Oh, actually I have joined the Heath Hospital only today. My Hospital I.D. will be ready tomorrow."

Vikram intervened, "No matter, we'll have the card issued when we come next time."

Then he turned to Nilofer, "Meanwhile you can use my card."

He took out his card from his wallet. Nilofer retrieved her passport and made to leave.

"Excuse me ma'am," the girl said, "I don't doubt your word. I'll make out the card presently."

She signed the card, stamped it, and handed it to Nilofer.

"Here you are, doctor, please enter your name, and address on it. You are now our esteemed customer."

Nilofer purchased her requirements, and they drove back to their house. While parking his car, Vikram suggested,

"Although it is a bit early, the dining hall must be open. Why don't we get done with our supper before we go to our rooms?"

The dining hall was almost empty at this time. They occupied a table at the back. As they were finishing their meal, Vikram said,

"Dr. Nilofer, I think it is not wise to carry your passport in your purse. If it gets lost, you may have to go through a tiresome hassle to have one re-issued. It is better to keep it under lock and key."

"I was following the instructions contained in the British Council brochure, which says I must always carry my passport."

"That applies when you are traveling. For the local purposes, it is okay to carry the I.D. issued by the hospital. Anyway, if you strictly want to adhere to the Council's guidance, you could carry a copy of the passport."

"I shall do that. I shall have a copy made when I go into the city next time."

"You don't have to go to the city for that," said Vikram, "I could copy it on my department's copier in the morning."

"That will be nice of you," Nilofer took out her passport and handed it to him.

Vikram made two copies of the passport. He handed them over to Nilofer along with the original the next evening.

"The extra copy could come handy," he said.

That evening Nilofer noticed a gross change in Vikram's behavior. He had so far been strictly formal with her, never asking a personal question, or making a personal remark. Since they had arrived at the dining hall that evening, she had caught him a couple of times, watching her intently. A smile played on his lips, and there was a glint in his eyes. Nilofer felt annoyed at this change. He leaned forwards and said, "Nilofer, have you always lived in Lahore?"

She was taken aback by the change from Dr. Nilofer to just Nilofer. She wanted to rebuff him for his attempt at familiarity, but refrained. She kept her voice frosty polite and answered,

"No, D...o...c...t...o...r Vikram, I spent some years in Karachi."

She did not elaborate any further. Vikram did not need Solomon's wisdom to sense her annoyance, and changed the topic.

Back in her room, Nilofer began a furious monologue in her mind. "*Ya Allah,* was the man about to make a pass at me? Perhaps it was a mistake to have maintained a week-long association with him. I should have accepted his help for a day or two and then parted company. Showing my dependence on him for all my needs seems to have put ideas into his head. I should get rid of him before he makes any further move at intimacy. However, I must break away from him without creating any bitterness."

She started framing in her mind the polite phrases she should use tomorrow, to tell him that she needed his help no more.

Next morning her phone rang. She looked at her watch. It could not be Vikram, she thought, It was too early for break fast. She picked up the phone. It was Vikram.

"Dr. Nilofer, Would you mind too much if I do not accompany you to the dining hall anymore. I am sure by now you have learnt the ropes and should be able to get along by yourself. The thing is that I am starting a new project at my department, and shall be keeping irregular hours."

Nilofer had not expected this. She felt relieved, infuriated, and intrigued, all at the same time. She would not have to give excuses for breaking with him. She was glad of that. However, she felt an eccentric sense of having been cheated of the opportunity of being the one who initiated the disassociation. Above all, she was intrigued at the turn of events. Was he a mind reader? "How did he know I wanted to break with him? I had given no such indications last evening."

For the next ten days, Nilofer did not even have a glimpse of Vikram.

After dissociating from Vikram, Nilofer was determined to fend for herself, and not to depend on help from others. Nevertheless, the very next morning she overslept. For the last six days, she had woken up to the ringing of the telephone at six sharp. Vikram knew she regularly said her morning namaaz – *Salat al Fajr.* Therefore, he had been giving her one full hour to get ready, and say her prayers before they went to breakfast at seven. Nilofer had not thought of setting her alarm clock. That morning when she opened her eyes and looked at her wristwatch, it said half past seven. "Gosh, I am going to be late for the ward rounds," she thought, "Cynthia will bite my head off."

She had a quick wash, dressed, and hastened to the hospital. She had to forgo even a cup of tea. She had been assigned the task of clerking. On the ward rounds, as the unit staff moved from bed to bed, Nilofer had to note down, in the patients' files, the instructions tossed at a rapid-fire speed by Dr. Joans. After the rounds were over, she had to fill in the request forms for the laboratory tests, and radiological investigations that had been ordered by the boss for various patients, and get them signed by the registrar. Back home, the ward servants carried these request forms to the lab and radiology. Here, the junior doctors had to do this job. By the time she had finished all these chores, it was lunch time, and her stomach was growling with hunger. Lunch was the first meal she had that day.

That evening Dr. Brackenridge, the senior registrar, was scheduled to lecture on abnormal fetal positions. She had two hours before that. She decided to use the interval for brushing up the subject of fetal positions. She went to the library and removed the volume of Whitfield's Obstetrics and Gynecology from the book stacks. She read until the lecture time. The attendance at the lecture was sparse. The lecture itself was insipid. Dr. Brackenridge went through it perfunctorily, just wanting to be done with it, and be gone.

She returned to her room, feeling low. She said her *Mugrib Namaaz*, and then went to the dining hall for supper. The menu that evening did nothing to raise her drooping spirit. The duck preparation was almost inedible. She purchased a couple of vegetable sandwiches from the counter and ate them slowly. She was missing the company of Vikram, but would not acknowledge it, even to herself. She recalled his attempt at familiarity and thought, "I did right in getting rid of him. I do not want intimacy with anybody, least of all with an Indian and that too a Hindu." However, an inner voice kept on pounding at her, "Was he really trying to be intimate? What made you think he was?" She could not give an honest answer to herself. What exactly had he done? She tried to think back. He had looked at her with a peculiar expression on his face. Was that a lewd look? After almost a week's association, he had dropped the title of doctor from her name, and called her just by her first name. Was that an indecent act? He had only inquired about her sojourn in Lahore. Was that a coarse inquiry? Perhaps she had been unfair to him. "Forget it," she said to herself. "Anyway, I did not discard him. It was he who did not want to keep the association," she tried to justify herself. "I don't have to be friendly with him, just because he gave me a bit of help, that too at the instance of my professor," she continued the monologue in her mind; "I did not go begging for it."

With all her self-justification, she could not get rid of a feeling of remorse. She decided to go to the common room. A little entertainment would change her mood, she thought. The common room was crowded, and full of cigarette smoke and noisy cheering. A rugby match was being telecast. She backtracked to her room, changed into her nightdress, and retired to bed. She lay awake for a long time taking stock of her situation. She had come to this country, ostensibly in pursuit of an academic career. The real purpose was to flee from that brute of her newly acquired husband. She had hoped to find, although only temporarily, a sociable environment where she could forget her misfortune. However, the situation here was not very comfortable. The weather was depressing. The people were not very friendly. Professor Wise was a sweet person, but he was far too senior to her, in age as well as position. There was no question of socializing with him. At the most, she could go to him occasionally for help and guidance. Ditto for Dr. Cynthia Joans. Then there was Dr. Brackenridge, the Senior Registrar. Though not too senior in age, he was out and out a disagreeable person. She had heard nurses sniggering behind his back and calling him a sour-faced Scot. The Registrar, Dr. Jason Rolfe was a cordial young Irishman, quite eager to make friends. Unfortunately, he did not live on the campus. He lived in rented quarters in the outskirts of the town with his wife and son. The first senior house officer, Dr. Katy Beckham was what the books described as typically English. She was the same age as Nilofer, and correctly polite to her when they were at work. Outside the working hours, she ignored her totally. She had not yet met the second senior house officer. She was on leave. She had heard some staff member referring to her as Pamela. She was due in a couple of days. "There is no one with whom I can share my thoughts and feelings," she thought desolately. Her thoughts un-intentionally returned to Vikram. She pushed them away resolutely. "I do not intend to socialize with an Indian Hindu." The Pakistani media often referred to the Hindus as a treacherous race, although she did not subscribe to that belief. She pulled the blanket up to her chin, and closed her eyes.

Nilofer was in a pitch-dark tunnel. She was stark naked. She was running to escape from the pursuing demon. She ran fast but could not shake off the pursuer. She could hear its panting, and its scampering feet right behind her. She ran even faster, but the pursuer kept right behind her, its panting becoming harsher. She stumbled and fell on her face. She shrieked, but no sound came out from her parched throat. She turned on her back to ease her breathing. The fiend jumped on to her chest. It was crushing her under its weight. She smelled its foul breath. She was choking under its massive bulk. She tried wriggling out, but found herself pinned down. She put both her hands against the hairy chest of the beast, and pushed with all her might. *Yaa… illaaaa…hi...hi...hi...hi…* she shrieked, and woke up from the nightmare. She was bathed in cold sweat, and out of breath. She lay there, whispering the words of the *Kalma, Laa ilaaha illal Lahoo Mohamed ur Rasool Ullah.* This helped to calm her down, but she found it impossible to go back to sleep. "I thought I had left this scourge of the nightmare back home," she said to herself.

She got out of bed and washed her face at the washbasin. She looked at her watch. It was half past four. Although it was a bit too early, she spread her musalah and offered the morning namaaz. She took out a *paara* of the holy *Quraan*, touched it to her eyes and lips, and did the *talawat,* recitation, until daylight.

*****

It was Friday. Nilofer reached the outpatient department ten minutes before the scheduled time. Only the nurse had arrived, and was laying out the sterilized packs of instruments needed for the internal examination of patients. She acknowledged her greetings, and took a chair in the senior registrar's room. After a few minutes, a frail looking girl in white coat breezed in.

"Good morning Sally," she tossed the greetings at the nurse and then turned to Nilofer,

"Ah, a new face!"

Nilofer had been appraising the newcomer. She was a sparsely built girl of around twenty-four. Her features were distinctly Asian, and her complexion a bit pallid. Nilofer could not decipher her accent. It was certainly not Asian.

"You must be the second S.H.O," she said to the new girl.

"Correct the very first time. I give you full marks. Pamela Lahore is the name and you can call me Pamela," her verbal strafing amused Nilofer.

"I am Dr. Nilofer Khan, and you can call me Nilofer."

Dr. Brackenridge arrived at this juncture, followed immediately by Dr. Cynthia Joans. There was no further talk between Nilofer and Pamela. At the end of the outpatient session, Pamela, who had been assisting Dr. Joans in the inner office, emerged and approached Nilofer.

"Coming for lunch Dr. Khan?"

Nilofer got up quietly and accompanied her new colleague to the hospital dining hall. The menu for lunch was egg Afrikan, broccoli, and the ubiquitous potato chips. Nilofer picked up a cheese sandwich from the shelf and obtained the egg preparation and broccoli from the counter, and they both occupied an empty table.

"Do you hail from Lahore in Pakistan?" Nilofer asked.

Pamela burst out laughing. "I think I must carry a placard around my neck saying, I am not a Pakistani."

Nilofer gave her a questioning look, "The name Lahore…" She did not finish her question.

"Oh that? Let me explain. I am from Barbados, West Indies. I look Asian because I am of Indian stock, although I know nothing about India. Generations back an ancestor of mine was brought from India to the West Indies as an indentured laborer. I have no idea to which part of India he belonged. All I know is he was a blacksmith. I am told a blacksmith in the Indian language is called a *lohar*. Most of the migrants had inter-marriages with the locals and lost their Indian identity, but there are a few families who marry only into the migrant families. They still give their children Indian names. My parents named me Prameela, Prameela Lohar. When I joined school, my father registered me as Prameela Lahore, a much more respectable name than the lowly Lohar. In the final year of my school, my parents decided to send me to Britain for further studies. I decided to change my name to an English sounding one – Pamela. That's how Prameela Lohar became Pamela Lahore."

Nilofer found that the only common links between her and Pamela were their complexion and their profession. There was no common social ground. This she discovered the next day. It was a Saturday. The surgery list on Saturday was that of the Senior Registrar. Pamela assisted Dr. Brackenridge in the innucleation of a uterine fibroid. After handing over the patient to the recovery room staff, Pamela and Nilofer went for a quick cup of coffee at the O.T. canteen.

"Are you coming to the disco tonight?" Pamela asked.

"I've never been to one,"

"Then you must come tonight. It is fun really, and helps you unwind."

Nilofer wanted to refuse. The clergy of her community prohibited participation in dance and music, calling these activities un-Islamic. She did not concur with their view. However, as she belonged to a family involved in politics, music was not permitted at home, lest it affected the family vote base. When she was residing in Karachi, she had owned a record player, and she and her friends used to listen for hours on end, to the *ghazals* and songs sung by Ghulam Ali, Noor Jahan, Runa Laila, and other popular singers. Occasionally, they would manage to lay hands on the records smuggled from India, and listen to the melodies of the famed Lata Mangeshkar and other famous Indian singers. Her favorites among these were Talat Mahmood and Begam Akhtar. Once, one of her friends managed to obtain a couple of old records of a very early Indian singer, Sahgal. She fell in love with the melodious voice of the man. The only musical instruments used in his records were the harmonium and the *tabla*. His voice itself was an orchestra. She played one particular ghazal of Sahgal, *ghum diye mustakil,* over and over again, until the record wore out. However, going to a disco was not the same as listening to the *ghazals.* Though she had not been to one ever, she knew it involved dancing.

"I cannot dance," she put forth an authentic excuse.

Pamela laughed, "There is no real dancing involved in discos. All you have to do is to shake a bit in the company of your partner. And don't you worry; I shall find a partner for you..."

"No, no," Nilofer interrupted her hastily, and said in a panicky voice, "I am not permitted to dance with men."

Pamela looked at her quizzically for a few moments, and then raised both her hands in front of her as if to ward off Nilofer's protestations.

"Okay, okay, no dancing for you. You can sit on the sidelines and watch."

Nilofer agreed to go to the disco with Pamela that evening, partly out of curiosity, as she had never been to one before, and partly out of concern that her refusal might offend Pamela. She was the only one who had offered a hand of friendship to her, and she did not want to lose her. Nevertheless, she was not prepared for what she saw that evening. As they entered the hall, her ears were assaulted by the deafening sound of blaring music. The floor was crowded with couples, gyrating with their bodies indecently pressed against each other.

"I'll go and find my partner," Pamela shouted in her ear above the din of the earsplitting music, and disappeared.

Nilofer did not hear her. Her eyes were riveted on one particular couple. The girl wore a very short skirt, and the boy had put both his hands underneath it, locking them behind her buttocks, crushing the lower part of her body against his own. The sight of the so-called dancing and the stench of liquor made Nilofer's stomach heave, and she fled from the scene.

Nilofer ran the whole way back to her room. She dropped her coat into the nearest chair and flung herself onto the bed without changing out of the street clothes. She shut her eyes tightly and took deep breaths to calm herself. She wanted to get up and change her dress, but could not will herself to rise. She pulled the blanket right over her head and fell into a disturbed sleep.

The nightmare began again. The dark tunnel and the pursuing fiend. This time the fiend was not running silently. It was growling loudly. Its snarl momentarily seemed to change into the rumble of loud music. No, it was not music, but ringing of a bell. She opened her eyes. The telephone by her bedside was ringing persistently. Her room light was on and its blaze hurt her eyes. She looked at her watch. It was three in the morning. Who could be calling at this time? A stab of fear gripped her. Was it someone from back home? Would she be ordered to return? She picked up the phone and brought it to her ear.

"You silly girl," it was Pamela, "Where did you vanish? I had such difficulty finding a partner for you, and you were nowhere to be found."

"I am sorry," Nilofer managed to utter the apology, "The loud music made me sick."

"You'll learn to like it, dearie. Now go back to sleep."

Nilofer got up. Changed into her nightdress, switched off the light and went to sleep. She slept until one in the afternoon. When she got up and looked through her window, all activity in the dining hall opposite to her room had ceased. It was closing time.

"Oh shit," she said aloud, and then gasped in horror.

"*Tobaa, tobaa;* what pass I have come to; have learnt to use foul language in such short time, in this Godless country! Do forgive me, my Parvardigar." That Sunday she had to go without lunch. She stilled the pangs of hunger with a cold fish sandwich, and a mug of coffee.

*****

The next week began pleasantly for Nilofer. After completing the ward rounds on Monday, all the doctors gathered in the conference room attached to the wards. Dr. Joans had scheduled a case for discussion that morning, before submitting the patient to surgery. As they were taking their seats, a porter wheeled in a cart, bearing coffee and sandwiches.

"Help yourselves," Dr. Joans said.

As they trooped to the coffee cart, two senior doctors joined them. Nilofer had not seen them before, but the others in the room, seemed to know them. Dr. Joans introduced them to Nilofer,

"Dr. Khan, meet Dr. Lisa Sheen, our Senior Pathologist, and Dr. Patrick Adams, the Assistant Radiologist." Then turning to the new comers she said, "Dr. Khan is a scholarship holder from Pakistan, and shall be with us for a couple of years."

She proceeded to open the discussion of the case. The subject was a patient in her late thirties. She had been hospitalized the previous Friday, for irregular menstrual periods. Dr. Brackenridge narrated the patient's complaints, his own findings on physical examination of the patient, and then went on to project on the screen the laboratory reports, leaving out the biopsy and the sonography reports. Dr. Adams explained the sonography pictures. Dr. Lisa Sheen projected the slides of the endometrial biopsy. After she had pointed to various characters of the slides, she spoke in a measured tone,

"Dr. Joans, I have had a full discussion with my colleagues, and am sorry to report that we all are of the opinion that your patient is a case of endometrial carcinoma."

Nilofer was highly impressed by the proceedings of discussion. No one even once interrupted the speakers, or spoke out of turn. "We, back home, need to emulate this," she thought. At the end, Dr. Joans thanked the Pathologist, and the radiologist, and bade them good-bye. After they had left, Dr. Joans and Dr. Brackenridge discussed the line of surgery to be carried out. They both agreed on an extended surgery, removing the uterus along with the ovaries and the broad ligament, plus the draining lymph glands. Dr. Joans turned to the junior doctors,

"Does anyone have a question or comment?"

No one spoke for some time. Then very hesitatingly, Nilofer put up her hand. Being a visitor, she was not sure of her premise. Dr. Joans nodded to her.

"Ma'am…," Nilofer began.

All heads turned to her. Nilofer knew that the teachers in that country were not addressed as sir, or madam. Everyone in the hospital, including the under graduate students and nurses addressed the senior consultant as Dr. Joans or even just Cynthia. A day after joining the unit, Nilofer had gone up to her and said,

"We, in our country, do not address our teachers by their names, just as we do not call our parents by their names. Would you mind if I address you as madam."

Dr. Joans had just smiled and said, "Suit yourself, Dr. Khan."

Dr. Joans was smiling now. Nilofer went on nonchalantly, "Ma'am, would it not be advisable to decide the option of a limited or a radical hysterectomy after opening up the patient on the operation table. If the glands are not involved, could we not restrict the surgery to simple hysterectomy, along with the removal of ovaries and the broad ligament?"

"A well taken point, Dr. Khan. There are gynecologists who believe in performing a restricted operation, the way you are suggesting, when the glands are obviously not involved. However, experience has taught me, and many others like me, that even if you do not find enlarged glands during surgery, there is no certainty that microscopic off shoots of the cancer have not invaded the glands. We prefer not to take chances with the life of the patient."

As there were no more questions, Dr. Joans thanked the audience, and got up to leave. She took a step towards the door and then turned back to Nilofer,

"Dr. Khan, Dr. Brackenridge will be assisting me at the surgery tomorrow, would you like to join in as a second assistant?

"Yes Ma'am," Nilofer said eagerly. She heard a faint snigger from her right. Probably it was Katy Beckham. "I am going to stick to addressing my teacher 'Madam'. I don't care if others think it a laughing matter," she decided resolutely.

That afternoon Nilofer spent a considerable time in the library, going through the chapter on the Uterine Cancer in the latest editions of textbooks, and looking up the latest reports on its surgical management. She came across an article on the subject by Dr. Cynthia Joans, published in the British Journal of oncology, only a year back. In this report, she had made out a convincing case, citing facts and figures, for the radical surgical approach while treating patients with the endometrial cancer even in the early stages. She returned to her room, prepared a mug of coffee in the common kitchenette, and carried it to her desk. While sipping the coffee she put down on a sheet of paper the steps of operation for the radical hysterectomy. She had a late supper in the Hospital dining hall, said her *Ishaa* namaaz, and went to bed. That night she slept soundly and woke up to the ringing alarm at six in the morning.

She reached the operating area at quarter past eight, went to the women's change room and got into the theatre clothes, and put on a surgical cap and mask. She went to theatre three, which was earmarked for major gynecology surgeries. The consultant anesthetist, Dr. Chiang Lin and his registrar, Dr. Nathan had already arrived in the anteroom, where the patients would be put under the anesthetic. The Anesthetist technician, Joe, that is what everybody called him, was laying out equipment that the anesthetist would be using. The junior doctors came in one by one and went into the main theatre. Dr. Brackenridge arrived at exactly half past eight.

"Nurse, please get the patient in. Good morning Dr. Chiang, please put her under when she arrives. Dr. Khan you come in and wash with me," he fired his instructions like a volley from a machine gun.

Nilofer lingered in the anteroom until the nurse fetched the patient from the blanket area. She had visited Mrs. Cyrus yesterday, in her hospital room. The stoic woman was putting up a brave front, but Nilofer could see the apprehension peeping from her eyes.

"You know, Mrs. Cyrus, you are in very safe hands," she had tried to reassure her. "Dr. Joans is a very competent surgeon. She and you both shall come out as winners."

Her encouraging words had the desired affect on Mrs. Cyrus, but to a limited extent. This morning, the nurse had given her a sedative, an hour before she was shifted to the operating area. In spite of that, she was obviously tense. Nilofer went up to her, and gave her a reassuring smile. Mrs. Cyrus smiled back. Nilofer gave a friendly squeeze to her hand, and could see the tenseness leaving her face. Then giving a thumb up sign to her, she turned to go into the operating room. She noticed an appreciating smile on Dr. Chiang's face. Nilofer had picked up this small, but comforting gesture towards the distressed patients, from her teacher back in Lahore.

She joined Dr. Brackenridge at the multi-tap washbasin, and started to scrub. She had watched, during the last two operating sessions, the technique of scrubbing adopted by the staff of Dr. Joans. Every surgeon had his or her own method of scrubbing, and insisted that their staff follow their method. She applied ample soap on both her hands up to the elbows, and scrubbed them vigorously with a sterilized brush. Ten strokes on the outer surface of her thumb, ten stroke on the front, ten on the inner surface, and then ten on the back surface. She gave the same treatment to the fingers, one after the other, then the palm and back of the hand, and lastly the forearms, using long strokes of brush. When both her hands and arms had been scrubbed in this fashion, she rinsed them under the water tap, holding her arms bent at the elbow in such a way that water flowed from her hands to the elbows. She made sure that during the procedure her hands and forearms did not touch any object or any part of her body. Dr. Joans had joined them at the scrub basin, and as she scrubbed, she watched Nilofer unobtrusively, out of the corner of her eye. She was satisfied with what she saw. After scrubbing, Nilofer moved away from the washbasin, still keeping her arms away from her body, and bent at the elbow. A nurse, who was the first to have scrubbed, and had donned a gown and surgical gloves, handed her a sterilized napkin. Nilofer used it to dry first her hands and then the arms. The nurse held a sterilized gown in front of her and she thrust her hands into its sleeves. Another nurse came up behind her, caught hold of the strings on top of the gown and pulled it up on to her shoulders, and then knotted all the strings behind her.

"Your glove size?" inquired the scrub nurse.

"Seven," Nilofer answered.

The nurse held the right sided glove in front of Nilofer, stretching its folded rim. Nilofer thrust her hand into it, making sure that she did not touch its outer working surface with her own bare skin. She put on the left glove with similar precaution. While the operating team was scrubbing, the anesthetists had wheeled the patient into the theatre, and then, with the help of Joe, lifted her on to the operating table. One of the nurses removed the sheet covering the bare body of the patient; another sprayed her front, from knees to the collarbones, with an antiseptic solution. They waited for a few minutes to let the antiseptic dry. Then the senior nurse, Deborah Mushin, wheeled the instrument cart besides the operating table. Dr. Brackenridge and Nilofer took their places opposite to the nurse. Deborah picked up various folded drapes from the cart, one by one, and held out one end of it to Dr. Brackenridge while retaining the other end with herself. They deftly spread the sheets on to the patient's body, so that she was completely covered under them, leaving bare a narrow rectangular portion of her lower abdomen, where the incision was to be made to open the belly of the patient. A small trolley, covered with a sterilized towel, was arranged over the thighs of the patient, keeping it clear off the patient's body. Deborah placed, on this trolley, the instruments needed for the initial stage of the operation. She would keep replacing these instruments with those needed at subsequent stages as the surgery advanced. Dr. Joans joined them and took position on the left side of the patient. She motioned Nilofer to take position on the left of Brackenridge.

"All set?" she inquired, and put out her right hand.

Deborah put a knife in her hand, and the operation began. The surgery was completed in two-and-a-half hours. No one spoke a single word during the whole procedure except once, when Dr. Joans had addressed the anesthetist,

"How are we doing, Chiang?

"No problem."

Except these two spoken phrases, the procedure was completed in total silence. Nilofer had known surgeons who chattered away during surgery, sometimes even throwing tantrums, or cracking jokes. Dr. Joans did not have to ask for an instrument. Deborah had handed the right instruments to her, and to her assistants, at the right moment. Nilofer was glad she had read thoroughly the steps of operation, the evening before. Although her role in the procedure was a minor one, she kept the operative area free of blood, by deft mopping or applying mechanical suction. She used the retractors at the right places. After Joans had placed the last stitch, she moved away from the operating table, and a nurse untied her gown. She thanked everybody before she left the theatre. Dr. Brackenridge placed the dressings over the surgical wound, and one of the nurses sealed it off with the adhesive tapes. Dr. Nathan took over from here, initiating measures for the recovery of the patient from anesthesia. The patient was shifted on to the trolley cart and covered with fresh sheets and a blanket. Nilofer noticed that she had recovered enough to open her eyes. She went to her and held her hand. The patient gave her a look of recognition and pressed her hand. Nilofer continued to hold her hand as Dr. Rolfe and Dr. Nathan wheeled her into the recovery room. The recovery room staff quickly wheeled her cart into one of the makeshift cubicle, spoke a few words of assurance to her, and clamped an oxygen mask on to her face. They hooked her up on to the monitoring devices, and checked her vital parameters – blood pressure, pulse rate, oxygen saturation, and cardiogram.

"All O.K.," pronounced the senior nursing officer of the recovery room.

Nilofer, instead of going home, returned to the operation theatre. She wanted to talk to Nurse Deborah, who was actually a nursing officer with a postgraduate qualification in surgical nursing. She was of Jewish origin. Nilofer had heard of her disciplinarian trait. She was known to bite off the head of any of her staff, found to be out of step with the regulations. Even the senior doctors were wary of treading on her toes. Dr. Brackenridge, she was told, had faced her tongue lashing on a couple of occasions because of his brusque behavior. Nilofer now approached her gingerly.

"Yes, Dr. Khan, are you looking for someone?" she asked her.

"Oh, I just wanted a word with you, if you can spare a few minutes."

"Let's go to the staff room, and we can talk over a cup of coffee."

They collected their cups of coffee at the theater canteen counter, and went to the staff room. It was empty. Everyone had left for lunch. They took their seats, and Deborah looked at Nilofer with a questioning eye.

"How long have you been working in the gyne theatre, Miss Mushin?" Nilofer asked.

Deborah was taken aback by this curt and rather impolite question. She said sarcastically,

"Why, Dr. Khan? Why this interrogation? Do you intend offering me employment in your country?"

"Please, Miss Mushin, don't take my question amiss. Your handling of the operation fascinated me. Not once did the surgeon have to ask you for an instrument."

Deborah's ruffled feathers were smoothened by the praise.

"Well, Dr. Khan, I have been working in this theatre for the last eight years. By the way, it is Mrs. Mushin, but please do call me Deborah. Let me tell you, you too did very well as a second assistant. You could put our junior doctors to shame."

The compliment elated Nilofer, and on that happy note, her day's work ended. She suddenly felt very hungry, and made her way to the dining hall.

*****

Nine days after Nilofer and Vikram had parted company, she saw him again, but not in person. It was Thursday. She was returning from the Hospital after completing her post lunch session in the ward. She had taken the short underground route, which connected the various buildings of the campus to the Hospital. She saw large posters stuck at various points on the walls of the tunnel announcing a friendly cricket match. There was a team photograph with Vikram seated in the centre of the front row. She stopped to read the details. The match was to be a three day, one inning affair, Friday to Sunday, to be played at the University Stadium, between the University of Wales team lead by Dr. Vikram Kocher and the Glamorgan County team lead by Toby Alan.

"Ah, Dr. Khan,"

She turned and saw Dr. Pamela Lahore standing behind her.

“Are you a cricket buff, Dr. Khan?

“All Pakistanis are,” replied Nilofer.

Pamela heaved an exaggerated sigh.

“Lord, I would have loved to watch this match, but tomorrow and day after I have to be in attendance to our *Queen* Joans. Nevertheless, I am not going to miss the Sunday session. Will you be going too?

“Well,” said Nilofer, “I have no idea where the stadium is located.”

“It is not far, just a walking distance. Tell you what? Why don’t you come down to my room around nine? We could walk down together. I am in room no. 311 at the Llandaff House.”

Nilofer agreed and they went their ways.

On returning from her work the next day, Nilofer found a letter in her pigeonhole. It was from Naseem, her intimate friend, and college mate, back in Lahore. She snatched it up and hastened to her room. She ripped the letter open before she had unlocked her room. She threw her purse on the bed, and unfolded the letter. It was a lengthy note. Naseem had the knack of writing sweet nothings, and chided Nilofer for what she called her dry and tasteless two-word letters. Nilofer read with amusement the mirthful description of the events that had taken place in the college since she had left. She laughed aloud as she read Naseem’s account of hilarious situations created by a newly appointed junior lecturer, Shabana Banu. The poor woman’s knowledge of English was limited, and she often made sidesplitting gaffes. In her joining report to the Professor she had written,

“I have been ordered by the Dean to join your Department, so please joint me…”

Naseem went on to describe another scene. At the end of a teaching session, some one brought up the subject of the escalating inflation. Shabana’s contribution to the discussion was,

“In these ‘hard and fast’ times it is difficult to manage with a junior lecturer’s salary.”

Naseem had hidden her face against the desk to conceal her laughter. Shabana thought she was unwell.

"Oi Naseem, 'is your health not well'?"

There was some disturbing news at the end of the letter. Mahmood Khan was involved in yet another drunken brawl, this time, with a traffic cop, whom he had beaten up. Her uncle, Hameed Maamu, had to use his political influence, and quite a bit of money muscle, to keep the incident under wraps.

"Hameed Maamu Jaan has asked me to apologize to you on his behalf for not writing. He is very busy with his political work, what with the gathering clouds of a possible armed clash with India over the developments in the Eastern wing of the country." As Nilofer belonged to a family steeped in politics, she could imagine the possible disastrous outcome of the sabre rattling between the two neighbors. Added to this the news of her husband's misdeeds dispirited her.

She was still in this somber frame of mind when she went for her supper that evening. It being a Saturday, there were very few diners. Most of doctors had left for the weekend. Nilofer, wanting to be by herself, took her tray to an empty table at the back of the hall. She soon realized she was not going to be left alone. She saw Dr. Tameez-Ul-Islam, carrying his tray and determinedly heading towards her table. She was equally determined not to get involved with him. She was fully aware of his reputation as a womanizer. His acquaintances called him Tomie Slam, and some girls among the nursing staff and the maidservants of the dining hall referred to him as Tomie the Casanova. Like the historical Casanova, he too maintained a record of number of women he had 'conquered' and bragged about it to anyone who would listen. Now he approached Nilofer's table, with a loutish grin, and said,

"May I join you?" and then sat down without waiting for her response.

She ignored him and continued to eat her supper.

"I am Dr. Tameez-Ul-Islam from Peshawar," he announced, "Which part of Pakistan do you come from, Miss Nilofer?"

"It is Dr. … Mrs. … Nilofer Khan," she answered, laying stress on each word and not hiding her distaste for the conversation.

"But your husband is not here with you in this country…"

"So?" Nilofer interrupted him indignantly.

Tameez refused to give up,

"All I am saying is, you are my compatriot, and single at the moment, and I would like to invite you to spend tomorrow evening with me."

Nilofer's face went crimson with rage. She spoke in a slow and deliberately insulting tone,

"You say your name is Tameez-Ul-Islam, but you have neither *tameez* nor Islam in you."

Tameez gave a sneering laugh,

"There is no need to get worked up dearie. You must be feeling lonely without a male companion, and I am offering my company for the evening. Take it or leave it. It is as simple as that."

Nilofer rose without finishing her meal. She leaned on the table so that her face was inches away from him. She hissed in fury,

"You are disgusting, you dirty minded pig."

She turned, and walked away. She heard Tomie Slam swearing under his breath,

"Uncultured bitch!"

She halted in her strides. She was tempted to go back and slap the face of the swine, but then changed her mind. "I should not create a scene in an alien land." She resolutely strode back to her room.

"Uncultured bitch…Uncultured bitch…Uncultured bitch."

The words continued to echo endlessly in her mind. She was sickened to her soul. What culture are our youngsters imbibing away from home? She recalled an article by Nacheeze published in the *Kainaat.* He had lamented that our youngsters go to the western countries, away from home, with the intentions of pursuing academic careers, but many of them get enamored by the permissive society of the west. They fritter away their time and money in pursuit of what they call free love. They take delight in being part of Western culture, and deride those of their fellow compatriots who shun these frivolities. They tend to forget the purpose for which they have left their homes. Tameez-Ul-Islam had been in Britain, as a house officer, for the last six years, moving from one hospital to the next. He had repeatedly registered himself for sitting the examination for the post-graduate qualification of F.R.C.S., but had not taken a single exam in the last three years. When he was off duty, he spent his time gobbling booze and chasing *birds.*

"Well," she said to herself, "there must be many Tameezes out there. Why should I lose sleep over them?"

Thus, having decided to purge her thoughts of Tameeze, she washed and said her namaaz of Ishaa and went to bed. However, she was not yet fully rid of Tameez. He penetrated into her dream. She lay on the floor, and he stood towering over her, hands on his hips. He bent over her with a coarse smile on his lips. Nilofer raised her head and shoulders, and put out her fisted hands to defend herself.

"Go away," she screamed.

The scream died in her throat, as the face of Tameez suddenly transformed into that of Mahmood. Her body went limp, and she fell back with a thumping sound. She woke up. The sound had come from the adjoining room. The walls between the rooms were paper-thin, and she could hear giggles of a couple, and thudding of bed, against the common wall. Under ordinary circumstances, she would have just smiled at this disturbance, but the nightmare had frayed her nerves. She lay awake for a long time, and then fell into a fitful sleep. She woke up at six to the ringing of her alarm clock. She silenced the clock, pulled up the blanket over her head, turned on her side and went to sleep again. When she woke up next, her table clock said five minutes past eight. She threw aside her blanket and got out of bed. She was to meet Pamela at nine. It being Sunday, the showers in the house were not too much in demand. She had a quick shower, changed into fresh salwar and kameez, and prepared a mug of coffee. She breakfasted on finger cakes, biscuits, and cheese, and was on her way to Pamela's room at the Llandaff House.

Nilofer reached Pamela's room at few minutes before nine. Pamela opened the door at her knock. She was not alone. There was another woman standing in front of the mirror. Her back was towards the door. When she turned around, Nilofer saw that she was a pretty Asian girl, about her own age, or may be a couple of years older. Her complexion was silky white with light pinkish tinge. She had an oval face, haloed by jet-black hair, cut to her shoulders. Her arched eyebrows and the hairline formed a nearly perfect crescent of a forehead. The Arabic term *Mah jabeen*, meaning a moon-like forehead, came instantly to Nilofer's mind. A perfectly shaped, rather smallish nose rested above a perfect Cupid's bow upper lip. Her lower lip was slightly furrowed in the centre, giving it the appearance of two adjacently placed rose petals. She was wearing jeans, and a full-necked sweater, which enhanced her perfect figure. The only flaw, if one could call it that, was her rather short stature. She was barely five foot three or so, but her slimness, added to her diminutive height, gave her a dainty appearance. Pamela introduced them to each other.

"Dr.Khan, meet Dr. Rana, our brilliant pediatrician. She has recently obtained her membership in pediatrics, and has now landed the job of a tutor at the prestigious Children Hospital of Glasgow. She is due to leave us in a fortnight's time."

Then turning to Rana, she continued, "Dr. Khan is a scholar from Pakistan and would be spending a couple of years with us. By the way, Dr. Khan, our lovely pediatrician is from India, and naturally a cricket enthusiast. She is going with us to witness today's match."

Dr. Rana addressed Nilofer, "My full name is Rasila Rana, and I shall be glad if you call me just Rasila."

"And I would rather you call me Nilofer."

The trio proceeded to the stadium, and took their seats just before the Glamorgan County Team came out for fielding. There were not many spectators, only a handful of Caribbean students, and a comparatively larger group hailing from the Indian subcontinent. There were barely a few white faces to be seen. Nilofer glanced at the giant score board, and realized that the match was heading towards an early end. The County team had scored two hundred and twenty-one runs in their inning. The University Team had scored one hundred and fifty-seven at the cost of eight wickets, trailing by sixty-four runs. The batsman no. 5 and no.10 were to resume the batting. Nilofer saw Vikram and another player come out at the crease. Vikram had made 49 runs the previous day, while his partner had not yet opened his account.

"I don't think this match will last more than a few minutes," Nilofer said.

"Just wait and watch," said Rasila, "Vikram is still there."

They fell silent, as Vikram faced the first ball. The Glamorgan skipper was using spinners at both ends. Nilofer could see that Vikram was batting to a set strategy. He kept his partner away from the bowling for most of the time. He was a master of placement. He would score either a couple or a boundary and refused to run a single even if it was there for the taking, except on the last ball of the over. The opponent team would close in to prevent him from taking a single on the last ball. Vikram would lift the ball over the heads of close-in fielders, but would make sure it did not go to the boundary. He would then just stroll across to the opposite end to face the next over. Only on few occasions, he could not cross over on the last ball, and his partner had to face the bowling. Luckily, his partner survived the few balls that he had to face. This drama continued for almost three hours. Nilofer and her two companions got so engrossed in the game that they did not exchange a single word. However, Rasila went on whispering under her breath,

"Come on, Vikram... bravo Vikram ... go Vikram go..." Vikram's team ended up the winners. Vikram had added 53 runs to his overnight score of 49, while his partner at the other end contributed just 12 runs. When Vikram returned to the pavilion with a century, and a win under his belt, the sparse spectators gave him a standing ovation. Rasila turned to her companions,

"Vikram is known to snatch victory from the jaws of defeat."

"Yeh," said Pamela, "he is a great player."

"And a great playboy too," added Nilofer.

Rasila whirled to face Nilofer.

"What did you say? A playboy? Vikram?" She and Pamela burst out in a simultaneous and uproarious laughter. "Where did you pick that joke from?" asked Pamela.

"I am telling you from my personal experience," Nilofer explained, "he made a pass at me the other day."

"Lucky you!" Pamela said sardonically, "God, how I wish he would make a pass at me, I will give my right hand to be in his arms for once."

"May be he likes tall girls," Rasila could not help having a dig at Nilofer, "You, Dr. Lahore, are probably too short for his liking."

"Anyway, I am going to the dressing room to congratulate Vicky, and while I am at it, I shall lure him to make a pass at me," Pamela persisted in poking fun at Nilofer, "Would you two like to come?"

She started walking away without waiting for their reply. After taking a few steps, she turned and walked back to them.

"I have a lunch date with my boyfriend. I shan't be coming back with you."

"It's okay with us," Rasila assured her, "you run along for your lunch date."

Nilofer and Rasila returned to the Llandaf House. Nilofer wanted to say good-bye at the entrance of the house, but Rasila detained her,

"Could I offer you a home cooked lunch?"

Seeing a questioning look in Nilofer's eyes, she explained,

"I usually cook a couple of dishes on Saturday evenings and store them in the fridge. Today I can offer you only a vegetarian biryani for lunch."

"A vegetarian biryani? I have never heard of a veg biryani."

"Come, and see, and taste for yourself."

Curiosity drove Nilofer to accept the invitation. Even otherwise, she found Rasila's company agreeable. They went to Rasila's room. Nilofer looked around the room. It was meticulously neat. Everything was in its right place. They both went to the kitchenette, where Rasila removed a steel box containing the Biryani from the refrigerator, and steamed it in a pressure cooker. She ladled it out into two plates, and they carried them to the room. Nilofer noticed that the vegetarian biryani placed before her looked like the usual meat biryani, and tasted equally delicious. Instead of lamb meat, it contained mushrooms chopped up into small bits. She complimented Rasila for her skill at culinary improvisation. As they were eating, Rasila said,

"Nilofer, I am intrigued by what you said about Vikram making a pass at you. We do have a few Romeos from our part of the world, like Tameez-Ul-Islam, Ramesh Puri, and Shafiq Ahmed, who keep chasing girls with their tongues hanging out, but Vikram is a different man. People around here admire him for his helpful nature and his sportsmanship, but no one has ever linked him with a woman. A number of girls have made advances towards him, including a junior consultant surgeon, but he has always politely excused himself. His attitude has ruffled a few feathers inviting epithets like Bishop Vick, Fairy Vicky, and even effeminate dude."

"Well, I don't know about others," Nilofer said, "I can only speak for myself, and my…"

"That is exactly what I would like to know," Rasila interrupted Nilofer, "what did he actually say or do to you?

"He didn't say or do any thing. It is the way he looked at me. But why are you so concerned about him?" Nilofer was getting a bit edgy.

Rasila made no immediate response to Nilofer's angry comment. Her eyes looked troubled. They sat in silence for a while.

"I'll get the dessert," Rasila said and went off to the kitchen.

She returned after about ten minutes with two dishes of hot *gajar halwa*. They ate the sweet in silence. Then Rasila said hesitatingly,

"You have spoken for yourself. Let me tell you my personal experience of Vikram." She fell silent for a while as if deciding in her mind how much she should confide in the girl, whom she had known only for a few hours. Then she began haltingly,

"I have known you only for a few hours. There is some thing in you, which pulls at the chords of my heart, and I feel a sense of instant bonding with you. I feel obligated to defend Vikram, and disabuse your mind regarding him. The only way I can convince you is by divulging my past, which I had managed to bury in my mind, with great difficulty."

She fell silent again; she seemed unsure whether she should continue. Then she took a deep breath, and spoke unfalteringly.

"I have known Vicky for the last eleven years. We were together, first at the science faculty, and then at the medical college in Baroda, back home. Vicky, or Vikrambhai, as he was commonly called, was good at studies and I often sought his guidance at the time of examinations. His hometown is Ahmedabad, while I lived with my parents in Baroda. I am the only child of my parents. My father was a dentist, with a modest private practice, and we lived in a modest house, in a modest locality of Baroda. I had introduced Vikram to my parents. My father and Vikram hit along well. My mother, on occasions, invited him to share meals with us, so that he could have a break from the dreary hostel meals. In the third year of my medical studies, my father died suddenly, of a massive heart attack. After that, Vikram's visits to my home became more frequent. He helped my mother with the sale of my father's clinic, and in settling various investments that my father had made during his lifetime. After he had put my mother's financial affairs on track, his visits to our home tapered off. He had only one passion – to excel in studies and he avoided everything that could hinder this pursuit, including attention from some fellow female students. He had two diversions, playing cricket and playing the market. He bought and sold shares in small denominations. He seemed to be a shrewd investor, and made profits. He deposited the profits from the share market into a bank account, which he never used for his personal expenses. He used this account to help needy people around him: nurses, ward servants, and even students. A nurse or a ward servant, in a financial crisis, would approach him for a loan, and he willingly advanced the required amount. If the borrower forgot to return the amount, he never reminded him of it. He was astute at judging the persons who came asking for help. He pointedly refused a loan to frivolous borrowers.

Rasila halted in her narration. There was a look of hesitation in her face. After a few seconds of silence she went on,

"In my final year, I developed relations with one of our classmates, whom I shall call M, and we decided to get married after graduation. M and Vikram were on friendly terms. After completing MBBS, Vikram joined postgraduate course in surgery, while I opted for pediatrics. Vikram did not intend to complete his surgical course in Baroda. He wanted to have a year's experience in the subject, and then go to Britain and obtain Fellowship of Royal College of Surgeons. M took up the job of a tutor in ophthalmology. Being on the teaching staff, M was allotted living quarters on the college campus, while Vikram and I had to stay in the postgraduate hostels. M and I often spent our free time in the privacy of his quarters and indulged in physical relations. As we were sure to marry, we did not always take precaution. I got pregnant. When I told the news to M, he seemed somewhat perturbed, but assured me he would soon visit his parents in Nagpur, and would discuss the subject of our marriage. I was sure my mother would happily agree to this union. I decided to wait for M's return from Nagpur, before I broke the news of my pregnancy to my mother. When M returned, I went to his quarters, hoping to hear the good news of his parent's consent. Instead, he had returned, bearing not the consent of his parents, but a photograph of a girl with whom he was engaged to be married. He said his parents had forced him into it. I was aghast. How could he do this to me? He was sheepishly apologetic, and said he could not defy his parents. I suggested that I accompany him to his parents, and sort out the matter with them. He would have none of it. He had made up his mind to ditch me. Unashamedly, he informed me that his fiancée was a daughter of Mr. Ram Narayan Moonga. I knew then that no amount of my pleading would move him. Becoming a son-in-law of a nationally renowned business tycoon was a bounty for which discarding me was an insignificant price for him. Very graciously, he offered his help in taking care of my pregnancy. 'We could have it discreetly terminated,' he said. My fury knew no bounds, but all I could do was to slap his face and then burst into helpless sobbing. He told me to give a thought to his suggestion of aborting the pregnancy, and went off to the club, to play tennis. Driven by an insane fury, and utter desperation, I went to my department, wrote a prescription for a fictitious patient, and purchased a bottle of gardinal tablets. I returned to M's residence, wrote a parting note, and pinned it to the pillow. I swallowed the whole lot of twenty tablets, and lay on the bed, which I had, on so many occasions, shared with that swine M. I thought it a fitting place for committing my final sin. I became oblivious to what happened to me after that. Vikram told me about it, much later. M had returned from the club without playing tennis, as the courts had been watered that evening. He found me nearly unconscious, in his bed. He must have read my note, and seen the empty bottle of sleeping pills. In sheer panic, he rode his scooter to Vikram's room, pulled him out of his chair, telling him he needed his help urgently, and drove him back to his residence. M pointed to me lying in his bed, and handed him the empty bottle of the pills, but did not show him my note. Vikram comprehended the situation instantly. He quickly assessed my breathing and pulse. He asked M to stay back with me, while he rushed to the hospital. From the operation theatre, he collected the necessary equipment and drugs, telling the nurse in charge these were required for a dire emergency, and hurried back to me. He pushed a stomach tube down my throat, and pumped out my stomach thoroughly. Simultaneously he asked M to start an intravenous infusion, and add a heavy dose of a diuretic to it. They put a catheter into my bladder and ran speedily the infusion with the diuretics, keeping a close watch on my blood pressure and respiration. Vikram warned M that if my condition deteriorated, he would be compelled to shift me to the hospital, and to notify the police. M made no reply to this, but fear was written large on his face. Vikram instructed him to go and fetch my mother. When she arrived, Vikram explained to her the situation, assuring her that he was trying to keep the whole thing under wraps, but if the situation worsened, and I had to be moved into the hospital, it would not be possible to stop the publicity and the police procedures. Because of the timely stomach wash, and the forced diuresis, I recovered consciousness the next morning. Vikram instructed M to see that his house cleaner, who came every morning for work, was sent back with a plausible excuse. M went to the drawing room to await the arrival of the servant. My mother went to the kitchen to prepare meals, as no one had eaten any anything since the previous day. I was left alone with Vikram. I blurted out to him the news of my pregnancy. He showed no surprise, and advised me to say nothing to my mother for the time being, as this would only add to her distress."

At this point Rasila stopped speaking, her eyes shimmering with the brimming tears. Both the girls sat still for a long moment. Then Rasila rose listlessly and said,

"I'll get some coffee for us," and went into the kitchen.

Left alone, Nilofer reflected on Rasila's sad story. Then her mind went at a tangent. Vikram was an Indian Hindu, who had studied at Ahmedabad and Baroda, yet he spoke chaste Urdu. She had an impression that the Indian authorities had banished the language from their country. She wondered whether Ahmedabad had some Urdu schools, and whether a Hindu family would condescend to send their child to such a school.

When Rasila returned with two mugs of coffee, both of them sat there in a reflective mood without touching the coffee lying in front of them. Wordless minutes passed. Rasila handed a cup to Nilofer, picked up her own, took a sip from it, and with a wan smile resumed her story.

"I stayed at M's quarter that day, and night, accompanied by my mother. She went about her chores of cooking and feeding the three of us, without uttering a single word. I was too full of remorse to speak to her. On Vikram's instructions, she plied me with gallons of coffee for the whole day, and unflinchingly emptied bottles of my urine, which kept filling up at frequent intervals from effect of diuretics and coffee.

Next morning Vikram drove my mother and me in a borrowed car to my house. When my mother was out of earshot, he again advised me not to divulge my pregnancy to her yet. He said he would talk to her at the right time. Meanwhile he had typed a request to my chief, in my name, asking for sick leave. I signed it. He visited me, morning and evening, for the next three days and gave instructions to my mother regarding my medication and diet. She carried out his instructions silently. I tried to break the silence between us, but she was too grief-stricken for conversation. On the fourth day, when Vikram visited us, he pronounced me fully recovered, and laughingly told my mother to pay his fees in the form of a home-cooked dinner that evening. I knew instantly that he was planning to take up the matter of my pregnancy with my mother. He stayed late after dinner, and gently broke the news of my pregnancy to her. We both, Vikram and I, realized from my mother's demeanor, that she had already guessed that much. Vikram stressed the need for early and discreet termination, at a clinic away from Baroda. My mother nodded in assent. My mother and I went to Ahmedabad where a gynecologist known to Vikram performed the abortion in her private clinic. After a week's convalescence, Vikram urged me to join my duties. I was reluctant, but he impressed on me the importance of putting up a normal front. The façade of normality lasted for a couple of months. It was torn asunder, one morning, by a three-column news item in a popular daily, along with a photograph of M, announcing the imminent wedding of a small town junior doctor with the daughter of a nationally renowned business mogul. I had gone to my department, unaware of the press announcement. I noticed the oblique glances, and low whispers of my colleagues. At lunchtime, a friend handed me the newspaper. My affair with M was no secret. We had even entered in a competition for selecting the most handsome couple of the campus, and had won the title of *haseena aur albela,* cute and dude. The press release resulted in an inevitable tongue wagging. I put up a brave front and ignored the fuss. A month later, my bravado fell apart. M married, and brought his bride to live on the college campus. A vicious scandal mongering was let loose.

My associates brazenly labeled me as *ex* of M, and made oblique lurid remarks even in my presence. It did not take long for the gossip to reach the ears of M's bride. She turned out a reckless and brash woman, ready to discuss her husband's affair, with anyone who was willing to gossip. She even pried out of her husband, explicit details of some of our exploits behind the closed doors of our bedroom. Then she went around narrating to the campus folks the juicy scenes of the play enacted by *our own porn artists*, as she called us. In her extreme viciousness, one day she slung them into my mother's face, calling me a crafty slut. My poor mother, she was from a conformist family, from a very conservative region of Kutch. The disgrace and humiliation brought on an attack of cerebral stroke, and she succumbed to it in four days."

Tears were rolling down Rasila's cheeks. She said between sobs,

"I felt like a murderer, the murderer of my unborn child, and of my poor mother."

She halted her narrative again, and sat motionless with an anguished face. The dead stillness lasted so long that Nilofer thought she had forgotten her presence. Then she shook her head a couple of times, as if trying to banish the pain in her heart, and resumed her story.

"My mother's funeral was sparsely attended. The younger brother of my father and his wife came down from Bhuj, some of my colleagues and staff members from my department, and a few neighbors of my mother joined in. Vikram did all the legwork for the funeral. At the end of thirteen-day mourning, my uncle and aunt left for Bhuj. They did not bother to ask me my plans, nor made even a formal offer of help. After their departure, I was alone in the house. That night I lay in bed, ditched by those who till a few days back were my loved ones. I felt as if God too had abandoned me. Next morning I did not get out of bed, and just lay there wallowing in self-pity and self-revulsion. The doorbell rang around noontime. I ignored it. I was in no condition to face anyone. The person at the door was persistent, and kept ringing. Grudgingly I opened the door. It was Vikram. He had come with food and provisions. I thought he'd slam me for my unkempt appearance. He casually laid the bag containing the food and fruits on the table, and told me he was leaving, and would return in half an hour, that in the meantime I was to have a bath and change into fresh clothes, and that we would eat when he returned. He came back in half an hour. I had reluctantly bathed and put on a fresh indoor dress. I laid out the lunch and we ate in silence. He left, saying he would be back at nine in the evening, and we would go out for diner. When we returned to my house, after eating out that night, he did not come into the house, but told me in a commanding tone that he would expect me at the hospital next morning, and that I was to have my meals at the hostel mess. I tried to protest, but he was gone before I could say anything. Next morning I joined my duties at the hospital, and returned to my hostel room. However, I knew this was not going to work out. The college campus was rife with stories of mud slinging matches between M and Mrs. M, and some of the mud spattered on to Vikram. Mrs. M had given me the epithet of Dr. Hussy. Many campus inmates started using the nickname behind my back. While on a ward round, I heard one of the undergraduate students, whisper to his companion,

'Poor girl, she has been demoted from *hasina* to hussy.'

"Life became intolerable. In two days, I ran back to my mother's house, and did not report on duty without a leave of absence. I was on the brink of a nervous breakdown. In the evening, Vikram came to see me. His frequent visits to me had started fresh malicious gossip. As soon as he entered, I flung myself on his neck, and broke into sobs.

'I can't stay in Baroda,'

"He led me to a chair and took one for himself in front of me. He held my hands, and said, 'I agree that you should leave Baroda, but where can you go?' I had no answer to that. He told me there was only one way out. I should go abroad and continue my career there. He told me he could try to get me a job in one of the hospitals in Britain, if I was willing to go there. 'Think about it,' he said, 'meanwhile let us eat. I am famished.'

"I agreed to go to Britain, if he could fix a job for me. He said he would start his efforts right away, but took a promise from me that meanwhile I would continue to attend my present duties at the hospital. I could understand he did not want me to bury myself in my house, and become a recluse. I kept my promise and attended my duties regularly, but it was not easy, what with my colleagues losing no opportunity to throw barbs at me. Vikram, perceptive as he was, went all out to give me company whenever we could take a break from our duties. His effort to keep up my morale was denting his own reputation. Unruffled by the gibes, he helped me in collecting various documents necessary for applying for a job in Britain. A doctor relative of his, in Leicester, managed to have my application processed speedily at the home office, and in two months' time I received a call to join the Geriatrics Department of the Birmingham Hospital. Geriatrics was the last thing I would have liked to work in, but at the time, it was a Godsent boon. Arriving here was like deliverance from hell. As I had nothing to distract me, I put all my time and energies in my work. My consultant was pleased with my work, and on his recommendations I landed a job at the Liverpool Children's Hospital, first as a senior house officer, and then as a registrar. Six months back I obtained my membership in pediatrics. Meanwhile Vikram, after completing one year at the Baroda Hospital, got a job at the University Hospital of Wales in Cardiff. He arrived here a little over two years back. He visited me in Liverpool on a couple of weekends. He always stayed at a bed and breakfast joint. I would have been glad if he had chosen to stay with me in my room. I would have happily given myself up to him. In fact, I unashamedly offered myself to him, body, soul, mind, and heart. He just smiled and said, 'You haven't learnt your lessons Rasila, nor have you understood me. I shall get involved only with my soul mate, and I have not found her yet. Save yourself for your soul mate when he comes along.'

"I have been here, in Cardiff for the last three months, doing a locum job as a senior registrar. I do not get to see Vikram too often. He keeps a respectable distance from me. And here you are, claiming he made a pass at you! Or may be," she said laughingly, "he sees his soul mate in you."

"Well," said Nilofer, "I don't claim to be infallible. I may have made a mistake in judging him." She got up to go. "Thanks for the lovely lunch. Do look me up before you leave for Scotland."

As she walked towards her quarters, she reflected on Rasila's story. Is this girl, Rasila, in love with Vikram? She makes him out to be an angel. She almost worships him. Maybe, her feelings only reflect her indebtedness towards the man, for the help she had received from him. What about her story, that she was willing to have physical relations with him, and he had spurned her? The girl is exceptionally pretty. Men would fall over each other to be in her company, leave aside an opportunity to have physical relations with her. If Rasila's story is true, the man must be either of exceptionally high character, or incapable of physical relation. The picture of her last meeting with Vikram came to her mind. Wasn't there a yearning in his eyes? On the other hand, had she misread his eyes? Doubts assailed her mind. The man had a helpful nature. He did help her to settle down in a strange place in such short time. "Perhaps my behavior towards him had been unwarranted, and unfair," she thought.

On an impulse, she decided to make amends for the wrongs she might have unwittingly done to him. She decided to meet him. She had a plausible excuse for the meeting – offering him personal congratulations for his performance at the cricket match this morning. She looked at her wristwatch. It was approaching four in the evening. Instead of going to her room on the first floor, she climbed up to the second, and knocked at Vikram's door.

"Come in," Vikram called from inside.

She opened the door, and entered. He was sitting at his desk, an open textbook in front of him.

"Oh, Doctor *Sahiba*, it is you! Welcome to the poor man's abode, *khush aamdeed gareeb khane pe aap ka khairmaqdam hai.*

His sarcastic gallantry, and the use of most formal manner of address in Urdu, irked her.

"*Tashreef rakhiye,* Please be seated." He indicated the chair besides his own.

He removed an Urdu magazine that was lying on the chair, and placed it on the desk. She noticed that it was *Kaainaat,* a monthly published from Lahore. It was her favorite periodical, and she had been its regular subscriber, back home.

"I dropped in to congratulate you for winning today's match," she said.

"I thank you from the bottom of my heart," he again used the polite Urdu phrase *tah-e-dil se shukriya.*

He was persisting in using the most formal polite Urdu phrases, in order to mock at her earlier umbrage at his attempt at informality. She chose to ignore the taunts. "I have only myself to blame for his attitude."

"Will you like a cup of coffee?" he asked, but made no move to get it.

She politely declined the ritual offer. There was silence for a while. She had nothing further to say, and he too made no effort at further conversation. She was eyeing the magazine, lying on the desk.

"I see that you subscribe to *Kaainaat,*" she found a subject for conversation.

He said nothing.

"May I borrow it? I shall return it tomorrow," she attempted to carry on the dialogue.

"Please do," he said, "You need not return it. I have finished with it."

She returned to her room a bit annoyed, and feeling let down at the cold shouldered response of Vikram. She could not explain to herself her renewed keenness to befriend him. She changed into a housecoat, and picked up the magazine she had borrowed from Vikram. She quickly turned the pages to see if there was a write up by Naacheez. There was one. A short poem titled *my star.*

In a corner of my sky, there was a little star
Not like any other; a very special star
It was my star; my own star
Was near to me, yet very far

Played with me hide and seek
Behind the clouds it would sneak
When I spied it, it shed its veil
In its twinkle, I saw it smile
Peals of laughter came over the gale
....
Then all of a sudden one ungodly night
Ugly dark clouds covered my sky
They hid my star out of my sight
An eternity I waited it did not appear
My bliss was over my heart cried
For In my breast I felt the spear
It was lost to me I bowed to fate
Months went by and the years
With the time did the memory fade
An eon later, I looked up the sky
My heart leaped it did serenade
There it was my twinkling ally
It wasn't as bright as it used to be
Its glow had ebbed its twinkle weak
When I beckoned, it shrank from me
I smiled at it, it chose to flee
Behind the clouds back it went
Leaving me aghast and stunned

Nilofer was mildly surprised. This was not Naacheez's style of writing. She had read almost everything that he had contributed to the magazine during the last two years. He usually wrote articles on changing social life the world over, and poetry in the *Sufia* style. This somewhat childish and romantic poem from him was unusual. On the next page, she saw a notice announcing a convention of poets, a *mushaaira,* to be held under the aegis of *Anjuman-e-Traqqi-e-Urdu Britannia,* at the Royal Albert Hall in London, on Saturday, a fortnight on. Many prominent poets from the Indian subcontinent were listed as participants. Naacheez's name was among them. She felt excitement rising within her. She had always wanted to see her favorite writer in person. She decided to make the trip to London. "Who knows, I may get an opportunity to talk to him, and may even get his autograph," she thought.

She sent a cheque for five pounds to the organizing secretary of the mushaaira for reservation of a seat, hoping to get a front seat, on the first come first served basis. She also sent another cheque for four pounds to the Indian Y.W.C.A. of London, requesting reservation of a room for the day. She would have preferred a Pakistani Y.W.C.A, but the London Guide Book listed no such hostels. She passed the next thirteen days in an excited frame of mind and anticipation.

On Saturday, she had an early breakfast and then took a bus to London. She took a taxi to the Y.W.C.A. The girl at the counter gave her a practiced synthetic smile. She handed to her the key to her room on the second floor, and a terse notice that the lunchtime was one to two in the afternoon. The room was a tiny affair, with a narrow bed, two chairs, and a tiny desk. Nilofer had to push the chairs and the desk against the wall to make room for saying her namaaz of Zuhr. She went down for lunch precisely at one. In the dining hall, an amusing menu for lunch confronted her. It read,

"Chapaties: Limited to only two per head. Rice, daal and vegetable: unlimited."

A middle-aged Indian woman was serving the meal at the counter. She was wearing a shirt, and jeans, which compressed her ample rump so tightly that Nilofer feared a slight movement might rip it. She put two misshapen *chapaties* on Nilofer's plate, and added a helping of cauliflower cum potatoes, and a bowl of *daal.* Nilofer looked around for a seat, and noticed a young couple, eating at a table at the end of the first row. The girl was wearing kameeze and salwar similar to her own, and was looking at her intently. She walked up to their table and sat down, after asking permission to join them. It turned out, that they too had come to attend the Mushaaira. They introduced themselves as Zahira and Akram, hailing from Kenya. They were students of Pharmacy at the Exeter University. They readily agreed to Nilofer's request to let her accompany them to the Hall. They left at half past four, after the evening tea, and traveled by the tube. Akram was conversant with the London map. They reached Bayswater well before the program started. Nilofer's seat was in the front row on the balcony, while her companions had their seats in one of the back rows. Nilofer thought she had done well to obtain an early booking. V.I.Ps and people holding the high priced premium tickets occupied the seats on the ground floor of the hall, level with the stage.

Precisely at six, the organizing secretary of the function appeared on the stage. He introduced himself as Jagan Nath Fatehabadi, a name Nilofer had not come across before. From the comments she overheard from the adjoining seats, it seemed the man hailed from the province of Madhya Pradesh of India, and had settled in Southhall, jokingly called the little India of London. He gave a short account of the activities of the Anjuman, aimed at the advancement of the Urdu language in the U.K. He thanked those who had enrolled as its members, and appealed for more to join. He thanked the poets who had agreed to participate gratis in the mushaaira. He informed the house that collection from the sale of tickets would go into the coffers of the Anjuman, and made a fervent appeal for donations. Then he invited the chairperson of the day's session to begin the proceedings.

The well-known poet of Pakistan, Gulzar Azad, came to the lectern, and without much ado announced that he felt honored to have been given the task of chairing the session, and was pleased to introduce the learned poets of that evening. He read out each name in the alphabetic order, gave a short review of his work, and then welcomed him on to the fore stage. Some of them were familiar faces to Nilofer, some she knew only by names. She had no eyes for them. She was impatiently waiting for the announcement of Naacheez's name, so that she could see her favorite writer in person. Then she heard the chairperson saying,

"Now *Haazreen*, I present to you the youngest poet of the evening, who has created a niche in the world of Urdu literature by his unmatched writings. He has won many a heart among the young as well as the not so young readers. I give you, one and the only one, Naacheez!"

Nilofer leaned forward and craned her neck as a young man emerged from the backstage. She froze in her stance. "*Vikram*!" She said wordlessly, opening her mouth and then shutting it tightly. She sat there like a statuette, as Vikram took his seat to a mild applause from the audience. The chairperson continued to call the participants, but Nilofer became oblivious of the going on around her. Her eyes remained glued to Vikram's face. Vikram was scanning the audience for familiar faces. His eyes came to rest on Nilofer. Their eyes remained locked for a few seconds, and then he turned his gaze away. The first participant was called to present his gazal. His words hardly registered in Nilofer's ears. The second participant offered a few couplets on modern life. It must have been a hilarious piece, judging by the giggles of the audience. Nilofer sat there utterly oblivious to the participant presenting their work. She was watching Vikram, who was intent on doodling on the back of his copy of the program. Gradually she recovered her composure, and the words of the poet currently presenting his piece, began to register on her mind.

"And now ladies and gentlemen," announced the chair person, "*Hazrat* Naacheez will present his *nazm*, the title of which is *Meri sukadti duniya,* my contracting world.

Vikram walked to the lectern, stood silently for a long minute, and then said into the microphone,

"Mr. Chairman Sir, I am sorry, I have left my *sukadti duniya* in my hotel room."

There was silence as it took some time for the people to realize that what the poet standing at the lectern was actually saying was, that he had forgotten his notebook in the hotel room, and could not recite his piece. The participants sitting on the podium broke into subdued laughter, and the chairperson joined in the merriment. Vikram waited for the mirth to die down and then said,

"Mr. Chairman Sir, may I be permitted to present my latest creation?"

"*Irshaad,* proceed please," said the chairperson.

Nilofer saw Vikram turn slightly, and look at her as he said,

"The title of my new nazm is *aaj mein jeeo,* live for today."

"Irshaad," said many voices in unison.

Continuing to look at Nilofer, Vikram started his recital.

Beeta kal to beet chuka, us ko yaad kyun karte ho
Agla kal abhi aaya nahin, us se abhi kyun darte ho
Hamein aaj jo dene wala ho kadwa ho meetha pyala ho
Khushi se us ko pee lien hum aao aaj mein jee lein hum

He halted momentarily. Then looking straight into Nilofer's eyes, he resumed.

Aaj ko jee lo jee bhar ke, phir yeh kal mein badlega
Yeh abhi tumhaara apna hai, kal ise kaal nigal lega
Aaj ki uthti lahron mein jeevan ki kashti behnein dein
Ahtmaad ke chappu se is kashti ko khe lein hum
Aao aaj mein jee lein hum, aao aaj mein jee lein hum

As he recited, he went on looking alternately at Nilofer and the program in his hands. Nilofer knew he was unobtrusively reading what he had spontaneously scribbled at the back of the program, while waiting for his turn, and his words were aimed at her. She was disconcerted at the uncanny ability of the man to peek into her mind. "He is telling me to live for today, to forget the past, and not be afraid of the future. How in the name of God does this man know that I am troubled by my past, and scared of my future?" As she mulled over this, she temporarily lost the link with his recital. She recovered her composure, and heard the concluding lines.

The present only matters.
The past has gone. The future is only a vision.
Do not carry the corpse of the past on your shoulder,
Bury it in the pages of history.
Let your life flow with the stream of the present.

Live for today.

Vikram returned to his seat. There was a thunderous applause from the audience. When it died down, the chairperson announced a forty-five minutes break for refreshments. Nilofer waited for Zahira and Akram to join her and the three of them went to the cafeteria attached to the hall. They purchased sandwiches and coffee at the counter, and sat at a nearby table. Nilofer nibbled at her sandwich absently. Her mind was in turmoil. For the last two years, Nacheez's writings had been appearing regularly in *Kainat*, published from Lahore. She had presumed he was a Pakistani. The philosophical tinge in his work had created a picture of a middle-aged author in her mind. He had turned out to be a young Hindu doctor, with whom she had been having a sweet-sour relation for the last few weeks. The voice of a high school teacher from the past rang out in her ears,

"The *kafirs* of India are destroying the Islamic culture and its Urdu language."

Here was her favorite Urdu writer, her idol, a *kafir*? No, no, she would not permit these thoughts to smash her idol.

Nilofer noticed that the participants and the organizers were having their snacks in an adjoining smaller cafeteria, separated from the main cafeteria by a glass door. She begged her companions to excuse her, and walked resolutely towards the adjoining cafeteria. She removed her diary from the pocket of her jacket and went through the door. Nobody stopped her. She saw Vikram sitting at a table with the chairperson of the evening, and another man. She approached the table, and when its occupants looked up, she raised her right hand to her forehead in the customary Muslim salute, *aadaab,* and it was acknowledged in similar fashion. She extended her diary towards Vikram and said,

"Nacheez Sahib, may I have your autograph please?"

Vikram got up, not showing a flicker of recognition, took the diary from her hand and said,

"Would you please come this way, *mohtarma*?"

He led her to a vacant table, motioned her to a chair, and took the opposite one himself. He took out a pen from his breast pocket, held the diary in front of him and asked,

"How have you come?"

"By bus."

"Alone?"

"Yes."

"Where are you putting up?"

"At the Indian Y.W.C.A."

"When are you returning?"

"Tomorrow."

"May I offer you a lift in my car?"

"*Zahe naseeb*, I shall be honored, Nacheez Sahib," it was her turn now to jab him with the formal phrases.

He accepted the dig with a smile and said,

"I shall pick you up at eleven in the morning."

He wrote in her diary,

Yesterday is ashes, tomorrow wood.

Only today does the fire burn brightly.

Under the ancient proverb, he wrote his pen name in Urdu, "Nacheez".

Next day when Vikram arrived at the Y.W.C.A, he found Nilofer waiting in the reception hall, packed and ready. He picked up her bag, and put it on the back seat of his car, while she took the front passenger seat. Vikram drove carefully through the morning traffic of London until they came onto the newly built Motorway M 4. Then he picked up speed and drove steadily at seventy miles an hour. Nilofer noticed that he was not inclined to engage in conversation while he drove. For the next one hour, they exchanged only a few words. Then he announced,

"We are approaching Bristol. We'll make a halt there for lunch."

They entered Bristol around one in the afternoon. Vikram seemed to know the town well. He drove straight to an Indian Restaurant called "The Raj". A security man in the Eastern regalia – *chudidaar* and *shervani*, complete with a *kullah* turban, opened the door. Nilofer noticed that the lights were soothingly dimmed, and classical Indo-Pak music was playing at a subdued volume. The wallpapers had blown up pictures of Indian historical monuments. Nilofer recognized a few, the Taj Mahal, the Qutab Minaar, the Red Fort, and the Gateway of India. Like the doorkeeper, the serving staff too wore the Indian ceremonial dress. They were shown to a table at the back, and two copies of menu placed before them. Nilofer started scanning the menu, while Vikram did not open his.

"I am going to order a Gujarati *thali*," he said, "please order what you want."

Nilofer was surprised,

"Gujarati *thali*? I didn't know that the Gujarat district had any special dishes of its own."

Vikram gave a short laugh, "I am not talking of the District Gujarat of Pakistan, but of the Gujarat state of India."

She gave a sheepish smile. She thought, "This man knows so much about Pakistan, while I know so little about India." Vikram was saying,

"This is the only restaurant in this country, which serves a Gujarati *thali*. When ever I get nostalgic, I come here to refresh the taste of my home made food."

Nilofer shut her menu decisively,

"In that case I too would like to sample the Gujarati food."

"Mind you," Vikram warned her, "it is a totally vegetarian fare, and it may not suit your taste buds."

Nilofer smiled; the same smile, starting from the eyes, and spreading slowly to the lips. It never failed to jab Vikram's heart. She said,

"I will take my chances."

Vikram ordered two *pannas* as starter, to be followed by two *thalis*. Nilofer liked the taste of panna. It was a sweet-sour concoction made from raw mangos. It left a mild tingling after-taste on the tongue. As they were finishing their drinks, a bearer placed two over sized metal plates, containing arrays of small metal bowls or *katoris*. Nilofer was struck by the variety of food, neatly arranged in the big plate.

There was the ubiquitous daal, curried potatoes, fried okra, a variety of mixed vegetable, which Vikram informed her, was called *undhiyun.* There were sprouted green grams, curried peas, yogurt, *bhujias,* rice and small paper thin chapatis, mango pickle, a couple of *chutnis* and salad, all in small quantities. In a bigger bowl there was a sweet dish called *basundi.* It was lunch, cum snacks rolled up in one. To her amazement, Nilofer found that the daal and all vegetables had sugar added to them. Vikram was right. The taste of food was nothing to write home about. She tasted each dish in turn. None appealed to her taste buds. Undhiyun was tolerable. She ate a small amount of it with chapaties. Bhujias were good, so she finished them all. Yogurt was fresh and to her taste. The rest of the items remained uneaten. She relished the sweet dish, basundi, and polished off the whole bowl. This much was enough to satisfy her hunger. She again glanced at each item in the plate, and as a professional in health, had to admit that what was lying in the plate in front of her, was a correctly balanced diet having all essential dietary ingredients. She noticed that Vikram had eaten up every thing on his plate, but had refused any extra helpings. At the conclusion of the meal, the bearer brought Calcutta *paans* on a silver platter. She took one, and placed it in her mouth. When she saw Vikram declining his, she asked the bearer to wrap it in a tissue paper for her. Calcutta paan was a rare luxury in her country.

When they left Bristol, it was past two in the afternoon. They re-entered M4, and crossed the Savern River, driving over the famed suspension bridge and entered South Wales at Monmouthshire. They arrived at the Radnor House around three. Vikram parked his car, and carried their bags upstairs. Nilofer considered asking him to let her carry her own bag, but then thought better of it. Vikram deposited her bag at the door of her room and said,

"Here you are doctor sahiba," and made a move to leave. Nilofer's words stopped him in his tracks,

"Do we always have to be that formal, Dr. Vikram?" There was a note of pleading in her voice. He turned back and looked into her eyes.

"I am Nilofer," she said in the same pleading voice.

"And I am Vicky," he said with a smile.

She smiled back. "Shall we have a cup of coffee, before you leave?" She said, inserting her key into the lock.

"That's a fabulous idea."

He waited in her room while she went to the kitchenette to make coffee. When she returned with the coffee tray, he was sitting very still in a reflective stance.

"A penny for your thoughts," she said.

"Oh, it is nothing, only a bit tired after driving,"

After Vikram left, Nilofer started pacing the floor of her room. She replayed the events of the last evening and this morning in her mind. Her discovery that Vikram was the writer she had adored was startling as well as delightful. His unassuming manner when she asked for his autograph had won her admiration and respect. Hence, she had accepted his offer of lift back to Cardiff with alacrity. During the journey, he had behaved as if they were long-term friends. "I do want us to be friends. Has he really accepted me as a friend?" She asked herself. The expression she had seen on his face, a few minutes back, was disconcerting. It certainly was not a look of tiredness. What was it? It was more as if he wanted to say something, but could not bring himself to articulate. "Well, leave it to the future to tell." She said to herself. At this thought, the line from Vikram's poem rang in her ears,

"Tomorrow is not here yet, why worry about it?"

She laughed aloud, "I am going to live for today," she said to the room at large. She flung herself into her bed without changing her outdoor dress, and in minutes, a deep, dreamless slumber engulfed her, from which she woke up late next morning. She had slept for fifteen hours. Her stomach was growling with hunger. She had not eaten her supper the previous night.

Nilofer did not see Vikram for one whole week after their journey together from London. There was an inexplicable expectation in her heart that he would come to see her. When he did not, she chided him in her mind, and in frustration called him names, stuck-up egotist. She knew well he was busy preparing for exams for his fellowship. "Even otherwise, why should he come to meet me? Who am I to him, or he to me?" She argued with herself. She wanted to remain busy, so that she did not have too much free time for fretting. With that in her mind, she had gone to Dr. Cynthia Joans one evening and made an unusual request,

"Madam, I know in my present assignment I am not permitted to attend emergencies. But may I be allowed to remain present when obstetric emergencies are being dealt with by the medical officer on regular call?'

Dr. Joans seemed pleased by her request,

"I like your ways of thinking. Tackling obstetric emergencies is a vital part of the training for our specialty. What I shall do, is to instruct Jason to give you a ring whenever he gets an emergency call, so that you can join him while he is tackling the case. But please remember you are not permitted to handle any case independently."

Thus, she started attending emergency cases twice a week. This extra work was now keeping her busy. Added to that, her resolve to live for the present had helped her in putting away the unpleasant thoughts of her conjugal life back home. She had organized her daily routine; getting up at the scheduled time, going for daily early morning walks, regular baths and prayers, timely meals, punctual attendance of hospital duties, and frequent visits to the library left her no time for gloomy thoughts. The unsettling nightmares that had earlier marred her sleep, stopped altogether. She was a rejuvenated person.

She still dreamed. But they were pleasant dreams, dreams from her childhood, dreams of her father riding a mare, with herself sitting behind him, her tiny arms wrapped around his waist; dreams of her *Naana*, the Grandfather, proudly presenting his doctor grand daughter to his friends. However, most of the times it was Vikram who visited her in her dreams. She talked to him in an endless chatter, while he sat listening to her, with a smile on his lips. When she woke up in the morning, she could not recall a single word of what she had said to him in the dream. He was almost constantly in her thoughts. She would banish him from her mind, but he would return unobtrusively and reoccupy her thoughts. She could not understand this obsession on her part. There had not been the slightest intimacy between them. "We are just colleagues, working at the same place, and that too just for the last few weeks," she thought. "In fact, we know almost nothing about each other. Then why do his thoughts refuse to leave my mind? Perhaps the dramatic way in which his identity, as a poet and writer, was revealed to me has influenced my mind. True, his writings had always appealed to me. May be that makes me think he is not a stranger." She went on, in this manner, making excuses for being attracted to Vikram. She refused to admit to herself that she had fallen madly in love with him.

A week later, on a Sunday morning, she ran into Vikram as she was leaving the house for her morning walk.

"Good morning Vikram," she said, "Are you going for a walk?"

"No, I'm out for a swim."

"How nice," she said as they started walking side by side.

"Do you like swimming, Dr. Nilofer?" he asked.

"I was very keen on learning swimming as a child, but my learning was cut short by an accident. By the way, I thought I had been promoted from Dr. Nilofer to plain Nilofer"

"I am sorry. By the way Nilofer, you were talking of an accident."

"Oh, I almost drowned in the water canal of my village, and after that I was forbidden to go near water."

"That is why I feel everyone should learn swimming. One could, some day, save someone's or even one's own life. Besides, it is an excellent exercise. Sorry for sermonizing though," he apologized.

"I entirely agree with you. It was a childhood friend's swimming skill that had saved me from drowning."

"Then why don't you learn swimming?

"You should know better than to ask that," she said. "A woman in a bikini would be stoned to death in my country."

"At present you are in Europe, not in Pakistan, and you don't have to wear a two piece bikini, we could buy a decent swim suit for you," he continued his reasoning.

Nilofer did not fail to notice his use of 'we' when he talked of buying a swimsuit.

"But Vikram, learning to swim at my age...," she trailed off.

By now, they had reached the gate of the swimming pool. Vikram invited her in. The gatekeeper came forward to open the gate,

"Good morning doc," he said to Vikram, and then looked questioningly at Nilofer.

"Oh Bill, this is Dr. Khan, she would like to have a look at the pool."

"Okay doctor, she is welcome," said Bill and waved them in.

They climbed up the steps, and Vikram led Nilofer to a poolside granite bench. Nolofer noticed that the pool was fairly large.

"Its dimensions are of international standards," Vikram informed her before she could ask.

The water was sparkling blue. Only two of the bathers were engaged in active swimming, one performing free style laps, and the other butterfly strokes. Nilofer saw a little girl, hardly three years old, in the shallow side. A man in his early thirties, probably her father, was coaching her. A little further, a young strapping man was instructing a rather bulky middle-aged woman. In him, Nilofer correctly recognized the official coach.

"Vikram," Nilofer said in a resolute voice, "I would like to join the pool."

Vikram turned to her. He saw the determined look in her eyes and said

"I would suggest you take a little time before making a final decision. If by tomorrow evening you don't change your resolve, we shall go and buy you a bathing costume."

Vikram knew it was an audacious act by a Muslim woman from a conservative family of Pakistan to don a swimsuit in a public place. He wanted her to have time to mull over her decision so that there should be no regrets afterwards.

Nilofer joined the swimming pool on the next Tuesday with one stipulation. Vikram would have to instruct her, and not the professional coach. Vikram demurely accepted the pleasant assignment. Nilofer was ill at ease in her swimsuit, only for the first couple of days, and then took to swimming like the proverbial fish taking to water. Every morning Vikram would knock at her door, precisely at quarter to six, and would find her ready with her kit bag. They would arrive at the pool at six. On most of the days, they were the first to arrive, and would have the pool to themselves. They spent an hour at the pool on working days, and a bit longer on weekends. Nilofer was a fast learner, and did not need much coaching. She had purchased a booklet titled *Learn swimming in three days.* She literally did that. With only a few lessons from Vikram, she started venturing into the deep parts of the pool, in less than a week. Vikram consciously avoided unnecessary body contact while instructing her. He laid emphasis on her learning how to float on her back, in case of muscular cramps or any other injury while in water. For this exercise, he had to support her shoulders and waist for a few times, and to his relief, she showed no embarrassment or awkwardness. Once she was able to keep afloat effortlessly and had learnt to hold her breath and stay under water for a full minute, he stopped his surveillance over her and let her be on her own. He had to confess to himself that in such short time of learning, her free style had become as good, if not better, than his.

Nilofer had laid one condition for herself, which she never breached. She never went swimming except in the company of Vikram. If for some reasons he were not able to go, she too would stay away from the pool. Vikram did not approve of her missing her routine exercise because of him, but she stuck to her guns.

Nilofer and Vikram imperceptibly grew close to each other, and a bond of friendship and mutual respect grew stronger by the day. However, Vikram took care that apart from visiting the swimming pool together, they were not seen together too frequently. At no time, he overlooked Nilofer's conservative background. He was particularly wary of his Asian co-workers, and wanted to avoid any gossip about Nilofer and himself in that group. He had vetoed Nilofer's suggestion that they have breakfast at the Hospital dining hall after their daily swim, and then return to their rooms. She had perceptively understood his reluctance, and her respect for him grew even more. Their early visits to the pool went unnoticed by their compatriots, as none of them used the pool, and hardly any of them was an early riser. As such, the Asian doctors working at their hospital could be counted on fingers of one hand.

*****

It was Thursday, 31 March 1966, Nilofer's twenty-sixth birthday. She did not rise at her usual early hour that morning. There was not to be the routine swimming session that morning, as Vikram was away in Swansea, and she never went swimming alone. She was feeling a bit down in the dumps. She offered her usual morning namaaz of *Fajr*, had her breakfast, attended her indoor duties at the hospital, had her lunch at the hospital diner, and returned to her room like a robot. She was badly missing Naana, her grandfather. She had spent sixteen happy years with him in Karachi. Every year, on this day, he had celebrated her birthday on a grand scale until the year he died. He had a large circle of friends, and threw lavish parties on his Shahzadi's birthdays at their mansion. She used to have a gala time with her friends, who were inevitably all girls. Her family was conservative, and it was inconceivable for a girl of her clan to have a male friend. Male and female guests assembled in different but adjoining rooms, and partook of the fares of the evening. After her Nana died and she shifted to Lahore, nobody even remembered her birthday. Her *Maamu* Uncle and *Maami* Auntie with whom she was living, did not believe in celebrating the birthday of a female child. They continued to celebrate the birthdays of their own two sons. What particularly annoyed Nilofer today, was that even her best friend Naseem seemed to have forgotten the occasion. Nilofer had not returned to the hospital after lunch. She had sat near her telephone, as she was sure Naseem would call. It was a quarter past six in the evening now, almost midnight in Pakistan. She gave up hope of hearing from Naseem. She had looked for her mail on her way up. There was no letter either. "Why do I bother whether any one remembers my birthday or not?" She said to herself, "I do not care whether somebody does or does not utter a few words of greetings." It was only a show of bravado. She sat dejected, and engulfed by a sense of gloom.

A knock at the door roused her from her reverie. Wearily, she got up and opened the door. Vikram stood there with a bunch of red roses in his hand, and a wide smile on his lips.

"A very happy birthday to you, Nilofer," he said offering the flowers.

She was so surprised that for a long minute she neither uttered a word of thanks nor accepted the flowers. Then she did an unexpected thing. She put her face against his breast, and broke into uncontrollable sobs. Vikram stood there rigidly. He wanted desperately to put his arms around her, and console her, but he restrained himself and kept his hands hanging by his sides, and let her cry. She wept for a long time, long enough to wet the front of his shirt with her tears. When her sobs subsided, he held her by her arm and led her to a chair. He sat facing her and said,

"Unfulfilled expectations give pain. Keep your expectations at the zero level, and you will find that even small mercies that the Almighty bestows on you will bring immense pleasure with them."

He kept talking to her in this refrain, in a low measured tone until she got hold of herself. She got up, went to the washbasin, sprinkled water on her face, and wiped it with the towel. She filled a glass from the water tap and drank thirstily. She was wondering, how he knew her expectations have been shattered today. Instead, she asked,

"How did you know today is my birthday?"

"Your passport had divulged the well-guarded secret." There was a mischievous twinkle in Vikram's eyes.

Nilofer's sense of humor had returned.

"I had given you my passport to make a copy of it, not to dig out my secret life."

Both of them laughed and the atmosphere brightened. Vikram got up and said breezily.

"Okay Madam, I am going to my room and shall be back in precisely ten minutes. You have until then to change. We are going out."

"Where to?" she inquired.

"Yours is not to ask where and why," he said over his shoulders and left.

Nilofer obeyed. She was ready when he returned. They drove to the city centre. Vikram parked the car in the paid parking lot, and they walked down to an exclusive garment store. Vikram led Nilofer to the jeans stand.

"I want you to select a pair of jeans for yourself."

She turned to him in utter astonishment,

"You know I don't wear jeans."

"Yes, I know, but I want to gift you a pair anyway."

"But why give me something which I'll never use?" She looked visibly baffled.

"Just do it, please, to satisfy a friend's whim," he persisted.

Nilofer gave in, "Okay, but this is going to be a wasteful expensive whim."

She went to the jeans section, and started scanning the price tags. Vikram beckoned to a middle-aged saleswoman who was standing at a discreet distance and watching them unobtrusively.

"Excuse me. Will you be kind enough to help this lady here, to select a pair of jeans and a T-shirt to go with them?"

"Yes sir," the woman said looking at the salwar-kameeze clad Nilofer.

"Do you have a price range in mind, sir?"

"Let her have the best,"

The sales woman removed three pairs of jeans from the stand. She and Nilofer disappeared into the measurement cabins. They emerged half an hour later, Nilofer clad in jeans and T-shirt.

"Here we are sir," the sales woman addressed Vikram, "your lady looks so attractive in this outfit. Doesn't she?"

Vikram gave a brief casual once over to Nilofer. She looked a bit self-conscious without her duppatta. He had to admit that, with her height and strikingly feminine figure, she did look very pretty indeed. However, he refrained from making any effusive comments. He very well knew that in the conservative families of the east, comments by a male, on the physical appearance of a woman was an anathema.

"The dress becomes you," was all he said.

Even this mild compliment raised the color in her face. She changed back into her own clothes, and had the dress packed. While Nilofer was away in the change room, Vikram obtained the page of the slip book, on which the sales woman had noted down Nilofer's measurements, and pocketed it.

While they were driving back, Nilofer was thinking why Vikram had insisted on giving her a dress which she would never wear. She had never worn anything except kameeze and salwar. Of course, as a young girl, she had felt jealous of some of her Christian schoolmates who looked very smart in their skirts and blouses. The *Qaazi Saheb* at Masjid had branded such western dresses as satanic. She wondered what the Qaazi would think of the dress that lay on her lap now. "At present you are in Europe, not in Pakistan, and you don't have to wear a two piece bikini," the words of Vikram seemed to ring in her mind. She had not considered the swimsuit as an indecent dress, then how could she label a pair of jeans indecent? Almost all women here wore trousers. "It is rather I, who looks an odd one out in my salwar -kameez," she thought. Vikram broke into her daydream.

"Here we are." He had parked the car.

She looked out, but could not recognize the place. Vikram got out of the car, and Nilofer followed suit. They walked down the road, and turned into the second street on the left, marked the Whitchurch Street. Vikram led her to a small, neat looking eating joint. The sign displayed on the front read *Zaaika–e-Afghani*, in English as well as in bold Urdu script. As they entered, a burly bearded middle-aged Afghan, supporting a turban with a *turrah,* emerged from behind the counter. He noticed the traditional eastern dress of Nilofer and greeted them with the conventional *aadaab,* raising his right hand, with the palm upturned, to his forehead, and bowing slightly at the waist. Vikram and Nilofer acknowledged the salutations in similar fashion. There were about a dozen tables covered with sparkling white tablecloths. Only three of them were occupied. All occupants were from the east, and none of them was a woman. The ubiquitous music in the eating-places was conspicuously absent in this one.

"It doesn't seem to be a very popular place," Nilofer remarked under her breath.

"Ah, you should come here after ten. You will not find an empty seat. The British youngsters love the dishes offered at this place."

A bearer appeared at their table. He placed two copies of the menu before them with exaggerate deference, and withdrew. Nilofer did not open her menu, and said,

"Will you please select for me?"

"Sorry Madam. It is your night, and besides, the names of the dishes are likely to be more familiar to you than to me."

Nilofer took up the menu and started scanning it. The waiter had re-appeared, and stood patiently with his pencil poised over the order book. After a rather prolonged study of the menu, Nilofer looked at the waiter and said in Urdu, "To begin with, bring us the *Kaarach Shorma*. After that, we shall have *Chelo Nachodo* and *Obi Naan*, and at the end please bring *Chalow* with *korma.*

While they were waiting to be served, Vikram brought up the matter of the examination again.

"What have you decided about sitting the MRCOG Examination?"

She had almost forgotten their earlier talk on the subject, and took some time to reply,

"I am not sure whether the rules of my scholarship permit me to take an exam."

"As I understand, in your country, a six months internship in Rural Medicine is mandatory after completing MBBS."

"Yes," said Nilofer, "I have done that."

"I have gone through the rules of the commonwealth scholarship. There is no clause that prohibits a scholarship holder from taking an exam. You have registered with the GMC, and are undergoing training in Obstetrics and Gynecology in a teaching institution for a period of two years. Add to that your six month internship, and that will make two and a half years." Vikram stated the facts.

"By my calculations, you should be eligible to take the exam for the membership. At the most, you may fall short of the required period of training by a few months. The scholarship rules permit a holder to have his tenure extended by six months. I do not see any difficulty in your sitting for the exam. Still however, we could talk the matter over with Professor Wise.

There it was again. '*We*', not '*you*'. Nilofer felt the imperceptibly growing bond between them. At this point, the waiter appeared with two bowls of shorma. It was steaming hot. Vikram gingerly swallowed a spoonful of it. He licked his lips like a child. He had never tasted a mushroom soup as delicious as this one. Nilofer knew how to select from an Asian menu. As they ate their soup, Vikram reverted to the topic they were discussing.

"What I suggest is that you start preparing for part one of the examination, and aim to take it this October."

Nilofer thought for few minutes and said diffidently,

"How can I be ready in just six months?"

"It should not be too difficult," Vikram said in a reassuring tone, "You only have to brush up your basic sciences. You know, the course for the part one in all specialties is more or less the same. I have taken my part one last year. I have a lot of reading material stashed away, and we can procure some more for you. If you start preparing right away, I am sure you can be ready for the test in six months. In any case, if you feel you are not ready by then, you can sit the exam in April next year."

Their main dish of Chelo Nachodo and Obi Naan arrived. Chelo nachodo looked like any other chicken stew, but had a mouth-watering aroma, and tasted even better. The spices used for seasoning were so well proportioned that they enhanced its taste without making it too hot. The sparse tiny particles of ginger left a slight tickle on the tongue. They ate in silence, their thoughts traveling in their separate channels. Nilofer was thinking, "Here is a man, a stranger, whom I met only few weeks back. We know practically nothing about each other's background. There has always been hostility between our countries. We have already fought two bloody wars in the span of eighteen years, the last one only six months back. Our communities have harbored mutual abhorrence for centuries. He is a *kaafir*, an infidel in the eyes of the clergy of my community. The priests of his community call us *maleksh*, the unclean. Here I am, celebrating my birthday in his company without any qualms whatsoever. Why do I feel happy in his company?" She could not find a convincing answer to her own questions.

Vikram's thoughts too were about Nilofer, "The girl is passing through difficult times. There has been some tragic incident in her life. She is on the verge of a nervous break down. I must keep her mind occupied, so that she gets little time to dwell on her misfortunes, whatever they are. She looks so forlorn. I should not let her be alone."

"*Khatoon,* will you like some dessert?" The bearer's inquiry to Nilofer broke into their thoughts. Nilofer felt a bit annoyed as the chain of her thoughts was broken by the interruption. She recovered her composure quickly and ordered *Sheer Payra* without consulting Vikram. He, on his part did not mind her minor slip, and took it as a good sign of her getting hold of herself. If there was any remnant of annoyance, it evaporated with the very first spoonful of the dessert. The cardamom fudge just melted in his mouth.

Next day, on Vikram's advice, Nilofer approached Professor Wise and obtained his formal permission for taking the exam. Vikram gave her a list of books she should read and some material he had collected for his own primary fellowship.

"Tomorrow is Saturday," Nilofer said to Vikram, "The library will close early, will you mind if I read in your room on weekends. I loath being alone while studying. I promise not to disturb you in your own preparation for the exam."

Vikram laughed, "You have only one day, tomorrow, on which to disturb me. The day after, I am leaving for London for sitting the exam. Next week when I return I will be glad of all the disturbance."

When Nilofer went to Vikram's room next afternoon, he was busy packing his things. She offered to help, but he declined saying,

"You will only be in my way. You do not know what I need to pack. You better sit over there and start reading."

Nilofer noticed that Vikram packed his things so quietly, that sometimes she had an impression of being alone in the room. After finishing packing, he went to the kitchen and came back with two mugs of coffee.

"You shouldn't have bothered," Nilofer said, "I could have got the coffee."

"From now on you will only concentrate on reading, and I shall ply you with loads of coffee, to keep you from dozing off."

While they were eating their supper in the dining hall, Vikram informed Nilofer that he would be catching the 11.10 train for London.

"May I accompany you to the railway station?"

"It shall be my pleasure, madam, if you will drive me down to the station." There was mischievous tone in his voice.

"Don't mock me, sir, you know I can't drive," she answered in the same tone.

"Then better learn driving," this time there was a serious note in his voice.

"Oh Vikram…"

Vikram cut her off. "You can accompany me to the station."

Next morning, as Vikram was ordering a taxi on the phone, Nilofer walked into his room, wearing the jeans and the T-shirt he had gifted her three days earlier. There was not the slightest discomfiture in her demeanor. He was delighted, but again avoided making any comments. However, Nilofer saw the admiring look in his eyes. Before they went down to board the taxi, he handed her a slip of paper on which he had written the name of his hotel and the phone number. Nilofer phoned him regularly twice a day; in the morning to wish him good luck, and in the evening to inquire how he had fared at the exam. On Thursday he told her that he had finished his theory part, and the oral test was scheduled for next Monday, that he intended to spend the intervening time doing shopping and visiting a couple of picture galleries.

"But Vikram, you can do the shopping here in Cardiff as well. Why not come back and return on Sunday afternoon?"

Vikram tried to reason with her that it would be a tiresome exercise to be traveling on two days in order to be in Cardiff just for one day. Nilofer acquiesced very reluctantly. "How can I tell you how much I miss you?" were her unspoken words. On Monday evening Vikram called,

"Nilofer, I am through."

She was delighted, but could not find words to express her elation. "Congratulations, Vikram," was all that she said, "When are you returning?"

"At the moment I am at the post exam dinner with the other successful candidates and the examiners. The get together is expected to last until late in the night. I intend to take an early morning coach to Leicester, to see my local guardians. I shall be with you at dinner time tomorrow."

Next day was Tuesday, the out patient day of Nilofer's unit. She left the hospital before noon, and walked down to the city center. At the Marks and Spencer's grocery counter, she picked up a small sized broiler. Next, she visited an Indian grocery shop, and purchased a pound of *Basmati* rice, a pack of semi baked *Naans*, tomatoes, onion, ginger, garlic, chilies, spices, and other cooking ingredients, making sure she forgot nothing. On the way back, she picked up a packet of fish and chips from a Chinese shop. By the time she reached her room, she was dog-tired. The long walk had taken its toll. It made her think of Vikram's advice to learn driving. She ate the fish and chips, and rested in the reclining chair. After refreshing herself with a light nap, she went into the kitchen in a bid to rediscover her cooking skills.

Vikram arrived around half past seven in the evening. He went straight to Nilofer's room, carrying his suitcase, and rang the bell. The door was promptly flung open. Nilofer stood there with a beaming smile on her face. She opened her arms, and took a step forwards as if to hug him. She hesitated, and then ended up holding both his hands and congratulated him effusively.

"Oh Vicky, I am so happy for ...for us," she said.

Although they had agreed to call each other Nilofer and Vicky, she had called him that for the first time. The excitement had brought a rosy flush to her cheeks. Added to that, her peculiar smile sent Vikram's heart racing. He opened his mouth to speak and then shut it resolutely. After a while, he said,

"I am famished, let's go for supper."

"No, my dear Mister Kocher," Nilofer laid stress on 'Mister.' Because having qualified as a surgeon, from now on he was to be officially addressed as Mr. and not Dr., "Tonight you shall have to be satisfied with a frugal meal cooked by yours truly."

She went on to produce the dishes she had spent four hours to cook. First, she brought in the thick, gingered tomato soup with floating bread crumpets. This was followed by a chicken preparation and naans. The chicken was a Mughlai preparation, with nuts and grated desiccated coconut.

"It is called *Noor Jehani Murg,*" Nilofer enlightened him. Finally, she produced chilled *kheer*, the rice pudding with liberal sprinkling of resins.

"Where did you learn to cook such delicious preparations?" Vikram inquired.

"Under the tutelage of my *Maami Jaan,*" she replied.

After they had eaten, Vikram opened his suitcase and brought out a shopping bag.

"This is for you," he said, handing it to her.

It contained two dresses, a pair of jeans and a tee, and a pair of grey trousers with a white shirt. Nilofer looked up reproachfully and started to protest, but Vikram cut her off,

"You can't wear the one pair of jeans every day. And please," he went on in a mock stern tone, "from now on, you'll have to buy your own stuff. I don't own the *Haroon's* treasure."

He handed her the slip bearing her measurements, which he had taken from the woman, who had sold them her first pair of jeans. He did not give Nilofer an opportunity to say anything further. He picked up his suitcase, wished her good night, and left.

Next morning Nilofer took a bold step. She went to the hospital in the trousers and shirt Vikram had given her. Most of her colleagues made appreciative comments on her new appearance. Even her consultant, Cynthia Joans gave an approving smile, and a friendly wink. Pamela Lahore was the most vociferous in her compliments.

"You look gorgeous," she said, "why have you been hiding your charms behind that dowdy dress of yours?"

That evening Nilofer took another even more drastic step. She went and purchased half a dozen new dresses, and before she retired to bed, she packed up all her old dresses in a plastic bag, and placed it in the far corner of her wardrobe.

For the next three weeks, the time flew for Nilofer. With the task of reading for the exam, added to her hospital duties, she was left with very little free time. Into this busy schedule, she had squeezed in two hours of weekly driving lessons. She did not mention her driving lessons to Vikram. All this time, not once the bitter memories of her past entered her mind. As a result, her general health improved considerably. Vikram, who had kept a watchful eye on her, noticed that her sallow complexion had given way to a pinkish skin tone. There was á springy bounce in her steps, and she smiled a lot more. That smile of her never failed to create a turmoil in his heart.

It was the end of the first week of May. They were in Vikram's room for her post-supper reading session. Nilofer was discussing with Vikram the anatomy of the uterine ligaments as approached from the vaginal route. The telephone rang. Vikram answered it. Nilofer heard Vikram telling the operator,

"Put me through please." Then after a few seconds, she heard him say into the phone,

"*Pairi pona Bauji.*"

Nilofer realized it was a call from his father, and she got up to leave the room. She did not want to eavesdrop on a private conversation. Vikram waved her back into the chair. Nilofer tried not to pay attention to the one sided conversation of Vikram, and tried to concentrate on her reading. She failed in both. Snatches of Vikram's talk penetrated her ears. "That's wonderful...I'll be there...no, no, I'll try to reach a couple of days earlier... I'll call you as soon I have booked my air ticket, failing that I'll send a cable." Vikram ended the call with, "take care Bauji."

Nilofer turned to him. Her eyes looked troubled.

"Are you planning to go to India?"

Vikram had failed to notice the concern in her face, and said with enthusiasm,

"Yes Nilofer, my parents are celebrating the silver jubilee of their marriage. It is going to be a grand celebration."

Nilofer stood there, color drained from her face, tears welling in her eyes. Vikram noticed her plight and went to her,

"What's the matter, Nilofer?"

She flung her arms around his neck and started sobbing. "Don't go away Vicky, please," she said between sobs, "don't leave me alone, I'll die without you."

Vikram held her in his arms, and tried to calm her down,

"It is a matter of just ten days, and I shall be back before you start missing me."

She raised her face, wet with tears, pulled down his head, and kissed him on the lips. It was an awfully awkward kiss of a novice. Vikram tightened his hold on her and returned her kiss. He felt her body quiver with excitement. They remained in that position, locked in each other's arms, oblivious of the passing time. When her tears ultimately dried, Vikram wordlessly led her to his bed. That night she did not return to her room, and slept in Vikram's arms after they had made tender but passionate love. She woke up in the middle of the night feeling cramped. She had lain in the same position for a long time. Vikram's arm was still loosely draped around her. She badly needed to change position but refrained from doing so, lest she woke him up. Vikram withdrew his arm and turned on his back, as if he understood her need even in his sleep. She shifted in a comfortable position, and watched Vikram's face in the subdued light of the night lamp. He, her love, looked an innocent child sleeping besides her. She closed her eyes, and relived in her mind the bliss she had experienced in Vikram's arms. She had read somewhere that love between man and woman was never complete without the physical union. Now she had experienced the bliss that had made her totally oblivious of any consequences.

Her thoughts traveled back in time to that fateful night, her *shab-e-aroos,* her nuptial night, when she had sat in her elegantly decorated bridal chamber, waiting for her bridegroom. She had read so many romantic stories woven around the *hujra-e- aroosi,* the bridal chamber, and had been excited and apprehensive at the same time. She had rehearsed in her mind for the umpteenth time what she would say to *him,* and had made countless guesses of what *he* would say to her. "One thing I shall make clear to him," she had thought, "we should plan not to have children for the first two to three years." She had been sure he would happily agree. Time had passed, first in pleasurable anticipation, then in annoying frustration, culminating in heart breaking disappointment. The clock on the wall of chamber had shown well past midnight and *he* had not shown up. The wedding ceremonies of the day had tired her, and now so late in the night she found it difficult to keep awake. She had removed most of the bridal finery, donned a nightdress, and had stretched herself in the bridal bed. She had promptly fallen into a fitful sleep. A tug on her pajama cord woke her up. She opened her eyes with fright. *He* was sitting on the edge of the bed with one end of her pajama cord in his hand, which he had pulled loose. Stark naked, he looked, in the dim glow of the night lamp, like a grizzly bear with thick growth of hair all over his body, from neck downwards to his legs. Before she could react, he tried to pull down the dress, ripping it in the process.

"No!" her scream had been barely audible.

"Why not?" He said in a slurred drunken voice.

"Not this way, please," she had pleaded in a hoarse trembling voice.

"Tell me how then," his lips had twisted in an amusing smile. "Tell me, how else does a man take a woman?"

Nilofer was shocked to her core. A man taking a woman! Is that all a marriage is supposed to be? Before she could recover from his verbal assault, he had roughly lifted her from the waist with one hand, and had jerked her torn pajama away with the other. He was a hulk of a man, and she was half-dead with fear and shock. He had spread-eagled her and taken her. She was pinned down under his massive weight, and she thought she would choke to death. Abruptly he had slipped off her, and lay besides her. In no time he was snoring away, whisky fumes from his breaths filling the bridal chamber. The bride lay there paralyzed with shock, stripped of all dignity, battered, and bleeding. The act of taking was repeated the next night, and the night after that. Her heart and soul were filled with hatred for the man, and for the act, which he had called taking, and the romantic fools of the world called lovemaking. Animal, animal, animal, her mind shrieked in helplessness. No, the brute is worse than even an animal. She had never seen a male animal forcing itself on an unwilling female.

Now as she lay there, besides Vikram, her initial sense of utter bliss was assaulted by the memories of the nights, when that brute of her husband had forcibly and repeatedly, made her a receptacle of his filthy semen. Her body shook with sobs.

Vikram woke up with a start, and turned to her. She had her back towards him. He put his arm gently around her, and asked hesitatingly,

"Are you feeling remorse for tonight?"

She jerked around to face him, "No, silly," she said, "You don't know what you have done. You have cleansed my heart and soul of long pent up pollution. I feel liberated."

"Then why the tears, my love.?" His use of the endearing address drove away all the bitterness from her heart.

"You know Vicky, I once saw a prisoner who was sentenced to death by the trial court cry his heart out when set free by a higher court."

Vikram was about to say something when he felt Nilofer's hand on his lips. "No more talk," she said, "hold me, and put me to sleep." Vikram too thought it prudent not to probe any further.

When Vikram woke up at his usual time at quarter past five the next morning, Nilofer was deep in sleep. Poor thing, he thought, remembering her bitter sobs of the last night. It was after two in the morning before he had succeeded in lulling her to sleep. Now she slept tranquilly, a faint smile playing on her lips. He decided to let her sleep, knowing well she would grumble missing her morning swim. He soundlessly brushed his teeth, then tiptoed out of the room to the bath stalls and had a hot shower. Next, he scrambled some eggs in the kitchen, prepared egg and cheese sandwiches, and carried them to the room. Nilofer stirred in the bed, and gave a gaping yawn.

"Good morning," he called out.

"Good morning," she replied languidly. "What time is it?"

"It's nearing seven.

She got out of bed, and reflexly walked towards the washbasin for brushing her teeth. She stopped short, realizing she was not in her own room.

"No tooth brush," she said to nobody in particular.

Vikram produced a new spare toothbrush and handed it to her. While she was brushing her teeth, Vikram went back to the kitchen, and in a little while returned bearing a tray with the tea things. Nilofer had never felt so hungry in her life, and attacked the breakfast greedily. In the middle of eating, she stopped abruptly, with the sandwich poised half way to her mouth, a frown in her face. She gave Vikram a perplexed look and said,

"Vicky, there is one thing I cannot understand."

Vikram smiled and said, "I know what you are thinking. Yes, I am twenty-seven. You are wondering how come my parents are celebrating their twenty fifth wedding anniversary."

Nilofer was once again wonder-struck by his uncanny perception. How could this man read her mind?

"For God's sake Vicky, how can you…" Vikram did not let her finish.

"How I can read your thoughts?" Well my dear, when you will start loving me as intensely as I love you, you shall get your answer."

Nilofer's cheeks glowed deep pink at Vikram's nonchalant confession of love for her. Her heart danced with joy, mingled with a trace of embarrassment. In her circle, maybe even in his, people usually did not declare love vocally. She feigned offence, glared at him with her large eyes.

"My dear *Majnu*, What makes you think my love for you is any less than yours for me?"

"Wait until your Majnu's adorations elevate you to *Laila's* position. You will not need to ask any questions then. Now to answer your earlier question, my parents who are to celebrate their twenty-fifth anniversary, are not my biological parents. In fact, I have two pairs of parents…"

"Two pairs of parents?"

Vikram continued as if he had not been interrupted,

"My biological parents and my foster parents. My foster parents are a childless doctor couple. My biological parents were their employees when I was a child. They had informally adopted me and educated me. Now I hold the enviable position of a lone child of two pairs of parents.

Both remained silent for a minute or so. Then Nilofer spoke in an emotional tone,

"You know Vicky, we have come so close, yet we hardly know anythingg about each other."

"You speak for yourself, my dear girl. As for me, I know a whole lot about you."

Joining the fun game, Nilofer asked, "What do you know about me? Out with it."

"Your name is Nilofer, you were born in the village of Uchaanwala, in the Gujarat District of the Province of Punjab of Pakistan. Your father's name is Wazeer Ahmed, Mother's Aneesa Bibi, and grand father's Mirdaad," Vikram rapid fired the information in one breath.

Nilofer clapped her hands, "Full marks to you for the accurate recital from my passport."

Vikram looked at her. There was intense excitement in his eyes.

"Let us see," he said. "Does your passport say that your parent's house is the largest building of the village, and that it is situated at the eastern end of the central street, next to the village pond, and that it is called *Daadu-di-haweli*?"

Nilofer was taken aback. "How do you know all this?"

Vikram said with mock seriousness, "There is a red corner warrant out for you, and the Interpol has passed on your dossier to my court."

Vikram stood in front of her, and assumed the posture of a stern prosecuting judge.

"Now, Dr. Mrs. Nilofer Khan, This court requires from you, honest answers to some serious questions. Remember, Dr. Khan, you are under oath, and I warn you that perjury in this court will attract harsh penalties. Let me ask you Dr. Khan, have you, or have you not, at one time or the other, been going under the name of Fatima?

Nilofer gaped at him. In spite of it being only a mock drama, she sat there, absolutely stunned, staring at Vikram, and then said in a stammering voice,

"That was my childhood name. I had almost forgotten it. How did you find out?"

"We have our sources of information."

Vikram continued to act a prosecutor. He turned and picked up a letter pad from the desk. He turned its pages, pretending to locate some information. Then staring down at her, he said,

"What about another name, *Jhalli Phatti*?"

Nilofer was completely bowled over by the question. She spoke like an automaton, "Only…er…he called me that, Jhalli Phatti, the crazy."

"Who is this 'he'?" Vikram said continuing his stern inquisition.

"A friend," she said, "a childhood friend, who once saved me from drowning."

"Does this friend of yours have a name?"

Nilofer's face had assumed a thoughtful look. She said haltingly,

"I can't remember his name."

Vikram clapped mockingly, "Bravo, Dr. Khan, someone saves your life, you call him a friend, and then you just go and forget his name!"

Nilofer flinched at his assault, and said apologetically, "It was so long back, and I was so…" Nilofer halted in mid sentence,

"Wait a minute, his name was … Kittu, no… it was Bittu…no, no, Bikku, yes, I have it now, it indeed was Bikku."

Vikram's next question brought an audible gasp from Nilofer,

"Are you referring to Bikku the Lizard?"

She leapt from her chair and shook Vikram by the shoulders, "How do you know all this? Tell me, how do you know?"

Vikram put his arms around her neck, and whispered in her ears, "I am that Lizard, Bikku… Bikki… Vicky."

Nilofer went limp in his arms, but only for a moment. Then she started banging Vikram's chest with both her fists, as she used to do when Vikram annoyed her in their childhood.

"Bikku, you idiot! You cheat! How long have you known about me?"

Vikram feigned to ward off her blows, and then lovingly clutched her in his arms. She raised her tear stained face and he kissed her repeatedly. Her agitation gradually subsided and she sank back into her chair. Their half-eaten breakfast lay in front of them. The tea had gone cold. She picked up the tray and said,

"I'll get us fresh tea. We both need it."

Sitting down with fresh cups of tea, they looked wordlessly at each other for a long time. Nilofer broke the silence,

"Tell me, when had you recognized me?"

"You know Nilu, actually when we first met, and I accompanied you from the office of Professor Wise, that mole on your nose, and your twinkling smile, the *tim-tim* smile had prodded my memory, but your name had put me off the track. Besides, I could not dream of Fatima, the unkempt lass of Village Uchaanwala, being a doctor."

Nilofer interrupted him, "You still remember my nick name, *Tim-Tim Taara*, the twinkling star?"

"How can I forget? After all, it was I who had given you that name."

"Yes, you had poetic leanings even as a child. Remember, I had made you promise, you will call me by that name only when no one else was around. I loved it when you called me that, Tim-Tim, and wanted no one else to have that privilege."

Vikram picked up where he had left off, when Nilofer had interrupted him,

"When I was making copies of your passport, the word Uchaanwala, your birth place, caught my eye. Your Father and grandfather's name made the whole thing clear. A daughter of Wazeer Ahmed bin Mirdad, bearing a mole at the tip of her nose, and smiling that twinkling smile, had to be my Phatti, my Tim-Tim, whatever name she might be going under."

"Then why did you keep away from me for so long?" Nilofer's voice was choked with emotion.

"My first impulse was to rush to you immediately. Then I remembered your somewhat detached attitude. I thought if I rushed to you and said, look here Phatti, I am Bikku, your childhood friend of Uchaanwala, and if you had denied knowing any Bikku, it would have been the end of the road for me. Therefore, I planned to approach you cautiously. I asked you places you had lived in, back in Pakistan. I had expected you would talk of the Village Uchaanwala and the childhood companions. If necessary, I would have nudged your memory about Bikku. However, as the things went, you showed a clear distaste of my attempt at informality. I won't say I was not hurt."

"May be he sees his soul mate in you."

Rasila's words echoed in Nilofer's mind. She squeezed her eyes shut in sheer agony, remembering how she had considered Vikram's conduct indecent.

A silence fell between them. Both were reliving those moments of mutual discord. Nilofer broke the silence,

"And was it my insolence of that day that gave birth to the poem, *My Star?*"

Vikram gave an imperceptible nod, and Nilofer continued,

"Do you remember my pleadings with you to teach me to read and write?

Vikram nodded again.

"Yes, the village girls were not permitted to attend school, and you used to pester me to give you lessons. I had to hold clandestine teaching sessions for you on the terrace of your house in the afternoons, when most of the household was having their siesta. And what a fast learner you were!"

"And you gave me your old Urdu Primer," Nilofer joined in the reminiscence. "I had written my name on it, the way you had taught me. You know, Vicky, I have preserved that primer to this day. The pages though have turned brown, and tend to tear on handling. I am going to add the copy of the magazine containing your poem, *My Star* to the primer as the second souvenir."

Thus, they sat there, oblivious of the passing time, reliving their childhood. Nilofer looked at her watch and exclaimed,

"It is almost closing time for the dining hall. If we don't look sharp we shall have to go hungry."

With a twinkle in his eyes, Vikram said,

"Don't you worry, Tim Tim, your Bikku won't let you starve."

Both laughed at the memories of the punishment that Nilofer, or Fatima at the time, had frequently suffered at the hands of her stepmother, Amina Bibi, Amina the witch, as the children called her to her back. Most of the times it was Fatima's cousin, Fazal Illahi – Phalloo, the Bully, who brought upon her the wrath of her step mother. He was two years older to Fatima, and was always on a lookout to pick up fights with her. He would object to Fatima's participation in the game of *gilli danda*. No other girl from the village was permitted to play outdoor games. Fatima loved to go out in the evenings and play with the boys. In this she had a tacit support of her father, who himself was an athlete, and champion horse racer of the district. Whenever the boys voted to exclude Fatima from the gilli danda game, Bikku too would opt out. This compelled them to let her play, as they could not contemplate a game of gilli danda without Bikku, the ace player. Her inclusion infuriated Phalloo. The teams would be formed by allotting players by the formula of *akkad bakkad bamba bo*. Whenever Bikku and Fatima were selected in the same team, their team invariably won. Fatima was a lissome, nimble footed girl, and a superb fielder. She brought about some excellent catches. Bikku was a hard hitter of the gilli and an expert at placing. On the other hand, when Fatima and Phalloo were selected in the same team, they invariably ended up quarrelling. Phalloo was a ponderous and unwieldy fielder, and Fatima lost no opportunity of mocking him, whenever he blundered on the field. Many a time they would come to blows. Bikku used to intervene, and shielded Fatima from Phalloo's punches. He had even coached her in counter attack. On occasions, when Fatima would get the better of Phalloo, he would rush to his Auntie, Amina Bibi, and make a whimpering complaint. Amina was ever ready to "discipline" Fatima. Her way of disciplining was to withhold food and starve the child, and confine her to an isolated room on the terrace. Vikram always came to know of this, as he lived next door, and invariably managed to smuggle food to her by scaling the back wall of Fatima's house. He was adept at climbing and had earned the epithet of lizard: Bikku, the Lizard. He would lightly tap at the window and whisper, "Tim Tim", and when Fatima opened the window noiselessly, he would pass the food to her through the iron grill, and then stealthily slither down the wall.

That day Bikku again fed his Tim Tim the Afghan delicacies at the Zaika-e-Afghan. The ambience of Afghan restaurant was in keeping with their current mood.

Both of them were busy for the next ten days or so. Vikram had to do his shopping, make arrangements for his trip to India, besides attending his hospital duties. Nilofer was even busier. However, in spite of her preoccupations, she had not forgotten to go on the pill after her next period. Pregnancy under the circumstances would have been a disaster. She had taken to reading in Vikram's room every evening after supper, until eleven, and then returning to her own room. During short breaks from reading she and Vikram would talk of their past, thus catching up with each other's life after they were parted at the time of the Partition of India, nineteen years back.

Shivram Kocher, of Uchaanwala village in Punjab, was an enterprising person. He had inherited a small business of *bajaji* from his father, wherein he would purchase, from the neighboring town, a few bales of various fabrics commonly used by the village folk, and then sell the stuff in pieces, from a tiny shop located in the centre of the main village street. The paltry income from this business left him discontented and frustrated. He decided to explore greener pastures. In the year 1937, he sold away, the not so productive ancestral farmland, and carrying the money thus acquired, he traveled to the distant town of Ahmedabad in the Bombay Presidency. Ahmedabad was the hub of the textile industry of the country. He purchased a large consignment of various fabrics from the wholesale market, with an extra benefit of ten per cent rebate for making a down payment in cash. He had the consignment transported to his village. Then carrying the samples of the fabrics, he cycled from one village of his tahsil, Phalia, to the next, and offered the material to the local retail cloth dealers at prices lower than the prevalent rates in the local market. He sold away the whole consignment in less than a week and made a decent profit. He made another visit to Ahmedabad, and this time returned with three consignments. Now he included the towns of the district Gujarat in his selling itinerary. In less than two years, he had opened a wholesale depot in the neighboring town of Mandi Bahauddin, the main trading centre of the district. He took in a partner, and employed two helpers. He enlarged his purchasing arena to other important textile centers like Surat, Bombay, Madras, Bangalore, and Banaras, and included ready-made garments and hosiery in his purchases. He stopped going out on selling trips. Instead, the traders and shopkeepers came down to his depot for making purchases, and placing orders of their requirements. He considered shifting his residence to the town. His wife, Mayadevi, vetoed his plan. She was happy with the simple village life, surrounded by friendly and ever helping neighbors. Their son Bikram, whom they affectionately called Bikku, was less than two at the time. Mayadevi wanted their son to grow up in the unpretentious village atmosphere. She promised her husband that she would not oppose shifting to the town after Bikku had completed his middle school education in the village. Shivram had laughed at his wife's promise,

"That will be eleven years from now, Madam, and who knows what can happen by then."

He could not have foreseen, in his wildest dreams, what was to happen by then. Because of his wife's stubborn attitude, he had to cycle to his depot in the town every morning, and return to the village in the evening.

The next six years were years of prosperity and happiness for the Kocher family. Shivram's business flourished, in spite of difficulties brought about by the ongoing world war. He renovated his village house on the model of city dwellings, with concrete pillars and slabs, albeit with the restrictions imposed by the lack of civic amenities in the village, like sewer lines and public water supply. They had to make do with a septic tank, and a hand operated water pump. Their son was now eight years of age, and did well at school. His teachers were full of praise for his ability to learn quickly. Shivram and his wife were leading a tranquil and carefree life. When the war ended in 1945, Shivram anticipated a healthy surge in his business. That was not destined to be. All his expectations were dashed to the ground. Soon after the end of the war, there was a mass movement for liberating the country from the British rule. A political strife hit the country. It snowballed into a communal divide. Large-scale riots, between Hindu and Muslim communities broke up in different parts of the country. The communal frenzy led to mass killings of members of both the communities, and ended up in the division of the country in August 1947 amidst lot of blood shed.

Shivram's district became a part of the newly created nation state of Pakistan. There was incessant news of mass migration of people across the borders. However, an uneasy calm prevailed in his village. Muslims and Hindus here had lived like good neighbors for generations. The Muslim headman of the village, *the alambardar,* had reassured the Hindu families of their safety, and pleaded with them not to abandon their homes. Nevertheless, the news of the roaming marauders, attacking the neighboring villages, kept the Hindu families on edge. On the midnight of the 29 August, Shivram woke up to the terrifying cries piercing his ears. He rushed to the roof of his house, and saw towering flames of fires rising in the western part of the village. That part of the village was entirely inhabited by Hindu families. His was the only Hindu house in the eastern sector. Actually, it stood between two houses belonging to prominent Muslim families of the village, Mirdaad's on one side and Saajid's on the other. Mirdaad was the most affluent farm owner, and Sajid the headman of the village. In the glow of the burning fires, he saw the silhouette of a man on the roof of the house to his right. It was Saajid. He was waving his hands frantically, and shouting. At first Shivram could not comprehend his words over the shrieks, and the din. He walked to the end of his roof to close the distance between them. Now he heard him,

"The raiders have attacked. Rush to my house with your wife and child."

Shivram did not wait to reply. He ran downstairs. His terrified wife met him on the staircase coming up. He gripped her arm, and hurried her down into their bedroom. He picked up his son who was still asleep, and shouted to his wife,

"Unlock the front door."

The next minute they were in the house of Saajid. He was waiting for them at the entrance. They had not stopped to relock their own door. Their house was ransacked in the night. They heard the mob, and the poundings of their destructive activities throughout the night.

Saajid told them to go into one of the inner room, and not to make any sound. They had become refugees in their own village.

Next morning the police arrived from the tahsil town of Phalia, and summoned Saajid to accompany them for assessing the damage done in the last night raid. He returned at lunchtime, and reported the spine-chilling damage to Shivram and his wife who were already scared stiff by the eerie silence in the village.

"Every single house in the locality has been burnt down. Not a single occupant of the houses has survived. Most of them were burnt alive inside their houses. Those who escaped the inferno were slaughtered, men, women, and children. You three are the only survivors."

Mayadevi fainted and collapsed on the floor. Shivram and Saajid lifted her on to a bed. Shivram sat by her side, and rubbed her palms. Saajid's wife rubbed her soles. Presently, she opened her eyes, looked in Shivram's face, and then cast her frightened eyes in all directions.

"Bikku is alright. He is sleeping in the other room," Shivram reassured her. She wanted to go to her son. Her husband persuaded her to remain in bed. She turned on her side, hid her face with her *duppatta,* and sobbed uncontrollably. Shivram let her cry. He turned to Saajid,

"My cousins Kharayati, and Harilal…" Shivram could not finish. He choked on his words.

"They are dead…their families too."

"Will the police permit me to go there?"

"There is no point. The bodies are charred beyond recognition."

"I must see to their cremation."

"The police will not permit that. After they complete all formalities, they plan to carry out a mass cremation of all the bodies."

An audible sob escaped Shivram. He had been trying hard to keep his emotions under control. Now he wept unrestrained. Saajid too broke into uncontrollable sobs.

"Pardon me my friend," he said between sobs, "I could not keep my promise of protecting the village."

He put his arm around Shivram's shoulders, and they wiped each other's tears.

"The police sub-inspector is insisting on evacuating you to the refugee camp of Mandi," Saajid said, "I think it will be prudent to go with him. The police van shall be leaving in two hours. I suggest you have your lunch, and then I shall accompany you to your house. We will see what can be salvaged."

Shivram fed his son. He had to be woken up from a brandy-induccd sleep. Bikram instinctively realized that some tragedy had gripped the village. He had heard snatches of conversation between Saajid Uncle and his father. His mother was sobbing, although his father's face was inscrutable. He had guessed they were in some sort of danger, although he could not guess its source. His father was urging his mother to eat.

"Eat a little. You will need your strength,"

Mayadevi refused to touch the food. Shivram forced a few morsels down his own throat, and went to inspect his house, accompanied by Saajid. At one glance, he knew there was nothing to salvage. Every bit of their belongings was either taken away, or burnt, or irretrievably damaged. The arsonists had spared the building as it was sandwiched between two Muslim houses.

The police van dropped them at the transient refugee camp in the Gurudwara of Mandi-Baha-uddin. Shivram and Mayadevi had tacitly agreed not to discuss, in the presence of their son, the gory details of what had happened back in the village. However, they could not prevent him hearing bits of it from other inmates of the camp. A week later, they were evacuated, across the newly demarcated border, to a refugee camp in Amritsar, heart broken, homeless, and penniless. The camp consisted of a large number of disarranged tents of varying sizes and shapes, pitched in a large open space fringed on one side by a large bricked building. The site was probably an old stadium. The facilities at the camp were over-stretched with large number of refugees pouring in daily. The dug up latrines were grossly insufficient, and men and children relieved themselves in the open. The stench was all pervasive.

The privacy for bathing and washing was almost non-existent. Most of the discarded clothes *donated* for the use of the refugees were threadbare and unusable. The old wornout bedding was insufficient to ward off the cold of the approaching winter. The most appalling sight was the community kitchen. The unhygienic cooking repelled many newcomers, like the Shivram family, who initially refused to eat, but later had to give in to the hunger pangs. Shivram could foresee an epidemic in the making. The first time his family stood in a queue and received an almost inedible fare of burnt chapattis, and water-thin daal, his wife broke down and wept.

"Yesterday we were feeding the hungry coming to our door, and today ..." She could not finish, overwhelmed as she was with grief.

"You have to forget yesterday, my dear, and start living in today."

"And what do you think today can give me?" She screamed at him in frustration.

"I don't know about you, but as for me, I have, today, asked the authorities to arrange to transfer us to the Ahmedabad camp in Gujarat."

There was a gleam of determination in his eyes, which went unnoticed by his wife.

"You think going from one refugee camp to another will improve our lot?"

"You are talking of tomorrow, which is not here yet," Shivram said enigmatically.

Mayadevi had often been disconcerted, in the past, by this type of utterances of her husband. Today it perturbed her even more, but she let it go at that. On the other hand, Bikram felt reassured by his father's words, though he did not fully understand them. His father was a believer of living for today.

Shivram was a stoic person by nature, with a steely determination and wisdom of Solomon. He refused to let despair overtake him. He started planning a new life for his family. He had traveled widely in connection with his business, and now when he weighed various options for a fresh beginning, one place kept coming to his mind -

Gujarat. His business instinct told him that Gujarat was the place for him. That day he had approached the camp authorities, and put in a request to transfer his family to a refugee camp in Ahmedabad. After the usual bureaucratic red tape, his request was granted.

Ahmedabad camp was drastically different from the one they had left in Amritsar. It was housed in a concrete building of an old, abandoned fifty-bed municipal hospital for women. It was situated in a locality called Daryapur within the city limits. There was no overcrowding. At thc time, it housed about a dozen refugee families. Shivram's was the only family hailing from the Punjab. The rest had migrated from the province of Sindh across the newly-drawn border. There were two main halls, which had served as general wards of the erstwhile hospital. There were half a dozen rooms of various dimensions, which must have been the private rooms and offices. These rooms were allotted to small families, while the larger families occupied the halls, which were sectioned off with portable screens. The old beddings of the hospital that were still usable were retrieved from the storage, and more were forthcoming from the welfare societies. Heavy beddings were actually not required as the weather in Gujarat was mild. The most gratifying feature of the camp was its hygiene and cleanliness. The able-bodied inmates and the local volunteers joined hands to keep the place tidy. There was no dearth of funds as large and small amounts of donations kept flowing. Three daily square meals were provided to the inmates. A local physician, Manubhai Patel visited the camp daily, and provided honorary medical care to the sick. He was a young man, in his early thirties, and was as jovial by nature as he was competent in his profession. His patients used to look forward to his daily visits. Barring a few minor skirmishes among the inmates, the camp, overall, had a very peaceful environment.

Being an able-bodied man, not given to idleness, Shivram started lending a helping hand in the camp activities, like assisting in the kitchen, attending the sick, carrying the genuine complaints of the inmates to the managing authorities. While performing these voluntary services, he came in close contact with Dr. Manubhai Patel.

He used to attach himself to the doctor during the latter's visits, and assist him in his work. He noted down the doctor's instructions to the patients, and made sure that they acted on them. On his next visit, he would report the progress of the patients. He assisted in dressing of the wounds and injuries, and helped in other small ways, like carrying the antiseptic bowl and towel for the doctor to wash his hands. Dr. Patel called him *my houseman.*

During their time together, Dr. Patel encouraged Shivram to talk about his past, and his future plans. He had once asked him,

"What made you select Gujarat for your new home?"

"You know, doctor, Gujarat is a place of opportunities, especially the city of Ahmedabad. I am hoping that I shall be able to rebuild my life here."

Shivram's reply had pleased the doctor.

A few days later, Dr. Patel had asked Shivram to accompany him to his private clinic. The clinic turned out to be a fair sized, two-storied hospital. The ground floor housed Dr. Patel's nursing home, while the first floor was taken up by a well-equipped and well-maintained compact maternity and gynecology hospital run by Dr. Patel's wife, Dr. Mehru Patel. A receptionist, on instructions from the doctor, had shown Shivram around on both the floors, while Dr. Patel had gone into his consulting room to see his waiting patients.

After the doctor had finished his work at the clinic, he had invited Shivram to accompany him to his residence, located in the posh locality of Shahi Baug. He had straightaway shown Shivram an outhouse attached to his bungalow. It had two rooms and a small kitchen. It was sparsely furnished, with old but functional furniture. The doctor had impassively told Shivram,

"If you agree to work for me, your family could occupy this house."

"And what work will I be expected to do?"

"Not you alone. Your wife too shall have to work. You see, my wife and I live in this big house all by ourselves. We have no children. We are both out at work the whole day. A cleaning woman comes every morning and tidies up the house. A part time cook manages the kitchen. We need a trustworthy full time housekeeper, who would oversee the work of the servants. I think your wife is well suited for the job. As for you, you will be required to do odd jobs for me, like paying the bills, insurance premiums, municipal taxes, etcetera. For this, you will be required to do a bit of cycling."

"Can I give you my answer by tomorrow? You see, I shall have to consult my wife first."

"Certainly, Shivram, You do that. But are you not going to ask me what wages you shall be getting?"

"If my wife agrees to your proposal, wages shall be of no consideration."

"Look here my friend, I don't like ambiguity. If you agree to work for me, this outhouse will come to you free of rent, all your meals will be on the house, you will eat what my wife and I eat, and you will be paid cash salary of three hundred rupees each."

When the doctor saw him nodding his head in comprehension, he added,

"There is one more thing Shivram, if later on you wish to leave the job, you can do so any time without giving notice. On my side, I shall not terminate your services before the completion of one year, and if I do so, I shall pay you and your wife, wages for the period by which your employment falls short of one year. I shall commit all this to writing.

The doctor's generous offer overwhelmed Shivram. Beating back the tears that threatened to spill over, he said in a choked voice,

"That won't be necessary, Doctor Sahib."

When Shivram told his wife of the doctor's offer, she said,

"It is better than nothing for now, but this petty job can't be our destiny."

"Mayaji, Mayaji, tomorrow is not here yet," Mayadevi frowned disapprovingly. She was getting tired of his absurd remarks.

Shivram got his family discharged from the camp, and he and his wife went to work for the doctor couple.

On the first day of their employment, Mayadevi took a leisurely tour of the house after the doctor couple had left for work. She noticed certain deficiencies in the way the household was being run. She filed them away in her mind, for future action.

On the first day of their employment, Shivram went around the rather vast compound of his employer's house and was appalled by the unkempt condition of the garden. He spent the whole morning planning its restoration.

On the first day of their employment, when Shivram and his wife were busy organizing their new home, their young child was sitting in the compound and doodling on the damp ground with a small stick. Dr. Patel called out to him,

"Come with me, son."

Bikram followed him to his study. As the doctor took his seat, the boy stood deferentially in front of the desk.

"Get a chair, and come and sit by my side."

The child obeyed wordlessly. The doctor talked to him for about half an hour, and learnt that the boy had completed his fourth class in the Urdu medium, that he was a rank holder in his school, and that he knew no English. He sent the child away with a friendly pat on his back, and then remained sitting thoughtfully in his chair, planning a meaningful education for the boy.

On the first day of the employment of the new servants, Dr. Mehru Patel had to grapple with a very thorny problem that her husband had created by telling the new employees that their meals would be on the house, and that they would eat what their employer ate. Doubtless, the employees could not eat before the employers did. If they were made to wait until their employers came home and finished eating, it would amount to offering them the leftovers. On the other hand, if they were to sit together at the table, it would be too much of a familiarity with the servants, and could be an unbearable embarrassment in presence of guests. She would have to discuss this seemingly insoluble problem with her husband.

The doctor couple held a conference of two, that afternoon, in the private office of the wife. The husband had agreed with the wife's evaluation of the situation. They concluded that they had three options. One, withdraw the offer of providing the meals, and enhance their wages. Two, give them the raw material and let them cook their own food. Three, accept their own slip-up and share the table with the servants. The first two options were abhorrent to the husband, as they amounted to his going back on his word. The wife too did not want her husband to lose face. Therefore, they bowed to the inevitable, and settled on sharing their table with their employees.

Shivram, in his wisdom, had anticipated the dilemma of his employers, and had discussed it with his wife, the previous evening. They had arrived at an inspired solution. When Mayadevi was laying the table for the dinner that evening, Shivram was nowhere to be seen.

"Where is Shivram?" Dr. Patel had inquired

"Doctor Sahib," Mayadevi tried to explain, "They are doing some thing …er… autoclaving, or something like that, at the hospital. He has stayed back to observe it."

"Oh," was all that Dr. Patel could say. He marveled at the foresight of the man, and at his plausible, but contrived excuse for bailing him out of a difficult situation. When Dr. Patel asked Mayadevi to have her seat, she demurred,

"I shall eat after *he* comes." Dr. Patel thought, another plausible excuse, but not a contrived one, this time. Many Indian wives did not eat until their husbands had eaten first. Dr. Patel was content with having Bikram sit by his side for his dinner.

The next evening, for the sake of form, Dr. Patel had inquired again, why Shivram was not present at dinner. Mayadevi again had offered a polite excuse. After that, no one alluded to Shivram's absence at the dinner.

On the Sunday morning following their employment, Shivram, his wife, and their son were all summoned to the doctors' study. When they arrived, they found the doctor couple engaged in an earnest discussion. Dr. Patel asked them to have their seats. Shivram and Mayadevi took the chairs across the rather large study table. Bikram chose to keep standing. Mrs. Patel noticed the civility of the child and was pleased. Dr. Patel opened the dialogue,

"I have called you here to discuss the plans for the schooling of Vikram."

Shivram noticed that the doctor pronounced the name as Vikram, with a V and not a B, but offered no correction. Dr Patel continued to speak,

"I have talked to the Principal of a good English medium school, who is on friendly terms with me. The difficulty is that the child has so far studied in Urdu and does not know the English language at all. I have called you to discuss how to overcome this obstacle."

Shivram and Mayadevi sat silently, looking anxiously at the doctor, who continued his monologue,

"There are six months before the commencement of the new school term. I have decided to give personal and intensive coaching to our Vikram in the use of the English language for this period, and Mehru is going to help me in this."

He turned to his wife, who smiled and nodded her head in agreement. Now he faced the parents of the child,

"For this, I need your wholehearted approval."

The doctor's kindly disposition brought tears to Mayadevi's eyes.

"We must have done some good *karmas* in our previous incarnation to deserve the kindness of angels like you two."

"Okay, then it is settled,"

Dr. Patel turned to Bikram, "Master Vikram, you shall come to my study every evening after dinner. We'll do our lessons for two hours. And you will have lots of homework to do during the day."

Bikram nodded his head wordlessly. This prompted the doctor to ask him,

"Now that you are going to be my student, what are you going to call me?

"*Teacher Ji,*" was the prompt reply.

"N…o...o...o...o, that sounds like a school master"

Bikram thought for a while,

"Then may I address you as sir?"

"No, that won't do either, it sounds too bossy. Let's see …." Dr. Patel assumed a thoughtful stance,

"You shall call me *Bapuji*."

Shivram and Mayadevi were first surprised and then pleased. Mrs. Mehru Patel had a somber look on her face. They had no child of their own, but was it wise to become so involved with a child they had known for only a few days? Mehru had never gone against her husband's wishes, and he on his part, had always consulted his wife before taking any weighty decision. This was the second time, in a week, that he had acted impulsively, first in inviting their new employees to share their meals, and now getting emotionally involved with their child. However, when she remembered how adroitly Shivram and his wife had extricated them from their earlier dilemma, she calmed down, and decided to go along with her husband's wishes. She said in an enforced bright manner,

"In that case you will have to call me *Baa*."

"Baa...Bapuji..." Bikram savored the two Gujarati words, on his tongue.

Next day, after the doctor couple had departed for work, and before the cleaning maid had arrived, Mayadevi went to her employer's bedroom. She noticed that the wardrobes, the steel cabinet, and the drawers of the writing table and dressing table, none were locked. The keys were left in their locks. She locked them up, and made one bunch of the keys in a key ring. She put the bunch under the mattress. Then she collected the garments, which her employers had discarded for laundering. She went through their pockets and found currency notes, in the breast pocket of Dr. Patel's shirt, amounting to three hundred and forty rupees. She put the clothes in the laundry basket. When the house cleaner arrived, Mayadevi was dusting the furniture of the bedroom. She remained present, while the maid swept and swabbed the floor. Mayadevi noticed her casting sideway glances at the wardrobes and the cabinet, now without the keys in their locks. In the evening when the doctor couple came to the dining table, Mayadevi casually handed the currency notes to Dr. Patel, saying,

"These were found in the pocket of your shirt."

As the days went by, Mayadevi noticed that there were no fixed hours for breakfast, and lunch, at Patels' home. Mrs. Patel almost never ate breakfast. She usually had a surgery session scheduled for early morning hours, and would hurry off after a quick cup of tea. The husband would leave around half past eight to begin his day. His breakfast consisted of some dry snacks, like *ganthia*, *chevada*, *khakhras*, *dhebras*, and such other knick-knack, purchased from the grocery store. The cook would arrive around eleven and would leave by one in the afternoon after cooking the meals and preparing a tiffin box for Mrs. Patel. A man from the hospital would come on a bicycle, and pick up the tiffin box for the Madam. The box would come back in the evening, with residual uneaten food, and on days even totally untouched. Dr. Manubhai Patel would return after three in the afternoon and the maid would serve him a cold lunch. At the most, the *daal* and vegetable would be reheated, but the doctor had to make do with cold, stiff chapaties, and cold clotted rice. After observing for few days, Mayadevi decided to bring about some radical changes in running the household. She would have to do this unobtrusively. She started by asking Mrs. Patel, one evening,

"Mem Sahib, what time tomorrow would you be leaving for work?"

Mrs. Patel looked up sharply. She was about to ask her, why she wanted to know, but then thought better of it and said,

"Around seven, and please stop calling me Mem Sahib, Mehruben would do."

Mayadevi just nodded her head. She was prone to use her voice box sparingly. Next morning when Mehruben came to the table at quarter to seven for her customary cup of tea, she found a hot cheese toast besides the cup. Her first reaction was to call Mayadevi, and ask her to remove the toast, but then she remembered her inquiry last evening about her departure time. She had planned to give her employer a hot breakfast, without her having a chance to decline. "I should not refuse such caring attention." She said to herself. She picked up a knife and cut the toast into two. "I'll have a bit just not to offend the good woman," she thought, but ended up eating both the pieces. When Dr. Patel came down for his breakfast, he found the jars containing his usual ganthia, chevada etc. missing from the table. Before he could react to this, Mayadevi placed a plate with two toasts and tea things before him. He hesitated only for a moment and then finished off the piping hot meal with gusto. The next day they were served *idli-sambhar* for breakfast, and the third day it was *gobhi paratha* with yogurt. From then on it was always freshly prepared hot breakfast.

Mayadevi worked out a plan to ensure that her employers ate hot lunch too. She instructed the cook to prepare only the daal and vegetable, and leave the rest to her. She shared her plan with the head nurse of Dr. Mehruben's clinic. Under this plan, a nurse would ring her up about forty-five minutes before Mehruben's surgery list was expected to conclude, and would dispatch a man to pick up the tiffin box. By the time the man arrived at the house, she would have made fresh chapaties, cooked fresh rice and heated up the daal and vegetable, and would have the tiffin box ready. The box would usually arrive just when Mehruben was finishing her surgery list. She would eat her lunch when it was still hot, before starting the out patient work. Mayadevi was gratified to see that the box came back with hardly any leftover. She served a similar hot lunch to Dr. Patel when he arrived home at about three in the afternoon.

This plan of Mayadevi for serving hot meals to her employers worked for a week before it had to be altered. Dr. Mehruben realized that she and her husband were being very unfair to Mayadevi. The poor woman was cooking two breakfasts, two lunches, and a dinner, just because Dr. Patel and she herself were keeping different timings for going to work. There was no reason why they could not readjust their schedule. After all, they were running their own private hospital, and needed no one's approval for altering their routine. Mehruben decided to change the time for starting the operation list to half past eight in the morning, and her husband decided to have his lunch added to the tiffin box that was brought to the hospital for his wife. That way, they could have breakfast and lunch together, and Mayadevi would be spared a lot of unnecessary labor.

The next two months went smoothly, but Mayadevi sensed bitterness brewing among the employees of the house. The cleaning woman, Sharda, had overheard Mehruben saying to her husband,

"Manu, in the last couple of months, Maya has thrice returned to us the money, carelessly left by you in the pockets of your clothes put away for laundering. It is not that you have become careless only recently. You must have been careless earlier too. How come, all these years Sharda has never found money in your pockets?"

"It is elementary, my dear wife, Sharda has been pocketing it herself."

"I wonder weather she has been pilfering the money found in the laundry alone. I have often been careless in leaving my purse around in the house, and so have you been with your wallet."

"And what about the wardrobes and cabinet left unlocked?" Manubhai aggravated his wife's misgivings. "We must ensure that they are kept locked."

"Mayadevi has taken care of that already. She locks them up before Sharda arrives. But it should be our responsibility to lock things up before we leave our bedroom."

Dr. Patel heaved a sigh.

"Maya is proving to be an asset. God bless her."

Sharda was furious, Damn this Maya, the offspring of Harish Chandra Satyavadi. Damn her to hell.'

She cursed Maya for depriving her of a fortune. She had been making a lot more than her salary, by using her nimble fingers on the wallet, and purse, which her employees had been leaving around carelessly. They never seemed to miss the few currency notes she had been pocketing from time to time. She was careful not to pilfer more than one or two notes at one time, though she took greater liberties with the *Sahib's* wallet. Men are such nincompoops, she had thought, he would have never found out. In addition, the money the fool left in his pockets, while leaving his clothes for the laundry. Well, that was a Godsent bonus, and quite a considerable lot at that.

It became untenable for Sharda to continue in the employment of the Patel couple. She was aware that the hawk eyes of Mayadevi followed her around the house, and she could sense the scornful looks that her employers cast towards her. She knew they were a kind and temperate couple, and would not outright fire her, and that it would be prudent to leave of her own. So one evening in a tactful move, she sent words to her employers, saying she was going away to her village, and was not sure when she would return.

"Good riddance," said Mrs. Patel, and promptly hired another young girl, Indu.

The cook too decided to follow the example of Sharda, and resigned. She too had been plundering her employers' kitchen, taking away a big chunk of the provisions she purchased with the money given to her by the mistress of the house. Mrs. Mehru Patel had been aware that the cook was pilfering the rations, but she considered it an unavoidable evil where servants ran the kitchen. However, it was only now that she had realized the extent of the loot. For the last two months, since Mayadevi had taken the purchase of the ration in her hand, their food bill had reduced to less than half, in spite of the addition of three more mouths to feed. The cook too had read the disapproval in the eyes of her mistress, who had always been considerate towards her employees. She still had some sense of dignity left, and decided to quit her job. Mehruben wanted to hire a new cook, but Mayadevi dissuaded her.

"I'll manage the cooking, with a little help from Indu."

Mehruben had already been aware that Mayadevi was doing most of the cooking ever since her arrival, and that she would not give that up even if a new cook were hired. Therefore, she acquiesced to letting her manage the kitchen, but decided to add the salary of the cook to Mayadevi's wages.

Shivram, as was his nature, was working unobtrusively at home as well as at the hospital. He had energetically taken up the work of revamping the garden surrounding the house. He drove the gardener hard, got rid of the dead plants, pruned the still redeemable ones, and had the deadwood clipped away. He had the lawn weeded out, mowed, and watered every night until it had the look and feel of a thick green carpet. He had the flowerbeds bordered off, to protect them from the intruding feet. He ordered new flowering and decorative plants from the nursery, and planted them at the vantage points. Shivram saw to it that the gardener no longer absented from duty and tended the garden daily. He himself nurtured each plant like his own child. The garden had a smartened up look within six months. Mehruben was exceedingly pleased with the *Raat Raani* planted on the two open sides of their bedroom. Its delightful fragrance floated over the nightly breeze. Shivram had a low grill fixed on the two sidewalls bordering the compound. He had Madhu Maalti creeper planted, and trained it to climb over the grill on the walls. The bloom of abundant red and white clusters of flowers gave a decorative look to the compound, and emitted a sweet fragrance in the night akin to burning of incense in a temple. Rose bushes were planted along the sidewalls of the compound, and were expected to come into bloom next winter. Along the front wall, Shivram had planted three bushes of Bougainvillea of different colors. Bunches of their decorative flowers had just started appearing at the tips of their branches. He had plans to fashion them in the form of arches, using the combination of pruning and training of the branches. Then only they would really become the glory of the garden. When his employers started having their daily evening tea on the lawn, he felt fully rewarded for his labor.

Shivram performed his other tasks with equal alacrity. Payments of electricity and phone bills, property taxes for the house and the hospitals, road tax for the car, premiums on the insurance policies of the house, the hospital, and the car, as well as the personal life insurance policies of his employers, were the odd jobs he was entrusted with. He had made a calendar for these tasks to ensure he missed no deadlines.

The Patels owned a Buick 46. They had hired a chauffeur to drive them around. There were very few cars on the roads of Ahmedabad in those days of the nineteen forties, and even fewer chauffeurs were available for hire. Ahmed Mian, the chauffeur, was a sickly looking middle-aged man, and frequently remained absent from duty due to ill health. This caused much inconvenience to his employers, especially to Mrs. Patel, who was not a skillful driver herself. Looking at their plight Shivram took lessons in driving, and soon obtained a driver's license. He took over as the locum driver whenever Ahmed absented himself. Later on, he was obliged to take on the job, full time. Ahmed had to be rested. He had contracted tuberculosis of the lungs. The Patels enhanced the monthly wages of Shivram by the amount equivalent to Ahmed Mian's salary. They generously continued to pay Ahmed his wages, and also helped him with the supply of medicines, and other expenses for his treatment.

Dr. Patel started tutoring Bikram, initially with a bit of misgivings, but as the days passed, he coached him with mounting enthusiasm. He had taken on himself a daunting task of training a nine-year-old in the use of English language in six months to a level, which the other children acquired in four years. After spending two evenings with the child, he had realized that his assignment was going to be easy, as also delightful. On the first evening itself, he had discovered that Bikram knew how to write the English alphabet in all the three forms. Not only that, he could write many simple two lettered and three lettered words. Although his school back in Pakistan started teaching English from the fifth grade, and he was still in the fourth, he had learnt to write the alphabet and some simple words from one of his friends two years senior to him. Dr. Patel set himself a two-fold task: one, to build his pupil's vocabulary, and second, to train him in spoken English. Dr. Patel was of the opinion that the best way to learn a new language was to persistently listen to it, just as an infant learns to speak his mother tongue by listening to members his family around him. Hence, during their training sessions, he spoke to Bikram in English, the way the parents spoke to their growing infant. Bikram on his part would grasp the words and phrases, and repeated them in similar nuance. Dr. Patel and his wife would always converse with each other in English when Bikram was around. After a month, Dr. Patel introduced storybook reading. He read the stories to Bikram, as a father reads to his growing child and Bikram heard them attentively. He clung to every word. The result was that in three months' time, he started expressing himself in the language, and became an avid reader of storybooks. When the time for admission arrived, the school principal admitted him to the fifth grade, without any reservations. His first year at the school was not a smooth sailing one due to lack of training in grammar, but in the next grade he procured the first rank in his class and then never let go of it. The kind doctor paid all his school fees, and refused to be reimbursed by Shivram,

"Vikram is as much my son as he is yours," he had said, "his education shall be my responsibility, and there shall be no future discussion regarding that."

The next two years were stress free for the Patel couple. Mayadevi had taken full control of the household, and was running it like a well-oiled machine. A shrewdly selected staff of two, a cleaning woman, Noor Bibi, and a kitchen help Shanti, aided her in the task.

*****

On a Sunday, in the month of May of 1951, Shivram made a request to Dr. Manubhai Patel, which was to set in motion events that were to slowly, and imperceptibly lead to a drastically altered relation between their families. That day Shivram presented two typed sheets to Dr. Patel for his signature. These were statements of emoluments paid by Dr. Patel to Shivram and his wife during the previous financial year. Dr. Patel was baffled.

"What are these for?"

"These are needed for filing our income tax returns."

"But surely Shivram, these amounts do not attract income tax."

"We have other sources of income," Shivram explained.

Dr. Patel was puzzled. Mayadevi never left the house. Shivram was in his sights for almost all the time. Then where did they get the extra income? He was too much of a gentleman to question Shivram on this. He quietly signed the statements. Shivram had seen the puzzlement on the Doctor's face. Therefore, a few days later, he showed Dr. Patel the income tax returns, which he had prepared with the help of a friendly clerk of a lawyer,

"Doctor Sahib, please have a look at these, and see if these are O.K. before I file them."

Dr. Patel scrutinized the returns. Besides the salaries, incomes from interest on bank fixed deposits, dividends earned on shares of companies, and capital gains from sale of shares were included. Shivram thought he owed an explanation to his benevolent boss.

"We have very few expenses. My family does not have to pay the house rent, nor spend on food and our son's education, thanks to you sir. Hence, a substantial part of our salaries remains unspent. We transfer half of the cumulated amount from the salaries to the bank fixed deposits where it earns good interest, besides remaining a liquid asset. I utilize the major part of remaining amount for buying shares of reliable companies. Besides getting dividend on the shares, I sometimes make profit by trading them on the market."

Dr. Patel was pleased by the acumen of Shivram in the management of his money, as well as his honesty. Who had ever heard of a man employed to do odd jobs in a household, paying income tax? Here was this man voluntarily offering to pay tax as soon as his earning had crossed the tax-free limit. Next day Dr. Patel handed over a file to Shivram.

"These are some share certificates of mine. I have purchased them from time to time, on advice of friends. I personally know very little about the share market. See what you can make of them."

Shivram went through the file. His employer's inept handling of shares dismayed him. It seemed he purchased the shares, filed the share certificates, and then forgot all about them. There were share certificates of a couple of companies, which had long ceased to exist. There were others of the business houses, whose balance sheets had been showing very little profit. However, to his delight, he found, in the file, substantial number of share of three blue-chip companies dealing in textile, steel, and cement. All the shares had been purchased from the primary market, so his employer must not have paid a very high price for them. There was however, no record in the file to show what premium, if any, had been paid on them. When he inquired from Dr. Patel whether he had kept any record of his investments, he received a negative reply. He advised the doctor to sell off the shares of those companies, which had not shown substantial profits for years now. Also not to keep the good ones locked up in the file, but to trade them when opportunity arose to make profit.

"Listen Shivram, I know very little about the share market. You keep the file. I am leaving it to you to deal with the shares the best way you can."

Shivram made a record of the doctor's investment, and with the help of his share broker friend, got rid of all the non-profit making shares. When he approached Dr. Patel for the signature on the transfer certificates, he tried to explain the incurred loss. The doctor waved him off, saying he needed no explanation.

On a cold morning in December 1951, Ahmedabad woke up to the news of the demise of Sheth Ghanshyamdas, one of the greatest industrialists of the country, and the chairperson of the Robust Group of Companies. For a whole week, the newspapers were full of stories of the rise and rise of Ghanshyamdas from rags to riches. He had established himself as an earner of wealth, not only for himself but also for the shareholders of his industrial empire. Whenever he floated a new company, its shares were fully subscribed in a matter of hours. Some of his companies gave its shareholders a two to three hundred percent return as dividend. About a month after the death of the industrialist, Shivram sold out all the seven hundred shares held by Dr. Manubhai Patel in the Robust Textiles Limited, one of the premier companies of the Robust Group. Around the end of the year, he repurchased five hundred shares of Robust Textiles in the name of Manubhai Patel, and another five hundred in the name of Mehruben Patel. When he presented the transfer forms for their signature, Manubhai said,

"Shivram, at the beginning of the year you sold off the whole lot of this scrip, and now you go and repurchase the same. Please do not think I am asking for explanation. I am only curious."

Shivram had to give a lengthy explanation,

"Doctor Sahib you have not been following the market. After the death of Sheth Ghanshyambhai, there was a tussle between his two sons for the chairmanship of the Robust Group, which was threatening to escalate into a proxy war. This type of situation always leads to a slide down in the share prices. Hence, before the proxy war started we unloaded our shares at two hundred and seven rupees. Since then the share prices have been constantly depreciating and have touched almost the rock bottom. Now the elder son of Sheth Ghanshyamdas, Amit, is in control of the Robust Group. He is an astute entrepreneur, and is expected to restore the prestige of his father's business empire to its original heights. The share prices of Robust Textile are sure to climb. Hence, we have purchased a thousand shares at today's price of thirty-one rupees. In this transaction we have made a profit of roughly one lakh and fourteen thousand rupees and increased our holding by three hundred shares."

"That was a smart transaction," Dr. Patel lauded Shivram's efforts.

"Actually, doctor sahib, a scrip of this group, Fortune Chemicals, is at present selling at a very low price and is expected to improve in the near future. I suggest we buy a thousand shares."

"This share business is beyond me. I have left it in your hands. Do what you think is right."

A fortnight later, another incident occurred, which prompted Dr. Patel to leave his entire financial management in Shivram's hands. Dr. Piyush Parekh, a friend of the Patels was preparing to migrate permanently to the U.S.A. He had put out his farmhouse, and a plot of land for sale. The plot of land was adjacent to the Patel house. Ten years back the two friends had purchased the adjoining plots with the intentions of constructing houses. While Dr. Patel had gone ahead and built his house, Dr. Parekh had deferred the construction pending his son's return from the U.S.A. The son had now settled permanently in the U.S.A. and Dr. Parekh and his wife had decided to join their son. Shivram advised Dr. Patel to purchase the Parekhs' property.

"What will I do with it?

"If you have the required funds, Doctor Sahib, it would be a very profitable investment. The prices of land are appreciating rapidly. Besides, there is the advantage to sell the land later to people of your own choice, so that you have amiable neighbors."

Dr. Manubhai Patel showed reluctance, but his wife grasped the merit of the deal, and decided to go for it. The bank accounts of both, the husband and the wife showed there was no dearth of funds. On the contrary, Shivram was appalled to see so much of money lying in their savings bank accounts, earning only a pittance of interest. Moreover, the money in the fixed deposits was invested for far too long terms, most of them for ten years, so that even though the present rates were high, the Patel couple was earning a low interest that was prevalent years back. When Shivram brought this to their notice, theirs was the stock reply,

"Doesn't a longer term deposit bring in a higher interest?"

"It is true for the first one or two years," Shivram explained to them, "but with the ever climbing inflation in our country, the deposit rates keep on rising, and if you have invested for too long a term, you end up earning interest at the old low rates."

"Look here Shivram," Manubhai said with a touch of exasperation, "I am a poor manager of finance. Here are all the bank accounts. Manage them your way."

Shivram's first impulse was to refuse. Managing the finances of his employers was too big a responsibility, fraught with the danger of it being misconstrued. Any bad investment of someone else's funds, even though made with the best of intentions, could invite censure. However, remembering their benevolence towards his family, he gracefully accepted the responsibility. His first act as their finance manager was to purchase the piece of land from Dr. Parekh in the joint names of Dr. Manubhai Patel and Dr. Mehruben Patel, after having scrutinized the papers. Next, he purchased ten twenty-gram gold coins of twenty-four carats, which the Government treasury was selling through the banks, although the Patels had shown a total lack of interest. These went into their bank locker. After that, he tackled their fixed deposits, which took some calculating. Those deposits, which were nearing the maturity date, he left them alone. The others he closed prematurely, and redeposited the proceeds for a period of one year, with the instructions for auto renewal at the prevalent rate of interest.

Shivram strongly recommended to Dr. Patel to buy Dr. Parekh's farmhouse too. His employer was unwilling to acquire property located so far out of the town. The jungle, he called it. Shivram could foresee the Sarkhej zone becoming the hub of Ahmedabad's commercial activity in the near future. The farmhouse was going at a throwaway price. When he could not persuade his employer to purchase it, he bought it for himself.

The land that the Patels had purchased from Parekh, adjacent to their own house, was a plot measuring a thousand square yards. It had six-foot high walls surrounding it with a metal gate. Shivram did not let it lie idle. He had a water line extended to it, and with a little help from their gardener, had converted it into a large kitchen garden. This kept the family supplied with fresh vegetables and even some fruits throughout the year. This further enhanced the talented image of Shivram in the eyes of the Patel couple.

After Shivram took over their personal financial management, the Patel couple gradually transferred other burdens onto his shoulders. They made him responsible for the payment of the salaries of hospital as well as domestic staff, the bills for the purchase of the hospital equipment, drugs, and other articles. Slowly they passed on to him the responsibility of looking after the maintenance of the hospital gadgets. Finally, they gave him the task of collecting the hospital charges from patients, and depositing the daily collections into the bank accounts.

Dr. Patel was quite aware of Shivram's increasing burden. He gave him a dignified designation of Hospital Administrator, and a handsome salary equivalent to that drawn by the superintendents of public hospitals. He allotted a personal office to him at the hospital, and authorized him to appoint an assistant for himself. For discharging these duties, Shivram had to obtain Patels' signatures on cheques for various payments. Manubhai suggested that he and his wife give a mandate to the bank to honor the cheques signed by Shivram. Shivram firmly vetoed the suggestion.

"It is very gracious of you to place so much trust in me, but I would rather remain within my limits."

The two land deals that Shivram had made with Dr Parekh, initiated him into the real estate business. He slowly picked up the elements of real estate deals. He would scout around for the land likely to come up for sale. He would estimate its potential value based on the information garnered about the future developmental plans of the area. He would then go in and purchase a piece that would suit his budget. He made sure that all the papers pertaining to his purchases were in order. Once the developmental plans of the area were made public, the value of the land would spiral up, and he would unload his piece at a handsome profit. He slowly promoted himself from small deals to larger ones, and by the year 1955, his name started appearing among the leading land dealers of the city. In seven years, he had rapidly climbed the rungs of the ladder of success. He was now well placed financially, and socially. He had kept his family undersized. When they had gone to live with the Patels, he had consulted his wife on the need of not having any more children, and had undergone the minor surgical procedure of vasectomy. They were more than happy with their only son Bikram, who was now Vikram in official papers. At seventeen, he had grown into a healthy, but wiry young man. He had, under the tutelage of Dr. Manubhai Patel, done very well academically. After he had completed his schooling with distinction, Dr. Patel had advised him to join the science faculty of the Baroda University. Here too he had done well, and was admitted to the medical faculty. Although Shivram and his wife would have liked their son to stay with them, and study in Ahmedabad, they had left his education completely to the discretion of Dr. Patel.

"I want to be a doctor like you, Bapuji," Vikram had decided his goal when he was still at school.

Dr. Patel had chosen Baroda for Vikram, for pursuing his medical career for two reasons. One, the Baroda College took fewer students, and two, there were a couple of friends of Dr. Patel on the faculty there, who were excellent teachers and would keep an eye on his progress.

*****

Shivram's wife, Mayadevi, was now a contented soul, what with their financial security, and their son's satisfactory progress in his education. She had become quite fond of Mehruben, and a bond of friendship had developed between them. Mehru had divulged to her, some of the intimate incidents of her life, some pleasant ones, and some not so pleasant. She had confided in Mayadevi how she came to marry Manubhai.

"Manu and I were classmates at the Grant Medical College of Bombay. Manu was shy by nature, and did not mix easily, particularly with girls. This trait of his, had earned him the nickname of Lajjamanu, after the sensitive plant *lajjamni* or *chhui-mui*. We came into intimate contact at the end of our final year of graduation, when we both were selected to perform the main characters in a play, to be staged at the annual function of the college. We were thrown together for long hours, for weeks on end, rehearsing our parts, quarrelling on slip-ups on our dialogues, mocking each other's false moves, and then patching up over a plate of sandwiches and coffee in the college canteen, at late hours in the nights. Before the play was staged on the appointed night, we had become quite fond of each other. Our mutual fondness grew unabated with the passage of time, and we fell madly in love. After finishing our post graduation, we decided to tie the traditional knot. That itself was a knotty problem. I come from a priestly Parsi family of Dastoors. My religion did not permit marriages outside the community. I knew my family would never agree to the union, and if I persisted with it, I would be excommunicated. I refused to abandon Manu, and we went ahead and obtained a civil marriage certificate. My family abandoned me. Manu and I decided to settle down in Ahmedabad, his hometown. My sister, Shireen, who is younger to me by three years, and very much devoted to me, came clandestinely to see me on a couple of occasions. She later got married to a Parsi barrister, a naturalized citizen of Australia. I have not seen her in the last fifteen years. I miss her intensely. Manu's family consisted of his mother and a younger sister, Saroj. His mother did not need much of persuasion to accept a Parsi girl as her daughter-in-law. She had adopted a fatalistic attitude towards life after her husband's death, two years earlier. Saroj and I had met a couple of times, when she had come visiting her brother in Bombay. She was thrilled to have a Parsi bhabi. The two of us got on admirably. Saroj married an intimate friend of Manu, Dr. Harshad Kothari, a general practitioner based in the U.K., and went to live in Leicester."

In three years of their practice in Ahmedabad, Manubhai and Mehruben had established themselves as capable doctors. Besides earning good names, they had earned a goodwill of their patients due to their charitable and caring nature. They decided it was time to start a family of their own. Mehru became pregnant in October of 1942, the year of the Quit India movement. They were very happy and eagerly waited for the arrival of the bundle of joy. They endlessly debated the name they would give the new comer. Both of them agreed that the name should reflect the national movement launched that year. After mulling over various names, they settled on Swaraj if it was a boy and Kranti if it was a girl. All their dreams came crashing down around them in the third month. Mehru, being a gynecologist herself, had started suspecting that all was not well with her pregnancy, when she was still in the seventh week. Her uterus seemed to grow too fast. She consulted a gynecologist colleague. They suspected an abnormal pregnancy, but decided to wait and watch for a while. The ultrasonic devices had not yet been invented, and an X-ray examination would be of no help at that stage. Her blood pressure started shooting up. Her feet swelled up and she vomited almost incessantly. Mehru was now sure she was having an abnormal placenta, and no fetus in her womb, a rare condition called hyditidiform mole, where a mass of grape-like tissue replaces the fetus. There was no doubt now that her uterus would have to be evacuated. A date was set in the next week for the D & E., dilating the cervix, and evacuating the uterine contents. The night before the scheduled day, Mehru had a bout of profuse bleeding, and the gynecologist decided on an emergency intervention. She feared it was an invasive mole, and may be difficult to evacuate completely by scraping. She decided to cut open her uterus, and remove the contents. The Patel couple's cup of misery spilled over when Mehru started bleeding profusely on the operating table. Their misfortune did not end there. As a last straw on the camel's back, the rare growth and the rare complication of massive bleeding was compounded by Mehru's rare blood type of O negative. Considering the uncontrollable bleeding, and the insufficient availability of blood of her type, an unfortunate, but unavoidable decision was made. Her uterus was removed. Manubhai was heartbroken, but he kept a stoic façade. He was worried how Mehru would react when she recovered from the anesthetic, and was told about the hysterectomy. She would be devastated, and he feared she might go into depression. He had no heart to tell her, and requested the operating doctor to break the news to her. Later that evening, when he went to her bedside, he could not control his emotions, and wept unashamedly. He was surprised to see his wife totally in control of herself. She wiped his tears, and said gently,

"We have each other."

He took heart at her brave front, and braced himself to take life as it came. A year later, Manubhai had broached the advisability of adopting a child. Mehru refused even to consider it. Four years later Bikram came into their life. They had taken the child under their wings, with the intention of preparing him for admission to school. It was perhaps a subconscious feeling of emptiness in their life that prompted them to tell the child to call them Bapuji, and Baa. However, as time passed, they were captivated by the child's intelligence and his endearing manners. They could not contemplate life without him. They had nurtured him with parental care, and shaped his life for a dignified future. They felt fulfilled to see that their efforts had borne fruit, and their protégé had reached the threshold of a medical career.

*****

By the end of 1956, Shivram thought the time was ripe to start a new chapter in their life. He purchased an eight hundred square yard plot of land in the affluent residential locality of Ambawadi, in the outskirt of the city. He had engaged an architect, and had a plan drawn up for the dream house for his family. He had gone to Dr. Patel's office intending to show the plan to him.

"Come in Shivram,"

He had welcomed him in his usual effusive way, but his manner changed the moment he saw the plan. A frown assailed his face. He folded up the drawing and handed it back to Shivram.

"We'll talk about it some time later," he said brusquely, and ended the meeting.

The uncharacteristic behavior of Dr. Patel baffled Shivram. The plan seemed to have annoyed him. No, it could not be the plan itself. He had barely looked at it. It has to be something else. Shivram could not put his finger on the cause of his employer's displeasure. He did not have to wait long to find out. The next day, when Mayadevi had served the Patels their evening tea, Mehruben had said in a grave tone,

"Maya, my husband and I want to have some serious talk with you and your husband. Please come to the study as soon as Shivram arrives."

Mayadevi, as usual, had nodded her head. Her nod had a grace of its own. Mehru could not help commenting teasingly,

"You prefer to shake your five kilogram heavy head, rather than sixty grams of your tongue."

When they met in the study an hour later, Shivram instinctively braced himself to face the unknown. Mehruben's forehead was wreathed with wrinkles indicating that a battle was raging in her mind. Dr, Patel opened the talk.

"The plan for the house that you showed me yesterday, Shivram, is a faulty one."

Shivram looked up sharply, but said nothing.

"It does not show a room for Mehru and me."

Shivram was quick to understand what Dr. Patel was getting at. They did not want to part from them.

"We are not planning to build the house immediately. May be, some years later…"

Mehruben interrupted him,

"We want you to have a house of your own, but we want you to live with us."

Shivram's quick wits deserted him at this moment. He could not follow the course of the paradoxical conversation. Dr. Patel saw his confusion, and said with an enigmatic smile,

"Yes Shivram, I have here a plan whereby you can build a dream house for your family, and still we can live together.

He handed a sealed cover to Shivram,

"Do not open it right now. Study it at your leisure, and we can talk later."

When he went back to his quarters that evening, Shivram opened the envelope. He found in it a legal deed whereby Dr. Manubhai Kesarbhai Patel and Dr. Mehruben Manubhai Patel, the joint owner of a plot of land, the particulars of which were given in the appendix, had gifted the said land to Mrs. Mayadevi Shivram Kocher out of natural love and affection …

He showed the legal document to his wife. She said,

"So that's their plan. They want us to build our house on the plot next to theirs. That way, we'll have our own house and yet we shall live together."

"But my dear, we can't accept such exceedingly expensive gift from them."

Next evening when the Patels had just finished their dinner, Shivram placed the document on the table, and stood silently in front of them with bowed head. Mayadevi, who had just cleared the table, came and stood by the side of her husband. Dr. Patel spoke gently,

"Do you remember Shivram, what advice you had given me when you had persuaded me to buy the plot?

Shivram did not answer, Dr. Patel continued,

"You had said that I could sell it later to people of my liking, and that way I could make profit as well as have neighbors of my choice. Today I have achieved both the goals. I have sold the plot to you at a considerable profit. We have preferred to make a gift deed in order to save the stamp duty, and avoid the hassle of registering a sale deed. The only irregularity I have committed is that I have fixed the price of the plot all by myself without consulting you. The price is yours and Mayadevi's five years salary. Both of you shall receive no salary for the next five years in lieu of the price of the land. Mehru and I have found our friendly neighbors."

The relation between the Patel and the Kocher families had, over the years, imperceptibly changed from the employer-employee standing to a mutually friendly bond. They were now more or less one family. Dr. Patel had lately been ill at ease while handing the salary cheques to Shivram and Mayadevi. He wanted to end this master-servant relation, but was afraid of losing them. He and his wife had even considered asking the Kocher family to move from the outhouse into their bungalow with them. They had held back as they knew that Shivram would not accept their offer. It could create an uneasy situation. When Shivram had decided to build his own house, the Patels had hit upon this inspired scheme for terminating their employer-employee relationship, and live together as a family.

The Kochers built a comfortable house on the plot. The wall separating the two houses was demolished, so that it became a two-wing resident block with a vast compound surrounding it. Vikram was ecstatic. He had two homes, and two sets of loving parents.

The transition from the rustic life in Punjab to the sophisticated set up of Ahmedabad, in Gujarat, had come easier to Bikram than to his parents. He was a quiet and shy boy. Providence had gifted him an extraordinary intelligence, and a robust health. He was only nine when the county was portioned, and his family had to abandon their home. He did not ever question the need for leaving their home. He had been listening to his elders discussing the inevitability of the migration of the non-Muslims from the newly formed nation state of Pakistan. The only question that seemed to worry the child's mind was how would the Muslims of his village manage their lives in the absence of their Hindu friends? Almost all Muslims in the village were un-lettered, as they started working in the fields from childhood. A few might have erratically attended the *Madrassa* for a couple of years. Very few of them could count beyond twenty. They had depended on their Hindu friends for reading and writing their letters, for writing petitions to the administration, and even for selling their farm products. He thought of the truncated teams of *gilli-danda,* without the Hindu children. He often thought of his playmates – Joginder, Dilip, Tarlok, Mahinder, Partap, Iqbal, Jeet, and Parkash. He wondered who out of these had come out alive, and to what part of the country they had migrated. Would he ever see any of them again? His parents had strictly avoided mentioning in his presence, the gruesome massacre that had taken place the night before they had left the village. He also thought of his Muslim friends – Ahmed, his closest friend, and Aslam, Shrif, Daara, Fazal or Phallu the Bully, and above all, little Fatima, the Star, Tim Tim

Tara. He packed away the old memories in a corner of his mind, and immersed himself in the activities of his new school. His father's philosophy of living for today had, to some extent rubbed on him. He had also imbibed his father's business sense. He had often listened to his father, discussing on the phone, the share market trends, and desirability of buying or selling a particular scrip. He made it a habit to study the business section of the newspaper every morning. By the time he entered the medical college, besides being good at academics and cricket, he was an astute market player. In a total confidentiality with a broker, he made small deals in shares. He parked the gains made from the share market in a separate bank account. He used the accumulated funds to help the needy around him. Besides the un-publicized monetary help to the needy, Vikram was prone to assist friends on the social front too, a trait of his, which became known in the first year of his postgraduate studies. A staff nurse had lodged a complaint against one of Vikram's senior colleagues, first with the Hospital Superintendent and then with the police for making lewd overtures towards her. The colleague was hauled to the police station and procedures initiated for booking him. Vikram had rushed to the office of the deputy superintendent of police, and persuaded him to stall the booking for a while. He had then talked the nurse into withdrawing her complaint conditional to the doctor giving a written apology. The nurse withdrew the complaint. However, the doctor's misery cascaded into a family discord. His wife, who was a tutor in the same college, and whom he had married only six months back, was so shamed that she left him, and threatened to sue for divorce. Vikram had to use all his persuasive skill to bring the doctor couple and the nurse together. The nurse charitably tore off the letter of apology and extended a hand of friendship to the couple. Then on, the three of them were frequently seen together, and the episode was forgotten.

Jealousy among the doctors is well known. Vikram helped resolve many minor discords between his fellow students, and sometimes between students and teachers.

His negotiating powers were put to a crucial test in late 1962, when Dr. Rajeev Kumar Prasad had to face the wrath of the entire student community of the college. Dr. Prasad hailed from one of the northern states of the country. He had been appointed, a couple of month back, professor of Preventive, and community medicine. He happened to be a close relative of a senior cabinet minister of the central government. He flaunted his political connections by throwing his weight around, and paying scant regards to rules and traditions. While conducting a class, he would use up a considerable time grilling the students who had missed his previous lecture. His lectures enlightened the students more on the prevalent political situations than on the community medicine.

One day in the last week of October 1962, Dr. Prasad came to the class, his face clouded with gloom. He did not take the customary roll call, and straightaway lunged into a furious commentary on the ongoing Sino-India war.

"It is a disgraceful day for the country. We have lost the Chip Chap valley to the Chinese. They have grabbed a large tract of our land. A handful of our soldiers are facing vast armies of the enemy. The brave sons of India are laying down their lives in defense of our motherland. Every state of the nation is contributing men and material towards the war effort."

He stopped for a while, and then continued in a slow deliberate tone.

"No, not all the states are doing so. Gujarat may be contributing material but no men."

Another pause,

"We have a Punjab Regiment, a Madras Regiment, a Rajputana Regiment, a Jaat Regiment, a Gurkha Regiment, a Sikh Regiment, a Maratha Regiment...," He reeled off a long list of various fighting units of the Indian army, and then stopped for a dramatic effect,

"Where is the Gujarat Regiment?"

He now had a smirk on his face,

"All that the people of Gujarat can do is to amass money, and expect others to sacrifice their lives to protect them, and their wealth. The timid lot!"

There was an audible gasp from the audience, and a few angry hisses. A girl stood up. Her face flushed with anger. She glared at the professor, and then walked out of the class. Another student followed her, then another, and another. The classroom was empty. Professor Prasad stood alone on the podium.

Within the hour, a notice was circulated asking all students, undergraduates as well as postgraduates, to assemble in the auditorium at half past nine, after dinner, to discuss a very grave matter concerning the honor, and dignity of Gujarat. At the meeting that night, the girl who had earlier led the walkout from the class, took the stage, and narrated the incident. The audience was outraged. A din of angry comments arose from all corners, threatening to break into a pandemonium. The Secretary of the students' union, Dilip Vyas went onto the stage and raised his hands, appealing for silence. When the noise died down, he said,

"Please, please, let us conduct this meeting in an orderly fashion. You have heard the sacrilege committed by Professor Prasad. We cannot take the slur he has heaped on the Gujarati community lying down. We have to take action. I request some amongst you to come up here and suggest the form of action that we should take." He scanned the audience and called upon four of them, one by one, to come up and give their suggestions. They made various suggestions. Boycott the Professor's classes; shut down the college; blacken the Professor's face; lynch the culprit. From the response of the crowd, it was obvious that every suggested action had its backers.

At this point, Gohil, a final year undergraduate student and president of the student's union, took over the microphone. Gohil came from one of the royal families of Saurashtra and had an unusual and almost unpronounceable first name – Gaaraanaad. The name was based on two musical notes – gaa and raa. His grandfather, General Varendrasinhji Gohil, an Icon of the family, was a music lover, and had given him that name. His college mates called him Grenade, which was easier on tongue and went well with his temperament. He was prone to lose his temper and explode at the slightest provocation, like a grenade with a short fuse. He now spoke into the microphone,

"Where is Vikram?"

Heads turned to scan the audience. Gaaraanaad spotted him, sitting in the last row.

"Vikram, will you please come over here and let us have some gems of your wisdom." Gohil and Vikram were intimate friends, and did not let go any opportunity to pull each other's leg.

Vikram briskly walked over on to the podium and addressed the audience,

"I am sorry I arrived here late, as I was assisting an emergency surgery. I do not have the full details of what transpired in Professor Prasad's class, but what I have heard in the last few minutes is enough to show that what the professor has said is very unfortunate, to say the least. It calls for action, and we must act. However, I suggest we act in an orderly manner, with restraint and civility. As a first step, I think two or perhaps three of our representatives should meet our dean tomorrow morning, and see what he has to suggest. We should assemble again tomorrow night to decide our further move. Meanwhile no one should attend Professor Prasad's classes."

Vikram had the knack of putting a situation in a nutshell. There was no voice of dissent. Gohil came back on the stage.

"Do I take it you agree with the plan of action suggested by our trouble-shooter?"

There was a loud "yes" from the gathering. He then went on,

"I would suggest Vikram as one of our representative and our spokesman. As the President of your union, I put forward my name as the second representative. I invite our women students to depute one from amongst them for the job."

Shrill shouts of "Zeb…Zeb..." erupted from the audience. The tall, sturdy, affable final year student, Zeb-Un-Nisa Saiyad, was the unanimous choice for the job.

The delegate thus appointed, met Dean Dr. David Benjamin. He already knew all about the Prasad episode, and the subsequent meeting of the students. He led the trio into his office, and told the doorkeeper they were not to be disturbed. He asked them to be seated.

"What happened yesterday, in Professor Prasad's class, is certainly regrettable, but I appeal to you not to let the tempers run high. Put the unfortunate incidence behind you, and get on with your studies."

Dr. Benjamin was a sober and levelheaded man. He had given up his teaching job only a year back to take up the administrative responsibilities as the head of the college. He was loved and respected by his students who often referred to him as the Mask Face, because of his solemn and impassive countenance.

"Sir," said Vikram, "had the professor rebuked a student, or the whole class, or for that matter the entire student community, we, in deference to a teacher would have overlooked it. Sir, he has wounded the dignity of the entire people of our state. The resentment caused by his assault, at the moment, is confined to the students of our college. If the news of his attack on the honor of the state were to spread, it would become impossible to contain the anger of the people. We therefore urge you to intervene and see that the hurt is assuaged without delay."

"What do you suggest I do?" asked the dean.

"If you can persuade Professor Prasad to come to the general assembly of the students, and express an unqualified apology to the people of Gujarat, we three will try and persuade the students to forget the whole unfortunate episode."

The dean agreed.

"That's the least he should do. I shall have a talk with him presently. Meanwhile please see that nothing is done to disturb the peace of the campus."

Dr. Benjamin sent for Professor Prasad. He could sense immediately that the task was not going to be easy. The man exuded hostility and his body language was far from reassuring. His first words confirmed Dr. Benjamin's misgivings.

"So, I am summoned here to stand trial."

He looked first to his left and then to his right, and continued mockingly,

"Where is the dock? Where are the prosecutors? Where is the jury?"

"Have a seat Professor." Benjamin said in his most disarming tone.

At this juncture, the secretary came in with coffee.

"Aha, a drink for the sacrificial lamb before it is slaughtered." Prasad was at his sarcastic best.

As Prasad took the first sip of coffee, the dean said,

"Professor Prasad, yesterday you made some indiscreet remarks on the people of our state, in front of your students. Their feelings have been hurt. It would be in the fitness of things to make amends."

"Are you suggesting I crawl and grovel before my students, and beg their forgiveness?" Prasad's face was suffused with anger, and a fleck of froth had appeared at the corner of his mouth.

"It takes courage to own up one's mistake, professor."

"So, you are putting me in the dock, and trying to extract a confession out of me. All right, I confess that I have called the people of Gujarat timid. I believe in calling spade a spade. I have said nothing wrong, and I refuse to eat my words." He rose haughtily from his chair, and stomped out of the office with his chin in the air.

The dean summoned Vikram and his two associates, in the afternoon and reported his failure in making the professor see reason.

"In that case, sir," said Vikram, "we are left with no choice but to proceed on strike and call a press conference to let the public know of Professor Prasad's opinion of the people of Gujarat."

"I will not try to stop you from what you plan to do, but I request you to put off going to the press, for a day. I have to apprise the director of medical services and the health minister of the situation here, lest I be blamed for keeping them in dark."

The students met that night. Their representatives reported their discussion with the dean. Vikram spelled out their next move.

"We shall stay away from all classes from tomorrow, but shall not approach the press for one more day in deference to the request of our dean. I have one more suggestion. The matter has now become too tough to be handled by your three representatives. We are bound to have brush with the state authorities. My suggestion is, we form a wider action committee who will analyze the situation from time to time, and will advise the three of us on the stand to be taken at the meetings with the state authorities."

Four more members, Harbirsingh Bajaj, Jyoti Kothari, Bharat Dandekar, and Dilip Vyas were added to the previously selected representatives to form an action committee. As predicted by Vikram, an array of officials, including the state health minister, Mr. P.M. Mankodi, the health secretary and the Director of health services, Dr. M.V. Patel, descended on the college the next morning. No prior press announcement of their visit had been made. Vikram was bracing himself to face them, but to everyone's surprise, these dignitaries departed within an hour without meeting the student representatives. The dean informed them, later on, that the mule headed Prasad had brusquely brushed aside even the health minister's appeal to express regrets. The minister had left in a huff.

"We can now expect the man to be sacked soon," said Vikram.

The dean shook his head, "I wouldn't bet on it. The state cabinet runs scared of Prasad's uncle in Delhi. How else do you think he got a permanent appointment here without being interviewed by the Public Service Commission, and bypassing two senior contenders for the job?"

Vikram answered that question, "I understand, in him the state received a gift of an eminent scholar."

The dean burst out laughing. No student had ever seen the Mask Face laugh. Only few had seen him smile,

"Eminent? ... Scholar? Professor Prasad? The less said the better."

"Then what do you think will happen now?" asked Gohil.

"As I see it, the health minister will dump the buck in the lap of the chief minister."

The newly formed action committee of the students decided to maintain a status quo for one more day. When there was no further move by the state administration, the action committee met to chalk out their next step.

"Why has the administration suddenly gone silent after the initial flurry?" Zeb-Un-Nisa put the question to Vikram.

"It is a standard trick of politicians, Zeb. Whenever the discussions are deadlocked, they play a game of patience. They will now sit back and test our wits and patience. "

"What shall be our next move, Vikram?" This was from Harbirsingh.

"Take the bull by the horns. Give the authorities no respite. We call a press conference for tomorrow, and give them the story of Professor Prasad's outburst against the people of Gujarat."

"How do we go about calling a press conference?" Jyoti wanted to know

"We shall leave that to Bharat," said Vikram. Not many people knew that Bharat Dandekar's father was a noted syndicated columnist, who wrote under an assumed name, Pawan Dada."

"Done," said Bharat, "just give me the day and the time, and you will be the host to the entire media.

"For that," said Vikram, "we shall have to take a couple of preliminary measures. First, we will have to give a formal written notice to the dean of our intention of holding a press conference, and proceeding on an indefinite strike. Secondly, we'll have to make preparation for presenting our side to the press, so that its veracity cannot be questioned and it has a telling effect on the public."

"But Vikram, why should we bother to inform the dean regarding the press conference?" Gohil asked.

"Ask me that question later, after the dean responds to our notice. Meanwhile I have a task for Zeb."

"Shoot," said Zeb-Un-Nisa.

"Gather as many students as you can from amongst those who had attended Professor Prasad's class on that fateful day. Ask them, one by one, to repeat what the professor actually said. Then piece the story accurately without an iota of exaggeration. After you have done that, select a bright student with a reasonable ability at narrating things, and prepare him or her for presenting the professor's utterances in a very casual manner. There should be no dramatics, and no flourishes. In addition, please see that the person you select for the job is capable of facing a few questions from the press. You have only until tomorrow noon for the job."

The notice to the dean was prepared at once, and signed by Gohil and Vyas as the president, and the secretary of the student union. It was on the dean's desk within an hour. The dean sent back his reply with equal alacrity.

"The students are advised to desist from proceeding on strike. They are prohibited from holding a press conference. A strict action shall be taken against them if they try to hold a press conference on the campus."

The dean had sent a copy of his warning to the Director of Health.

"Do you now understand why it was necessary to inform the dean regarding the press meet?" Vikram asked Gohil.

"Yes, I do now. That was a smart move. You gave the dean an opening to demonstrate to the authorities that he was doing his best to thwart the students' protest."

Bharat rang up the local offices of almost all the daily newspapers. He gave them all an identical message:

"The students of the Medical College of Baroda have been on strike for the last two days in protest against a professor who has been degrading the people of Gujarat. The junior doctors of the hospital, attached to the college will join the strike from tomorrow. You are requested to attend a press conference this afternoon at three, at the band stand of the Commatee Baug gardens."

The press meeting was well attended. To the delight of the organizers, Mr. Ganesh Gandhi, a veteran journalist and the chief editor of *Sandesh* was among the first arrivals. He walked up to Vikram, shook hands, and patted his back. He was a patient of Vikram's Bapuji and a friend.

"Thank you Ganesh uncle, for coming all the way from Ahmedabad."

"Actually Vikram, I am in Baroda on a different mission. My local sub-editor informed me of this meeting. And here I am, ready to listen to your story."

They all stood in a group at the bandstand. Gohil thanked the press for responding to their call and then introduced the members of the action committee. The first question came from a young man, with a baby face, representing *Gujarat Samachar,*

"Why have you selected a garden for the meeting?

"We are sorry for keeping you standing." Gohil said. "We have been prohibited the use of College Campus for the meeting."

"Never mind, let's come to the battle ground," it was Mr. Gandhi of *Sandesh,* "What's the story?"

Vikram took over from here.

"We have a Professor, Dr. Rajeev Kumar Prasad, recently appointed to head the Department of Preventive Medicine ..."

Pawan Dada, the columnist, interrupted Vikram,

"Wait a sec Doctor, isn't this Professor a close relative of Shri Ganga Prasad of the High command at Delhi?"

Vikram had to appreciate the journalistic sagacity of Bharat's father in injecting the political tinge at this juncture.

"I wouldn't know much about that," Vikram said with a straight face.

There was a spurt of whispers, as the journalists shared the information among themselves. Vikram thought this was the right time to revert to Professor Prasad's misdemeanor, now that his political connections were established, thanks to Pawan Dada.

"This professor," continued Vikram, as if there was no interruption, "has made insulting remarks publicly about the people of Gujarat. I personally have not heard those remarks, but about sixty students of his class had the misfortune of being witnesses to his odious onslaught. Miss Rekha Mohite is one of those unfortunates. She will give you a first hand account of the incident."

Rekha came forwards and told the tale. She repeated the words of the professor almost verbatim, in a calm and steady voice. She spoke of the professor's allegation that the people of Gujarat did not contribute men to the armed forces. She recounted the professor's accusation that they were busy amassing wealth when the other people of the country were sacrificing their sons to protect Mother India. There was a tremor in her voice when she repeated the Professor's words that the people of Gujarat were a timid lot, expecting others to sacrifice their lives to protect them and their wealth.

After completing her recounting, Rekha stepped back, and stood beside Vikram. He put his arm around her shoulders to calm the turmoil raging within her, which she had kept under control so far. She let out a barely audible sob, which did reach the ears of a few journalists standing near her.

The woman representing *The Indian Express* said in an angry voice,

"If what this young girl has said is true, the professor has committed a contemptible crime against the people of Gujarat, and a punitive action is called for."

Rekha surprised everyone; she stepped forward, now fully composed. She raised her right hand dramatically in front of her, and said in a court room style,

"It is the truth, only the truth, nothing but the truth."

There were a few chuckles from the gathering, lightening somewhat the somber atmosphere. Vikram was pleased at the aplomb with which Rekha had carried her part.

Next question came from Mr. Ganesh Gandhi,

"Haven't the authorities taken any action?"

Vikram supplied the answer,

"The Dean of the college had tried to put an end to the whole matter by suggesting to the professor to tender an apology. Yesterday the health minister, the health secretary, and the director of the health services had visited the college to persuade the professor to apologize. He has stood by his statements, and refuses to express regrets."

"Damn him," said Mr. Gandhi, "the man has the cheek to defy such high authority."

"Why worry Ganesh Bhai," a young journalist shouted from the back of the gathering, "We shall soon puncture his inflated ego, and shatter his political shield thar he seems to flaunt so shamelessly."

"O.K. young fellas," said Pawan Dada, "we'll see what we can do in this matter."

On that note, the meeting ended.

Next morning almost all newspapers splashed the story of Professor Prasad's tirade against the people of Gujarat, and agitation by the medical students and the junior doctors on their front pages.

"The people of Gujarat are a cowardly lot – Says Professor Prasad"

"A servant of the People of Gujarat heaps insults on his masters"

"A professor drunk on political backing sullies the image of Gujarat"

"The Chief Minister of Gujarat watches helplessly when the state's honor is being dragged through the mud."

The most telling feature appeared in the *Times of India.* It read, **"Politically pampered professor spits on his hosts."**

The outrage in the press brought immediate response from the authorities. The dean's phone was ringing as he entered his office at nine in the morning. The personal secretary of the chief minister was on the line,

"Is that Dr. Benjamin?"

"Yes."

"The C.M. wants you to be in his office at half past five this evening, along with not more than three representatives of the agitating students."

The secretary disconnected the phone.

The Dean called the three representatives to his office.

"The C.M. wants the representatives of the students to see him in his office at half past five this evening."

"May we please see the orders?" Vikram asked.

"There are no written orders. He has conveyed, on phone, that I should escort the representatives, and there should not be more than three of them."

"We need time to consult our colleagues."

"Do as you wish, but please see that you assemble here before two."

The action committee met on a fifteen minutes notice, Gohil voted against the proposal of meeting the Chief Minister.

"He has not written to us. Why should we go?"

Vikram spelled out the answer,

"How could he write to us? Whom would he have addressed? As to why we should go, the answer is, for the sake of our dean. He is a subordinate of the C.M. His superior has summoned him, and asked him to bring us along. Our dean desires that we should accompany him. We should honor our dean's wishes."

It was decided that the three representatives should go. Vikram sounded a warning to his two companions, Gohil and Zeb.

"This meeting with the C.M. is going to be a tough job. The politicians are adept at stick and carrot games. They can induce you into commitments you had not intended to make. So do not make any hasty and unguarded comments. This goes particularly for you, Grenade Gohil."

"You do all the talking, Vikram," Zeb said, "We both will keep our mouths shut.

They reached the Secretariat in the Ambawadi area of Ahmedabad at the appointed time. The chief minister's receptionist asked them to wait in the outer office. A few minutes later, a middle-aged woman, perhaps a lower rung secretary, came up to Dr. Benjamin and said,

"Dr. Benjamin, the director of health is in the secretary's office. Would you care to join him there?"

"No, thank you, I am fine here."

The dean's gesture in refusing to leave their side touched the hearts of Vikram and his associates.

They were kept waiting for forty minutes, without a word of regret. This irked Gohil and Zeb.

"This is the stick for you. The carrot may come later," Vikram explained.

When they were eventually ushered into the Chief Minister's air-conditioned office, they saw an array of dignitaries sitting at the far side of a long table. The C.M, Mr. Bipin Varia, sat in the centre, dressed in a spotless white *khadi kurta* and *dhoti*, the trademark of the ruling party. He was flanked by the health minister on his right and a suave man in a suit and necktie on his left, probably the chief secretary. Dr. M.V. Patel, the director of health services, occupied the seat next to him. A man, similarly clad in suit and tie sat next to the health minister. Vikram assumed he was the health secretary. A young woman in a sari occupied the chair at the right end. Vikram failed to guess her position in the hierarchy. On the left end, there was an empty chair next to the director's, obviously for the dean.

When they approached the long table, the director motioned them to take seats facing the officials across the table. He gestured to the dean to come and occupy the empty seat next to him. The dean pretended not to have noticed his gesture and took a seat on the left of the students. The director grimaced at the dean's action, while the health minister gave an approving, but barely visible smile. The rest sat with stony faces. As they were taking their seats, Gohil whispered to Vikram,

"Why the full army?"

"It's for the effect," Vikram whispered back, "Aren't you intimidated?"

Nobody bothered about introductions. The chief minister took off his *khadi* cap, proceeded to fold it very elaborately, and laid it on the table. Then he removed his glasses with equal elaboration, polished them with his spotless white kerchief, and put them beside the cap. Having finished these seemingly crucial tasks, he started speaking in a typical public speech style,

"It gives me pleasure to be addressing young people like you, young people who are the future of our country, young people who are engaged in studies to become doctors, the noblest of the noble professions, which heals the pain and sufferings of the fellow men."

He paused for breath, and then continued,

"At the same time it pains me to see you frittering away your valuable time in unworthy and unproductive activities like agitations and strikes. I appeal to you to go back, call off this futile agitation, and get on with your studies."

He picked up his glasses and the cap one by one, and put them on as if he had finished with them and was preparing to leave. Gohil and Zeb were perplexed at such abrupt ending without giving them an opportunity to utter a single word. Gohil looked askance at his companions. Vikram patted his hand, indicating that he should remain silent. Vikram gripped the arms of the chair, as if to rise and said in a casual manner,

"We shall convey your advice to our fellow students, sir."

The minister removed his glasses with a jerk, dropped them on the table, and spoke angrily,

"Are you telling me, you are here as mere messenger boys?"

"No sir, there seems to be some misunderstanding. We are the delegated spokespersons for the students of Baroda Medical College, and we thought we were here to discuss a grave problem with our elected representatives."

There was a faint smile on the lips of the health minister, this boy can meet the Chief on his own grounds, he was thinking.

"What is the problem? Where is the problem? I don't see any," the primness had gone out of the C.M. "A professor has made an unguarded remark, and you people have made a mountain out of a mole hill."

"It was not just an unguarded remark Sir, The Dean, the Director, and the honorable health minister here will tell you that the man has repeated the contemptible remark against the people of Gujarat, more than once, and proudly stands by it."

The three witnesses named by Vikram, sat stiff and silent.

"All right, to satisfy you I am asking the Dean, Dr. Benjamin, to convene a meeting of all the students, tomorrow morning, and Professor Prasad will tender an unqualified apology."

Gohil, who was gnashing his teeth at the overbearing attitude of the minister, burst out,

"The time for an apology has passed."

There was a stunned silence.

Vikram whispered into Zeb's ear,

"This is an unguarded but welcome remark."

The dean, who sat next to Zeb, heard Vikram's whisper, and made an unsuccessful attempt to suppress a smile.

The chief minister was livid with rage. He sat there motionless, with his lips compressed with anger. Then he burst out.

"You, young man, you have the cheek to sit there and spar with me. I shall …"

Vikram intervened.

"Sir, I apologize for the unguarded remark of my companion."

The chief secretary, who had so far sat with a stony face, compressed his lips tightly to suppress a smile. The chief has found his match in this boy.

Vikram unobtrusively held Gohil by his arm and pushed him upwards. Gohil took the hint, rose to his feet and said,

"I am sorry sir. The casual way, in which the grave matter of disrespect to our state is being discussed, got my goat. Do forgive me."

The minister appeared to be mollified.

"We are not taking this lightly. We will issue an official reprimand to the professor, and he shall offer his apologies. What else do you want me to do?"

So, the bargaining begins. Vikram thought, and joined in the game. He said with a crafty casualness,

"Perhaps transferring Professor Prasad out of Baroda…"

Vikram's suggestion was left incomplete. The chief minister flew into a rage again.

"Now you will tutor me how to run my government. Will you, you wise guy?"

Vikram, who ordinarily was cool as cucumber, lost his poise at the outburst of the minister, and said in a slow deliberate voice,

"You had asked for our suggestion, and I offered one. Have I said anything to warrant the sarcasm?"

The others in the room did not fail to notice that Vikram had dropped the *sir* from his address.

"Let me tell you mister, the people have not put me in this chair to take suggestions from greenhorns like you."

Gohil could take it no more. The short fuse of the grenade had burnt out. He jumped up from his chair, and said with clenched teeth,

"If we are not to make any suggestions, then what are we here for? Have we been called here to be ridiculed and insulted?"

He gripped Vikram and Zeb, who sat on his either side, by their arms and yanked them up,

"Come on mates, let's be off before we are deprived of the last vestiges of our self respect."

There was a silence of dismay in the room. The Chief Minister's jaw fell open. He realized his blunder. He was not dealing with his subordinates, who took his rants lying down. These were his electorate, highly educated and enlightened ones at that. He could picture the headlines in tomorrow's newspapers, if the proceedings of the meeting got reported. Prasad's foul mouthing had already agitated the people. His own insulting attitude towards the delegates would add fuel to the fire. He cast his eyes to left and right as if seeking help from his staff. Dr. Benjamin came to his rescue. He addressed his students in his usual fatherly tone,

"Gohil, Zeb, Vikram, please resume your seats."

The trio sat down.

Vikram took the writing pad lying in front of him, lowered it in his lap, so that only Zeb and Gohil could see it. He wrote on the pad,

"We keep our mouths shut from now on."

The chief minister cleared his throat, and addressed Gohil.

"You do have a temper young man. Tell me, has your father never scolded you? Do you fly off the handle when he pulls you up for a mistake?

Gohil saw the carrot being dangled in front of him, but refused to take the bait. He kept mum. The minister continued,

"Your parents spend their hard earned money and send you to the college to study. As an elder, I advise you to concentrate on your studies and fulfill your parents' dreams and make your mark in life. At this stage, you should shun agitations, strikes and such other activities. I hope you will go back and give a thought to what I have said."

He picked up his cap and glasses, and rose to his feet. He seemed in a hurry to conclude the meeting.

He turned to the dean and said,

"Dr. Benjamin, will you please stay back for a while."

"Yes sir,"

The dean spoke to Vikram, "you can take my car. The driver will take you all back to Baroda. I'll come later."

"That is not necessary sir, we'll take the bus."

"All right, I'll see you tomorrow morning."

On the bus ride back to Baroda, Zeb asked Vikram, "What is to happen now?"

"I give you a bet of hundred rupees; the dean shall be carrying the transfer orders of Professor Prasad."

"But Vikram, What happened there at the meeting, has left me totally confused. You suggested transfer of the professor. That infuriated the C.M. Now you are predicting that he will act on your suggestion. Tell me how the transfer of that foul-mouthed professor from one college to the other, within the state, will assuage the hurt inflicted by him."

"Yes Vikram," Gohil intervened, "I too fail to understand, how an astute person like you could suggest merely a transfer. The striking students are certainly not going to accept it. We should have demanded his dismissal."

There was a twinkle in Vikram's eyes as he answered his friends.

"You are absolutely right. Neither the Chief Minister nor I am so naïve as to think that merely transferring the professor will solve the problem. Yes, the minister was livid when I made the suggestion. That was because he is not used to 'green horns' like us offering advice to him. Nevertheless, he soon realized that I had suggested him a way out of the situation in which he finds himself. I can bet, the orders will say the professor is transferred to Ahmedabad. Majority of the voters will be satisfied that the Government has taken *action*. The big boss in Delhi will appreciate the chief minister's cunning *inaction*. He may even think his relative's transfer to the state capital amounts to promotion. The chief minister's masterly inaction will ultimately satisfy everyone, including us."

Zeb could not contain herself any more. She burst out, shaking her head desperately.

"Including us? Damn you Vikram, don't talk in riddles."

"My dear fellows have patience for a couple of days. You shall get your answers.

Vikram's prediction was bang on target. The orders for the transfer of Professor Prasad to Ahmeabad Medical College were typed that evening. He was ordered to report on duty at his new posting within two days. The dean was entrusted with the task of handing the orders personally to the professor.

Two days later, Professor Prasad drove to Ahmedabad Medical College, to take charge at his new posting. His car stopped in the porch, in front of the college entrance. As he emerged from his car, a burly woman student materialized from nowhere, and stood blocking his way. She was carrying a large placard saying,

"**Professor Prasad, you are a persona non grata here. Go back where you belong.**"

The professor tried to sidestep her, and move towards the entrance of the college building. About thirty students came marching silently from the two sides of the building, and stood there blocking the entrance. More of them appeared and lined up flanking the professor. Prasad stared at the silent, sullen faces for a minute, then turned about, got back into his car, and drove away. He resigned his job, and left for his hometown, carrying bitter memories of his short sojourn in the state of Gujarat.

If the Prasad episode was a high point in Vikram's sagacity as an interlocutor, there was another, which put him into a very unenviable situation. Two dear friends and colleagues of his, Dr. Mahinder Sahgal and Dr. Rasila Rana were involved in this unfortunate incident. The duo professed undying love for each other, and indulged in premarital sex. All their friends expected them to get married. The undying love evaporated when a billionaire industrialist offered his daughter in marriage to Mahinder. He ditched pregnant Rasila, and tied the knot with the heiress. Rasila tried to commit suicide, but timely intervention by Vikram saved her life. Vikram's discretions prevented her pregnancy and her suicide attempt from becoming public, and reaching the police files. Vikram helped her with a covert abortion. However, pulling her out of mental trauma and impending depression was a daunting task. When the scorn poured over her by friends and foes became unbearable for her, he arranged for Rasila to migrate to the U.K., where she could start life afresh and pursue her career in medicine. Some months later, when he himself left for Britain to pursue his pre-planned career in surgery, some of his colleagues insinuated that he went chasing his friend's discard. Vikram could have never even dreamed that the fate was guiding him to a rendezvous, not with his friend's discarded love, but with a long lost childhood love of his own.

Mohammed Ashraf, a resident of Gujaranwala, was a minor legend around that region. He had two passions, rearing thoroughbred horses and experimenting in the cultivation of various varieties of cotton. With some help from his father, he had developed the expertise of cultivating a special variety of long staple Egyptian cotton. As long as his father was alive, this highly profitable farming skill was kept confined to the family, but after his death, Ashraf decided to disseminate the knowhow to his fellow cultivators. Within a few years, the whole district of Gujranwala was producing the famed Egyptian cotton that brought rich returns to its farmers. In the local market, the variety came to be known as the *Ashrafi* cotton. There was great demand for it abroad, particularly in Manchester. Gradually Ashraf acquired a commercial skill to supplement his farm income. He started working as an intermediary between the cultivators of his district and a commission agency in Multan, which supplied the *Ashrafi* cotton to an export house in Chittagong. In the early nineteen thirties, the labor unions had established a stronghold in India. They were quite active in Bengal. Frequent strikes disturbed the commercial activities of the province, and the shipping from the Chittagong port was recurrently disrupted. The cotton remained unlifted from the fields and the godowns. Ashraf went to Karachi, and met a leading commission agent, Tikumal Bijlani. He set up a new export house in partnership with Tikumal, which would exclusively export the *Ashrafi cotton* from the port of Karachi.

His love for the horses stemmed from his brief friendship with Shahid-ul-Zaman, an Afghan horse trader from across the Khaiber pass. Ashraf had attended a horse show cum trade fair held annually at Multan. Shahid had entered two horses in the competition, a tartar, and a habash. The tartar was a small, sturdy, and speedy animal. Shahid called it *Mushki*, the Blackie. It was quickly picked up by a buyer, for a handsome price, as the tartars are well suited for the *neza baazi* competition. This equine game is popular in the Punjab, and is akin to *Buzkushi* of Afghanistan. The habash was in a different league, a great Arabic mare. She had a long, strapping, slick, white body with black spots. Shahid entered her in the show, under the name of *Gul Badan.* He rode her, bare back, and without a bridle. She sped away like a typhoon and disappeared into the dust cloud raised by her clattering hoofs. She returned presently, emerging out of the dust cloud like an apparition. Shahid made her dance to the drumbeat, and she performed many other tricks at the wave of his hand. The watchers were spellbound, but nobody offered to buy her. She would allow no one to come near her, leave alone ride her. Shahid held her by her mane, and started to lead her out of the arena.

"How much would you take for her?" Someone in the crowd asked.

Heads turned towards the speaker. It was Mohamed Ashraf from Gujranwala. Shahid named a figure.

"It's a lot of money."

"Gul Badan is a lot of a mare, my friend."

Ashraf walked up to Shahid, and said, "It's a deal, but on a condition."

"Speak."

"You shall have to accompany Gul Badan and me to my farm house in Gujranwala, and be my guest for three days."

"Agreed."

When they reached Ashraf's farmhouse, he asked Shahid to tie the mare up in the stable, where a couple of native horses were already sheltered.

"If I were you, I wouldn't do that," said Shahid.

Ashraf thought for a moment and then agreed to leave her untied.

For the next two days, Ashraf worked on Gul Badan, to a well thought out plan. Whenever the caretaker went to feed her, wash her, or carry out other ministrations, he and Shahid would stand on either side of her. Both would keep petting her. At the end, Ashraf would offer her *gurh*, the unrefined sugar lump. Gul Badan refused the treat for the first two days. On the third morning, when Ashraf extended his hand with the sugar lump, she started licking it hesitantly. Then she raised her snout in the air and let out a short, low-pitched neigh of happiness. With one sweep of her tongue, she lifted the lump into her mouth.

"Atta girl," said Ashraf.

"Atta boy," said Shahid to Ashraf, thumping his back. "I can now leave happily. I am sure you and Gul Badan will get along fine. However, before I go, I would like to give you some tips. Gul Badan does not like a bridle. It is not necessary. Never take a whip or a stick to her. She follows her rider's body language. If you ride her with your legs relaxed, she will go at a trot. You squeeze her flanks with your knees and she'll fly. Put you right or left hand on her shoulder and she will turn in that direction. Put both your hands on her neck and she will halt instantly. You yourself seem to be a good trainer, and she is a quick learner. You'll make a good team."

They did make a good team. Whenever Ashraf-Gul Badan combination entered a race, they invariably lifted the trophy until one day, in 1937, when a young man from a comparatively small village of Uchaanwala appeared on the scene. That year, a *neza baazi* event was held at the vast farmhouse of Mohamed Ashraf, in the outskirts of Gujranwala. It was a District Gujarat versus District Gujranwala competition. A flat wooden peg, two inches in width, and painted white, was driven into the ground, at a fixed angle so that its face was tilted slightly skywards. The peg had a two-inch-long pointed lower end which went into the ground and the remaining eight-inch rectangular portion remained visible above the ground. The rider carrying a standard sized spear took his position behind the starting line, at half-a-mile's distance from the peg. At the given signal, the rider raced down the tract, and tried to carry away the peg on the point of the spear. If a rider pierced the peg, a new one replaced it. It was mandatory that the interval between the signal *go*, to the piercing of the peg should not be more than one minute. It meant he had to ride at an average speed of more than 30 miles an hour. The riders who failed to reach the prescribed speed, or failed to carry the peg in the first round were eliminated from the race. Those who passed the first round entered the second, and so on until the three finalists remained. The final race consisted of three rounds. The winner, the first and the second runner-ups, were decided on the speed of the rider and the number of successes in piercing the peg.

In that particular race, in 1937, the three finalists were Mohamed Ashraf of Gujranwala, Shibbir Mohamed of Village Mianwali of District Gujarat and Wazeer Ahmed from the village of Uchaanwala, again of District Gujarat. The first two were veterans of the game. Wazeer Ahmed was participating for the first time. Ashraf eyed the newcomer with admiration. He was a handsome, broad shouldered youth, in his early twenties, oozing confidence from every pore of his body. In the final race, Shibbir pierced the peg twice but his speed was the lowest. Ashraf too managed to lift the peg twice. His speed was the fastest. Wazeer carried away the peg all the three times and won the trophy. Ashraf was the first runner up, and Shibbir the second.

This was for the first time in the last seven years that Ashraf-Gul Badan combine had lost a race. Ashraf knew the reason; age had slowed down his reflexes. His spear had come down a fraction of second too late. "Perhaps the time has come for me to hang my boots," he thought.

He went down to the young winner, and shook his hand, congratulating him profusely. In the course of their conversation, Ashraf learnt that Wazeer was a son of Mirdad of Uchaanwala, a leading farmer of that area, owning vast tracts of farmland. Ashraf had met Mirdad once, at the cotton market of Mandi Bahauddin, a prominent trading centre of District Gujarat. Ashraf invited Wazeer and Shibbir to his *haveli* for dinner that night.

Wazeer arrived at Ashraf's mansion a little before sunset. The gate was open and he walked into the large courtyard. He noticed that a *tandoor,* the traditional Punjabi clay oven for baking chapatis was lit up on the right side of the courtyard, and a young girl in her late teens was feeding it with the firewood. On hearing his footsteps, the girl turned to face him. It was an attractive face, with a red glow in the cheeks, probably due to the heat from the *tandoor.*

"Aslaam Alaikum," he called out, "I am Wazeer. Is Mian Ashraf at home?"

Alaikum Aslaam," she returned his salute, and then called out, "*Abbaa Jaan,* some one has come to see you." Her voice was as sweet as her face.

Ashraf came out and greeted his guest. As he led him to the *baithak* hall, a middle-aged plump woman emerged from the house. Ashraf introduced her as his wife, and they exchanged the traditional greetings. She left without any further word to join her daughter at the tandoor.

Shibbir arrived soon after. As the dinner was being laid, a young man joined them. Ashraf introduced him as his son, Hameed. Wazeer noticed that although the two women of the house did not observe *pardah,* they did not join the men folk in conversation. They silently served the food, and left them as soon as they had finished eating. The conversation during the meals had mainly been about horses, and farming. Hameed took very little part in the conversation. His interest lay elsewhere. He had started dabbling in politics, and had become an active member of the *Harkat-e-Ittehad-e-Musalmeen-e-Hind.* His activities had come to the notice of Mohamed Hayaat Khan of Lahore, a prominent leader of the party. Hayaat was increasingly impressed by the political maneuvering skills of the young man, and had appointed him the vice president of the Harkat's youth league of Punjab. Ashraf was unhappy, as his son seemed to be slowly losing interest in the management of the family's vast farmlands.

When the guests were leaving, Ashraf escorted them to the gate of the haveli. Wazeer saw Gul Badan being given a rub down by her keeper.

"Uncle, will you be interested in selling Gul Badan?" Wazeer asked Ashraf

"No son, she is not for sale. Besides, you won't be able to handle her."

"Well, if you are not going to sell her, my skill at handling her becomes irrelevant."

Ashraf had the feeling that the young man was capable of handling any horse. Before saying good-bye, Wazeer extracted a promise from Ashraf that he would make a reciprocal visit to his family in Uchaanwala soon.

In the first week of December, that year, Ashraf took his wife Mamtaz, and daughter, Aneesa to Uchaanwala, ostensibly to witness its famed *Tazia* procession of Moharram. Aneesa was looking forward to watching the run of the *Duldul,* a symbolic historical horse of *Imaam* Hussein. They stayed for two days as guests of Wazeer, at the house of his father Mirdad. During one of their conversations Mirdad said,

"Ashraf Mian, before this day we were just acquaintances, I am glad now we have become friends."

"I suggest we go one step further and become relatives." Ashraf suggested.

Mirdad failed to comprehend Ashraf's hint

"I offer my daughter Aneesa in marriage to your son Wazeer."

Mirdad was taken by surprise at such a forthright proposal. He promised to confer with his family and get back to him. Wazeer agreed to the proposal without hesitation. His mother not only gave her consent but also insisted the marriage take place at an early date. She was bedridden with a serious heart condition, and wanted to see Wazeer married before she went to her grave. His elder brother Abdul Kadar was indifferent to the proposal, but Kadar's wife Rahima Bibi was keen for this proposal to go through. She had been managing the house alone, but since the birth of her first child six months back, she was finding the task difficult. She wanted another woman in the house to help her. Above all, the good looks, and mild manners of Aneesa had won her approval. Ashraf placed twenty-one rupees on the palm of Wazeer indicating that he was spoken for. The wedding, *Nikah,* took place on 7 February 1938. Ashraf gave Gul Badan in dowry to his daughter. Wazeer's mother died, a happy woman, two months later.

Wazeer's married life had a fantastic start. The day after he brought his bride home, his family invited the women of the village for viewing the new bride for the *muhn dikhai* ceremony. All the women, without exception, declared the new bride the prettiest woman of the village. Wazeer was ecstatic. Aneesa did not show the slightest vanity at being so idolized. She and Wazeer made a happy couple. Their happiness knew no bounds when sixteen months later Aneesa got pregnant. Rahmat Bibi, the village mid wife, delivered Aneesa of a baby girl on the last day of the month of March 1940. Mirdad's house, the *daadu-di haveli,* as it was called, erupted with merriments and celebrations. However, the festivities did not last long. By the nightfall, Aneesa started showing signs of serious illness. She became deathly pale. Her breathing became labored. The village *hakeem,* Sujaan Singh was summoned. He had one look at Aneesa and said,

"She is bleeding."

"No sir," said the midwife, "she has not bled unduly."

"She is bleeding internally. She should be shifted to the town hospital immediately."

Aneesa died before they could begin the arrangements for shifting her to the hospital of the neighboring town. Nobody expected the newborn girl to survive. Rahima Bibi, the elder daughter-in-law of the family volunteered to look after the infant. With the help of Rahmat Bibi, she found a wet nurse, Khatija, who agreed to come and live with the family for three months. Khatija came from a poor family of shepherds, and had a month old daughter of her own. She was a godfearing honest young woman, and made all efforts to see that her new ward thrived. While feeding the two babies, she showed complete impartiality. She gave one of her breasts to her own daughter Fatima, and the other to the newborn whom she started calling the *chhoti* Fatima. The two girls came to be known, in the house, as the Big Fatima and the Little Fatima. Initially the Big Fatima howled with resentment at getting the reduced quota of her feed, but the things were set right by the *Hakeem,* who put Khatija on milk augmenting herbal preparations, and a supplementary diet. Khatija stayed on for six months instead of the initial contract of three, and both the Fatimas thrived. After the departure of the wet nurse, Rahima Bibi took over the care of the baby. They continued to call her Fatima. Nobody bothered to give her another name. Fatima turned out a precocious child. She spoke her first two words, *Amma* and *Abba,* imitating her two years old cousin, when she herself was six months old. She started walking at the age of seven months. When she was one year, her father, who called her my princess, took her for frequent horse rides, holding her in his lap. She enjoyed the rides immensely and loved her father for them.

*****

By the year 1946, when the British parliament resolved to grant India its independence, the demand for a separate sovereign state for the Muslims of India was becoming shriller by the day. The Hindus in the Muslim majority provinces, particularly of Punjab and Sindh were getting increasingly apprehensive. Tikumal, Ashraf's business partner in Karachi, thought it prudent to shift his commercial activities to a safe Hindu majority province. For this, he selected the city of Surat in the Bombay Presidency. He wrote to Ashraf informing him of his intention of leaving Karachi, and suggested termination of their partnership. He gave Ashraf the options of taking over the entire business or dissolving it. Ashraf left the management of his fields and the steed farm in Gujranwala in the hands of his son Hameed, and went to Karachi. He bought Tikumal out, and became the sole proprietor of the export house. Shortly afterwards, when Tikumal migrated to Surat, Ashraf purchased his elegant residential house too. His wife Mamtaz joined him there. Meanwhile, with the merger of the Punjab's *Tehrik-e-Kaashtkaar* into the *Harkat-e-Ittehad-e-Muslmeen-e-Hind*, Hameed's role in the politics of Punjab became increasingly important, and the high command of his party asked him to shift to Lahore. He, against the wishes of his father, sold off the steed farm, leased the farmland to a cousin and moved to Lahore.

When Fatima reached the age of two, often referred to as terrible twos, her aunt Rahima Bibi found it difficult to manage her. She threw tantrums, and got peeved for no obvious reasons. On top of that, she and her cousin Fazal, who was now four, fought pitched battles over toys, and for Rahima's attentions. If Rahima had a pair of knee-length trousers stitched for Fazal, Fatima would want one too. All explanations that girls did not wear knee-length trousers would be in vain. The fights between the two occasionally ended up in physical injury to one or the other. Rahima pestered Wazeer to get married again, and bring home a mother for Fatima. He was reluctant to give his daughter a stepmother. Eventually, he succumbed to the insistence of the family, and married Amina, the daughter of a local petty farmer. Amina Bibi took good care of Fatima for the initial few months and then her interest in the child gradually wore off. The girl often remained unkempt, with unwashed clothes, and uncombed hair, and went out into the streets without shoes. Not a day passed without the child getting physical punishment for doing something or the other, which annoyed the quick-tempered Amina. Her father left the house early in the morning for the farmhouse, and returned late in the evening. He hardly got to see his princess. Rahima's heart went out to the little creature, but she made no effort to help lest she be accused of interference. She did interfere, though cautiously, on occasions when the stepmother kept the child without food, as punishment for a *misdeed.* She would furtively pass some eatables to the girl when the stepmother was out of sight. One of Fatima's playmates, Bikku, who lived next door, was another source of help. Whenever he came to know that the *witch* was starving his friend, Fatima's friends had given that name to her stepmother, he invariably managed to smuggle food to her, without anyone ever finding out. Fatima tried to avoid the wrath of Amina by keeping out of her sight. She stayed away from home as much as possible, playing with other children and taking surreptitious tuitions from Bikku in reading and writing, and learning arithmetic. She often prayed to Allah to make her invisible to Amina Amma, or give her a flying mat so that she could fly away, far away, out of the reach of her stepmother. One day she did go away, far away, but under tragic circumstances.

*****

It was a pleasant morning in the month of July 1948. A fine drizzle had started. Wazeer was getting ready to leave for the farmhouse. Fatima, who was eight year old now, went up to him and said,

"Abba, Take me with you to the farm house."

"No my *Shahzadi*, I shall be very late coming back, and you will get bored there all alone. Tell you what; let me give you a long ride before I go to the farms."

Wazeer took his daughter on a long ride. The drizzle changed to steady rain. He dropped her back home. He gave a gentle kiss on the tip of her nose before leaving. There was a very, very tiny mole at the tip of Fatima's nose. Whenever he saw it, Wazeer felt a stab in his heart. His late wife Aneesa too had a similar mole exactly at the same location. Fatima, with the passing years, was acquiring the pretty looks of her mother. While riding to the farms, he recalled the happy days he had spent with Aneesa. By the time he reached the farmhouse, the rain had changed into a downpour. The deluge continued unabated for the whole day. The fields were heavily flooded and so were the surrounding low lands. Wazeer decided to stay overnight at the farmhouse. This was not unusual. He often spent nights at the farmhouse, particularly during the monsoon season. The farmhouse was built at a safe height, and was well stocked with provisions. One or the other woman servant would rustle up a workable meal for him. The animals were herded up inside the covered backyard. The servants slept in the hall, and Wazeer took up the private room meant for the family members.

In the middle of the night, one of his guard dogs, a Doberman, started growling fiercely, and woke Wazeer up.

"Shut up Sheroo," he shouted through the open door.

Instead of quietening down, the dog's growling got even louder. He got up to investigate the cause of the ruckus created by Sheroo. As he walked out through the door in the darkness, he stepped on a soft rope like object. Next moment a sharp excruciating pain in the left leg assailed him. He jumped back, and let out a piercing shriek. A couple of farm hands heard the scream and came running.

"Get a lamp," Wazeer spoke through clenched teeth from pain, "Some creature has bitten me."

One of the workers brought the lamp and looked at Wazeer's leg.

"It's a snake bite." He pronounced. He shone the light on Wazeer's face. He had a vacant look and his eyes did not seem to focus. The servants held a hasty consultation, and decided it would be quicker to ride to the village and fetch the *hakeem*, rather than to try to get their master to the village. One of them rode to the house of Allah Rakkha. It was an excruciatingly slow ride through the floodwaters. The Hakeem, when told about the snakebite, hurriedly collected the necessary remedies and rode back with the messenger. Before leaving, the hakeem instructed his son to carry the news to Wazeer's family. By the time Allah Rakkha arrived, Wazeer was almost unconscious and his complexion had taken a blue tinge. He was muttering one word repeatedly, *Shehzadi.* Allah Rakkha's shrewd eyes told him it was a cobra bite, beyond his competence. He also realized the condition had reached an irretrievable stage. He applied a salve at the bitten area just for the appearances, and tried to pour a concoction into the patient's mouth, which he failed to swallow. Wazeer breathed his last before any of his family arrived.

The distance between Karachi and Uchaanwala prevented Ashraf from attending the funeral of his son-in-law. He came down three days later and offered the prayer of *Al-Fatihah* at his grave. That evening when he sat down for meals with Wazeer's father and brother, he hesitatingly made a request.

"I solicit your permission to take Fatima with me to Karachi."

After only a moment's reflection Mirdad said,

"Perhaps that would be better for the poor orphan. I am sure you and your wife will give her much better care than what she can hope to get here."

Nothing more was said in the matter. Next morning Aunt Rahima told Fatima she would be going to Karachi with her *Naana*. She packed her few dresses and toys in a small suitcase, and told her she could pack any other things she wanted to take with her. Rahima was surprised when the girl discarded the toys, and put in a slightly torn Urdu Primer and a slate. In the afternoon, Fatima left the abode of her *Daada*, the paternal grandfather to go and live with her *Naana*, the maternal grandfather. They had to travel for almost sixty hours by train to reach Karachi.

"Why have I left my home in the village?" She asked herself, as the speeding train was carrying her away. Then she remembered her friends, who too had left the village suddenly some months back. Her family had kept the news of the massacre from the children.

"Where have they gone?" she had asked her cousin Phallu.

"I don't know."

"When will they be back?"

"They will never come back."

"Why have they gone away?"

"Abba says they were afraid."

"Who were they afraid of?"

"I don't know."

Now that she herself was going away, she thought, "I was afraid of my stepmother, still I had never thought of going away. I had my Abba, Daada, Kadar Chacha, and Rahima Chachi. They protected me from my stepmother. None of my friends had a stepmother and still they went away. In one way, they were luckier than I am. They went with their families. I have left my dear ones behind. Phallu was saying my Abba went away to Allah's home. He will never come back. Now I am going to Naana's home. Will I never go back to the village?"

Lost in these thoughts, sleep overcame her, and she slumped against her grandfather sitting next to her. He eased her head gently on to the berth and placed a pillow under it. He straightened her feet to a comfortable position and she slept. She dreamed that she was playing the game of Gillidanda with her friends and had dropped a catch. Bikku shouted

"You, *Jhalli phatti,* idiot!"

For Fatima, traveling from her tiny village of Uchaanwala to the metropolis of Karachi was no less than Cinderella's ride to the palace. She had never before gone out of her village. She had never seen a train. Bikku had once shown her a picture of it in his schoolbook. Now she was actually riding in one. When they changed trains first at Laalamusa and then at Lahore, she watched in amazement the vast network of tracks, coming and going of so many trains, which gorged and disgorged huge crowds of people. At the Karachi railway station, she witnessed another marvel. Her grandfather led her to a shinning strange looking contraption. He opened a door on its side and said,

"Get into the car, child."

She had only heard about cars from her Kadar Uncle. He had been telling the children about the carriages in the cities, which drove off by themselves, without the horses or the bullocks pulling them. This one ran with great speed, and emitted a strange smell. The man sitting in the front was holding on to a wheel, and turning it from side to side.

The house of her grandparents too was no less than a dream palace to Fatima. It was a big two-storey building, sitting in the middle of a large compound, which surrounded it on all the four sides, and had numerous pretty looking plants and flowering bushes. Fatima had seen only brick and mud houses in the village. This house was painted red and white, and was called the *Laal Bangala*, the Red Mansion. Fatima recalled a line from a song she had heard on the gramophone of her Abba,

"*Ik bangala bane nyara,*"- let us build a matchless mansion.

Fatima soon got used to the magical mansion, where the lamps lit up, and the fans started whirling, just at the push of a button. Her grandparents gave her unrestricted freedom, and fathomless love. She quickly learnt to handle the electrical gadgets; to sit on the table and eat from the crockery; to instruct the servants, and above all to groom herself. The most testing task for her was to learn to sleep alone in her own large bedroom. In a few weeks' time, she got so familiarized and acclimatized to the new place that anyone would think she had always lived there.

When her grandfather informed her that he intended to send her to school, she jumped with joy. Next day she found herself facing the headmaster of the Allavi Primary School, run by a Shia Education trust. He asked her,

"Which school have you attended before?"

"I have not been to any school."

"Not been to any school? Why not?

The grandfather explained,

"She was in a small village, where the parents do not send the daughters to school."

"What's her age?"

"Almost eight-and-a-half years."

The head master shook his head.

"At this age she should be in the fourth grade. I cannot let her join the little girls of grade one?"

"I know all the lessons of the first grade," Fatima volunteered.

The headmaster gave her a look of scrutiny, then handed her a sheet of paper and a pencil. He dictated a few simple words and numbers. He inspected what she had written and asked,

"Can you do arithmetical sums?"

"Only sums of addition and subtraction."

The headmaster tested her mathcmatical skill and seemed satisfied.

"You said you did not attend any school. Where did you learn this?'

"A friend taught me."

The headmaster agreed to admit the child in the second grade, with the condition that the grandfather would hire a tutor, who would cover the course of two years in one. At the end of the year, she would sit the examination along with the students of the third grade. If she passed the exam, she would be given a double promotion to the fourth grade. That way the girl would be only one year older than her classmates. The headmaster recommended Walayat Khan, the class teacher of the third grade, for the home tuition. In the application form for the admission, her grandfather wrote down her name as Nilolfer. He thought Fatima was too old-fashioned a name. That is how Fatima of Uchaanwala village became Nilofer of Karachi.

At the end of the academic year, Fatima, now Nilofer, sat for the exam first with the students of the second grade, and then with those of the third grade. In both the exams, she was the top scorer.

In the year 1950, she finished her primary education. She joined the Husseini High School run by the same trust. She passed her Matriculation in 1955, topping the state list of successful candidates. Almost all newspapers carried her photograph and her success story. She was the first girl student, so far, to have topped at the board examination. The principal of the school, Mirza Mehndi Ali visited her home to congratulate the family, and had tea with her grandfather.

"So Nilofer, what's your next target?" the Principal asked.

"Get married, and raise a family. What else?" The reply came from the grandfather.

"Allah forbid! Ashraf Sahib, are you planning to snuff her God given talent in the bud? For God's sake, don't do that. You are one of the enlightened members of the community. Do rise above the orthodox beliefs, and don't deny your granddaughter to prove her worth just because she is a girl."

"What will she do even after obtaining a university degree? Certainly, she cannot serve in offices. If ultimately she is going to be a housewife then how does it matter whether she is a matriculate or a graduate?"

"Naana jaan," Nilofer intervened politely, "If you permit me to study further, I would like to do my intermediate in Science, and join a medical college to become a doctor. I am not interested in any other course."

"How many years will it take for you to become a doctor?"

"Seven more years."

"You will be 23 years before you become a doctor. Where will I find a husband for you at that age?"

Mirza tried to reason with him,

"Ashraf Sahib, you must know that in our community many more boys than girls study to become doctors. Usually the doctors prefer doctor wives. If our Nilofer becomes a doctor, there shall be no dearth of suitable boys for her."

Ashraf found logic in Mirza's reasoning. He gave Nilofer permission to pursue further studies. In 1958, Nilofer established another record by being the first girl in the state to top the list of successful candidates at the Intermediate Science Examination. She joined the Karachi Medical College for Women.

When she finished her pre-clinical course, and started attending the hospital for her clinical training, Nilofer came into her element. She followed a set routine for studying applied medicine. In the outpatient clinics, she listened attentively to the symptoms of the patients, and watched her teachers carry out their physical check. She listened carefully to her teachers, and junior doctors, discussing the possible diagnosis, and ordering relevant laboratory and radiological investigations in order to reach the final diagnosis. She went to the library and read up the medical conditions that she had witnessed in the out patient clinic that morning. Armed with the knowledge she had gathered from her teachers and from the books, she went to the wards and carried out her own examination of the patients that had been admitted there from the out patient clinic. She checked the patients' files to see whether all the relevant investigations had been ordered, or whether any unnecessary tests were included. She also scrutinized the treatment that had been prescribed, and compared it with that suggested in the textbooks. Next morning, during the ward rounds, she politely questioned the teachers to clarify points on which she had doubts. She subconsciously studied the ways her teachers spoke to the patients, and their general approach to the sick. In a very short time, she herself had developed endearing bedside manners. She unhesitatingly asked the senior nurses to instruct her in certain procedures, which the medical teachers did not teach. She learnt from the nurses, dressing and bandaging, giving enemas, preparing patients for surgery, and many other mundane procedures. She willingly went to the wards at odd hours to learn various routes of injections, and minor surgical procedures, from the junior resident doctors. She fully immersed herself in the study of medicine to the exclusion of all other activities. The result was that two years before she was due to qualify as a doctor, she knew more medicine than a fresh fully qualified doctor would know. Once, Dr. Mubarak Hussein, a teacher of internal medicine, while conducting a clinical session had commented on the proficiency of Nilofer.

"If it were in my powers I would award this girl the postgraduate degree in medicine today itself."

The praises and admirations did not go to her head, and she always maintained a gracious and modest bearing. Neighbors and family friends started visiting Nilofer's home seeking her advice for one or the other ailments. She willingly examined them and even suggested remedies for minor ailments. However, if she diagnosed a major illness, she would tell the patient to seek treatment from a qualified doctor.

"But Doctor *bitiya,* if you know my ailment why don't you prescribe the medicine?" She had become doctor *bityia* to the elders and doctor *aapa* to those who were younger to her.

She often volunteered to take them with her to the hospital and got them treated by her teachers. Gradually the number of people seeking her help increased and there was hardly a day when one or more patients did not accompany her to the hospital. Her grandfather's car, which used to drop her at the hospital every morning, came to be known as Dr. Nilofer's ambulance. Poor driver had now the extra duty of waiting until her patients had been attended upon, and then ferry them back to their respective homes. The grandfather too, was often denied the use of his car. When her uncle Hameed Maamu came down from Lahore in February 1962, to attend a convention of his party, he was surprised at the number of people coming to her for advice and help.

"You are still to qualify as a doctor, yet you have such a large following. You could become an invaluable vote bank in politics."

"Can you not think beyond your petty politics?" said his father.

"Petty politics!" exclaimed Hameed, "Abba, you can't even begin to imagine how lucrative the business of politics has become in this country. The popular doctors, sports persons, cine artists and the like are big assets in this business."

"God forbid that I shall ever become a pawn in the hands of politicians," Nilofer said, but only in her mind. She could not anticipate, at that time, that one day she would be obliged by the circumstances to offer herself as a pawn in politics.

Her grandfather, Mirdad of Uchaanwala village, died in November that year. Nilofer insisted on accompanying Ashraf Naana on the long journey to the village to offer condolences to the family of her late father. She was returning to the village fourteen years after she had left it as a child of eight. She had only vague memories of her childhood. They alighted from the train at the Mandi-Bahauddin railway station, and took a horse carriage to the village. When the carriage crossed the bridge over the canal on the western boundary of the village, an old memory flashed through her mind. She was sitting on the edge of the bridge when some one, probably her cousin Phallu, had pushed her from behind, throwing her into the deep water. She vividly remembered, even now, the horrifying choking sensation of drowning. A friend of hers had jumped in, and had rescued her. She tried to recall his name, but in spite of prodding her mind hard, she could not remember it. On arriving at the haveli, her luggage was taken to the terrace room, where she was to put up during her stay. A faint musty smell assailed her nostrils as she entered it. It had not been aired sufficiently. The window was shut to keep the winter chill out. She pulled open the shutters. Involuntarily, her hand shot out through the grill. Then she slowly withdrew it. She closed her eyes. The picture of her childhood friend passing a food packet through it arose in her mind. She pensively walked out onto the terrace and peered into the compound of the adjoining house, half expecting to see her friend. No one was there. She again strived to remember her friend's name. She could not. She had completely forgotten it.

She had almost forgotten her own name. It was only when her relatives started addressing her as Fatima did she remember that it was her name until she had left the village. Her stay in the village was short; only three days, but for those three days, she had become Fatima again.

*****

She completed her MBBS in 1964, again with the top rank. She was given a provisional certificate of having passed the examination, and was allowed to use the title of doctor, and write prescriptions for the patients. Nevertheless, as the rules required, she had to put in six months of a rural internship before the degree would be conferred on her. Her grandfather threw a lavish party to celebrate the occasion. Hameed Mamu came down with his family. He again repeated his opinion about her being a potential vote bank. This time it was not a casual remark but a serious proposition.

"You come down to Lahore and I will build a hospital for you. A bit of charity work by my niece would enhance my vote bank considerably, and would boost my standing in the party high command."

"But Mamu Jaan," said Nilofer, "in order to run a hospital I shall have to study for three more years and specialize as a gynecologist."

"You come down to Lahore, and I shall see that no one prevents you from further study."

Nilofer had no desire to go to Lahore, and help build her uncle's vote bank. She had decided to do her post graduation from Karachi itself. However, for the civility's sake she said,

"I am not sure whether the Lahore University will give me an eligibility certificate if I was to migrate from the Karachi University"

"You leave all that to your uncle. I can pull all the necessary strings."

"Uncle, I still have to complete six months of rural service before I get my degree. I can apply for migration only after that."

"That's fine by me. You make the application after you get your degree and send me a copy of it. I shall do the rest."

"I shall do that," Nilofer said without the slightest intention of doing it. She was happy in Karachi with her doting grandparents. Little did she know that she would be compelled to do exactly that before the year ended.

On a cold winter night of December, the same year, Ashraf Naana died in his sleep. She was heartbroken, but had to put up a brave face for the sake of her grandmother, who was inconsolable in her grief, and needed all the moral support that Nilofer could give. Hameed Mamu flew in from Lahore for the funeral, and to be by the side of his mother and niece. After the mortal remains of his father were consigned to the grave, and other rituals completed, he held consultations with his mother and Nilofer about their future. It was obvious to the three of them that Nilofer and the grandmother could not continue to live in Karachi by themselves. It was equally obvious that they would have to shift to Lahore with Hameed. It was decided to wind up Ashraf's business and sell the house. This should take about six months, and this interval would give Nilofer the opportunity to complete her internship. Gul Mian, the loyal manager of Ashraf, and a good family friend, was given the task of winding up the business, and disposal of the house. Gul Mian offered to buy the business for himself, provided the family agreed to a piecemeal payment in easy installments. This the family readily agreed to. The house was put up for sale, and a sale deed was finalized in just two months, with an understanding that the possession will be handed over in the month of June. Nilofer completed her internship in the first week of June 1965. She applied to the Karachi University for permission to migrate to the Lahore University to pursue her postgraduate studies. She made a similar application to the Lahore University, and requested for an eligibility certificate. She was afraid the action on her applications might be delayed, because of the ongoing Indo-Pak hostilities. Fortunately, due to the political influence of her uncle Hameed, there was no hitch, and on the first day of July, she joined her duties as a junior house officer in obstetrics and gynecology at the Medical College for women and the Mohamedia Hospital of Lahore.

Nilofer saw an announcement, tucked in a corner of the college notice board, inviting applications from the postgraduate students of obstetrics and gynecology for a two-year scholarship of Commonwealth University whose offices were located in London. That afternoon she obtained a copy of the relevant brochure, and a form of application from the college office. She was going through the brochure while sipping tea in the college canteen, when Naseem walked in, and threw herself in the chair next to her friend, with an audible sigh.

"I am so-o-o-o tired," she said, "What are you reading?" Naseem was the senior house officer in the same unit in which Nilofer was working, the unit of Dr. Nikkhat Aazmi, an honorary Obstetrician and gynecologist attached to the college and the hospital.

"These are the rules for the commonwealth scholarship."

"Are you going to apply for it?"

"Yes."

"Will your parents agree to send you abroad?"

"I have no parents. I live with an uncle and aunt. As to whether they will agree to my going abroad, well, I don't know. I do not even know whether I will be awarded the scholarship. Nevertheless, I do know that I should apply. Rest is for the future to decide.

She had hardly completed three months at her new posting when an unforeseen hurdle was put in the path of her career. Her auntie informed her that a proposal was being considered for her marriage into the family of Akbar Ali, a prominent political leader of the area, and a heavy- weight member of the party. Nilofer was aghast.

"But auntie... my studies...?" She stammered in anguish.

"Tell that to your uncle. It is he who is so keen on this marriage."

She hesitatingly took up the matter with her uncle.

"Uncle, please let me finish my studies first," she pleaded.

"Rest assured girl, the marriage will not come in the way of your studies. Your in-laws are agreeable to your continuing the studies after marriage."

"But what is the hurry, uncle?"

"Look here Nilofer, I cannot miss this opportunity. You do not understand what this bonding of our two families would mean to me in the political hierarchy. You too stand to gain immensely. Mahmood is the only son of his parents, and an heir to a farming empire."

Nilofer needed no pecuniary gain from marriage. Her grandfather's bequest had left her comfortably off. However, she could see that her uncle had made up his mind, and no pleading on her part was going to budge him from his resolve. She compressed her lips and rolled up her eyes in futile anger and despair.

"So I am to be a pawn in the game of politics," Nilofer thought. For the first time she felt envious of the girls of the western world, who decided for themselves when and whom to marry. Here she was being compelled to marry when she was not ready for it, and to wed a man she had never met. All they told her was that her prospective husband had received education up to matriculation, and that he was a handsome and healthy young man. As a gesture of concession to her, they showed her a photograph of his. He did look handsome and young in the picture.

"Do you, Nilofer Banoo, daughter of Wazeer Ahmed, agree to be bound in marriage to Mahmood Khan, son of Akbar Ali against a *mehr* of ten thousand rupees? *Aap ko qubool hai?*" The cleric had asked her at the ceremony of *Nikah*,

"Yes," Nilofer had replied.

"If you are agreeable to this union, Banoo Nilofer, please say *qubool hai.*"

"Qubool hai," she had said

Thus, she was bound in marriage to a Mahmood Khan, an entity she knew nothing about.

Choudhry Akbar Ali was a middle rung but influential farmer of Shekhupura. His influence emanated from his political standing. He was the elected representative of *Tehrik-e-Kaashtkaar* of the district. He and his close relatives owned large farmlands in the surrounding villages of Mianwala, Shah Kot, Jaranwala, and Bhai Pheru. The Sikh Farmers of the region owned much larger farmlands in these villages. In 1945, the merger of the Tehrik-e-Kaashtkaar into the Harkat-e-Ittehad-e Musalmeen-e-Hind enhanced the political influence of Choudhry. He was elevated to the position of one of the three provincial general secretaries of the party. He had a further and much bigger windfall when the new nation state of Pakistan was carved out of India, and the Radcliff Award for drawing its boundaries was announced. Shekhupura District was allocated to Pakistan. This led to a widespread communal strife, and the Sikh farmers fled their homes, abandoning their vast farmlands and crossed over to the Indian side. Using his political power and bribing the *patwaris,* Choudhry got the land records doctored to show the larger of the abandoned farms as his own, and his relatives' properties. The fraud came to the notice of the authorities in January 1951, and they ordered the setting up of an inquiry commission. By this time, Akbar had acquired a very influential position in his party, now renamed the Harkat-e-Ittehad-Musalmeen-e-Pakistan. The first elections for the provincial assembly of Punjab were held in March 1951. Akbar Ali contested the election from the rural constituency of Lahore, while Hameed, who was the provincial president of the *Harkat,* contested from the urban constituency. Both of them won with large majority. Both put up claims to the chief minister's chair. Hameed had the support of his mentor, Mohamed Hayaat Khan, the national president of the party. Choudhary knew that with Hayaat backing Hameed, his chances were dim. So, shrewd politician that he was, he met his adversary, one to one, and offered to withdraw from the contest on the condition that Hameed help him with the inquiry commission. Hameed gave his word. As it transpired, the provincial government never came into existence. The whole election was countermanded amidst charges of rigging. Nevertheless, Hameed kept his promise. He used his proximity to the officialdom, and made sure that the inquiry commission never materialized. All the related files disappeared, leaving Choudhury unblemished and a millionaire in the bargain.

To remain at the centrestage of politics, Chowdhry decided to shift from Shekhupura to Lahore. He built a large, tastefully planned, and elegantly furnished house in the exclusive residential locality of Gulberg, and named it Nehmat. He shifted his family from Shekhupura to the new house in Lahore on 6 June of 1956, the twentieth birth anniversary of his son, Mahmood.

*****

Twenty years back, when Chowdary was still an average farmer and a novice politician of Shekhupura, the birth of a son on 6 June 1936 was an occasion for rejoicing for the family. On three earlier occasions, when his wife Rehana Bibi was pregnant, he had hoped for the birth of a son. Each time he had been disappointed with the arrival of a daughter. When Rehana was expecting the fourth time, her husband remained on edge throughout her pregnancy. He was convinced that his wife was incapable of producing a male child. After she had borne three daughters one after the other, he had even contemplated taking a second wife. The thought of hurting the tenderhearted Rehana, who had served him devotedly for almost fifteen years, had deterred him from translating the thought into action. When against all hopes, the midwife in attendance at Rehana's labor, announced the arrival of a son, he promptly left his house and went to the eatery adjoining the main mosque. He ordered feeding of all the beggars who had queued up in front of it. He then entered the mosque and asked the *Mullah* to offer a special namaaz of thanks for the boon of a son Allah had bestowed upon him. He deposited one hundred rupees into the coffers of the mosque and returned home to view his son. Forty days later, the town quazi, after offering prayers, breathed into the child's face and named him Mahmood Khan. This was followed by the *sunnat* of the child, the mandatory circumcision. Akbar Ali celebrated the occasion by inviting relatives and friends to a grand feast in the evening.

Infant Mahmood became the centre of the family's attention. He was the apple of his mother's eye. Her life now revolved around him. Her eyes were constantly on the wall clock. She saw to it that the maidservant massaged him twice daily on schedule, with the scented oil especially brought from Lahore, that she bathed, fed, and put the child to sleep according to a fixed timetable.

Mahmood was growing into a robust and healthy infant. His first birth anniversary was celebrated on a lavish scale. Many of the friends and relatives who attended the function commented on the good looks of the birthday baby. About a fortnight after the festivities, the child started running a mild fever. The local medical practitioner tried various remedies but the temperature did not go down. Akbar Ali thought of consulting Dr Bhagatsingh, a famed physician of Lahore. Rehana insisted on taking the child to the monk, Fakeer Saain Khuda Baksh of the village Bhai Pheru. She was convinced a pat of the *saain* on the child's back would rid him of the evil eye which some guest must have cast on him at the time of his birthday fete. The next day they placed the child at the feet of the *fakeer* invoking his divine intervention in banishing the evil eye. The *fakeer* closed his eyes, and murmured a prayer under his breath. He then gave a gentle thump on the child's back and bellowed,

"*Jah Bachche, teraa Allah Beli*"

Akbar put his hand in his shirt pocket intending to offer money to the fakeer. The fakeer shooed him away with a loud "*Allah hoo Akbar.*"

As they were returning home in a horse carriage, the child suddenly became stiff in the mother's lap, and started convulsing. Rehana shrieked in fright. Akbar looked at his quivering son in disbelief and helplessness. The shuddering soon subsided and the child went limp. By the time they reached back home, the child had recovered considerably. The local doctor advised them to take the child to a hospital in Lahore without delay.

The next day Akbar Ali and his wife boarded a bus with their child, and after three-hour journey arrived at the Sir Ganga Ram Hospital, attached to the Balakram Medical College, on the Queen's Road of Lahore. They had never been to such a large hospital before. Akbar Ali had to stand in a serpentine queue to have a new case paper issued. Then he was guided to clinic No. 3, exclusively meant for children. Here, after a long wait, Mahmood was examined first by a group of medical students, and then by a junior doctor before being sent to the specialist's chamber. The pediatrician, Dr. Prahlad Bedi looked at the notes made by his junior and carried out a quick check up of the baby. Then he turned to Akbar and said in a sympathetic tone,

"I am sorry to inform you that your child is having a serious infection of the brain. We need to admit him to the hospital for treatment, and for carrying out necessary tests on him.

"Doctor, how long will he have to remain in the hospital?" Akbar asked.

"Well, it could be a week, may be ten days, and even two weeks, depending on how he responds to the treatment."

Akbar agreed for the hospitalization. A hospital attendant accompanied them to the children's ward, and handed them over to the nurse in charge. Akbar noticed that all the beds were occupied, and a couple of children were lying on beddings spread on the floor. A ward servant spread similar bedding on the floor, and the nurse instructed Akbar to lay the child on it. He requested her to allot them a bed, considering the child's age and the seriousness of his illness. The nurse expressed her inability to do so. When in the afternoon, the junior doctor came to the ward, Akbar pleaded with him for the allotment of a bed. The doctor too ignored his request. Leaving his son and wife in the ward, Akbar went to meet Akhtar Hussein, the current chairperson of their party, *Tehrik-e-Kaashtkaar*. Fortunately, Akhtar Hussein lived nearby and was at home at the time. He was aware of the influence that Akbar wielded over the farmers of the Shekhupura District. He greeted his visitor warmly. Akbar apprised him of the difficulties he was having at the hospital,

"My one year old child having a serious brain disease has been dumped on the floor of the ward." Tears welled up in his eyes as he narrated his plight.

Without a word, Akhtar Hussein picked up the telephone and dialed a number. When it was answered, he said authoritatively,

"This is Akhtar Hussein of *Kaashtkaar*. Get me the Director of the Medical Services." After a short wait he spoke again,

"Dr. Sodhi, a dear friend of mine has brought his seriously sick little son to the Gangaram Hospital. The child is not receiving proper care. See that he is looked after well."

He listened for a few moments, before speaking again,

"The father's name is Chowdhry Akbar Ali. He is from Shekhupura." He hung up.

Akbar Ali noticed that during the whole conversation with the Director, Akhtar had not uttered a single word of salutation, nor so much as a *please* or a *thank you*. It was a rude terse order.

When he returned to the hospital, he did not find his child and wife in the ward. The nurse hurried to him and said with deference,

"Sir, the child has been moved into a special room. May I please show you to the room?"

Akbar found Mahmood lying on a freshly-made bed in a comfortable well-furnished room with an attached bath. There was an extra couch for the attendant, a small table, a couple of padded chairs, and a chest of drawers. There was a bell push to summon a ward servant, or a nurse. Akbar marveled at the power that the politicians wielded. That day he made a decision. He would take a more active interest in politics.

The next morning a whole string of doctors descended upon Mahmood, and gave him a thorough check up. When they had finished, the junior doctor stayed back and talked to Akbar Ali.

"We will be sending Mahmood for an X-ray check up. We will also get his blood examined. We need to tap his spine. For that, we need your permission. Will you please sign this consent form?"

The doctor saw a look of incomprehension in Akbar's face, and hastened to explain,

"We'll introduce a fine needle in his spine and withdraw a small amount of fluid that covers the brain. This will be examined in the laboratory to find out the type of infection that Mahmood is suffering from."

Akbar signed the proffered paper.

A few days later, an eye specialist was called in to examine Mahmood. Akbar had known Dr. Jasbir Singh only by his reputation. He held a British qualification, and was perhaps the best eye specialist of the province. He had very pleasing manners that put the patients and their relative at ease. After examining the child, he made some notes in the case file. Then putting his hand on the shoulder of the distraught father he said,

"Have faith, the almighty *Waheguru* will be compassionate."

When all the reports were in, Dr. Bedi called Akbar to his private office. The doctor asked him to take a seat. Akbar Ali guessed, from the doctor's demeanor, that he was about to deliver bad news.

"We have now all the reports of your son. They indicate that the child has tuberculosis of the brain…"

Akbar felt faint, but kept a brave face.

"…The infection has affected the nerves of his eyes, and he has lost his vision…"

Akbar could no longer keep control on his emotions. He lowered his head on to the doctor's desk. His shoulders heaved, as he sobbed. The doctor came round the table, and laid his hand on Akbar's shoulder.

"... Dr. Jasbir Singh is a very competent eye specialist. His opinion is that if we quickly bring the infection under control, your child has good chances of recovering his eye sight."

Akbar struggled to recover his composer. He raised his head, and looked pleadingly at the doctor. Dr. Bedi resumed his seat.

"Trust us Akbar Sahib, we have already started a vigorous treatment, and we'll do all that we can for your child. Have faith in *Parmatma*, the merciful."

Mahmood stayed in the hospital for over a month. His mother grumbled that the doctors had turned her little baby into a sieve, piercing his body with countless needles. She cursed the nurses for stuffing the little one with so many medicines. Nevertheless, as the days went by, Mahmood, who had been reduced to a bag of skin and bones, started putting on weight, and showing general improvement. The doctors tapped his spine two more times during the month, and the last report declared the spinal fluid free of infection. His eyesight returned too, though the ophthalmologist was unable to pronounce the degree of recovery. That will have to wait until the child was old enough to participate in the tests. Dr. Bedi permitted him to leave the hospital with the strict instructions to the parents to continue the treatment for at least nine more months, and bring him to the hospital for periodical check ups. At the age of two years, the doctor pronounced him free of the disease.

"Doctor, my child is two years now. He has not yet spoken a single word. Don't children usually start speaking at an earlier age?" A worried Rehana Bibi had asked Dr. Bedi.

"Don't worry Bibi, some children do start late."

Mahmood spoke his first word "*Aana*" at the age of twenty-seven months. He probably was saying *Rehana.* That was what he had been hearing his father call his mother. The child, to all appearances, progressed like any other child, except that he stammered a bit when he was excited or angry. His father admitted him to a school at the age of five. His progress at school was tardy. He was always among the lowest ranked students at the exams. His father blamed the poor performance of the child on his mother's pampering. By the time he reached the fifth grade, his teachers gave him up as a hopeless case. They stopped taking interest in him, but continued to promote him to the next grade for two more years because of the growing political influence of his father. The annual examination for the seventh grade was conducted by the District Education Board. The headmaster of the school urged Mahmood's father to withdraw him from the school, telling him that the child could never clear the board exam. Akbar consulted Dr. Bedi who had treated Mahmood in his infancy. The doctor studied the old file, and said,

"My professional opinion is that the infection in his childhood has partly damaged that part of his brain which is linked with intellect. My advice to you is not to push the child too hard in his studies. He should be capable of performing non scholarly tasks without much difficulty."

Akbar Ali was heartbroken, but he was a man of practical wisdom. He discontinued Mahmood's school and started taking him to the farms with him. To Akbar's delight, his son took interest in farming right from the first day. The teachers at school had complained that Mahmood lacked concentration in his lessons. Here at the farm, he listened attentively to his father issuing instructions to the farm hands, and watched keenly various tasks being performed by them. By the age of fifteen, he could affectively manage the farms when his father had to be away on his political tours. By this time, the family's holding of farmlands was the largest in the Shekhpura district by virtue of Akbar acquiring, illegally though, the fields of the Sikh farmers who had fled their home after the partition of the country.

Mahmood's father taught him horse riding, so that he could easily move from farm to farm, and commute between his home and the farms. Although the boy now could run the day-to-day chores of farming, his father had one major worry. Mahmood lacked initiative and imagination. He carried out the routine chores, and could perform the tasks, which he had seen others perform, but taking a decision on his own was beyond him. He could only tread the beaten tract.

Akbar recalled Dr. Bedi's opinion on the intellectual capabilities of his son.

Mahmood was in his nineteenth year when he had his first episode of epileptic seizure. He had not liked the lunch that his mother had placed before him. He flew into a rage. This was nothing new. He often lost his temper at seemingly insignificant matters. That day in the middle of angry ravings, he abruptly fell silent. His mother looked up sharply and saw him lurch on one side and fall to the floor. Before she could react, her son went into a fit of convulsions. She screamed, and her husband hurried into the kitchen. He saw his son's condition and quickly removed one of his own shoes and held it to his son's nose. Within a few minutes, the seizure subsided and Mahmood went limp. Shortly he opened his eyes and then slowly sat up. His father helped him to his bed and asked him to lie down, and covered him with a light blanket. Mahmood slept until next morning.

Akbar Ali decided to have Mahmood checked up at the same hospital of Lahore where he had been treated in his childhood. He had to hunt for his old file all over the house. He and his wife were sure they had preserved it, but could not remember where. After two hours' hunt, they found it in an old metal trunk along with the toys, which they had purchased for baby Mahmood, sixteen, seventeen years back. The file bore the faded name of Sir Ganga Ram Hospital, and contained reports yellowed by age. Akbar knew that the hospital had been renamed as Fatima Jinnah Hospital after the new nation state of Pakistan had come into existence. Dr. Bedi, who had treated Mahmood earlier, and most of other old doctors were not there anymore. They had crossed over to the Indian side. The hospital was still one of the largest hospitals in the country. Akbar took his son and the file to the senior most physician of the Hospital, Dr. Imtiyaz Saiyad, who received him with deference. This time he did not need a recommendation of any politician. He himself was well recognized as an eminent member of the Harkat. Dr. Saiyad read the old file, gave Mahmood a thorough check, and ordered some investigations, which included an electro encephalogram, a newly added gadget to the hospital. He patiently explained to Akbar that the seizure was an aftermath to the brain infection that Mahmood had had in his childhood; that the seizures were likely to recur, but could be kept under control by medication which he would have to take all his life.

"But doctor, isn't there a permanent cure?" Akbar had asked.

"No, as of today, there is no permanent cure of his condition."

"Is the condition dangerous?"

"If the seizures continue unchecked, they can be dangerous. They can result in further damage to the brain. They can even be fatal. I suggest that you start with the prescribed medication right from today. If he gets another seizure, come back to us and we will readjust the dose. One thing more, Akbar Sahib, keep him away from fire and machinery."

Akbar returned to Shekhupura with his son, a heavy heart, and a new file, which bore the name of Fatima Jinnah Hospital. The first line, on the first page of the file read -An old case of Koch's meningitis, treated by Dr. Bedi of Gangaram Hospital in 1937.

In the next six months, Mahmood had two more attacks of seizure, once at a wedding party and second time at the farm. The people around had started talking about Mahmood getting attacks of *mirgi*. Akbar and his wife feared that if their son's condition received a wide publicity, it would have an undesirable affect on the prospect of his marriage. They decided to leave the town and move to Lahore where they had already built a large house. The large city would offer Mahmood a better cover from the prying eyes of friends and relatives, and better conditions for his treatment. They moved to their new house on Mahmood's twentieth birth anniversary.

Around this time, Mahmood started drinking in the company of a couple of young farmhands. To the delight of these farm workers, Mahmood replaced their country hooch with the Scotch Whiskey. Mahmood had seen his sister's husband, Major Bashir consume the brand. Though he still had seizures, they were now infrequent and far apart. He never had one while riding a horse or the bike. Actually, in five years time he promoted himself from riding a bike to driving a jeep. He was now almost twenty-six. His parents had not yet found a suitable bride for him. By now, most of their close relatives and friends had come to know of his *mirgi*, and were unwilling to offer their daughters in marriage to him. When Akbar and Rehana had almost given up hopes of acquiring a daughter- in- law, one was offered to them unsolicited. It was an invaluable gift presented to them on a gold platter.

*****

It was the evening of the Thursday, 23 September 1965. The core group of the *Harkat* had met at the residence of Akbar Ali to discuss the fall out of the cease-fire between the Indian and Pakistan forces, under the aegis of the United Nations. They were concerned about the Soviet Union's conciliatory moves in the matter. At the conclusion of the deliberations, when Akbar was seeing Hameed off, a fast moving jeep came to a screeching halt before the gate of the house. A handsome looking young man alighted from it and walked into the compound. As he approached them, he wished them with a polite Aslaam alaikum.

"He is my son Mahmood Khan."

Akbar had made a perfunctory introduction and the youth had walked on into the house. The next day Hameed had made discreet inquiries about Mahmood from a couple of young members of the party. They could not tell him much, except that he was the only son of the family; that he was still unmarried; and that he spent most of his time at Shekhupura, managing the farms of his father. For Hameed this much information was more than enough. Mahmood was still single, and a handsome son of the general secretary of the party, and sole heir to a farming empire. It sounded a sweet music to his ears. He took an instant decision, and made an appointment for meeting Akbar.

"I have come to put a proposal to you," he had said to Akbar, when they met.

Akbar became instantly alert. He very well knew Hameed's political maneuvers. He wondered what game he was up to.

"Let's have it, friend." He had said, keeping a cautious façade.

"I don't like you calling me a friend."

This unusual and rude statement by his party co-worker took Akbar aback.

"Are you proposing that we break our friendship?"

"Allah forbid, Akbar Sahib, what I am proposing is that we promote ourselves from friends to relatives."

"Pardon me, I don't understand."

"Alright, let me put it concisely, and precisely. I am asking for your son's hand in marriage for my niece."

Akbar did not make an immediate reply. He sat in a thoughtful pose for a while. Then looking into Hameed's eyes, he asked,

"Isn't your niece a doctor? A match between a doctor and a school drop out...."

Hameed did not let him finish,

"What has education to do with bringing up a progeny? Besides, Akbar Sahib, think of the power we two will wield in the party once our families are thus united."

Akbar reflected for a while and then asked,

"Do you think we should let the two see each other?"

"That's not the done thing in my family, Akbar sahib. If your son wants to see Nilofer, I can arrange for him to view her, without her being aware of it,"

"That won't be necessary, but we should at least let them see each other's photographs."

"My family shall have no objection to that."

Three days later, a brief function was held at Hameed's residence. Only the women relatives of Akbar and Hameed were present. Mahmood's mother had draped a red *chunni* over Nilofers head, put a sweet *bataasha* in her mouth, and placed gifts in her lap, thus solemnizing the betrothal of her son Mahmood to Nilofer. The male relatives had a separate meeting later, and fixed a date for the *Nikah* a fortnight on.

Within days, friends and relatives of both families started arriving, and the ceremonies and the festivities were in full swing. Akbar's youngest son-in-law, Bashir Ahmed arrived from Muridabad with his family. He was a major in the Pakistan Army, and had obtained a five-day leave with difficulty because of the ongoing Indo-Pak hostilities. He was aware of the ailment from which Mahmood had suffered in his childhood, and the consequent epileptic seizures. On gentle probing, he discovered that Mahmood was quite ignorant about the physical relation between man and woman. True to his army training, he took an instant decision. He took Mahmood to the *kotha* of Zohrabai in the red light area of Lahore. Zohrabai was a cream of the crop prostitute, and catered to the customers only from high society of the city. When she was informed that the son and the son-in-law of Akbar Ali wished to see her, she presented herself immediately.

"The slave awaits your orders sir." She bowed low to her visitors.

Bashir Ahmed began in a measured tone, "This is my brother-in-law, Mahmood. He is to get married in a couple of days. He is innocent of ...ah... of man woman relation. Will you instruct him... in...in..." He failed to find subtle words for what he wanted to say, and blurted out, "Instruct him in what he is supposed to do ... on his nuptial night."

"It shall be the slave's pleasure, sir." Then holding Mahmood by his arm, she said, "Please come with me, my charming prince." She took Mahmood with her to her chamber.

Once inside her chamber, Zohra dropped all pretence at politeness. "So young man, you need instructions on how a man takes a woman on the nuptial night?"

Ten minutes later Zohra was back in the presence of Bashir.

"Rest assured sir, the bridegroom is fully instructed, and quite capable of performing the rituals of the *shab-e-aroosee.*" She did not lack delicate vocabulary.

The Quazi pronounced Nilofer and Mahmood as husband and wife, after extracting *qubool hai-* "I accept" from both of them. The *nikah nama*, the marriage certificate, was issued on 23 September of the year 1965, the day on which the five-week war between Pakistan and India ended, and all battlefields fell silent. That night Nilofer's mind became a battleground, where a relentless hostility erupted against the male dominated society. It started when her bridegroom wielded his skill at taking a woman instantly, a skill that Zohra bai had taught him in the ten minute tutoring session.

When the bridegroom had started snoring, a stunned Nilofer had got out of bed and walked into the bathroom. She had torn her pajama top off in a fit of revulsion and had stood under the shower for a long time, her tears getting lost in the gush of the shower as rain drops get lost in a flowing river. She felt invaded and defiled. She scrubbed herself, repeatedly, inside and out. She almost scraped the skin off her body, but there was no way of decontaminating her soul. She squatted on the floor of the bathroom and wept silently until the light of dawn came filtering through the ventilators.

She changed into fresh clothes and listlessly descended the stairs. Her mother-in-law was already up, and was brewing tea. She handed a cup to Nilofer and said,

"Mamdoo must still be sleeping." She called her son *Mamdoo* when she wanted to show indulgence towards him.

Nilofer could only nod her head in confirmation. She sat down on a chair and took a sip from her cup. She choked on it, and almost threw up. She swiftly left the kitchen to hide her distress from the mother-in-law.

Nilofer remained in a daze for a couple of days, incapable of thinking straight. She moved around in the house like a ghost. She silently watched the childish behavior of her husband, throwing tantrums over small matters, and refusing to eat meals when an item of his liking was absent on his plate. His mother fussed over him as if he was a three-year-old child. Nilofer noticed that she had to coax him every morning to take some medicine, and then put a tablet wrapped in a paper in his breast pocket, before he left for the farm, and pleaded with him not to forget to take it in the evening. When he returned in the night, she checked his pocket to make sure he had taken it. Nobody bothered to tell Nilofer what medicine her husband was taking. Neither did she care. She had a pressing problem of her own, which she had to take care of. On the second day following the wedding, when the male members had gone to the farm, she went into the hall, where the telephone was kept. She rang up her unit at the hospital, and asked for Dr. Naseem, her close friend. When she came on the line Nilofer said,

"Naseem this is Nilofer…"

"So the brand new bride at last got the time to …" Naseem started excitedly. Nilofer cut her off.

"Listen Naseem, and listen carefully…" Naseem sensed the grimness in her friend's voice. Nilofer was saying,

"Don't make any comment. Just listen and do as I tell you. I want you to come to my in-laws' place as soon as you can, and bring with you a set of cervical diaphragms of all the three sizes, and a tube of spermicidal jelly. I also want a three-month supply of contraceptive pills. I will be in my room upstairs." She disconnected the line.

When Naseem arrived, she asked Nilofer,

"Why this multi-pronged assault on your reproductive system?"

"You know Naseem; I intend to finish my postgraduation without any hindrance. I cannot risk pregnancy."

"But my dear friend, you very well know that the pills by themselves are quite an effective protection against conception, then why the diaphragm, and the jelly?"

"I want to make it cent percent safe."

"Have it your way," Naseem said, "I still say the diaphragm and the jelly are not necessary."

Nilofer very well knew that the pills were sufficient to protect her against pregnancy. What she could not tell her friend was that she had resolved not to permit a single droplet of the semen of that brute of her husband to enter her system. After the departure of her friend, Nilofer tried on all the three sizes of the diaphragm, and found that the medium size fitted her snuggly. She went on the pill immediately.

Every night of the week, following her marriage, Nilofer suffered the humiliation of *being taken.* Every night her husband – she hated even to think of him as husband – every night he would come home late in the night, when Nilofer was already in bed, half dead with fear of the impending defilement of her body and soul. Every night he wordlessly pulled down her dress and *took* her before falling to sleep. It was like a daily chore for him, like brushing his teeth before going to bed. Every night she used the diaphragm and the jelly. Every night she washed herself thoroughly, after her husband had fallen asleep.

By the end of the week, her leave of absence from duty ended, and she went back to her work at the hospital. Her in-laws were very unhappy at the resumption of her studies, but Hameed had, at the time of Nilofer's betrothal, extracted a commitment from Akbar that he would permit her to complete her post graduation. Initially Akbar had balked at the idea of his daughter-in-law continuing her education, but when Hameed had unfolded his political plans in which his niece would play a significant part, he had relented.

"My plan is to create a trust in yours and my name, Hameed-Akbar Charitable Trust. Then set up a free hospital for women in Shekhupura, under the aegis of the trust. By the time we build the hospital, your daughter-in-law will have qualified as a gynecologist. We will appoint her the superintendent, and the chief gynecologist. We could invite a couple of other gynecologists to join as honorary staff. I have already discussed the plan with Altaf Ali, the chief advisor to the President, General Ayub. He has assured me that once we get our trust registered, he will persuade the president to allot the required land from the government holding. The fund raising for the project shall be no problem for you and me. Imagine the political gains that you and I stand to gain from this project. The hospital will cater to the whole countryside around Shekhupura. General Ayub, I am told confidentially, is planning to lay down his office, and call for the general election in two years' time. By that time, we will have created one of the largest vote banks in the state through this project."

Akbar Ali was thrilled with this plan. He readily agreed to let Nilofer continue her studies.

Back on duty, Nilofer had tried to drown her sorrows by flinging herself whole-heartedly into the grueling routine of a junior doctor. Naseem, her friend and colleague had noticed the sudden change in Nilofer. She had been an outgoing chirpy girl before she had gone on leave to get married. She had returned, a dejected, and gloomy shadow of her earlier self. Something inside her has died, Naseem thought. She recalled her earlier visit to Nilofer's house, when she had gone there to deliver the contraceptives demanded by her. Even then, she had noticed signs of melancholy in her colleague. She was certain her friend was not happy with her marriage. What had gone wrong? She considered asking her, but then decided against it. Some things are better left unspoken.

In the whole month of October, Nilofer was off duty only on two Sundays. She was loath to spend these two days at home, but decided not to stay away in order to avoid offending her in-laws. On the first occasion, she had to suffer the nightly humiliation at the hands of her husband. The second time, she was mercifully spared, as that day Mahmood did not return from the farm.

In the first week of November, she received a communication from the Commonwealth University of London, offering her a two-year scholarship. She was given a fortnight to confirm her acceptance. She was filled with hope and despair at the same time. Here was a hope of being spared the humiliation, at least for two years, and desperation at the thought that the family would never agree to her going abroad. For a full day, she mulled over the situation. She could not let this god sent opportunity slip through her fingers. "I must get away if I have to save my sanity. Only Hameed Mamu can prevail upon my in-laws to let me go, but why would Mamu intervene? He has no other interest except his political career." She decided to play on this weakness of her uncle. The next evening she invited herself to dinner at his house.

During the course of the meal, as Nilofer had expected, her uncle brought up the subject of the proposed hospital.

"When this dream hospital of mine becomes a reality, I want you to make it the most prestigious and sought after institution. I want the people of Shekhupura to be proud of the first Gynecologist of their district."

"Rest assured uncle," Nilofer said cunningly, "I will do everything in my power to come up to your expectations. But tell me uncle, how will your voters feel if your niece, managing your dream hospital, was to be a foreign trained gynecologist?"

Her uncle bit the bait.

"Is there any chance of your being trained abroad?"

"Well uncle, if you were to help me, I could train in Britain."

"What do you want me to do?"

Nilofer knew she had her uncle hooked. She decided to exploit his vanity.

"You know uncle; your niece…" She deliberately went on, referring to herself as his niece,

"...Your niece has been a meritorious student throughout her studies. The Commonwealth University of London has recognized her merit, and has offered her a two year scholarship at any hospital of her choice in the U.K.…" She persisted with half-truths.

"…You could help your niece in two ways. The first one is a left hand play for you, but the second may be a bit difficult even for you."

Nilofer noticed that she had succeeded in hurting her uncle's sensibilities.

"Come on girl, nothing is difficult for your uncle. Just say what you want me to do."

"You will have to expedite my relieving orders from the health ministry, and you will have to convince my in-laws for my going."

"You start your preparations for going. Leave the rest to me."

Having thus been maneuvered by Nilofer, her uncle went, full stream into action. Driven by his prodding, the health department cleared all her papers in just over a month, and issued a relieving order for 13 January.

As Nilofer had expected, there was an almost inflexible opposition from her in-laws to her leaving the shores of the country. However, Hameed dangled the same carrot of political gain in front of Akbar, which Nilofer had dangled before him. Akbar ultimately gave in, and his wife had no choice but to follow suit. To the utter surprise of Nilofer, nobody had bothered to ask for the opinion of her husband. He did not seem to count, and he appeared unconcerned.

Nilofer made an appointment with the British Council, and visited its office. She informed them of her plan to take a flight to London on 15 January. The Council had her passport stamped with the entry pass by the British High Commission, and also instructed their travel agents, Thomas Cook, to purchase her ticket for the BOAC flight that would leave Lahore on the morning of 15 January.

Nilofer had flown into the Heathrow Airport on the night of the fifteenth, and was in the office of Professor Wise in Cardiff, the next morning. Here she had met Dr. Vikram Kocher.

It was the night of 21 May 1966. After having her supper in the dining hall, Nilofer had gone to Vikram's room to help him pack. He was due to leave for India the next morning. The packing did not take long, as Vikram had already sorted out the items that had to go into different bags. In just over half an hour, his suitcase and duffel bag were packed, locked, and put aside. He left the handbag un-zipped, as a few items of daily use would have to be put in, the next morning. Nilofer had kept chattering about inconsequential matters all the while. Vikram knew her babble was a shield for the pain in her heart at the impending parting from him. She was resolutely holding back her tears. Once the task of packing was over, she could not hold back anymore. She turned her back to Vikram to hide the tears from him. He held her by her shoulders and turned her to face him. Lifting her chin, he brushed her lips with his, and then drank at the twin streams running down her cheeks. She gazed into his eyes for a long time before speaking.

"Tomorrow …" Vikram interrupted her,

"Tomorrow is not here yet, Nilu."

She smiled through her tears. Vikram never let her forget the virtue of living for today.

"That's my girl."

That night the two of them slept locked in each other's arms until the soft chimes of the alarm clock woke them up at half past five.

Vikram had booked, the previous day, a ticket for the rail cum coach service from Cardiff to Heathrow. He had ordered a taxi for going to the railway station. It arrived precisely at seven. He dissuaded Nilofer from accompanying him to the station. He arrived at the

Bombay Airport at five in the morning on 23 May, and was with his family, in Ahmedabad, the same evening.

The silver jubilee of the wedding anniversary of Dr. Manubhai Patel and Dr. Mehru Patel was celebrated on a grand scale. The function was held on the lawns of the Law Society Club. Almost the entire medical fraternity of Ahmedabad had turned up. Some of their old college mates who had settled in various towns of Gujarat, Maharashtra, Madhaya Pradesh and Rajasthan came down to felicitate the couple. The most heart-warming moment for Mehru was the arrival of her younger sister, Shireen, from Australia. After almost twenty years, Shireen's barrister husband, Aspi Abuwala had decided to ignore Mehru's excommunication from the Parsi community. He had not only permitted his wife to attend her sister's party, but had chosen to accompany her. This change of heart had occurred because of their daughter, Mehtab. She was an intellectual and lively girl, with liberal leanings, and a zest for life. She was the apple of her father's eyes. He loved her to the level of adoration. She fell in love, head over heals, with an Australian boy. They decided to get married. Her mother did not raise serious objections, as unlike her husband, she was not steeped in the orthodoxy. The father initially refused to approve the union of his daughter to a non-Parsi man, but ultimately gave in to the pleadings of his pet daughter. His capitulation to his daughter's will made him feel guilty towards his sister-in-law, with whom he had refused to have any dealings, because she had wed outside the community. As a gesture of atonement, he had now decided to travel to India, and attend her marriage anniversary celebrations.

Vikram and Mehru had received the couple at the airport. Vikram was struck by the resemblance of the two sisters, although Shireen was heavier, and looked older than her elder sister. Shireen was happy to see the mother-son relationship between Vikram and her sister. She had known that Mehru and her husband had undertaken the education of one of their employee's son, but now she saw that the relation between them went much beyond the benefactor and the benefited. When she heard Vikram addressing her childless sister as *ba,* she blessed the boy in her heart.

The attitude of Manubhai's sister, Saroj, towards this relationship was totally in contrast to that of Shireen. She winced at her brother calling Vikram *deekra,* son, or Vikram addressing him as *Bapuji*. Right from the beginning, she had disapproved of her brother's decision to take on the responsibility of educating a servant's son. When he had rung her up, in Leicester, and had given her the news of Vikram qualifying as a doctor, she had mocked him,

"Congratulations brother, there are plenty of beggars in the city of Ahmedabad. Why don't you pick one more and make him an I.A.S. officer?"

Manubhai had known his sister's disapproval of his and his wife's proximity to Shivram's family, yet her sneering remark had hurt him to the core.

"You are incorrigible," he had said and hung up.

Vikram was quite aware of her disapproval of himself, yet he had gone to see his *auntie* at her Leicester house, when he had arrived in Britain, three years ago. She had given him a cold reception, but her husband, Dr. Harshad Kothari had welcomed him warmly, and had asked him to call upon him for any help that he might need in the new place. Vikram had visited them on few more occasions when he had happened to be in their vicinity.

Now when Saroj arrived to attend her brother's function, she was appalled at the closeness between her brother and his servant, Shivram. She rubbed her eyes in disbelief when she saw the impressive house of Shivram standing next to that of her brother's. She said to her brother, within the hearing of Vikram,

"So brother, your servants first played on your sympathy, and induced you to finance their son's education. Now they are exploiting your penchant for charity, and are plundering your wealth."

"What makes you say that?'

"You tell me, Manubhai, from where did the wretched servants of yours get so much money to build such luxurious house."

"You keep calling them my servants. Let me tell you Saroj, they are my servants no more. They are masters of themselves. Let me also tell you, Shivram is not plundering my wealth. He is actually augmenting it."

"You expect me to believe that?"

"No, I don't. Still however, I will tell you that he earns for Mehru and me as much as we two earn for ourselves from our profession, if not more. This should give you an idea how much he must be earning for himself."

"And what does he do to earn that much?"

"He deals in real estate. Besides, he invests in profitable ventures."

"Does he invest your money too?" Without waiting for his answer, she continued,

"In that case your cheque books must be in his possession."

"Yes, cheque books, bank pass books, and all account books too."

"Then what can prevent him from transferring money from your accounts to his own or his family accounts?"

Manubhai was getting exasperated at his sister's inquisition, but continued to speak in a placating tone,

"You know Saroj, we wanted to give our banks a mandate to accept cheques signed by him on our behalf. The man firmly turned the suggestion down. He is honest to the core."

Saroj laughed wryly,

"O my poor simple-minded brother, you don't understand the craftiness of these scheming servants..."

"For heaven's sake, stop calling Shivram a servant," Manubhai had had enough. His anger overflowed the dam of his patience, "He is more than a brother to me. And if you think that your brother is a congenital idiot, please leave him to his fate."

Saroj had never seen her brother lose temper. She was aghast at his fury. At the same time, she was quick to realize that she had crossed the bounds of decency in persistently denigrating Shivram. She had failed to gauge the bond that had developed between him and her brother.

"Do as you wish. Who am I to interfere in your affairs?" She said with a poor grace, and marched off to the guest room.

Barring this fracas between Saroj and her brother, the function went off splendidly. Manubhai and Mehru moved around mixing with the guests and receiving their greetings. One of their friends, Dr. Shashank Shah who had come down from Nairobi, recited a short poem composed by him in Gujarati, wishing the couple a long companionship of seven lives. Mehru's eyes brimmed with tears. Her husband lovingly took her in his arms, and the guests applauded. A performing troup entertained the guests for the next one hour and then the guests moved into the dining enclosure. The buffet dinner consisted of the Gujarati, Punjabi, south Indian, and Mexican dishes. A police band played popular tunes while the guests helped themselves at the food counters. By the time the last guest had departed, it was almost midnight.

The next two days went in bidding goodbyes to the guests who had come from various places of the country, and from abroad. Saroj and her husband, Harshad, took the train to Bombay on the twenty-ninth night, and flew to London the next morning. At the railway platform, Mehru had wanted to offer some conciliatory words to sulking Saroj to mollify her, but Manubhai had dissuaded her with an imperceptible shake of his head. He knew Saroj would never understand their relation with the Kocher family.

Vikram had a whale of time in the company of Ba, Bapuji, Beji, and Bauji, for the next three days. He was due to leave on the night of 2 June. Mehru's sister, Shireen and her husband Aspi had stayed back, and Vikram drove them around the city for shopping. The most pleasant time for him was when the three families sat at the dining table, and exchanged pleasantries. At one of these sessions, Shivram had asked his son,

"Now that you have qualified as a surgeon, what are your future plans?'

"I don't know about future, I can only talk of the present."

His mother gave a sardonic look to her husband. Their son was parroting his father, making those absurd remarks that he used to make in his younger days – Mayaji, tomorrow is not here yet. Start living in today my dear.

Vikram was now addressing his Bapuji,

"I have applied for a registrar's job in plastic and reconstructive surgery. I am certain I will be selected. I hope to get my degree in two years' time. After that we shall see what the future holds for me."

Vikram's expressed desire to specialize in plastic surgery prodded Dr. Patel's memory and took him back to an incident that had taken place eleven years back. Vikram was then a sixteen-year young lad and was a witness to an unpleasant episode. He was just out of school. It was vacation time. He had accompanied Dr. Patel to his clinic as he frequently did in vacation. He sat quietly on a chair, and watched Dr. Patel deal with his patients. His Bapuji listened to them ever so patiently, put them at ease with his gentle talk while examining them. He often refused the fees when the patient was poor. In the course of his consultation, that morning, the nurse had ushered in a young man, around twenty-five years of age, and dressed in a farmer's attire. Dr. Patel addressed him by his name,

"Come, come Veljibhai, how is your son?"

The man did not answer. He walked up slowly and came to stand before the doctor's table. Vikram's keen eyes noticed the despair reflecting in his face. Dr. Patel asked him to sit down. The man took the seat, but remained silent. The doctor did not rush him into speaking. He too had fathomed his distress. The man put his hands on the table, crossed his wrists, lowered his head on to them, and burst into sobs. Dr. Patel came round the table and silently placed a gentle hand on the back of the sobbing figure. He had presumed that the man's child had died.

About a year back, Velji had brought his newborn son to Manubhai. The child had been born with a defective palate, a condition called the cleft palate. Manubahi had given Velji a note on Dr. Bhavan Jani, a specialist in plastic and reconstructive surgery. Now, after a year he was sitting in Manubhai's consulting room and sobbing

Velji slowly regained control over his emotions. He raised his head and said,

"My child is well doctor, but..." He could not continue.

Dr. Patel went back to his chair. Velji gradually collected himself and told his story.

Last year, when Manubhai had sent Velji's son to Dr. Bhavan, he had advised Velji to bring the child for surgery when he attained one year's age. Velji had asked him what the cost of the operation would be, and he had quoted five thousand rupees. Two weeks back Velji had returned with the child and Dr. Bhavan had operated on him. The parents were happy with the results of the surgery, but when Velji went to the administration office for making payment, the accountant handed him a bill for forty thousand rupees. He stared at the bill in disbelief.

"I...I was told the surgery would cost five thousand rupees." He was virtually stammering.

"Who told you that, and when?"

"Dr. Bhavan himself had given me that figure when he had advised surgery, last year."

"You know my friend, a lot of water has flown under the Ellis Bridge in one year," the man went on with a sarcastic smirk, "If you haven't noticed, let me tell you, this hospital has undergone a sea change in the last one year. It is no more a small clinic. It is now a super specialty hospital. Naturally, the costs have gone up. Your bill includes the super specialist's consulting fees, the operation charges, the operating theatre charges, the ten day stay charges, the nursing charges, the laboratory charges, the drug charges, the intra venous infusion charges, injection charges etc."

Velji comprehended very little of the list of charges reeled out by the accountant. All he knew was that he had expected an expense of around five thousand rupees for his child's surgery, and he had barely managed to put together a sum of eight thousand rupees. He offered seven thousand to the accountant and promised to pay the remaining later on.

"You make the full payment, and we shall discharge your son from the hospital," was the curt reply.

A helpless Velji returned to his village, and mortgaged his house. This fetched him a sum of twenty-five thousand rupees. He now had just over thirty two thousand. He offered the sum to the hospital, begging the accountant to forgo the remaining eight thousand. The accountant remained unmoved.

"Look here brother, this is a hospital, not a Friday Bazaar, where you can haggle. If you keep delaying the payment, the daily charges will keep on adding to your bill."

As a last resort, poor Velji had gone to Dr. Manubhai Patel, and had sobbed out his sad story. Vikram was listening to him as keenly as was his Bapuji. His face first showed an expression of bewilderment, then of sadness, and finally of anger. He was wondering how his Bapuji was going to react. Dr. Patel was sitting motionless with a reflective look in his face. He asked Velji to go into the reception room and wait. He picked up the intercom and asked Shivram to come to his consulting room. When Shivram arrived, he gave him the gist of Velji's story.

"Shiv, I want you to go with Velji to Dr. Bhavan's hospital. Make full payment of the bill with cash, not with a cheque. I do not want Dr. Bhavan to know who made the payment. After you have done that, I want you to drive Velji's family to Sanand, and retrieve his mortgaged house."

After Shivram had left, Dr. Patel instructed the nurse not to send in the next patient for a while. He leaned back in his chair and closed his eyes, his face wreathed with anguish. He soon recovered his composure, and finished his out patient work with his usual equanimity. When Vikram was sure that his Bapuji was his usual self, he asked him,

"Bapuji, why does Dr. Bhavan charge his patients so exorbitantly?"

Dr. Patel gave him a rather lengthy explanation but steeped in a tranquil voice.

"Bhavan had come to Ahmedabad about four years back after qualifying as a plastic and reconstructive surgeon from London. He had applied for a job at the medical college. He was turned down, as he had crossed the prescribed age for a government job. He then decided to set up his own practice. The people here knew nothing about him and his work, and no patient went to him for months. Dr. Bhavan approached various medical consultants and begged them to refer patients requiring reconstructive work to him. Some of us started sending patients to him, and were more than satisfied with his work. His skillful work gave him a good name and his practice flourished. However, his greed earned him neither good will nor respect. He is the only plastic surgeon in the whole of Gujarat, and exploits his monopoly. He has steadily increased his charges over the last two years, and hands his patients ridiculously inflated bills. We are loath to send patients to him, but we have no choice. The alternative is to send them to Bombay, but that would be extremely inconvenient to patients and the accompanying relatives and friends. We keep on sending patients to him and helplessly watch them being fleeced. This case of Velji is reprehensible."

Vikram pondered over Dr. Bhavan's unscrupulous dealings, and then surprised Dr. Patel by his next query.

"Bapuji, how many more years will I need to study if I want to become a plastic surgeon?"

Dr. Patel gave him an indulgent smile and said,

"Let us see; you'll need to put in two years of science, then five years for MBBS, three years of general surgery, and two more years of specializing in plastic surgery...um, how many year would that be?"

Vikram, who had been computing rapidly in his mind as his *bapuji* was giving out the duration of various courses, supplied the answer instantaneously.

"Twelve years."

"O yes. Quite a long duration, isn't it?"

Ten years had passed since then. Dr. Patel had almost forgotten his conversation with a sixteen-year-old Vikram. Now his expressed decision to specialize in plastic surgery brought back the memories of Velji's case. He understood the reason for Vikram's resolve.

"Look here son," he said, "We do not have to join issue with Dr. Bhavan Jani."

"No Bapuji, I have no intention of joining issue or competing with anyone. I only want to see that there are not too many Veljis around."

Vikram's reply had gladdened Dr. Patel's heart. He had turned to Shivram and inquired,

"Shiv, have you sold out the land that you had acquired at Sarkhez?

"No brother, it is still in my possession."

"Hold on to it. Our son may need to build a hospital on it in the near future."

Vikram smiled. He was tempted to say, the future is not here yet, but he held his tongue.

Vikram flew back into the Heathrow airport on 3 June. It was eight in the evening, London time. By the time he arrived at the Cardiff railway station, it was past midnight. He wondered whether a taxi would be available at the railway taxi stand, or would he have to phone the taxi service for one. His luggage was light, just a suitcase, and a carry bag. The empty duffle had gone into the suitcase, which itself was almost empty but for a couple of packages containing eatables. His mother had prepared *pinnis,* enough to last him for a month, and *Ba* had procured green *Chevda* from Baroda. He was so fond of that snack. He himself had picked up a dozen records of the choicest songs of Lata Mangeshkar, and Akhtari Begam's ghazals. These were a gift for Nilofer. He slung the carriage bag on his shoulder, picked up the suitcase and walked out of the station. The place was practically deserted, except for a young woman, probably French. She wore a full flowing knee length skirt, a wide lapelled shirt, and a Garbo hat. He could not make out the color of her dress, as it was indistinguishable under the sodium light. She must have come to pick up someone, he thought. He was the only passenger to alight from the train. Perhaps her passenger has missed the train. Poor girl! Coming out at this ungodly hour, only to be disappointed, he thought sympathetically. He noticed a couple of taxis in the stand, and started to walk towards them. As he drew near to the woman, she said,

"Want a lift monsieur?" Her speech was slurred.

Vikram thought, "My God, a hussy, soliciting at a British Railway station! It was an unheard thing. The British Police would never permit soliciting near a public place." He continued to walk, ignoring the woman. As he went past her, she started giggling, and then broke into a full-fledged laughter. Vikram stopped in his tacks. It was the tinkling laughter of his Nilofer. He dropped his luggage and swerved on his heals. Nilofer ran into his arms. They held on to each other for a long time, their lips locked together, oblivious to the time and the place. Vikram disentangled himself from her embrace, and held her at an arm's length to scrutinize her. Her face was radiant with happiness. Inexplicably, she looked a bit taller. Then he noticed her high heels. The lemon yellow skirt gripped her narrow waist, and hugged her not so narrow hips, bringing out her comely figure. The pink of her shirt was reflected in the delicate skin of her cheeks. She had learnt to dress well.

Vikram picked up his luggage and started walking towards the taxi stand.

"This way monsieur," Nilofer said pointing towards the car park. "Remember, I have offered to give you a lift."

"You have brought the car?" Vikram asked incredulously.

"Yes boss, I received my driving license this morning. Your lawful chauffeur is at your service." She bowed to him in mock humility.

"You don't seem to stop surprising me."

"Why, what other surprise have I given you?"

"The skirt…the high heels...and…" Nilofer interrupted him,

"Well, blame it on yourself. It is you who have made me so shameless, first the swim suit, then the trousers, and now kissing in public."

"Now, now, madam, don't you go about giving me the credit for everything. The skirt and the high heels is your idea."

"And kissing in public, whose idea is that?"

"I own up half the guilt, your ladyship." Vikram bowed low in mock humbleness.

Nilofer burst into her peculiar tinkling but subdued laughter. Vikram put his free arm around her waist and gave a gentle pressure. She led the way to the car. Vikram noticed her confident springy stride. How a happy frame of mind can alter the physical appearance, and the behavioral pattern in a person, thought Vikram. Gone was the sickly complexion, and the perpetual scowl from her face. Vikram had deliberately nudged her to take up swimming, modern dressing, driving, and acquiring prestigious professional qualification. These were small pushes to help her gain confidence in herself, and make her own decisions. They put Vikram's luggage on the back seat, and Nilofer drove them to their quarters. Vikram had had supper on the flight. He declined Nilofer's offer for food. He was tired. He took a hot bath and slept in Nilofer's bed that night. She watched him sleeping tranquilly for a long time. Just watching him made her heart flutter with happiness. She had missed him so much these last ten days.

Next morning Nilofer woke to the melodious tune of Lata Mangeshkar singing *Jaago Mohan pyaare.* She was thrilled to receive the gift of the records. Later, when Vikram served her breakfast of a pinni and green chevda, she was overcome with nostalgia, and tears rolled down her cheeks. The memories of her grandmother, and Karachi flooded her heart. Mamtaz Naani was so adept at making pinnis, and Nilofer had relished them so.

*****

Vikram's tenure as a registrar in general surgery was to end on 30 June. He had applied for the position of registrar in plastic and reconstructive surgery at three major hospitals of London, as well as at the University Hospital of Wales in Cardiff. He received intimations from the Lister Hospital and the Highgate Hospital, both of London, that they had short-listed him for the job, and would send him an interview call soon. He would have loved to spend the next two years in London. However, his true love was based in Cardiff. Hence, when the Cardiff hospital offered him the job, he accepted it unhesitatingly. He also let go his privilege for a free of rent room, and opted for a two-room apartment for which he was required to pay rent at a subsidized rate. The apartment building was a two-storey block, set slightly apart from other buildings of the campus. It consisted of four fully furnished residential flats with private showers and kitchens.

On 1 July, Vikram shifted to his new quarters on the first floor of the apartment building. Nilofer made the kitchen of Vikram's new quarters her personal fief. She started cooking all their evening meals there, except on the two days in the week when she was on call. Those two days, she had to remain near the phone, in her own room. They stacked up the small storeroom, attached to the kitchen, with groceries, and went shopping on weekends to replenish the refrigerator with vegetable, fruits, meats, eggs and other provisions. Having lived at the coastal town of Karachi in Pakistan, Nilofer was adept at cooking fish. The sizeable variety of fish available in Britain gave her many opportunities to dish out to Vikram a surprise assortment of seafood.

For the initial couple of weeks, Nilofer used to return to her room on most of the nights. Gradually, the new quarters of Vikram became a home for her, and she imperceptibly slipped into the role of a housewife. She was usually the first to return from the hospital. She used to promptly get into her working clothes, offer the Mughrib namaaz, and get busy in the kitchen. By the time Vikram arrived, she would have done most of the cooking. He would join her in the kitchen, but Nilofer would not brook his intervention in the cooking. He lent his helping hand in other chores, like laying the table, doing the dishes after meals, and keeping the flat tidy. After supper they would, over a mug of coffee, share their day's experiences. Nilofer had strictly set apart two hours in the evening for reading for her exams. By then it would be time for her Ishaa namaaz. The duo would retire to bed by eleven. They continued their routine of rising early and going for a swim. Back after the swim, Nilofer would offer the morning prayer, while Vikram would set their breakfast. They would get dressed and go off to work. On the working days, Nilofer had to miss two of the Namaazez. However, on weekends she offered all the five. Vikram did not engage in any rituals, though he was a staunch believer. Nilofer never commented on his attitude towards religion. On the other hand, if Nilofer failed to notice the time for her prayers, Vikram would draw her attention to it.

Vikram was in constant touch with his family in India. He exchanged weekly letters with them. He talked to them on phone only on occasions, as the trans-continental phone calls took time to get through. Nilofer on the other hand wrote to her family back in Pakistan only sparsely. When she did, it was to uncle Hameed and father-in-law Akbar Ali. However, she never failed to send greetings on various Eids to her in-laws and to her uncle's family.

Now that Nilofer was virtually living with Vikram, she had moved a major part of her wardrobe to the apartment, leaving a bare minimum requirement in her own room. Vikram, a great believer in living for today, never analyzed his relation with her. He loved her, and at the time, she was with him. That was all that mattered. Nilofer on the other hand, was not that philosophical. Occasionally when she was alone and unoccupied, her thoughts would stray into future. She dreaded the thought of going back to her old life, back home. Just thinking of Mahmood sent an icy shiver through her. Nevertheless, she tried to keep the past at bay, and warded off the thoughts of future. The moment she came in the presence of her Bikku – she had now started calling him by his childhood nickname – she would forget all her miseries, and her face would light up with the glow of happiness. Vikram was not unmindful of her periodical, though rare spells of melancholy, but he steadfastly refrained from making any comments. He was extremely perceptive of her moods. He could accurately judge her frame of mind at a given moment. When she was in a reflective mood, he would leave her alone. When she was inclined to talk, he would sit and listen to her endless chatter. He could accurately read her vibes when she was in the mood of making love. In matter of sex, she had not shed her conservative approach. She would not put her desire into words. He would read her body language, and initiate the foreplay. He never took the initiative unless he perceived her desire. He had not forgotten her sobs on their first night together in bed, and had intuitively known that she had had some unpleasant experience, and needed a delicate handling in the matter. As such, she was not a highly sexed woman, and the frequency of their lovemaking was moderate. Nilofer too had realized that Vikram did not make the first move in the matter, but never failed to sense her desire. Right from their first meeting she had noticed his uncanny ability to read her mind.

One Friday night, in the month of September, the ringing of his bedside phone woke Vikram up. He picked it up at the second ring. He did not want Nilofer to be disturbed. They had gone to bed late after midnight, as Nilofer had continued to read until then for her approaching exam. His luminous watch said half past one. He talked into the phone in a hushed tone. Nilofer rolled over on the bed, and switched on the bedside light. He said into the phone,

"O.K. I am on my way," and hung up.

As he was dressing, he spoke to Nilofer.

"It's an emergency case of a severed hand. The relatives of the patient have brought the detached hand, packed in ice. My boss is attending the case himself. In case the hand is viable, the surgery for its re-attachment could be a prolonged affair. If not, I shall be back in an hour's time."

Nilofer woke up at the usual time of half past five. Vikram had not yet returned, so there would be no swimming session. Her unit had not scheduled any surgery for the day. She did not have to attend the hospital either. She went back to sleep, and woke up again at seven. Vikram had still not come. She rang up the operating rooms' desk. The surgery was still in progress. She had her breakfast and lunch alone.

Vikram arrived at six in the evening, after assisting his boss in a marathon operation of sixteen hours. Nilofer was alarmed at his haggard appearance.

"I'll have a bit of shut eye, Nilu," he said as he walked lethargically towards the bedroom.

She followed him.

"You first go and have a hot shower while I get you something to eat. You are not going to sleep on an empty stomach." She handed him a fresh towel.

Vikram obeyed her wordlessly. While he was having his shower, she took out fresh pajamas from his wardrobe, and draped them over the radiator to warm them. She hurried to the kitchen, scrambled three eggs, baked two parathas, and put the kettle on for tea. She was laying the table, when Vikram entered the kitchen looking reasonably revived. She sat in front of him and watched him tenderly as he ate. When he had finished eating, she poured him a cup of tea, and took one herself. She thought of asking him about the surgery, but refrained from burdening him with the details in his present condition. Her caring and tender ministering stirred Vikram. He found himself being sexually aroused in spite of the fatigue. He resolutely suppressed the urge. He finished his tea, and proceeded to the bedroom. For the first time, Nilofer could sense his desire, and followed him into his bed. Later, as she lay besides the sleeping figure of Vikram, she reflected, "How did I fathom his need? It has always been he, who had been reading my mind." Vikram's words rang in her mind. "When you will start loving me as intensely as I do you, you shall get your answer." Then the revelation came to her, when you love and care for someone wholeheartedly, you become one with him, body, heart, soul and mind. Her thoughts went back to the incident when she had wanted to part ways with Vikram, and he had pre-empted her. "He must have loved me intensely even then. Of course, at the time he knew my identity. Does that mean he had loved me even when we were children back in the village?" Lost in these memories, she fell asleep. From that night on, they were two bodies with one soul.

Nilofer's exams for the primary MRCOG were scheduled for Monday and Tuesday, 3 and 4 October. Vikram decided that they should spend the rest of the week exploring London. They put in requests for leave of absence for the week. They took the 14.21 train to London on Sunday, and then a taxi from the Paddington station to Piccolino Hotel in Sussex place. This hotel was easy on budget and was located at a walking distance from the Royal College of Obstetrics and Gynecology, where the exam was being held. Out of prudence, they booked into two separate rooms. To Nilofer's delight, all the four examination papers were easier than she had anticipated. On Wednesday morning, they purchased two five-day tourist tickets for the tube trains, and a tourist map of London, and went on a sightseeing spree. On the first day, after they had breakfasted at the hotel, they went to the Trafalgar Square, and spent hours at the National gallery, viewing the work of Vincent Van Gogh, da Vinci, Botticelli, Renoir, Constable, and other masters. In the afternoon, they took the tube to the Oxford Street, and strolled down the Gainsborough Road to the Hyde Park. On the way, they had picked up a couple of *keema parathas*, and some *Shami Kababs*, from a Pakistani eatery, and made a picnic lunch of them on the vast lawns. Nilofer was keen to see the famed Speaker Corner, but was disappointed to discover that it was only a small protrusion of the main park. They watched the renowned horse riding show, which awakened in Nilofer, a faint memory of her childhood, she riding behind her father, astride his favorite Gul badan. They took a cruising round of the Serpentine Lake, and then went to a Parsi eating joint in the Brook Street, where Nilofer tasted, for the first time, the typical Parsi dish of *Dhan Saak*. They returned to their hotel around eleven at night.

On Thursday morning, they visited the houses of Parliament, and saw the world famous clock tower of Big Ben, on the Bank of the river Thames. Nilofer wanted to see the residence of the British Prime Minister, so they went to the Downing Street. To her amazement, the house number ten, the famous "Ten Downing Street" looked, from outside, like any other British house. The unpretentious door had the figure 10 inscribed above it. A casual passer by would not have given it a second look, but for the lone security guard standing in front of it. She could not help comparing it with the pretentious bungalows of politicians of her own country, with an array of guards. Around mid-day, they visited the Buckingham Palace and watched the changing of the guards.

Nilofer had made an appointment, for half past three that afternoon, to meet Sir James, the Director of the association of Commonwealth Universities. While she went to his office in Tavistock Square, Vikram chose to wait for her in a coffee house nearby. When she rejoined him, she was grinning from ear to ear.

"You know Bikku, this was meant to be a mandatory meeting to get introduced to the Director. However, Sir James was gracious enough to tell me that Professor Wise has been speaking highly of me. Sir James has offered to bear all my expenses if I decide to attend a conference in any country of Europe, barring the communist ruled ones."

They had earmarked Friday for a visit to Oxford. Vikram had made an advance appointment with Dr. Rodney Coal, a reconstructive surgeon at the John Radcliff hospital. Coal was doing a facial reconstruction that morning. They spent the morning in the operating room, watching the surgeon transplant various tissues on to the face of the patient damaged by extensive burn injuries. Vikram watched assiduously every step of the procedure that the surgeon carried out with admirable dexterity. Later, Dr. Coal took them to lunch at the University Cafeteria, where they had smoked salmons and cheese sandwiches, it being a no-meat day. They spent the afternoon walking on the bank of the Isis, a section of the Thames, famous for its canoe racing.

On Saturday, they visited Madame Tussauds, and the Chambers of horrors on Marylebone Road. Nilofer was fascinated by what she called the living statues. Vikram stood for a long time, in front of Mahatma Gandhi's statue, as if willing it to speak. Nilofer was thrilled by the figure of Garfield Sobers, frozen in his bowling action. They had a self-serviced lunch at a Wimpy bar nearby, and then watched the final show at the celebrated London Planetarium.

Sunday morning they took the tube to the Tower Hill and visited the Tower of London. Here, housed inside the tower, they saw the Crown Jewels, which include the heirlooms of the British Royal family, and the war spoils from the British colonies all over the world, during the days of the great British Empire. Vikram pointed out to Nilofer the priceless 105-carat Koh-e-Noor diamond, brought from the undivided India, and now embedded in the Queen's crown. They also saw the celebrated 503-carat Star of Africa, perhaps the largest existing diamond of the world. They returned to Cardiff in the evening and resumed to their duties on Monday morning.

*****

Life for Nilofer was now like a perpetually pleasurable dream. "Can heaven be any different from this?" She often asked herself. She recalled the sermons of the *maulanas,* telling their audience that if they lived their lives according to the Allah's commandments, they would attain, after death, the paradise, where there would be everlasting happiness and they would have company of *hooris.* She used to wonder, if pious men would find *hooris* in heaven, what about the pious women? Why did the maulanas say nothing about the pious women finding angels in heaven? "It does not matter what the maulanas say," she would say to herself, "I have found my paradise in this life and the company of an angel." Every moment of her life was filled with heavenly bliss. Once or twice, the thought of returning home in less than two years, and facing the hell of her future life did cross her mind. She resolutely shut the door of her mind on that thought, and resolved to keep it shut. "I am going to live for today," she had said to herself. "I shall not allow the thought of future to over shadow my present. I shall savor every moment of togetherness with my soul mate, and I shall stretch every moment to a lifetime. That way I shall live in my paradise for eons."

She now had only two aspirations, preparing for her final professional exam, and caring for her beloved Bikku. Immersed in this rapturous existence, she became oblivious to the passing time. She was jolted out of her pleasurable oblivion, on a September evening, when she received a circular from the Royal College of Obstetrics and Gynecology, announcing the schedule for the final MRCOG exams, and the dates for registering the candidates. The exams were due to be held from the fifth to the ninth February.

"Gosh," she said to Vikram, "My exams will be in February, and my scholarship is due to expire on the fifteenth January. I should have written, last month, to Sir James for extending it."

"Don't get perturbed Nilu. Give me the scholarship file. I'll draft and type the letter to Sir James. I shall mail it tomorrow morning."

He read through the five-page file. The regulations attached with the letter of award of the scholarship had a clause that if the awardee so desired, he could ask for an extension of six months by writing to the director, six months before the date of expiry of the scholarship. Further extensions could be considered on merit. In the file, Vikram found an envelope containing spare passport/size copies of Nilofer's photograph. Vikram typed out the required letter, and gave it to Nilofer for her signature. He put the envelope containing the letter in his jacket pocket. He also removed a copy of Nilofer's photograph from the file and pocketed it too. Next morning he dropped the letter in the mailbox. Then took the photograph to a studio and asked to have an enlargement made.

Sir James reply came promptly. Nilofer had found the letter in the cubbyhole assigned to her in the department office. She had carried the letter home, without opening it. She went to the flat, changed into pajamas, sat in an armchair, and opened the letter. The message was short. Her scholarship had been extended up to 15 July 1968. The sight of a concrete date for her departure came as a stab to her heart. Living, as she was, in a happy and serene world of her own, she had forgotten that one day she would have to part with Vikram. She put the letter back into the envelop, and slumped in the chair. Vikram came home and was alarmed to see her in that condition. He reached her in two long strides.

"What's the matter, Nilu?" he whispered.

Then he saw Sir James' letter lying in her lap.

"Has he refused the extension?" He picked up the letter and read it.

For the first time he failed to understand her. He looked, by turns, first at the letter and then at Nilofer, with puzzled eyes.

"You've got what you wanted. Why do you look so upset?"

Her reply surprised him. It was so much out of context.

"Bikku, I don't want to be separated from you." She was trying to hold back her tears.

"Why are you talking of separation? We are together today."

Vikram's remarks filled her with annoyance. She sat up straight.

"Please Bikku, put this living for today aside for the moment, and listen to me. I cannot live without you."

"But I am here Nilu, and you are here."

"For how long, for God's sake?"

She snatched the letter from his hand and held it in front of his eyes.

"This here says, up to fifteenth July."

When Vikram did not reply, she wiped the tears from her cheeks, and spoke pleadingly.

"Isn't there some way we can get married, and you can take me to India, when you return there?"

Vikram started laughing.

"This is no laughing matter," Nilofer said with annoyance. "I am serious."

"I am not laughing at your suggestion. I will tell you something. When I was seven, one of my cousins was married to a girl of the Village Murala. When the *baraat,* marriage party, returned to our village with the bride, a *muhn dikhai* function for viewing the bride was held for her. The bride sat on a cot, her face covered in a *ghoongat,* the veil. All the women of the village had gathered there. I had accompanied my mother to the function. Each woman, by turn, went up to the bride, lifted her veil, passed a comment on her looks, and then placed a gift in her lap. Every woman, without exception, after seeing the face of the bride, had turned to the mother-in-law, and had said. Your son has brought the prettiest bride in the whole of the village. When I returned home with my mother, I said to her,

'Beji, I will bring a bride prettier than that of cousin Krishan.'

"My mother had smiled indulgently, and said,

'Yes son, I will select a very lovely bride for you'

'But Beji, I have already selected a pretty bride for me.'

'And who is that lucky girl. Tell me.'

'It is Phatti,'

'Phatti? Who?'

'Fatima, our next door neighbor.'

'Oh, my silly child, you cannot marry that girl.'

'Why not, Beji?'

'There is a wall between her and you.'

'I know Beji, but I have climbed over that wall so many times. I am Bikku the Lizard,' I had said with pride.

'I am not talking of the wall between our houses, my child.'

'What wall are you talking about then?'

"My mother had remained silent for a while, undecided whether to continue the dialogue. Then she said in a slow speech, which she usually employed when she told me a mystery story.

'The wall that I am talking about is invisible, and you cannot climb over that.'

'But Beji, how can there be a wall that cannot be seen?'

'Wait until you are a little older, my son. Then you will understand what I am saying.'"

Vikram sat down beside Nilofer, held her by the shoulders, and turned her to face him.

"Now, you and I both know what wall my mother was talking of."

They fell silent. Both lost in their own thoughts. After wordless minutes, Nilofer spoke hesitatingly.

"Can I not ask for divorce?" She sounded unconvincing to herself.

"You know better than to ask that question."

Nilofer thought of the tough Muslim laws for a woman seeking divorce, and heaved a deep sigh.

Vikram put his arm around her shoulders and spoke tenderly,

"Listen Tim," he used her rare nickname, which he had given to her in their child hood,

"Destiny has provided us the opportunity to get around the

insurmountable wall between us, and be together, although only temporarily. We have had a blissful time together for the last two years. Let us live each of the remaining moments to the fullest, and harvest enough happiness to last us for our lifetime."

Nilofer snuggled up to him and put her head on his shoulder. Vikram put his arm around her waist. They sat like that, without a word between them. Nilofer's mind was empty of any thoughts. Vikram's mind was in turmoil. It was a long time before they became aware of their surrounding. The room had become dark. Vikram peered at his watch.

"Gosh, it is six o' clock."

He jumped up, and switched on the light. Nilofer tried to collect herself.

"O Nilu, you silly girl, you have starved me. My stomach is growling with hunger." He said with a mock accusation.

Nilofer looked up with a start. She felt guilty. In her dwellings on the impending return home, she had forgotten to cook lunch. She hurried into the kitchen and put the kettle on the stove. Vikram joined her and they made some cheese toasts. The frugal meal became their lunch cum supper for the day. Neither of them really had any appetite.

Nilofer went into the living room and picked up a copy of British Journal of Obstetrics and Gynecology. She held the open journal in front of her and pretended to read. Vikram went along with her sham, and left her alone. Palpable waves of anger assailed her mind. "Why is there so much discrimination against women in my community? Why a man can divorce his wife even on frivolous grounds, just by uttering the word 'Talaque' three times, while a woman cannot unshackle herself even from an unbearable bond? Why is a woman made to feel so helpless? A woman may be physically weaker than her male counterpart, but intellectually and mentally, she is no less than a man. I want to be with my loved one, and I cannot, just because I am a woman." The storm in her mind suddenly abated.

"**Because I am a woman, I shall have my way**," she said to the empty room.

She had shouted the words aloud. Vikram was in the bedroom. He heard her muffled shout, and hurried into the living room.

"Are you alright Nilu?" He inquired anxiously.

"Oh, it's nothing." Vikram saw a Madonna-like enigmatic smile on her lips. For the second time, that day, he had failed to read her thoughts. A plan was taking shape in her mind. Once the plan had taken a concrete shape, she felt lighthearted. She put out the lights of the living room and joined Vikram in the bedroom. She slept like a baby.

Next morning she was back to her usual self. When Vikram joined her in the kitchen to help her prepare breakfast, he was happy to hear her humming, repeatedly, a couplet of the poet Kaifi Aazmi, sung by the famed ghazal singer Akhtri Begam.

Ik tum ke tum ko fikr nasheb-o-faraaz ka
Ik hum ke chal pade to bah har haal chal pade

The couplet was the essence of the resolve she had made last night. She was not going to let any wall stand between her Bikku and herself. She was determined to breach the wall. As a first step in that direction, she went off the contraceptive pill, and started charting her ovulation calendar, and maintaining her daily body temperature chart. She also started monitoring changes in the appearance of her cervical fluid. She had always had very regular menstrual cycle of twenty-eight days. "I must be ovulating on the fourteenth or the fifteenth day," she had concluded. She started looking for signs of ovulation, the liberation of an egg from her ovary. She kept Vikram in dark regarding her scheme.

In the month of September, she felt a brief twinge of pain on the left side of her lower belly on the fourteenth day of her menstrual period. She put a blue dot against that day in her daily temperature chart. Her cervical fluid appeared to be the thickest on the fourteenth as well as the fifteenth day. These were charted as two red dots against those two days. She thought her breasts were a bit tender on those two days, but she could not be sure. Nevertheless, she put them down as two green dots on the temperature chart. At the end of her menstrual cycle, she reviewed the record. Her temperature chart showed a marked spike on the fourteenth day, a rise of one and a half degree. By the month of December, she was in no doubt that her ovary liberated the egg on either the fourteenth or the fifteenth day of her cycle. By her calculations, her fertility time was from the thirteenth to the seventeenth day. She made sure not to indulge in sex on those days for the next four months.

She took her exams, which were scheduled for February fifth to ninth, and was declared successful. Vikram wanted to take her to Paris, for a couple of days, to celebrate the occasion, but she pleaded with him to postpone the merriment for the time being. At this time, she was in no mood for festivity. Her mind was occupied by conflicting thoughts of hope and despair.

Her menstrual calendar showed that her next ovulation was due on 11 February. She contrived to have sex with Vikram on the tenth and twelfth, willing herself to get pregnant. She was disappointed when her next cycle commenced on schedule, but she did not give up hope. "I will succeed whatever it takes." She said to herself. When she failed to conceive even next month, she got a bit worried. She still had over three months time. What if it does not come about in that time? Doubts assailed her mind.

"Bikku, do you think Sir James would agree to extend the tenure of my scholarship for a second time?" She had asked Vikram.

"Well…er… I cannot say with certainty…er…perhaps he may." Vikram knew very well that there was no chance of her getting further extension, now that she had cleared her exam.

It was Tuesday 8 April 1969. Nilofer was at the outdoor clinic. Around quarter to ten, she felt a sharp pang in the right side of her lower abdomen. She had no doubt it was the pain of ovulation. She knew that viability of her egg was for twelve to twenty-four hours only. She decided to act immediately. She went to her boss, Cynthia

Joans, and asked for permission to leave. Cynthia did not bother to ask the reason for her request. She just nodded her assent.

Nilofer hurried home. She rang up Vikram's ward and asked to speak to him.

"Bikku, please come home immediately." There was a frantic note in her voice

"What's the matter, Nilu? Is anything…?" She cut him short.

"Please don't ask questions, and hurry."

"O.K I am leaving now".

Nilofer undressed quickly, and put on a negligee. When Vikram arrived, she was in bed, curled up into a fetal position, and covered with a blanket up to her chin.

"What's the matter?" He was alarmed at the sight.

"Please Bikku, lie down besides me, and hold me tight." There was urgency in her beseeching.

Vikram had seen her, on previous occasions, getting distraught because of their imminent parting, but it was never that bad. He silently undid the tie, removed his jacket and shirt. Down to his vest, and trousers, he lay down besides her, and put his arms around her. She encircled his neck with her hands, and let go a shower of kisses. They ended up making love. She surprised him by her unusual frenzy in bed. She had always been a model of a tender partner. After remaining in bed with her for about half an hour, Vikram got up, washed himself, and dressed.

"How about lunch?" He asked.

"Oh Bikku, I am in no mood to cook."

"Shall we eat at the dining hall then?"

"Please Bikku, would you mind eating alone. I am not hungry. I would like to rest a bit."

"She does need to rest in her present frame of mind," Vikram thought, and went alone to lunch at the hospital dining hall. After finishing his day's work, when he returned home around four in the evening, Nilofer was still in bed, lying on her back. She did not get out of bed, but kept smiling at him. It was a disconcerting smile.

It remained confined to her eyes, and did not touch her lips. She looked like a Cheshire cat that had swallowed a canary. She got out of bed around eight and prepared a light supper – rice and curry. Next morning she woke up at the ungodly hour of four, and wanted to make love again. Vikram thought her new sex drive was subconscious amour against the mental agony at the thought of parting from him. Again, she did not get out of bed that morning, and telephoned the receptionist of her department for leave of absence for the day. To the utter amazement of Vikram, she incited him that night again into another session of lovemaking. He observed another change in her. She had always slept on her side. She would not remain on her back for more than a few minutes. Now uncharacteristically, she had not only made love three times in a span of thirty six hours, she had, after making love, turned on her back, and remained in that position for hours, as if to prevent the semen from flowing out. He watched her face trying to read her mind. She noticed his frown. She rubbed his forehead with her fingers, to smoothen the furrow that had appeared between his eyebrows.

"What are you scowling at?" She asked.

"Had I not known better, I would have thought you were trying to get pregnant."

The peals of her laughter had filled the bedroom.

"You should know better than that silly," She had said.

Of course, Vikram knew. Under no circumstances, could she permit herself to get pregnant. She knew the disastrous consequences of such an event. His misgivings disappeared when Nilofer appeared quite herself the next morning, perhaps a bit extra cheerful.

On Saturday, that week, when Nilofer and Vikram were having their breakfast, they heard voices outside their door. Vikram went to inquire. The door of the second flat on his floor was open, and two young men were piling up luggage in front of it. He recognized Dr. Thomas Douglas, his former house officer.

"Hi Tom," He greeted him.

"Oh hi, Vicky. Vicky, meet my friend, Mark Swift. Mark is going to be your neighbor. He is the new senior registrar of ophthalmology. And Mark, this is Mr. Vikram Kocher; he is registrar in the reconstructive surgery." Vicky and Mark shook hands, and then went into their respective flats.

"We have a new neighbor." Vikram informed Nilofer, as he rejoined her to finish his breakfast.

Around four in the afternoon, their doorbell rang. Vikram opened the door.

"Hi Vicky," a girl in her early twenties stood before him. He could not place her immediately.

"I am Pamela Lahore." Vikram recognized her now. The famed flirt from the West Indies.

"May I use your telephone, please? The housekeeper seems to have forgotten to get our phone line connected. I must speak to her before she leaves for the day."

She entered without waiting for Vikram's reply and made straight for the living room. Nilofer was in her housecoat, reclining in the easy chair. She was in a reverie of her own, and did not even look up when Pamela came in. Pamela stopped in her tracks on seeing Nilofer. "So the sour nun has conquered the reverend bishop," she thought. Aloud she said,

"Hallo there, you day dreamer, what goes with you?"

Nilofer came out of her trance with a start. She quickly collected her wits and greeted her colleague politely. She was annoyed. Pamela had seen her in the housecoat in Vikram's flat. On second thought, she took the matter philosophically. "It had to happen one day. Our relation cannot be kept secret indefinitely. Luckily, Pamela does not know my marital status. Only Professor Wise and Dr. Joans know about it, and they are not likely to talk." After Pamela had finished her phone call, Nilofer offered to make coffee for her, which to Nilofer's relief, she declined and left. "So, our neighbor is Pamela's latest boy friend," she said to herself.

On Monday, 14 April, Nilofer was talking to a patient in her ward, when she had a sudden spell of dizziness, which passed in less than half a minute. She felt slightly queasy. She went into the pantry, and had a glass of water. She felt better, and resumed her work. A couple of hours later, she felt a funny sensation in her pelvis, as if an ant was crawling in her womb. She instantly recognized these as signs of implantation of embryo. She was sure she was pregnant. She felt a thrill pass through her, but she had to make it doubly sure. She took out a lab requisition form and filled it up with her details, the name, age, and address. She put down the test required as HCG levels for that day and for the19 April, six days later. It was a reliable test for recognizing early pregnancy. She was tempted to sign the requisition herself, but refrained from doing so. She was not legally authorized to order any investigation. The registrar signed all the lab requests, and that position, at the time was that of Dr. Pamela Lahore. Perhaps it is for the better. She thought. "Pamela already knows my relations with Vikram, and is not likely to raise eyebrows at the request." She went to Pamela's desk, where she was busy signing the lab requests filled up by the house officer. She placed the form in front of her. Pamela glanced through it, looked up, smiled at her, and affixed her signature on it. Nilofer went to the lab, and had her blood sample drawn. She visited the lab again after six days to give the second blood sample. Next Monday morning, Pamela handed her the report without a word. She was pregnant. Pamela had expected an unhappy reaction, as she thought it must be an unwanted pregnancy. She was ready to help arrange an abortion. Instead, she saw a radiant smile spread over Nilofer's face, as she read the report.

"Thank you." Nilofer said, and vanished.

When she returned home Vikram had already arrived, and was busy writing. His pen traveled from right to left as he wrote, so she knew he was writing in Urdu, probably his next contribution to *Kaainaat.* He looked up as she entered, and she smiled. It was the same enchanting smile, starting from her eyes and spreading down to her lips. Vikram had been yearning to see that smile for the last few weeks. She seemed to be in some sort of euphoria. He wondered what had made her so happy today. She went straight to the telephone. After referring to her diary, in which she had noted down important phone numbers, she dialed.

"This is Dr. Khan from Cardiff," she spoke into the phone. "May I please have a word with Sir James?"

Vikram stopped writing. He looked at Nilofer with compassion. "Poor girl," he thought, "she is going to be disappointed. Sir James will not extend her stay here any further."

"Good afternoon Sir James," she was saying. "Sir, I had completed the tenure of my scholarship on the fifteenth of January. You were kind enough to grant me a six month extension until the fifteenth of July…"

Vikram held his breath. He saw the disappointing moment arriving. Sir James would surely refuse a further extension of her stay. Nilofers next words took him by utter surprise.

"Sir James, for a pressing domestic reason, I am required to return home immediately. Do I have your permission to leave?

She listened for some time, and said,

"I shall contact the British Council's office. Thank you Sir James."

She hung up. She looked at Vikram, who was leaning forward, with his mouth open.

"What are you up to, Nilu? Until yesterday, you were hankering after a further extension of your stay here. Now you go and cancel the few weeks that you still have. Why Nilu?"

"My dear clever Bikku, you always have known my mind, why can't you guess my motives now?"

Vikram let out a sigh, "I have lost you these last few weeks. You have been behaving illogically these days. I confess I can't understand you any more."

"O.K," she said with her jingling laughter. "Let me give you some lessons in logic."

She pulled a chair opposite to him and sat down.

"Now tell me why I wanted to extend my stay here?"

He watched her quizzically, and did not answer. She answered her own question.

"I wanted the extension so that we could be together a bit longer."

"And now you have decided to get away from me without any delay."

"No Bikku, I am not getting away from you. I am making sure to have you with me always,"

Her seemingly incomprehensible answers were exasperating Vikram.

"Can't you give a sensible answer to a sensible question?"

"Okay, okay! Let's see whether you can make sense of this."

She leaned forward and gazed into his eyes. He saw the twinkle in her eyes. She spoke slowly and deliberately.

"I … am … taking … you … with … me."

The meaning of her words brought a feeling of icy cold in the pit of his stomach. He found it difficult to breath. His mouth went dry. He spoke with difficulty.

"Are you…"

"Yes," she said as she handed him the pregnancy report. "You are now a prisoner inside me, and when I set you free, you shall be with me, always."

Vikram recalled her unusual behavior in bed.

"Oh God," he moaned, "I have been a blind idiot these last few days."

"Why Mister Kocher, you said you knew better." Nilofer reminded him mischievously.

Vikram sat up straight and said in a commanding tone that brooked no arguments,

"No Nilu, I can under no circumstances permit you to commit a hara-kiri. You know what shall befall you when your people come to know this. You have to get the pregnancy terminated before you leave here."

Nilofer was incensed at his suggestion.

"Now you *are* being idiotic. You are asking me to destroy something which is more precious to me than my own life. Moreover, what is going to befall me if my people come to know that I became pregnant soon after my return home? Or when I go into labor a couple of weeks prematurely?"

"But that would amount to..." He stopped abruptly. He was about to say that it would amount to a fraud. "Hasn't our relation itself been a fraud?" He thought. "No, no," he argued with himself. "To me Nilu has been my Phatti, my childhood soul mate. Destiny has returned my love to me. Does it matter if the world knows her as Mrs. Khan and not Mrs. Kocher? We love each other with our soul, body, and heart. Our love recognizes no boundaries, no bonds."

Nilofer broke into his thoughts. She put her hand on his shoulder, and said,

"I had to breach the wall between us. Please Bikku; do not trouble your heart. Let us rejoice that in your offspring, you will be with me, always."

Vikram stood up, and pulled her to himself and held her to his breast.

"Yes, my love, yes," he said, "I shall always be by your side."

That night, they lay awake for a long time, discussing the future for the first time.

"Nilu," Vikram said, "Our closeness these last two years has given us immense happiness. I do not want it to become the cause of your unhappiness in future. We must promise ourselves that once you return home, we shall not try to contact each other, nor try to find the whereabout of each other. You shall carry no photographs, and no other evidence linking you to me. Under no circumstances you will reveal to our child the identity of its father."

Nilofer agreed to all these suggestions, but asked for one concession.

"I shall write to you just one letter, informing you of the arrival of our child. After that I shall not try to contact you any time."

The only documentary evidence of her association with Cardiff, which Nilofer took with her, was a group photograph of the staff of the unit headed by Dr. Cynthia Joans, and one of herself with

Professor Wise. She had asked the British Council to book her on the first available flight to Lahore. The next day the air ticket arrived. She had been booked on a BOAC flight leaving Heathrow on Wednesday, 23 April. Early next morning she landed at the Lahore International Airport. Her father-in-law and his personal driver met her at the airport, and drove her home.

The Nilofer that returned home was not the same Nilofer that had left for the U.K. less than three years back. She had undergone a radical metamorphosis. She had left home with a numbed heart and a despondent mind. She had returned with a joyous heart and a resolute mind. She was no more a meek and compliant girl, ready to do the bidding of elders without a question. Her disastrous marriage, imposed upon her by her uncle Hameed, had plunged her into dark despair, and brought her to the brink of insanity. She had come back with a firm resolve, never again to permit anyone to mess with her life. She intended to plan her own future. "You take care of today and tomorrow will take care of itself," Vikram's words echoed in her mind. "What shall be my present task?" She asked herself. She set three immediate goals for herself – pursue her professional career, nurture her love growing inside her, and unchain herself from Mahmood. As a first step towards building her professional career, she reported on duty to her old department at the medical college on the second day of her arrival in Lahore. This was a lucky move. The college was collecting applications for the postgraduate examinations. The cut-off date for applying was only two days away. She submitted her application for taking the exam for the master's degree in obstetrics and gynecology, with barely a few hours to spare. The exams were due in June. She had calculated that the right time to declare her pregnancy would be mid June. Until then she would have to endure Mahmood. After that, I shall exclude him from my life. She said to herself determinedly.

On 27 April, she discreetly discarded a sanitary pad into the garbage bin. She intentionally had made her action not so unobtrusive as to escape the notice of her mother-in-law. She had poured on to the pad a small amount of milk to which she had added an equal amount of tomato ketchup. She hated this charade. It was alien to her nature, but it was a vital step in her plan of action. She repeated the farce for three more days. Her action, outwardly appeared unobtrusive, but she made sure that one or the other women of the house noticed it. After four days of simulated menstruation, she washed her hair to indicate the end of her menses. Neither her mother-in-law nor any of the woman servants saw her dispose off a sanitary pad in the month of May. At the end of the first week of June, she told her mother-in-law,

"Ammi Jaan, I think I am pregnant."

Rehanabibi was sitting on a *charpoy* in the courtyard of their house, cooling herself in the evening breeze. She looked up sharply, putting aside the *duppata* on which she was doing embroidery work. She caught hold of Nilofer's hand and seated her gently by her side.

"Allah be praised *dulhan*, are you sure?"

"I shall have some tests done tomorrow to confirm it. But I am quite certain."

"May Allah shower his bounties on us, and grant the gift of an heir to our family."

Rehanabibi invited the women of her neighborhood, friends, and relatives to share the news of the imminent new arrival, and some dainty dishes at her *dastarkhwan*. Nilofer would have ordinarily hated the public proclamation of her condition, but under the circumstances, she welcomed it.

Nilofer's exams, went smoothly that month. With the recent reading that she had done for her Membership exam, she had no difficulty writing her papers. She sailed through her oral test. Her MRCOG qualification had over awed the examiners. They asked her only a few perfunctory questions and declared her successful.

With the exams out of the way, she turned her attention to Mahmood. She knew that the task of keeping him out of her life was not going to be easy. Recourse to legal action was out of question. It would be impossible to get a divorce, she thought. "I must find some other way to unshackle myself from him. Perhaps I could persuade him to take a second wife, thus deflecting his attentions away from me. For the present, I shall reason with him, and persuade him not to share my bed during my pregnancy. After that, I shall find some lasting solution." As it turned out, the solution presented itself without her having to make any effort.

Two days after Nilofer had completed her exams, Mahmood returned from the farms in a foul mood. He had, while trying to overtake a truck, damaged his jeep. The truck driver had hurled the choicest of Punjabi abuses at him. Halfway through his supper, he had picked up his plate and flung it across the kitchen. The rice was under cooked. In the bedroom, while undressing he ripped his favorite silk *kurta,* and let out a stream of profanity. Nilofer watched him with contempt. When he had undressed down to his trunks, he seemed to shrug his shoulders a couple of times, then all of a sudden dropped to the floor. Nilofer turned around, and saw him convulsing. She thought he was having a stroke brought about by a head injury that he might have suffered at the time of the jeep accident that evening. She was about to shout for help when she realized it was not a stroke, but an epileptic fit. He had urinated and defecated in his trunks, and the room was filled with fetid stink. Nilofer stood rooted in dismay and watched the convulsing figure on the ground. In a few minutes he became still, and gradually opened his eyes, gazing unseeingly into space. Slowly his eyes focused on Nilofer and she saw self-pity in them. She too recovered from her initial alarm. She walked out of the bedroom, and went to the guest room on the same floor.

After his wife had left the bedroom, Mahmood remained on his back on the floor for a while. This was the first time his wife had seen him in this condition. He felt humiliated at having lost control of his sphincters. Earlier when that happened, his mother or a servant used to clean him up. Tonight he lay there alone in his own filth. His wife had, by walking out on him, made it clear that she had no intention of scavenging him, or even remaining around in that filthy atmosphere. He got up gingerly, and removed his under pants. He carried them into the bathroom, and washed them, as well as himself. Then he mopped the soiled floor of the bedroom. He went back to the bathroom and cleaned its floor thoroughly. He put on fresh pajamas and went to sleep.

Nilofer did not get a wink of sleep. She lay in bed in the guest room, and relived the ghastly scene she had witnessed. Surely, that epileptic fit was not the first episode. It does not come about suddenly at his age. He must be an old case of epilepsy, she reasoned with herself. "Was he having the malady before he was married to me? He must have." Now that she thought of his behavior all along, she felt certain he was epileptic since before marriage. The whole thing had been kept under wraps. A horrifying thought came to her mind. "Did my uncle Hameed know about this before he fixed my marriage to him? No, no," she rejected the possibility. "He may be a selfish politician, but he could not be that heartless. He could not condescend to be a willing accomplice in such cruel deception on his own niece. He too must have been kept in dark." She resolved to find out the truth.

Mahmood felt too embarrassed to face his wife. He did not come home for a whole week. He camped at the farm under the pretext of supervising the pre-monsoon ploughing. He arrived home the following Sunday, very sober, and wearing a sheepish look. After having a late supper, he went to the bedroom. Nilofer was reading in bed. He took a chair besides the bed and sat without a word for a long time. Nilofer could see that he was too embarrassed to say whatever he wanted to say, but she decided not to help him. She pretended to be absorbed in her reading. At last, she shut the book and lay it on the bedside cabinet. Mahmood spoke up haltingly.

"Bibi…" This was the first time he had addressed her by any title ever since they were married.

"Bibi, I… need your… help." He was stammering.

Nilofer made no reply.

"What happened the other day … when it happens… I am totally unaware of it at the time…Later on when I come to, I feel ashamed… You are a doctor. Can't you help me out of this misery?"

He stopped talking and looked at Nilofer with eyes of a pleading pup.

"How long have you been having these…episodes?" Nilofer tactfully avoided calling them fits.

"It happened the first time about twelve or thirteen years back…" He seemed in a hurry to unload his mind. "…I have been taking medicine since then. Initially the fits were not that frequent and I… did not…defecate. Lately they have become more frequent, and more severe."

He was silent for a while and then said,

"I feel so humiliated… Please help me." There was anguish in his voice.

Pleading was not in Mahmood's nature. To Nilofer he seemed suddenly to shrink in his stature. A feeling of pity diluted her hatred for him.

"Who has been treating you?" she asked him.

"I don't know the name of the doctor, but it is all there in the file."

"Bring the file to me tomorrow, meanwhile I have to ask you to go and sleep in the guest room." She told him in the tone of a doctor issuing instructions to a patient.

To her relief, he obeyed her meekly, and left.

The following evening when she returned from the hospital, and went to her bedroom to change, the file was lying on the bed. It had been issued by the Fatima Jinnah Hospital, and contained the case history of Mahmood. The first page was dated 1955. The first line read old case of Koch's meningitis, treated by Dr. Bedi of Sir Ganga Ram Hospital – 1937. Nilofer scanned the file in dismay. Mahmood's brain had been damaged in infancy. He had been having epileptic fits since the age of nineteen. Yet his parents had shown no qualms in getting their mentally impaired son married off, that too to a doctor! Bile rose to her throat, and her body shook with futile anger. She felt utterly helpless. Three years back too, she had sat helplessly, and uttered *qabool hai*, I accept, when the qaazi had given her the option of accepting or rejecting Mahmood as her husband. She put her hand on her abdomen, bent her head down, and whispered to her unborn child,

"I shall never let this happen to you."

As she studied Mahmood's file, she felt purged of all the hatred for him that had accumulated in her heart. It was replaced by a feeling of compassion and pity towards him. Poor man! How could he be blamed for his hideously irrational actions? He, with his damaged brain had only a limited reasoning power.

That night she spoke to her husband in the compassionate bedside manner of a doctor.

"Look here Mahmood Khan; I can help you, but I shall need your full co-operation."

"Tell me what I have to do."

"I can treat you affectively and mitigate your sufferings. But before I begin the treatment, you have to agree to certain stipulations."

"I will do whatever you say. Please help me out of my misery. I don't want to live this undignified life."

"Wait, don't make commitments before you hear the conditions. These will not be easy to adhere to."

"Tell me please."

"Listen carefully. If I am going to treat you, the relation between you and me will be purely that of a patient and a doctor, not that of a husband and wife. We may maintain an outward façade of a married couple, but there shall be no physical relation between us. If you wish to take a second wife, I shall give my consent, so that there is no objection from the community and the clergy. Nor shall I object if you would want to have a discreet relation with another woman out of wedlock."

Mahmood was visibly disconcerted at this unexpected and strange condition. He just stared at his wife without a word. Nilofer let her words sink, and then continued with the same clinical inflection.

"You must understand that you will have to consume the prescribed drugs regularly for the rest of your life, just as you consume your food.

Then there is the matter of your drinking. You will have to scale it down. I shall not insist on a total abstinence, but it shall have to be in moderation. If you get drunk any day, I shall withdraw from treating you. Lastly, this is equally important; you shall have to control your temper. I know it won't be easy. I shall prescribe drugs to help in this, but you will have to make conscious efforts to stay cool."

Nilofer saw that she had his full attention.

"I don't want your commitment right now. Take time to think. When you have made up your mind, come back and tell me."

She got up and went to the bathroom to change. When she came back, she was gratified to see Mahmood gone from the room. That night again, he slept in the guest room.

The following night he stood before Nilofer like a beggar seeking charity.

"I will do as you say. Please help me."

"Tomorrow I shall procure the necessary medicines and shall instruct you in their use."

Mahmood made to leave. She stopped him.

"Stay for a few minutes. I want you to witness an act of mine."

She went to the shelf on which a copy of the Holy Quraan lay covered under a green silken drape. She removed the drape and spread it on the bedside table. Then she lifted the holy book, and touching it with her lips and eyes placed it reverently onto the drape. She placed her right hand on the book, and spoke slowly and deliberately.

"In the name of the Holy Quraan, I make this vow of chastity and celibacy for the rest of my life. If I break this vow any time, may I burn in the fires of hell. So help me Allah."

Mahmood, with his limited intellectual faculties, could not grasp the enormity of the vow of celibacy by a woman at the young age of twenty-nine. All he understood was that his wife had slammed a door into his face, and put a seal of finality on his exclusion from any physical contact with her.

Nilofer put Mahmood on a new regime of treatment the next day. She felt that the anti-epileptic drugs that he was already on were the right ones, but the doses needed to be enhanced. She increased them by fifty per cent. She added a small daily dose of a tranquilizer. For a moment, *only a moment,* she considered including an anti-libido preparation, but she resolutely discarded the thought. Chemical castration was for habitual rapists. Although what Mahmood had done to her since their nuptial night, amounted to rape, and she had, at the time, considered him a rapist, now in the light of her recent knowledge regarding his intellectual deficit, she had absolved him of the misdeed.

Mahmood, on his part, made an honest effort to keep his side of the agreement between them. He started sleeping in the guest room, though initially he did not move his things from the bedroom. The news of his sleeping apart from his wife reached his parents' ears in a matter of weeks, and the mother angrily confronted her son with it.

"However great doctor your wife may be, she cannot take away your conjugal rights."

"Damn it *Ami,*" Mahmood growled, "it is my decision, and I don't want any one interfering. Do you understand?"

His ferocious tone made the mother shut up. "These two seem to have quarreled. We shall let them reconcile themselves." The parents decided. Now that the whole thing was out in the open, Mahmood moved his things out of Nilofer's room into the spare guest room. Weeks later Nilofer was relieved to hear a heated, but hushed argument between Mahmood and his father regarding Mahmood's relation with a middle-aged woman employee at the farm.

"For God's sake keep it discreet," the father had pleaded

In the matter of drinking, Mahmood occasionally breached the limits of discretion. Nilofer usually ignored the transgression. But whenever under the influence of alcohol, or otherwise, he lost his temper and resorted to ranting, all Nilofer had to do was to say firmly,

"Mahmood, you know anger is not good for your health."

The reprimand never failed to work, and he would cool down immediately.

*****

On 5 January in the year of 1970, Vikram's thirty-second birth anniversary, Nilofer wrote to Vikram, her first and the last letter to him.

"Dear Bikku,

This morning the Almighty bestowed on us the bounty of a son. I have named him Waqaar Ahmed. I fondly call him Vicky... yours Nilofer."

Waqaar Ahmed's was a trained scientific brain. He set about searching his father with an organized plan in his mind. His first step was to determine the date of his own conception. He jotted down on a piece of paper.

Date of birth: January 5, 1970

Likely date of conception minus 266 days

Around April 14, 1969.

The next step was to find where his mother was on or around that date. He knew that she had gone to the U.K. in 1966, for a period of more than two years. On what date did she return from there? "That date is going to be the crucial clue in my search," he thought. He opened the cabinet in which important family documents were kept, and removed his mother's passports from the folder. There were three of them, two that had expired, and a current one. He took up the one that had been issued in1965, and scanned the visa pages. There it was

Departure Lahore	January 15, 1966
Arrival Heathrow	January 15, 1966
Departure Heathrow	April 23, 1969
Arrival Lahore	April 24, 1969

It was a catch 22 position for Waqaar. In the medical science, it was not possible to precisely pinpoint the date of conception from the date of birth. At best, it could be fixed within the limit of a fortnight. From the data that Waqaar had jotted down, all he could say with certainty was that he was conceived either a few days before his mother left the shores of Britain, or within a couple of days after arriving back home.

He applied logic to the situation. "I am not Mahmood's offspring. In Lahore, there has never been another man in her life. Not a whiff of misdemeanor on her part has ever been smelt. Therefore, Ammi could not have conceived me after she arrived back from Britain. She conceived me in that country, a few days before she departed from there." His mother's words rang in his mind. *"Your birth was a very carefully planned event."* He wrote at the bottom of his jottings.

The answer lies in the U.K. – QED.

He based his next conclusion on deduction. "My mother is fair complexioned, and I am dark. My father could not be a white man. He has to be of a colored race. He is very likely to be a Pakistani whom my mother came in contact while she was in the U.K. I must go there at the earliest opportunity." That opportunity did not arrive until two-and-a-half years later. He had promptly applied to the Home Office of the U.K. for the position of a senior house officer in surgery, in any hospital under the National Health Scheme. He had received an equally prompt reply expressing regrets. There was already a long queue of applicants for the post and no further applications were being considered for the next three years. He had then applied to the Commonwealth University, London, for a scholarship in surgery under the Commonwealth Scholarships Program. He had to send the application through proper channels. He heard nothing about it even after more than two years. It was probably buried in the files of the health ministry of his country. He had obtained his Master's degree in Surgery by then.

One day while scanning the pages of the British Journal of Medicine, he came across a notice inserted by the Royal College of Surgeons, London, inviting applications under the ODTS –The overseas doctors training scheme. He applied immediately.

It was Thursday, 19 September 1996. He had come home for lunch, and found a letter lying on his table. It was from the Royal College of Surgeons of London. With excitement of anticipation, he tore it open. He was offered a placement in the ODTS. He was overjoyed. He showed the letter to his mother. She had smiled – that angelic smile and said,

"This will be good for your future career."

"It shall help me find my father," he said to himself.

He was required to apply for registration with the General Medical Council, London. The formality took some time. He received a letter in April 1997, listing nine centers from which he could opt for, one for his first placement. He went about selecting the centre with the primary purpose of his visit in mind. From a family album, he removed a photograph that his mother had brought from Cardiff. It was a group photograph of the staff of Dr. Cynthia Joans, with whom his mother had worked a quarter century back. There were six of them. Only two of them were of oriental origin. His mother sitting at one extreme, and another young woman, tagged as Dr. Pamela Lahore, at the other end. It sounded like a Pakistani name. "If anyone can tell me about my father, it has to be this woman, Pamela Lahore," He said to himself. He searched the internet on his computer for Dr. Pamela Lahore. There she was – now a consultant Obstetrician and Gynecologist at the Royal Hospital, Manchester. The nine centers listed by the ODTS director included Manchester. He opted for it. Next, he had a copy made of the photograph to go with him to Manchester.

Waqaar reported to Mr. George Collier, the senior consultant in surgery at the Royal Hospital of Manchester on 13 July. He received a courteous, but a rather cool welcome. Dr. Collier personally gave him a tour of the department, and introduced him to his staff. He instructed his secretary, Mrs. Helen West to see to Waqaar's professional insurance, and then turned to him,

"Dr. Ahmed, it'll take a couple of days or so before your insurance policy is issued. Until then you are welcome to attend the department and observe our routine. Once your insurance procedure is complete, you will be assigned your duties, which will be the same as that of a senior house officer."

After a few days of working with Dr. Collier, Waqaar realized that he was unlikely to benefit professionally by the training program. First, the volume of work here was much smaller compared to that back home. Secondly, the surgical skill of the senior staff was nowhere near that of his postgraduate teacher, Dr. Aklhlaq of Lahore. Lastly, one did not see here the variety of surgical diseases compared to those, which they catered to in his own institution. "I shall quit this program, once I achieve my primary goal." To accomplish that goal he had to meet Dr. Pamela Lahore. "Should I ask her for an appointment? Alternatively, should I stage a casual bumping into her?" He debated, in his mind, the merits of both the approaches. Excuse me madam, Are you Dr. Pamela Lahore…My mother knew you a quarter century back…Don't you remember Dr. Nilofer Khan of Pakistan…She had worked with you in Cardiff…Oh, you don't remember? A staged chance meeting could end there. The other approach, of setting up a formal meeting, could yield more desirable results. He rang up the Department of gynecology, one afternoon. A secretary answered it. He asked to speak to Dr. Pamela Lahore.

"Yes… this is Pamela Lahore."

"Good afternoon Dr. Lahore. My name is Dr. Waqaar Ahmed. I work here in the surgery department. I would like to meet you."

"What is it about, Dr. …er…Ahmed, if I may ask?"

"An old friend and a colleague of yours has asked me to look you up."

"An old friend, you say, who?"

"Could we please meet and talk."

"Oh well...Dr. Ahmed…by the way, have you had your lunch?'

"Not yet."

"Well then, I am going for lunch at the consultants' dining hall. Please meet me there in fifteen minutes, and I shall buy your lunch."

"Thanks Dr. Lahore, I shall be there." Waqaar was happy the talk had ended on an informal note.

Both of them arrived at the dining hall almost at the same time. While they shook hands, she said,

"You talked about an old mutual friend. I had expected to see a middle-aged man. And here you are a fledgling young boy."

"I am sorry. I did not mean a mutual friend. In fact, she is my… ah…teacher. Dr. Nilofer of Pakistan…when she came to know I was coming to this country, she asked me to look you up."

"Nilofer…Nilofer…" Dr. Pamela Lahore frowned in concentration "I can't remember knowing anybody of that name."

Waqaar took out the group photograph from the inner pocket of his jacket and handed it to her.

"This may perhaps jog your memory." He was getting a bit apprehensive that his search might end before it had even begun.

"Ah, Dr. Khan, the sour nun!" Pamela exclaimed.

"The nun?" Waqaar said in surprise. He himself had, on occasions, called his mother that, but only in his mind.

"Yes, we jokingly used to refer to her as the doleful nun, because of her puritanical and melancholic behavior in the initial stages of her tenure here. Initially she used to wear dresses, which were not much different from a nun's habit. She shunned male company. Actually, she seemed to have some sort of grudge against male species. Why, she even avoided any entertainment…" Pamela chuckled as she delved into the old memories. "… I once invited her to a disco, thinking a little entertainment would lift her low spirits. You know, at the sight of dancing couples, she fled from the scene, and…"

The maid arrived at their table, and read out the menu for the lunch in a bored practiced tone. They gave their orders. Pamela did not resume her narration. She seemed to have forgotten why Waqaar was there. He nudged her to resume.

"You said Dr. Khan's initial behavior was puritanical. Did she…" he purposely left his query unfinished.

"O, the silly girl, one day, went and accused that angel of a man… what was his name…the captain of our university cricket team… O yes, Vicky…she went and accused him of making a pass at her…"

Waqaar felt faint. His heart was thudding against his rib cage. Vicky… that angel of a man… His mother's words reverberated in his mind. "*Vicky my son, I cannot and will not tell you his name. However, this much I shall tell you, he was an angel, and my soul mate…*" He was brought back to the present by what Pamela was saying.

"…out of the blue, she goes and marries him."

Waqaar, in his present state of mind, had lost the thread of Pamela's recounting.

"Married whom?" He asked

The maid placed their lunch plates in front of them. Pamela attacked hers with the zeal of a famished wolf. Waqaar had lost all appetite.

"You mean she married the man who had misbehaved with her?"

"Misbehave? Dear Vicky could never misbehave. He was too much of a gentleman. Dr. Khan must have realized her mistake. Of course, it was much later, maybe more than a year, before they got married. Why, I am not sure they really were married. They might have been just living in. Nevertheless, she was a lucky girl to have landed Vicky as her husband or boyfriend. We girls used to vie with each other for his attention. He always put us off with a polite smile. By the way, Dr. Ahmed, your teacher must be having a young son, or a daughter… um…let us see…around twenty-four or so. She was pregnant when she left Cardiff."

"Yes she has a son. My age, and he too is a doctor." There was a catch in Waqaar's voice, which Pamela failed to notice.

"Some people have all the luck. She was so keen to get pregnant. You know, she came to me for the pregnancy tests, barely a week after she must have conceived. And how thrilled she was when the tests turned out to be positive."

"*You are not a by-product of your parents' lust. Your birth was a very carefully planned event.*" Waqaar recalled his mother's pride-filled words.

Pamela had finished her meal. Waqaar had hardly touched his.

"Oh dear boy, you have hardly eaten anything. Do finish your lunch, and please excuse me, I have a meeting in ten minutes. Do give my regards to your teacher." And she was gone. Waqaar sat there staring at his uneaten lunch. His deductions were proved right. His mother had met his father in Cardiff. Whether they were married or had a live-in relationship, either way she had lived in sin. "*He was my soul mate. I shall worship him until the doomsday,"* she had said.

He left the dining hall in this somber mood, and walked slowly to his room. He spread the *mussalah* on the floor and stood at its edge in preparation to say the afternoon prayer, *salat ul asr*. His mind was in turmoil. The words of the namaaz kept jumbling up in his mind, and getting entwined with those of Pamela Lahore, "*how thrilled she was when the tests turned out positive."* He could not recite a single phrase of namaaz. In utter bewilderment, he knelt down and touched his fore head to the ground. *When one goes down in sajda or obeisance, one offers oneself, body, soul, and mind,* the words of a quranic scholar floated in his mind. "That is what my mother had done. She had offered her whole self to her soul mate. That cannot be a sin. No, I shall never think of my mother as a sinner." His mind cleared, and his distorted thoughts came into focus. "I am here to find my father, not to investigate the conduct of my mother." He stood up and folded his hands in front of him. The words of the *namaaz* flooded back into his memory, and he serenely offered his prayer. His appetite returned, and he satiated it with a snack, and a cup of cold coffee from the refrigerator. He sat down at his desk, and tried to recollect the information that he had extracted from Dr. Lahore. He jotted it down on a piece of paper.

1. Vicky
2. Angel
3. Cardiff
4. Cricketer – Captain of the university team

This was not much of information, but enough to make a beginning. Waqaar had wanted to ask Dr. Lahore the full name of Vicky, and the department he had worked in. He had refrained for fear of rousing suspicion in her mind that he was fishing for information.

The following morning he used his department computer and searched for Dr. Vicky on the internet. The search threw up three doctors by that name. One was a physician in the U.S.A., the second a dentist in the U.K., and the third a nutritionist of the U.K. All the three were women.

Next, he searched the net for the Cardiff University cricket teams. All he got was the schedule of the next match to be played between the Cardiff and the Newport teams, and the squads that will participate. There was the news of the present Cardiff team being crowned the British Universities Champions, and two of its player being selected to be part of the M.C.C. No information was available on the past teams. "The information that I want may be lying in the archives of the Cardiff University." Waqaar decided to get his next posting in Cardiff. That would have to wait for another four months.

He wrote to the director of the Program, requesting for his next posting in Cardiff. His request was granted. He landed in Cardiff on Tuesday, 13 January 1998, and went through the usual drill of meeting the senior consultant in surgery at the University Hospital of Wales, taking the tour of the department, and receiving instructions on his duties. He was assigned a room in the Radnor House. He was unaware of the fact that his mother too had lived there thirty years back. She rarely talked of her sojourn in the U.K.

Waqaar let a week pass. Once he had familiarized himself with his present set up, he decided to resume the search for his father, whom he now knew as Vicky. "Had Ammi given me the name Waqaar on purpose, so that she could call me Vicky, and keep alive the memory of her…soul mate?" He could not bring himself to say *her husband.*

He rode a bus to the University, located in the Cathay's Park, and presented to the librarian his I.D. card, issued by the hospital. He was promptly enrolled as a member and was issued a membership card. The librarian, Mr. Perry Horton, in his early fifties, was a friendly soul. He took Waqaar around and showed him various sections of the library. Waqaar noticed with satisfaction that a separate room was marked as the records.

"Mr. Horton, do we have here, records of the past university's cricket teams?" he made the question sound casual.

"O yes, we have a meticulously maintained record of all the teams, right from the year 1909 onwards. Before that they went under the name of Cardiff Cricket Club."

He led Waqaar into the record room, and walked straight to the sports section. He indicated a row of neatly bound volumes, and said,

"Each volume is for a decade, and gives comprehensive information on the teams, and the matches played by them. You will find all that you want to know in those volumes."

The librarian went back to his cabin. Waqaar extracted from the row the volume marked University of Wales, Cricket chronicle, 1961-1970. He looked at the page of contents. The teams were listed in chapter seven, page 302. There were full-page photographs of the teams. The tenure of the teams was give at the top, and the names of the players at the bottom. Waqaar turned the pages until he came to the page number 307. The photograph showed a non-white player seated in the middle of the first row. He stared at the name printed at the bottom. It read, Dr. Vikram Kocher (c). Vikram, Vikram, Vikram. He repeated the name again and again. This cannot be true. Vikram is a Hindu name. He willed it not to be true. He tried arguing with himself to prove it untrue. It must be the wrong team. He looked at the date – October 1965 to May 1966. His mother had arrived here in January 1966. The last name – Kocher, "Yes, yes, I had a schoolmate, Aaftaab Kocher. Kocher is a Muslim family name. Vikram Kocher must be a Muslim." He clutched at straws, but he knew in his heart that his reasoning was futile. In desperation, he turned to the pages, which listed the captains individually. There he was again, the photograph and the biodata.

Full name: Vikram Shivram Kocher

Date of birth: 05. 01. 1938

Nationality: Indian.

Waqaar could not go on. The tears stung his eyes. Even through his tears he could see how closely he himself resembled the photograph in front of him. He closed the volume, and slumped on to the table. He remained in that position until he felt drained of all emotions. Then he stood up, wiped his face with a kerchief, placed the record book back in its shelf, and left the library. He wanted to be alone. He did not take a bus, but walked all the way to his room and flung himself into his bed. He went without supper. He had a troubled sleep, interspersed with dreams of his father, holding him by the hand and walking him in a park, teaching him how to hold a cricket bat, carrying him on his shoulders. The face of his father, in the dreams, kept transforming from Mahmood's to Dr. Kocher's, and back to Mahmood's. He woke up in the wee hours of the morning, but remained in bed until it was time to get ready to go to the hospital.

The whole morning he worked in the ward. His heart was not in what he was doing. At lunch break, instead of going to the dining hall, he headed to the departmental library. No one was there. He uncovered the computer and went on the Internet. He entered Dr. Vikram Kocher, and clicked the *search* button. What he saw took his breath away. There was a long list of pages on the web site.

Dr. Vikram Kocher, Waqaar Charitable Hospital for Plastic and Reconstructive Surgery, Ahmedabad, India.

Dr. Vikram Kocher, Muskaan Hospital for Plastic and Reconstructive Surgery, Ahmedabad, India.

Dr. Vikram Kocher, M3 Trust, Ahmedabad, India.

Dr. Vikram Kocher, Biographical notes.

Dr. Vikram Kocher, the cricketer.

Dr.Vikram Kocher, His Urdu Writings.

Dr. Vikram Kocher, Press Reviews.

Dr. Vikram Kocher, Television Coverage.

There were a number of other pages listing his training, the conferences attended as a faculty, awards, and honors, etc. It would have taken hours to read all those pages. Waqaar could not have monopolized the computer for that long. He made prints of the pages, and read them later. The personal information on Dr. Vikram, revealed by these pages startled Waqaar.

"Dr. Vikram Kocher, the compassionate healer, popularly called V.K. Sahib, was born on January the fifth, in the year 1938, in the tiny village of Uchaanwala, in the district of Gujarat of Punjab, now a part of Pakistan…

Uchaanwala? "Uchaanwala is the place of birth mentioned in Ammi's passport too. Did Ammi and Abba know each other since their childhood?" Waqaar was oblivious of the fact that in his thoughts, he had referred to Dr. Vikram Kocher as *abba, father.* He read on.

"…He was just nine at the time of partition of the country. His family had to flee their home. He and his parents arrived at Ahmedabad, penniless and homeless, and took shelter in a refugee camp. Here they came in touch with Dr. Manubhai Patel, a philanthropist physician. The kindly doctor gave shelter and a job to the refugee couple, and undertook the education of their child. The intelligent and diligent child has arisen to become perhaps the most gifted surgeon of the country. His benefactors, the Patel couple were killed in 1985, when the terrorists had blown off, mid-air, the aircraft in which they were returning from Canada. His father's rag-to-riches story is no less spectacular. He had an astute businessperson's mind, and from a penniless refugee, he moved on to become one of the richest builders of the state, before he died. The Patels, as well as his father had left their total assets to Vikram in their wills. Dr. Vikram has never forgotten the generosity shown to him by Dr. Manubhai Patel and his wife Dr. Mehru Patel, whom he called *Bapuji* and *Baa* during their lifetime. He has set up the Mannu and Mehru Memorial Trust in their honor to carry forward their philanthropic work…

…The doctor is an amateur painter and an ardent admirer of Urdu poetry. He writes in that language, under the nom de plume of Naacheez... *Naacheez?* "My God! I had thought he was a Pakistani." The biographic notes had one or two more surprises for Waqaar.

…When once asked why he had given a Muslim sounding name, Waqaar, to his charitable hospital, the good doctor had replied that he was an admirer of Urdu language, and Waqaar in Urdu means *honor, dignity.* 'In this hospital, we repair the defects with which the children are born, so that they can live and grow up with dignity.' A journalist had once asked him why he had not married. His answer was that it would have been an act of unfaithfulness towards his beloved. When asked who his beloved was, he had jestingly replied, 'you can see her in Waqaar.'"

Waqaar now had in front of him, a plethora of information on his father. He could piece together almost the whole story of his parents.

"My mother was married in September of 1965, and just three months later had left for the U.K. She must have been running away from her marriage. How could she have ever been happy with that almost unlettered and half-witted husband of hers? God knows under what circumstances she came to marry Mahmood. Initially she must have found no solace in the inhospitable atmosphere of the new place. Waqaar recalled the words of Dr. Lahore. *We used to call her doleful nun. She had some sort of grudge against the male species.* Later on, she must have met Abba" – Waqaar now unhesitatingly referred to Vikram, even in his thoughts, as his father. "They must have, somehow recognized each other. Meeting the child hood mate must have rekindled in Ammi the zest for life. They must have loved each other intensely, but could not bind in a legal wedlock, nor could they have remained together for long, even out of wedlock. Ammi had to return home. They must have planned my birth so that my mother could remain united with her loved one through me. The diplomatic answer that Abba gave to the journalist was a pointer to that, *you can see her in Waqaar.* I am the bond between them. Ammi has me to live for. Abba might have no one. I must go to him. *I shall see him.*" Waqaar. made another promise to himself.

From the website of Dr. Vikram, Waqaar had obtained information about his professional work. He was running two large hospitals in Ahmedabad, one named the Waqaar Charitable Hospital for Plastic and Reconstructive Surgery, the other the Muskan Hospital for Plastic and Reconstructive Surgery. Both were managed by a trust called the Mannu and Mehru Memorial Trust, or M3 Trust in short, of which he was the founder chairperson, and the managing director.

The photographs and the write-ups on the website showed that the two hospitals were mirror images of each other. They were housed in large buildings surrounded by well-kept lawns and plants. Both were staffed with dedicated medical, paramedical, nursing, administrative, and unskilled personnel. Both had state of the art equipment and facilities. Both received patients from all over India, as well as from the neighboring countries. Nevertheless, there were three differences. Although the patients of both the hospital received the standard bills for the treatment, the bills issued by the Waqaar Hospital were stamped "*PAY WHAT YOU CAN AFFORD*", and the payment was made by dropping the afforded amount into a box fixed to a wall in a small cubicle. The patient had a choice to pay cash or by a cheque. The bill issued by the Muskan hospital had to be paid in full, and only by a cheque. The rent for the rooms let out to the accompanying relatives, and the food served at the canteen attached to the Waqaar Hospital were heavily subsidized, although these services were of the same standard at both the hospitals. No cosmetic surgery was permitted at the Waqaar Charitable. There was one inviolable rule. No patient was scheduled for surgery, at either hospital, unless Dr. Vikram had personally seen the patient, and discussed the proposed surgical procedure with the operating surgeon. A patient was never discharged unless Dr. Vikram had seen him, and permitted him to go. The rule was overlooked only when he was unable to come to the hospital.

Waqaar learnt from the website, that the M3 Trust offered a limited number of sponsorships to surgeons from India and abroad. The sponsored doctors could visit the hospitals to observe their working, for a limited period of one to four weeks. The website gave the address of the trust where the application and the bio-data of the applicant could be sent. Waqaar thought obtaining the sponsorship for a visit would be a sure way of meeting his father. Should he apply for it while he was in Britain, or should he apply after returning home? He could not let his mother know that he was searching his father. It was best to apply while he was still in Britain. He promptly sent in his application for the sponsored visit for one week. He knew of course, that obtaining visa to India was going to be the greatest hurdle in his plan, looking at the strained relationship between India and his own country. He received a reply to his application telling him that he was welcome to visit the Hospitals anytime after July 1. He wrote a letter to the Pakistan High Commissioner, soliciting his help to get clearance for traveling to India. He enclosed copies of his application to the M3 Trust and their reply. He received a note from the secretary of the Ambassador, asking him to come down to the embassy next Monday at eleven.

Waqaar took leave of absences from his department for Monday, and presented himself at the embassy in Lowdes Square of London, a few minutes before the appointed time. The receptionist directed him to the secretary's office. The officer asked him to have a seat as he picked up the intercom.

"Sir, Dr. Waqaar Ahmed is here." He listened for barely one second, replaced the instrument, and rose from his chair.

"The High Commissioner will see you now. Please come with me."

The secretary escorted him to the Ambassador's Office. He opened the door, announced Waqaar, motioned him to go in, and withdrew. Waqaar noticed that the door and the walls of the office were padded to make it sound proof. The High Commissioner, whose name, Waqaar knew was Tahir-ul-Zamaan, came round the table and shook his hand saying

"*Khush Aamdeed*, Welcome, Dr. Waqaar Ahmed. Please be seated."

From his accent, Waaqaar construed that Tahir probably hailed from the Sind province. He was a tall handsome man, in his early thirties, with pleasing features, and intelligent looking eyes. Waqaar had not expected to see so young a man in charge of such vital office, looking after the interests of his nation in an all-important country like the U.K.

"May I see your passport, doctor?" He came straight to the point.

Waqaar handed it to him. He glanced at the last page, and returned it to Waqaar.

"What is the purpose of your intended visit?" His question was succinct and sounded grim to Waqaar.

"Sir, the two hospitals that I wish to visit in India, are being run on a unique strategy. I call it a *Robin Hood Strategy.* Taking from the rich and giving to the poor. On the face of it, it looks simple. Treat the rich patients in a posh hospital, charge them full fees, and plough the money into a charitable but equally posh hospital. However, the whole mechanism of running them must be quite complex, needing an astute and dedicated management. Frankly, sir, I am as interested in studying their organizational aspect as the technical side. I do not know how much they will permit me to delve into their management, but I do want to study whether it will be possible to replicate the set up in our own country.

"To do that job, don't you think doctor, we should send an economist?" There was a scornful inflection in the High Commissioner voice. "He is trying to dissuade me in my venture," thought Waqaar.

"I beg to differ, sir," he said politely, "it is not merely a matter of economics."

"I thought you said you wanted to scrutinize their managerial aspect."

"I seem to have put it badly. Let me explain with a concrete example. If I had worked with Dr. Kocher for a few years, any number of corporate hospitals would try to lure me to them, by offering me higher emoluments and better service conditions. I have read that most of Dr. Kocher's staff has been with him right from the inception of his hospitals. I want to see what makes them stick to him…"

"For that, one has to be a messiah, *a* prophet like him, keeping his flock together." The High Commissioner, uncharacteristically, interrupted him. His voice had gone soft.

"That's it Sir. I want to see that prophet." The pitch of Waqaar's voice had risen. He controlled himself, and asked,

"Sir, have you met him any time?"

"Yes, once." The ambassador said succinctly. He did not elaborate. He could not let any one know that only a year back, Dr. Vikram had operated upon his son, after a failed surgery for a bad hypospadias. The child was born with a defective urethra, and the local surgeon had botched up the reconstructive surgery. Only a few people in the administrative ranks knew that Dr. Kocher had performed the revised surgery. Had this become public, there would have been a furious outcry. Soliciting help from the *enemy* country would have been considered an unpatriotic act.

Suddenly the High Commissioner seemed keen to end the interview. He said,

"Doctor, your passport has been endorsed as invalid for travel to India. I shall have to get a clearance from our ministry of foreign affairs to have that endorsement cancelled. I do not foresee much difficulty in getting it though, thanks to the ongoing bus diplomacy between our country and India…" He stopped as he saw a puzzled look in Waqaar eyes. "Oh, the bus diplomacy… You must be aware that our Prime Minister, *Janaab* Mian Mohamed Nawaz Sharif and his Indian counterpart, Mr. Atal Behari Vajpayee are engaged in a confidence building drive between our two countries. A bus service has been introduced between Delhi and Lahore. Actually, the Indian Prime Minister was one of the passengers on the first run of the bus, and was cordially received at Lahore by our own Prime Minister. The two governments have, to some extent, liberalized the rules for travel between the two countries. You have good chances of getting clearance for traveling to India. Ring us up after a week, and we'll let you know the situation."

The High Commissioner got up to indicate that the interview was over.

Waqaar completed his tenure of training in the U.K. on 12 July 1998. By that time, the authorities of his country had cleared him for traveling to India, and he had obtained the visa from the Indian High Commission. It had taken two personal visits to the office of the High Commission at Aldwych in London, and a ten days' time to have his visa processed. He flew into the international airport of Bombay, renamed Mumbai on July 14. His travel agent had booked him on the Rajdhani Express train running between Bombay and Delhi, with a halt at Ahmedabad. The train was fully air-conditioned and his journey to Ahmedabad was quite comfortable. A courier from the M3 trust met him at the station and drove him to the premises of the Waqaar Hospital. He was ushered into a comfortable looking room in a two-storeyed building set apart from the main building of the hospital. The courier, who had rather a comical name of Baanke Bihari Lal, asked him whether he could get him something to eat. Waqaar declined. An appetizing dinner had been served on the train.

"Please be ready by seven. Dr. Deepak Bhatt will take you to breakfast. Then you are to meet V.K Sahib in his office precisely at half past eight."

After the courier left, Waqaar changed into his pajamas. It was past midnight, too late for the Ishaa namaaz. He brushed his teeth, and went to bed. He had not slept since he had left Cardiff about twenty-two hours back. Yet sleep was miles away from his eyes. Lying in a strange bed, in a strange place, in a country considered hostile to his own, he thought of the imminent meeting with a man who was his father, yet a total stranger to him. Not only a stranger, but of a community considered antagonistic to his own. He willed himself to expunge the word *kafir* from his mind. Conflicting thoughts churned within his head. "Will he recognize me? If he did not, how shall I disclose my identity? If he did recognize me but chose to feign ignorance what should be my response? Should I leave, and return home forthwith? In the first place, how would I know that he has recognized me? I cannot expect him to rush to me, and embrace me in the presence of people, and say look here folks, this is my son whom I had begotten illicitly, twenty-eight years back, by a Muslim concubine of mine, hailing from Pakistan. Was it a mistake to have come here? Must I catch the first train to Bombay, and fly back home? No, now that I am here, I shall see the whole thing through. Ya illahi, I have ensnared myself in an awful situation. Do help me my Parvardigar." He fell asleep in the wee hours of the morning.

That night, Vikram did not have a wink of sleep either. In the evening, when he was about to leave his office, his secretary had placed a manila folder before him.

"This is the file of the visiting doctor from Pakistan who is joining us tomorrow for a week's time."

Although the sanctioning of the sponsorships for the visiting doctors was the domain of Dr. Mayank Raval, the biodata of every visiting doctor was put before Vikram for his perusal the day before the visitor was due to arrive, because it was Vikram's task to welcome the visitor and introduce him to the staff.

"From Pakistan?" Vikram was surprised. Many doctors from the neighboring countries had taken advantage of the sponsorship offered by the M3 trust and visited the twin hospitals. None had come from Pakistan so far. The bitter relation between the two countries went back to the time of the partition of the Indian subcontinent in 1947, and had persisted unabated. "May be," Vikram thought, "this time the peace parleys between the prime ministers Vajpayee and Sharif are not merely a political gimmick." He picked up the file, put it in his bag, and hastily left the office. He was in a hurry. He had to attend a dinner at the Governor's house that night. He drove home, had a bath, and changed for the dinner. He made a mental note to read the file after he returned from his dinner appointment.

At eleven, before going to bed, he retrieved the file from the bag. Sitting down on the edge of his bed, he quickly turned the pages of the file and came to the prescribed form of application. He froze, and stared at the affixed photograph. He was looking at his own image of younger days. He felt faint. He gripped the edge of the bed for support. He closed his eyes and took deep breaths. He soon got a grip on himself.

"Can it be…?" Can it be…? He looked at the name – Waqaar Ahmed. The address – 5, Gulberg, Lahore.

Nilofer was there in the room. She was saying,

"This morning the Almighty has bestowed on us the bounty of a son. I have named him Waqaar Ahmed…"

He turned around. He was alone in the room. He sat there silently, staring alternately at the photograph and the name on the application. Why has Nilofer made the divulgence? Morbid thought assailed his mind, and it projected gloomy scenes. His beloved on deathbed, disclosing the truth to their son; or worse, Nilofer dead, and her will revealing the paternity of her son. What must he be thinking of his parents? He clutched at the straws. "May be, he does not know the truth, and his trip here is a mere coincidence? The first visitor from Pakistan turns out to be my son. It cannot be a coincidence." The whole night, he turned and tossed in his bed. He dragged himself out of his bed at five, and went for his morning walk. A cold bath and a hot cup of tea revived his spirits to some extent. During breakfast, his mother noticed that his mind was preoccupied, and he was eating mechanically. Halfway through the meal, the telephone rang.

"Ah, these blighted emergencies!" Exclaimed the mother disapprovingly. Vikram picked up the receiver.

"Sir, the doctor from Pakistan arrived last night. I have deposited him at the hospital guest house." It was Baanke Bihari Lal reporting.

"Thank you Baanke." Vikram replaced the receiver and returned to his partially eaten breakfast. His mother noticed a look of excitement on his face. He attacked his breakfast with gusto. He was not given to such abrupt changes of mood. His mother, who sometimes referred to him as the placid ocean, wondered what Baanke had told him that had created ripples in the tranquil water. Vikram was thinking, "My son is here today. That is all that matters."

*****

Waqaar woke up to a melodious azaan, the call to prayer for the devout Muslims, coming from a loudspeaker mounted on the minaret of a neighboring mosque. He got up, showered, and offered the morning namaaz. He felt calm, and ready to face the impending ordeal of meeting his earthly creator. He wondered whether there was a dress code for the doctors. He debated what to wear. To be on the safe side, he decided on a formal suit, although Ahmedabad was quite hot in that season. He chose the lightest of the suits, a white shirt, and a black plain tie. He dressed carefully, but left the jacket draped on the back of a chair. He intended to put it on when he went out for breakfast. Precisely at seven, there was a knock at his door. The newcomer, a young man in his early twenties, identified himself as Dr. Deepak Bhatt, an intern at the hospital. The name 'Bhatt' made Waqaar think, "we the people of Pakistan and India have common languages, common food, common music, common customs, and even common family names – Bhatts and Kochers, irrespective of our religions, then why is there the sabre rattling between the two governments?" Seeing that Dr. Bhatt was dressed casually in trousers and shirt, Waqaar decided to leave the jacket. He accompanied the intern to the cafeteria, where they breakfasted on omelette and toast, and filtered coffee. Dr. Bhatt then led Waqaar to the office of V.K Sahib at the hospital, precisely at half past eight.

Dr. Bhatt knocked at the door softly, opened it, and motioned Waqaar to enter ahead of him. Waqaar had his emotions quite under control, and advanced towards the desk to meet the man who had occupied his mind, heart, and soul every single moment for the last three and a half years. Two men were sitting on the far side of the desk.

A bearded man, wearing an open cream-colored shirt, was working on a computer, while the other was reading a letter, obviously one from a heap of mail lying in front of him. Waqaar looked around but his father was nowhere to be seen.

"Sir, our new visitor, Dr. Waqaar Ahmed from Lahore is here." Deepak announced.

The bearded man looked up. Waqaar saw the face of his father, partially veiled by a short-boxed salt and pepper beard, and a closely trimmed mustache. An instant gleam flared up in his eyes that were now riveted on his son's face. Waqaar had read of smiling eyes in books, and had wondered how the eyes could smile. He was seeing them now.

"Ah! Dr.Waqaar Ahmed, from my beloved homeland! You bring a whiff of *naseem,* the breeze of dawn of the Punjab. Come, come Dr. Waqaar, and have a seat.

"I wish you a very good morning, sir," Waqaar offered the formal greetings, and took a chair. Dr. Deepak Bhatt remained standing. Dr. Vikram introduced Waqaar to the other man at the desk as Dr. Mayank Raval. Then turning to Dr. Bhatt, he asked,

"Deepak, have you given our guest his breakfast, or have you kept him hungry?"

Waqaar gave the answer,

"Dr. Bhatt has been very kind. I have had a delicious breakfast. Thank you for your concern, sir."

Dr. Vikram went on effusively,

"You see, Deepak, Dr. Waqaar comes from my *maika,* my forefathers' abode. That makes him a relative of mine. I cannot let a dear family member stay in a boarding house. Will you please see to it that his luggage is shifted to my residence? He shall be staying with me. Do I have your consent, Waqaar?"

The transition from *Dr. Waqaar Ahmed,* to *Dr. Waqaar,* and then to just *Waqaar,* did not go unnoticed by the guest.

"I shall consider it a blessing of Allah."

"That's settled then. Now, let's go and see our patients."

Waqaar spent the next ninety minutes with Dr. Vikram and Dr. Rawal, making rounds of the wards. They visited each one of the patients admitted to the Waqaar Hospital. Majority of them had already been operated upon. The others were scheduled for surgery in the next couple of days. They were mostly children with various congenital defects. Vikram approached them with fatherly tenderness. He gave Waqaar a short résumé of each case, keeping his eyes glued on his son's face all the time. At the end of the ward rounds, Vikram said to him solicitously,

"You must be tired from the journey. You better go home, have your lunch, and rest a while. I have a couple of surgeries to perform. We shall meet in the evening."

Waqaar agreed readily. He badly needed some sleep. The chauffeur drove him to his father's residence. The house was one of the twin bungalows, surrounded by lush green lawns and flowering shrubs. As they mounted the steps on to a large porch, the driver shouted through the open door.

"Sakina Bibi, the guest has arrived."

A woman, past her youth, and dressed in immaculately clean, white *kameeze and salwar*, emerged from the house. A white duppatta covered her head, its two *palloos* neatly wound around her neck in the form of a simple *hijab*. She welcomed him into a wide, well furnished hall, and invited him to have a seat.

"Would you have some tea, or may be a cold drink?"

Waqaar politely declined. She called out to someone in a language of which only a few words were intelligible to him. He could understand that she was asking some one to come down. Later on, he was to know that it was Gujarati, the regional language of the state. Another woman, of nearly the same age, answered Sakina Bibi's summons. She held a duster in her hand. She must have been interrupted in her cleaning work. Sakina Bibi spoke to her again in the same language, and then said to Waqaar.

"Pushpa will show you to your room. *Sahib* said you need rest. Lunch will be ready in a couple of hours."

Waqaar silently followed the servant to his room. His luggage, which had been shifted earlier, lay on two low tables next to the inbuilt cabinet. He changed into pajamas and threw himself into the bed. In no time, he was fast asleep. He woke up at two, washed his face, and quickly dressed in trousers and shirt. He rushed down to the hall. Sakina Bibi was waiting for him. He apologized.

"Pardon me. I overslept."

"Do not apologize. You needed the sleep. Take your seat at the table. I shall bring your lunch."

While she was laying the table, he asked,

"Have others eaten?"

"There are not many to be fed here. There are only two family members, Doctor Sahib, and his mother, Beji. The old lady always eats at one O'clock. She wanted to wait for you. She was keen to see the visitor who has come from her *babul-ka-desh*, her fatherland. I persuaded her to eat and have her usual siesta. You will meet her at tea at half past five. V.K. Sahib eats his lunch at the hospital cafeteria, if he gets time in-between his operations.

"What about you? Have you eaten? Or have I kept you from your lunch?"

"I do not eat here. My husband and I, we both work here. Between the two of us, we manage the Sahib's household. My main job is to look after Beji during the day when Doctor Sahib is away at the hospital, besides supervising the general upkeep of the house.

After finishing lunch, Waqaar thanked Sakina Bibi, and retired to his room. He picked up the day's copy of *The Times of India,* the daily newspaper, from the hall and carried it to his room. He scanned the news items, but there was nothing to hold his attention until he came to the editorial. It was titled, 'nuclear tit for tat'. It was an in depth study of the present relations between Pakistan and India. The editor had decried the arms race between the neighbors that was eating into the meager resources of both the countries, the resources that could be used to better the lives of their poor citizens. However, according to the editor, there was a silver lining to the ominous clouds of this arms race. The retaliatory action of Pakistan in exploding a nuclear device in the Chagai Hills within a fortnight of similar explosion by India at Pokhran had made one thing clear to both the parties. From now on, neither could afford to go to a full-blown war against the other. They could do so only at the peril of mutual annihilation. The editor had gone on to suggest that now that both sides had the nuclear deterrent against any armed misdemeanor by either side, they should stop wasting their resources in purchasing arms, and should spend their energies in building up their economy. Pakistan would be the greater gainer from the cessation of hostilities. It is a much smaller country compared to India, and with much more limited resources. If it continues to strive to achieve parity with India in all fields, it is likely to meet the same fate as the Soviet Republic did while seeking equality with the more resourceful United States of America. Pakistan will, one day, have to learn to live as a younger brother of India. There is no shame in being the younger brother. The editor considered the ongoing peace parleys between the prime ministers of the two countries, Mr. Vajpayee and Mr. Sharif, a step in the right direction. Nevertheless, he expressed the apprehension that the hawkish generals in the Pak army might throw a spanner in these confident building efforts of the two statesmen.

Waqaar got so engrossed reflecting on the editorial, that he lost count of the time. A knock on his door cut through his reverie

"Sir, the tea is laid. Beji is waiting for you." It was Pushpa.

As he entered the hall, he saw a frail, fair complexioned elderly woman in a Punjabi cream-colored dress sitting at the dining table. She had a regal profile.

"Aadab, Beji," He said as he approached the table. She looked up, and started to reply to his salutations,

"Jeenvade ..." She was about to say *jeenvade raho,* the traditional words of blessings in Punjabi, but stopped midway. She groped for her spectacles that were hanging around her neck, on a gold chain, put them on, and peered at his face.

"Hai, mein mar jaanwan!" She uttered the Punjabi phrase of astonishment, almost in a whisper. Recovering quickly from her amazement, she went on in a normal tone.

"For a moment I thought I was seeing my *Bikku.* You look so much like him, when he was your age."

Waqaar understood that by Bikku she meant Dr. Vikram. She had noticed the resemblance. This disconcerted him briefly. He recovered promptly, and said laughingly,

"Beji, I thought you saw a ghost. Do I look like a ghost?"

"No, child, you are a handsome lad. At first sight, I thought you looked a lot like my son. At my age, the mind gets a bit muddled. Do pardon me."

"I am too young to be your son, but Beji, why don't you consider me your grandson? May I call you *Daadi,* my grand mother?"

"It would please me very much. You know, had Bikram married, after he returned from abroad, he would be having a child of your age… Come son, sit here besides me, and have your tea."

Waqaar took the chair next to her, and nibbled at a tomato-cucumber sandwich.

"Daadi, why did the doctor sahib not marry?" Waqaar knew it was not an appropriate question, but Beji's instant affection for him overcame his prudence.

The old lady grimaced, and said.

"As a dutiful mother, I had selected a fabulous girl for him, but he refused even to meet her. His late father, may his soul rest in peace, sided with him. 'Maya, he said, our son is of new generation. Give him the freedom to pick his own life partner.'"

"And he never picked one. Is that it, Daadi?" Waqaar had an inexplicable urge to egg her on.

"No he did not…" She started giggling under her breath, and said,

"Yes, he did once pick up a prospective bride for himself…" She laughed again. "He must have been a child of seven then…" She stopped, and frowned, as if trying to remember.

"His cousin had married a pretty girl. The village women were praising the good looks of the bride. My little Bikku proudly told me his future bride was prettier than that of his cousin. When I asked him who the lucky girl was, he told me he intended to marry his five-year-old playmate, the beautiful daughter of Aneesa Bibi, our next-door neighbor in the village of Uchaanwala. Poor innocent child! At that tender age, he didn't understand that centuries old impenetrable wall stood between him and his dream."

She picked up her silver handle cane and stood up. Sakina hastened to her side, and taking her arm led her silently to her room. The old memories had probably saddened her. Waqaar remained sitting there, lost in his own thoughts. Beji had said her son wanted to marry the daughter of their neighbor Aneesa Bibi. That was the name of his his mother's mother. "So Dad and Mom were childhood companions. There must have been a spark of love between them even at that tender age. They had drifted apart, like two clouds in the sky, blown away by the political storm that had ripped their country into two. Nevertheless, the spark must have endured. Twenty-one years later, the gentle breeze of fate had pushed the drifting clouds towards each other, and they came together in a foreign sky." Waqaar tried to picture the phenomenon of fusion of love, when the two of them had recognized each other. Was there a clap of thunder, and dazzling lightening, as the one brought about by the coming together of two clouds charged with electricity? Or, was the meeting of the two tender and caring mates a gentle drizzle of love? He remained immersed in his thoughts, oblivious of the presence of Sakina Bibi, who stood there mesmerized by the faraway look on the guest's face. He came to himself when the mild mannered maid removed his cup of tea, which had gone cold, and replaced it with a fresh hot one. He thanked her, and sipped the tea, still thinking of his parent's togetherness in the alien land. How painful it must have been when the time came for them to part again. His eyes became misty at the thought of his parents living the lives of monks, both drowning their personal feelings in the service of the sick. He himself was feeling sick at heart, and decided to have a stroll in the open.

"Sakina Aapa," he said to the housekeeper, "I am going out for a stroll."

"It will do you a lot of good, but please be back before dinner time. It is served at nine." Sakina was pleased at Waqaar addressing her as Aapa, the elder sister. His parents must have inculcated civility in him.

Waqaar took a long walk taking in, subconsciously, prominent landmarks, which would help him to return without losing his way. The walk revived his drooping spirits. He returned to the house at half past eight. Dr. Vikram was sitting at the dining table along with his mother. Sakina was arranging glasses in a tray. A familiar sound of a ladle stirring food in the pot came from the kitchen.

As he approached the group, Beji said,

"There you are, Wakker son..." She broke off realizing that she had mispronounced her guest's name. "Do pardon me son. This unlettered old woman finds it difficult to pronounce the modern names. In our times the names were so simple, like Phallu, Daulu, Mamdu, Amdu, and so on."

Waqaar realized she was referring to abbreviated names for Fazal, Daulat, Mahmood, and Ahmed.

"Don't worry Daadi; I too have a short name. You can call me Vicky. That's what my mother calls me."

Dr. Vikram was taken aback, first at Waqaar addressing Beji as Daadi, and then revealing his nickname. They looked at each other. There was an impish gleam in Waqaar's eyes. Vikram wondered what had passed between Beji and Waqaar to make them so informal with each other.

The cook came in, and announced that the dinner was ready. Sakina laid three plates on the table, and then went into the kitchen to fetch the food. She waited at the table as the trio ate in silence. When they had finished, Sakina left to join her family in the outhouse. Beji sent a barrage of questions at Waqaar.

"Tell me Vicky, have you ever been to my village of Uchaanwala? Do the youth still play the Jodi, the twin flutes? Do they still sing the

Heer, the *Mahiya,* and the *Mirza-Sahiban?* Do the young lads and lasses still dance the *Bhangda,* and the *Gidda?* Do the girls still sway on the swings during the month of Sawan?"

All Waqaar could do was to smile at the eager inquiries of his grandmother regarding the land she was forced to leave behind half a century back. He said,

"Daadi, come with me, and I shall take you to your Uchaanwala. Then you shall see the goings on there for yourself."

"How can I go with you? These *mar jaane*; the cursed politicians won't give me permit to enter my birth land."

"Rest assured Daadi, one day I shall take you to your Uchaanwala."

"I hope that day will come before I depart from this world."

She got up with a sigh. Waqaar handed her the walking stick. Vikram held her by the arm, and the old dame walked away to her room with a bowed head. The parting words of his grandmother had saddened Waqaar. He said good night to his host and retired to his room. Vikram was left alone in the hall, brooding over the evening's events. When the clock in the hall struck eleven, he got up and walked up the stair to the guest room where Waqaar was lodged. He saw a beam of light under the door. His son was still awake. He knocked gently, opened the door, and went in. Waqaar was stretched out on the reclining chair, reading *Train to Pakistan,* a novel by Khushwant Singh,which he had picked up from a bookstall on the Ahmedabad railway station. On seeing Vikram, he put aside the book and rose to his feet. For a minute the two stood there, father and son, facing each other, without saying a word. Vikram broke the silence.

"I came to see whether you are comfortable."

Waqaar looked into his father's eyes, and then lowering his own, he said.

"My mother says paradise is under the feet of one's parents. How can one be uncomfortable in paradise?"

Vikram saw tears roll down his son's cheeks. He could restrain himself no more. He stepped forwards and engulfed him in his arms.

The two held each other in an embrace for a long time, tears soaking their shoulders.

"Abbajaan!" Waqaar's voice came out in a squeak.

"My child!"

Vikram was first to control his emotions. He disengaged his son from his embrace, held his face in his hands, and kissed his forehead.

"How is your mother?" Vikram asked as he guided his son to a chair, took one himself, and sat facing him.

"She is well, and is..." He was about to say *and is lonely*, but checked himself and went on to say,

"She keeps herself immersed in work, at her charitable hospital."

"Does she know that you are here?"

"No, she doesn't. She has steadfastly refused to divulge your identity, and is, probably, unaware of your whereabouts."

Vikram had never doubted that Nilofer would keep her words to him never to divulge his identity to their son.

"Then how did you find me?"

"When my fa... when my mother's...er...mentally indifferent husband was dying of an accident, three years back, I came to know from his blood type that he was not my father. My mother refused to reveal anything about my real father."

A long sigh escaped Vikram. A mentally indifferent husband; so that was the cause of my Nilu's despondency. After a short pause, Waqaar resumed his narrative.

"A little working on the date of my birth led me to Cardiff where I managed to dig up your name. Rest was simple, thanks to the Internet. At the moment, Ammi believes I am in the U.K., and am due to return in about a week's time. I managed to obtain the visa for India at the Indian High Commission in London. I was afraid once I returned home, Ammi might not approve the idea of my meeting with you."

Waqaar looked into the eyes of his father. He saw utter sadness in them. Both of them were silent for a long minute. Vikram heaved a deep sigh, and said,

"I am sorry son. We both, your mother and I only wanted to avoid hurting you. We thought it appropriate to…" Vikram trailed off into silence.

"Let's not dwell on the past. Today I am with you. That's all that matters."

Vikram was surprised and pleased to see that his son had inherited his trait of living for today. Then a cry of pain arose in his mind, "God, what an unfortunate father I am to have missed the childhood of my son. Blessed is my Nilu who had the satisfaction of watching our son grow." He was jolted out of his thoughts by Waqaar's next words,

"Abbajaan, Ammi has been getting me photographed on my birthdays, every year. I shall E-mail you the album."

He has read my mind. His love for me is so intense. Vikram closed his eyes, and folded his hands in his lap and said a silent prayer, thanking the Lord for such handsome compensation for the long separation from his son. How thoughtful of my beloved to keep a pictorial record of the growing up of our son. She must have hoped for me to see the pictures some day. Vikram wanted to know a lot about her, but could not bring himself to ask Waqaar, lest the questions became embarrassing to both of them. There was very little further talk between them, but they remained sitting there, savoring each other's presence. It was well past two in the morning before Vikram went to his room.

Next day was Friday. A melodic, though a bit muted, *azaan* from a distant mosque woke Waqaar at half past five. Although he had slept for barely three hours, he felt fresh and rested, even a bit euphoric from the long session with his father. He stepped out of his air-conditioned room intending to go for a stroll. The July weather of Ahmedabad was sweltering even at that early hour. He went back into the air-conditioned, room, and had a leisurely cold bath. He offered the morning namaaz, put on a fresh shirt and trousers, and descended the staircase. As he entered the hall, the clock was chiming seven. Dr. Vikram entered the hall at the same time.

"Aadaab Abbajan," Waqaar said in a hushed tone. He knew it was imprudent, under the circumstances, to address his father as Abbajaan, but he could not resist the joy of using the endearing address. There was no one else within hearing. He felt like a small child pinching a delicious candy when no one was looking.

"May God bestow a long life upon you," Vikram gave his blessings.

They had their breakfast of stuffed parathas in silence. When they had finished, Vikram said to Waqaar,

"I am off to the hospital. There is a meeting of the Administrative Committee scheduled for half past eight. It shall last until ten. You can join the ward rounds after that. I shall send the car to fetch you."

"If it is permitted for a visitor to attend the meeting, I would like to come with you."

"There is no bar on visitors. But you might find the discussions boring."

"I am sure it will be quite instructive for me."

"Come along then. We ought not to be late."

Waqaar was in no way interested in the administrative aspect of the hospitals. He only wanted to stay close to his father as long as possible. When he had come to India to meet his father, he was not sure what the meeting would hold for him. He had expected, from the information gleaned from the Internet, to see a middle-aged man smug with self-esteem, reveling in his legendary work in the social and medical field. "Surely, he must have forgotten my mother and the child he had bequeathed her." All his doubts had disappeared the moment he had come in his presence. In spite of the eminence that he had reached in his profession, his father was living an unpretentious life. People revered him as a messiah of the sick, but he remained untouched by the adulations. He had received his 'son' joyfully, albeit covertly. There was an instant bonding between them. Today Waqaar was loath to leave his father's side even for a couple of hour.

His father was living a bachelor's life. Waqaar did not know whether to feel happy or sorry. His father still cherished his mother's love. That made him happy. But the poor man had been leading a lonely life for more than a quarter of a century. That saddened him. "My parents, the two lost souls are living on memories alone. This cannot be allowed to go on. *I shall have to bring them together*;" he made yet another promise to himself.

Vikram parked the car in the parking area reserved for the doctors. As they started walking, side by side, towards the entrance of the hospital, Waqaar was seized by an uncontrollable urge to hold his father's hand. As a child, he had felt envious of his friends, holding their father's fingers as they walked together. His "father" had never taken him out. At that moment, he felt like a little child in the company of a doting father. He impulsively moved closer to Vikram, and clutched his hand. Vikram comprehending the yearning of his son's soul gave an appreciative squeeze to his hand. They first went into Vikram's office, and donned white coats before heading towards the administrative wing of the hospital. On the way, Dr. Mayank Raval joined them. He too was on his way to attend the meeting. When they reached the central hall, covered by a huge decorative sky-light dome, Waqaar turned to Vikram and said,

'Excuse me sir, may I have the honor of getting photographed with you?"

Without waiting for a reply, he took out his single lens reflex cannon from his handbag, and handed it to Dr. Raval.

"Please Dr. Raval, if you don't mind."

He looked around, for a suitable background for the snap. By the side of the archway leading to the main hospital building, was a white marble statue of a female figure, clad in a flowing gown, with both hands raised in a pose of blessings. It was mounted on a low pedestal. It bore no inscription, but the local folk called it *Ayur Devi,* the goddess of health. A decorative steal chain cordoned off the sculpture. Waqaar went and stood in front of the statue. Vikram joined him. Dr. Raval, who was an amateur photographer, clicked the camera from different angles, and handed it back to Waqaar.

For the whole week, Waqaar hardly left the side of his father. Like Mary's little lamb, he accompanied him everywhere; to his office, to his outdoor clinic, on the ward rounds, in the operating rooms. He wanted to fill a quarter century's hiatus in his life in a week's time. During his childhood when his deemed father, Mahmood had shown no feelings towards him, he had felt miserable. When he was a teenager, he had felt ashamed of his half-wit "father". As he grew up, he became indifferent towards him. The indifference got tinged with pity when he came to know of his epileptic condition. When Mahmood died and he came to know that the man was not really his father; a sense of relief had swept over him. "Mahmood was no relative of mine. I am convinced he was no husband to my mother in the real sense." Now, in the presence of his biological father, all the emptiness of his life had disappeared. His heart was filled with pride as he observed his father's qualities. His authority and decisiveness while conducting an administrative meeting, his precision in scientific discourses, his expertise and dexterity in surgery, and above all his compassion towards the sick. "My father is a perfect human being. I do not care about the adage, which says no man is perfect."

His happiest time was the post-dinner hour, when he would cajole Beji to recount episodes from her son's childhood.

"Daadi," he would say, "Did doctor sahib ever laugh when he was a child?"

This would be enough to instigate Beji to embark on the flight of old memories.

"No, I don't think he has ever laughed a full throttled laugh, but he smiled a lot. He still does. Even as an infant, he was a happy, contented soul. You know, right from the time he was an infant; I have seen him cry only once. He must have been about five years old then. A scorpion had stung him. He was so brave; he did not howl or shriek. He could not hold back his tears though, and let out an occasional sob. Waqaar wondered how often his brave father might have shed silent tears after the sting of cruel destiny had torn him away from his love.

Waqaar wanted to know everything about his father. He kept on prying out of his grandmother, various incidents in his life.

"At every examination of his primary school in the village my Bikku scored the highest marks. His father would reward him with cash of few rupees. You know what he did with the money. He used to spend all of it to buy *rewadis* and other items of confectionery, and distribute the sweets among the neighboring family of poor *mirasis,* the village bards. The bard family used to assemble in the summer evenings, and sing *Sufi* verses. Bikku would sit with them for hours, and listen to the divine lyrics. That is how he developed a penchant for poetry."

When the grandmother would appear to trail off in her narration, Waqaar would egg her on.

"Come on Daadi, you want me to believe that a child gave away his sweets to grown ups."

"That is true. From his childhood, up to today, giving has been his religion. In the final four years of his high school, he won merit scholarships. He used the cash to pay fees for a poor classmate of his, while his own fees were being paid by Dr. Patel, our employer and benefactor."

From all these tidbits of information extracted out of his grandmother, and the details he had garnered in Cardiff, added to the details obtained from the Internet, Waqaar felt as if he had always known his father. He dreaded the day when he would have to part company with him, and take leave of his grandmother, with whom he had developed a special bond.

On Friday, two days before Waqaar was due to leave, he, and Vikram went to the city centre for shopping. They left their car in the parking lot of the railway station, and walked the length of the road up to the Lal Darwaza, passing through the Richie Road, the Manek Chowk, the Pankore Naka, the Teen Darwaza, and Khaas Bazar. At Richie Road market, Vikram purchased compact discs of gazals by Tallat Mahmood, and duets by Jagjit Singh and Chitra Singh. At Manek Chowk, Waqaar went into a large garment shop and selected a peacock colored woolen shawl for Beji. He also picked up a beautifully designed woolen cardigan for his mother from a Tibetan hawker at the Teen Darwaza. At Lal Darwaza, Waqaar saw glimpses of the Kali

Mandir, the Bhadra Fort, and the famed Siddhi Jaali, the exquisite lattice stone- work. People recognized his father everywhere they went, and greeted him with deference. They rode an auto-rikshaw back to the railway station and retrieved their car from the parking lot.

Waqaar was due to leave for Bombay by the evening train on Sunday. Beji came to know of it only on the morning of his imminent departure when he presented her with the shawl. She became distraught at the news. Waqaar put his arms around her neck to comfort her. Vikram captured the poignant moment with the click of Waqaar's camera. From the moment Beji had first set eyes on Waqaar, she had felt an innate pull towards him. His resemblance to her own son, and his spontaneously addressing her as Daadi had tugged at her heart. She could not resist looking at him as her family. Waqaar ached to go to her and say, Daadi, I *am* your grandson. He resisted the urge lest he might create upheaval in his parents' life. All he could do to stem his granny's tears was to promise her that he would come again, and soon. Then turning to his father, he said,

"When I come next time, I shall bring my mother along."

In the evening when it was time for Waqaar to depart, he insisted that Vikram should not accompany him to the railway station. They said goodbye at the gate of Vikram's bungalow. Both kept a stoic facade, keeping their emotions on leash, and their tears imprisoned within their eyelids. The driver accompanied him to the station and helped him board the train for Bombay. Next morning he took the London-Dubai-Bombay-Lahore flight of British Airways.

Waqaar arrived at the Lahore airport on Monday, the 25th of July at eight in the morning. It was well past nine before he reached home. He had not intimated his mother of his arrival. He wanted to surprise her. He was disappointed when he did not find her at home. Farzana, the maid, informed him that she had gone to Abbotabad to attend a conference, and would be back in three days' time.

After unpacking, Waqaar removed the film from his camera, and went to a photo studio to get it processed and prints made. The prints were ready in the evening. Waqaar ordered a few enlargements. As he inspected the enlargement of his own photograph in the company of his father, both in their white coats, the statue behind them attracted his attention. Its face bore a good resemblance to his mother. The almost imperceptible mole at the tip of its nose left no doubts in Waqaar's mind. Abba must have got the statue sculptured from a photograph of Ammi.

On Thursday morning when the doorbell rang, he knew it was his mother. He waved off the servant, and opened the door himself. His mother was surprised at his unannounced arrival but did not exhibit too much of excitement. She had never been demonstrative in her affections. "What is there for my poor mother to enthuse about?" Waqaar thought. "She was no better than a widow, even when she was married. Now when she is a widow, she, in a way, is still a married woman, married to man hundreds of miles away from her. What an irony! I shall have to alter this absurdity, and bring some colors into her life."

"Where are you lost Waqaar? Her mother's words interrupted his daydream. They were sitting at the breakfast table. His mother was still in her traveling clothes. She had not gone to her room to change.

"Was your trip to the U.K. gainful?" the mother asked.

"Yes Ammi, I achieved all that I had set out to."

"Good, may Allah grant you more achievements."

"I say Amen to that."

"By the way Vicky, what gift have you brought for me?"

"I have placed it on the desk in your room."

After their breakfast, Nilofer went to her room. She saw a slim rectangular parcel, wrapped in a gift paper, lying on the desk. She was tired from the journey, and did not open it immediately. She lay down in bed for about two hours, and felt quite rested. She picked up the parcel and ripped it open. Her eyes grew wide, and her breath froze inside her. It was a framed photograph of Vikram and Waqaar together, in doctors' white coats. Vikram was supporting a beard, but that did not prevent her recognizing her long parted love. She stared at the two faces. "God, where did they meet? In Britain? Has Vikram settled there? Have these two recognized each other? They must have. At least Waqaar does, or else why should he gift the photo to me? What must have passed between them when they met?" The thought of the moment when they must have met, made her dizzy, and beads of sweat appeared on her forehead. The faces in the photograph became blurred. She put down the photograph, and held on to the edge of the desk for support. She sank on to a chair slowly and looked at the photograph again. The two faces seem to be smiling at her. Slowly her vision cleared, and she noticed that the two men in the photograph were holding hands like friends. Then her eyes caught the statue in the background. She recognized herself in its face. "No, these two did not meet in the U.K. Why should there be my statue in a British hospital? The place is obviously a hospital, a hospital in which Vikram has a stake. That could only be in India." But there was no way Waqaar could have been to India. Or could he? She was very confused. It was then that she saw a small, flat, square cardboard box, without a wrapper, lying on the desk. She had not noticed it before. She picked it up. The label on it read, *Sur-Taal, Ahmedabad (Gujarat),* and it contained three audio compact discs. When she saw the names of the singers on them, she knew that it was a gift from her Vikram. Two things became clear to her. Waqaar had met his father in Ahmedabad, and the meeting had been amiable.

"Shall I serve lunch, doctor sahiba?

The servant's inquiry broke the chain of her thoughts. She instructed her to wait for half an hour, and then lay the table. She wanted to have a word with her son first. She went to his room. He was not there. She saw a couple of new framed photographs on his desk. One was of a majestic looking white building. The inscription on the top of its façade read 'WAQAAR CHARITABLE HOSPITAL'. She gaped at the three words as if mesmerized. After a while, she turned to the second photograph. Waqaar had his arm around the shoulders of a woman; his right cheek pressed against her left. The woman was an aristocratic looking dame of about seventy years, her head half covered with a white dupatta. The woman's features left no doubt in her mind that she was Vikram's mother. She let out a long sigh. "This boy has gone and found not only his father, but his complete family. Yes, 'his family' but could I call it 'my' family? He can call her grandmother, as her son is his father, but can I call her mother-in-law? Her son is not my husband." She could only smile dolefully at the paradox.

"Isn't she cute?"

Waqaar's voice had startled her. He had come into the room quietly, and was standing behind her.

"You know Ammi, when Daadi first set her eyes on me, she was dumbfounded. She thought she was seeing her young Bikku."

"How did you get to them?"

Nilofer asked almost in a whisper.

"I shall tell you later. Let us first have lunch. Farzana has laid the table and is waiting for us."

When they had eaten, and the servant had cleared the table, Waqaar gave her a succinct account of his search for his father, just as he had given it to Vikram.

"How is he?"

"How do you think he should be?" There was an inflection of resentment in Waqaar's voice, resentment against the cruel fate, "Living a stoic, but lonely life, immersed in his work to stifle the pain in his soul. You at least have me to lighten your misery, but that unfortunate man has spent almost thirty years seeking solace from a mute statue and an abstract name."

"Don't you dare use the word unfortunate for him." Waqaar was taken aback by Nilofer's intensity. "We both, he and me, are fortunate to have an eternally burning flame of love in our hearts. We can happily spend the whole of our lives living in the glow of that love."

"Ammi," Waqaar said in an emotionally choked voice, "I want you to emerge from that slender glow of memories into the boundless sunshine of togetherness."

"You know that is impossible."

"No Ammi, it is quite feasible, if you two agree. You could go to India on a visitor visa. Now that you are legally a widow, you can get married to Abbajan. After that you could apply for the Indian citizenship, to which you shall become entitled."

"You are looking at it only from the legal viewpoint. Have you thought of the social fallout of such an action?"

"I was in India only for a week, but Ammi I can tell you this much. In that country, although inter-marriages between Muslims and Hindus are quite rare, they do not generate as much furor there as they do here."

"You are forgetting one important thing. Vikram and I are prominent doctors in our respective countries. Can you imagine the amount of social hype such a union will create in both the countries? The media will go to town digging up our past. Can you imagine the damage it will cause to Vikram's social standing? And what about you? You will become a pariah, in your own country, a bastard of a Kafir."

Waqaar fell silent, reflecting on what his mother had said. Then he addressed his mother in a resolute tone.

"Alright Ammi, I see your point. I have an alternate plan, and I implore you not to veto it. I can persuade the Pakistan Surgeons' Association to invite Dr. Vikram as a faculty at our next national conference. When he arrives, I shall invite him to put up with us during his stay here. Alternately, you, or we both, could go to India on a visitor visa to attend professional conferences or even for pilgrimage, say to Ajmer Sharif. This way you two could be together at least for few days without inviting any inquisitiveness. Such occasions could be created frequently."

Now it was Nilofer's turn to fall silent, and give a thought to what her son had proposed.

"It still is risky, I shall think about it," she said at last.

Waqaar took this as an acquiescence of his mother and got busy arranging an invitation to Dr. Vikram from the National Surgeons' Association. He was certain that with the current peace parleys going on between the prime ministers of India and Pakistan, no obstacle would come in the way of to his father's visit to Pakistan.

The obstacles that did prop up blocking his father's entry into Pakistan were beyond the wildest imagination of Waqaar. These were the long stretched out human walls of India and Pakistan armies of hundreds of thousands soldiers facing each other eyeball to eyeball on the two sides of the border, and hundreds of booming artillery guns on the ground, and scores of bombers raining death from the skies. One day the governments of the two countries were holding peace parleys, the next day they were threatening each other of nuclear attacks. In the first week of May 1999, without any previous warning, the Pak army led by General Ashraf Rashid invaded the Indian territory of Kargil. This was in spite of the Simla agreement, which prohibited the use of force to settle any issue between the two countries. This reckless conflict, loftily named Operation Vijay (Victory) by India, and Operation Badr (Full Moon) by Pakistan, led to massacre of large number of soldiers on both side. While Waqaar was hoping his father could come to Pakistan, General Parvez Musharaff chucked out the country's own prime minister in a military coup. The High

Commission of the two countries stopped issuing visas to each other's nationals.

Waqaar's disappointment was boundless, but he was not discouraged. "I can wait," he said to himself. The situation shall change one day. Saner reasoning shall prevail. The war shall end. The mutual distrust between our peoples shall abate, and I shall bring my parents together."

While waqaar was hoping that the wall of hostility between the two neighbours would crumble one day, his mother was facing another impenetrable wall. The wall that she had erected herself; the wall of her oath of chastity and celibacy.

*****